THE VOICES ARE DRIVING HIM CRAZY. AND HE'S DRIVING THEM CRAZY, TOO.

For Noah Blake, pretending to be normal is getting harder by the day. A brush with death in Iraq has left him suffering from chronic auditory hallucinations. Ignoring the voices he hears isn't always easy, but Noah knows it's better than the alternatives.

Yet when a mysterious redhead hands him a seemingly innocuous business card, a new voice — that of a teenage boy — becomes too insistent to deny. It wants him to go to Tassamara. It swears he'll find help there.

It's bad enough to have hallucinations, but doing what they say is bound to lead to disaster.

Isn't it?

A GIFT OF GRACE

A TASSAMARA NOVEL

SARAH WYNDE

ROZELLE PRESS

Published by Rozelle Press
independent publisher of unexpected fiction
rozellepress.com

Cover design by Karri Klawiter, artbykarri.com

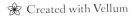 Created with Vellum

1

DILLON

Dillon had never seen so many ghosts in one place.

He came to a dead stop. His mother, oblivious, continued walking down the hallway of the federal courthouse, still talking on her cell phone. "It's a fishing expedition," she was saying. "The grand jury's calling everyone and anyone."

The hallway was crowded with the living, mostly men in suits. The lawyers looked sleek and comfortable, while the witnesses wore their ties like nooses, their suits like costumes.

Among them, ghosts wandered in uncanny profusion.

A translucent woman wearing long flowing skirts paced toward Dillon, her eyes empty. "*Sleep my love, and peace attend thee,*" she crooned a soft lullaby. "*All through the night. Guardian angels God will lend thee, all through the night.*"

Another woman, hair bundled into a knot on top of her head, scrubbed the floor on her hands and knees, heedless of the living legs walking through her.

An older man, head down, shoved through the crowd as if they were the ones who didn't exist, muttering furiously, "It's not right, it's not right."

Transparent blurs floated in the corners, wisps of white drifted along the corridor, balls of light bobbed in the air. Spirits — or the bits and pieces left of them after decades of slow erosion — were everywhere.

Halfway down the hall, Dillon's mom, Sylvie, stopped by a closed door. She spoke to the uniformed guard standing next to it, nodded at his response, and turned away from him. Moving across the hall, she settled in to wait. As she stood, her back against the wall, her eyes skimmed over the people around her.

Slowly, warily, Dillon made his way toward her. Should he tell his mom about the ghosts? In the weeks since he'd met her, she'd come to accept his presence, but he didn't think she'd be thrilled to learn that the courthouse was haunted.

Seriously haunted.

Like, haunted to the max.

Nah, he probably shouldn't mention it. But a thrill of anxiety tingled along the back of Dillon's neck. Ghosts could be dangerous, not so much to living people, but definitely to other spirits. He'd only been dead for six years but he'd already had a couple of bad experiences. Would this be another?

A soldier in desert camouflage was leaning against the same wall as Sylvie. He was young, his hair cropped short, and he looked as solid as a living person, but Dillon was almost positive he was a ghost. Next to him a woman in a long black robe, her hair covered by a tight scarf, crouched by a small boy in a brightly striped t-shirt, her head bent to him in conversation. They had to be ghosts, too. And the teenage girl sprawled across a bench, ignoring the men on whose laps her body rested, was definitely a ghost.

Had all these people died in the courthouse? As Dillon paused, uncertain, two living people walked through him, one offering low-voiced instructions to the other.

The soldier noticed. He straightened. "Hey, welcome to the party."

The girl on the bench sat up. She stared at Dillon, her gaze accusing. "Who are you?"

The scrubbing woman lifted her head to look at him. "Oh, dear, oh, dear," she mumbled before bending back to her work. "I'll never get this floor clean."

"Um, hi." Dillon gave a tentative wave in the direction of the soldier as he answered the girl's question. "I'm Dillon."

The soldier directed his thumb at himself, the woman in the robe, the boy, the girl on the bench, and the cleaning woman, and rattled off a list of names. "Joe, Nadira, Misam, Sophia, Mona. Don't worry about the others." He waved a hand through a ball of light drifting near his face, then gestured wide, indicating the rest of the spirits as yet another ghost, a man in a dirty white apron, emerged from the wall next to him. "Some of them say stuff, but they don't really talk. Not to us, anyway."

"It's nice to meet you," Dillon replied with automatic politeness, nodding at each of the others in turn.

"Salaam aleikum," the woman in the robe, Nadira, said, with a gracious nod of her own.

"Peace be unto you," the boy, Misam, offered with a wide smile.

"Uh, and to you?" Dillon answered.

From their closeness and matching dark eyes, they must be mother and son. Or maybe brother and sister? Now that they were looking at him, Dillon could see that Nadira was young, with clear unlined skin, bright red lips, and smudgy dark makeup around her eyes. She couldn't be much older than the soldier, if that. Still, the protective arm she had curled around the little boy looked maternal to him and so did the approving smile she gave his reply.

The girl perched on the bench, hands tucked around the edge of the seat as if gripping it, didn't look related to the others. With wrists like toothpicks and collarbones jutting forth from thin shoulders, she reminded him of a fledgling bird. Sophia, that was her name.

And Mona was the woman still scrubbing the floor.

The man in the apron gave Dillon a cheerful smile and said

something indistinguishable before strolling forward and disappearing into the opposite wall.

Joe chuckled. He nodded toward the wall. "That guy talks, but we don't understand much. We think his name is Chaupi."

"He doesn't speak English," the little boy volunteered. "I would teach him, but he doesn't want to learn. He is searching for something."

Dillon stepped closer. None of these ghosts seemed threatening, not even the nameless grumbling man, and his fear was dissipating, replaced by enthusiasm. Dillon knew he was lucky to have learned how to communicate with the living, but texting his parents was no substitute for talking, and he hadn't spoken to another soul in days. All the ghosts he'd met since leaving home had been faders, only repeating the same few words over and over again.

"So what are y'all doing here? Is this where you died?" he asked.

The teenage girl, Sophia, snorted. "Here? With all those metal detectors at the entrance? What do you think, bomb? Mass poisoning?" She rolled her eyes and flopped back down across the laps of the men sitting on the bench.

Joe's mouth twitched, but he answered easily, "No, we didn't die together. Except for Nadira, Misam, and me. We were in the same place."

"Not here, though?" Dillon asked.

"Nah. Long time ago, long way away."

Dillon glanced around the hallway, wondering what he'd missed. Ghosts were often trapped where they died. But if these ghosts could go anywhere, why choose the courthouse? "Why are you here, then?"

"We've been captured," Sophia said, without changing her position. "Taken prisoner." She was staring at the ceiling, but a lone tear rolled down the side of her face, and she sniffled.

"Captured?" Dillon's heart sank. For several years after his death, he'd been stuck in the car where he'd died. He'd only been free for a few months and he truly didn't want to find himself trapped again. "By what? The courthouse?"

4

"Not the building, no." Joe pointed at a dark-haired man sitting underneath Sophia. "By him."

The man had the finely hewn, perfectly even features of a male model, or maybe an actor on one of those teen dramas where all the kids looked way too old for high school and no one ever had a zit, but he held himself as if he would jolt upright any second, grabbing for a weapon he wasn't carrying.

A quick, unpleasant suspicion popped into Dillon's head. "Is he your killer? Did he murder you?"

"No, of course not." Joe gestured toward the woman in the long skirts, drifting toward them through the crowd of business-suited men. "What do you think, he was around for the Civil War?" He waved toward Mona. "World War II?"

"Oh, right." Dillon hunched his shoulders, sheepish. That should have been obvious. But he'd never heard of ghosts being trapped by a person before.

"Speak for yourself." Nadira rose, sweeping her hands down the sides of her robe.

Joe turned to her. "You know—"

"I know, I know," she interrupted him, flapping the fingers of one hand in his direction.

"Mama, you promised." The little boy, Misam, leaned into her side. "No fighting with Joe."

"Did I start?" his mother asked, spreading her hands.

Joe turned back to Dillon. "His name's Noah Blake. He was my buddy. The day we died, he did, too." Joe circled his finger around himself, Nadira, and Misam to indicate who he was talking about. "But they brought him back and we came with him. At least that's what we think happened."

Sophia heaved a melodramatic sigh. "He definitely didn't kill me." Tears started running down her face in earnest and she began to weep, her body shuddering with gasping breaths.

Two of the men on the bench didn't react but the one that Joe had pointed out shivered, pulling the collar of his leather jacket up around his neck.

Dillon was fascinated. He hadn't even known that ghosts could cry. Where did the tears come from?

"Come on, Sophia." Joe reached out and grabbed her hand, tugging her from the bench and upright. "You know it's not so bad. Walk it off." He gave her a gentle shove toward the lobby.

"You just want to get rid of me," Sophia said on a sob.

The cleaning woman scrambled to her feet and hurried to Sophia's side. She put an arm around the girl's shoulder and began walking with her, murmuring into her ear.

"Obviously," Joe said under his breath when the two were far enough away to be out of hearing range. He turned back to Dillon, his smile wry. "Sophia's a little temperamental."

"Temperamental?" Nadira said, her voice dry. "Is that American for sad? Depressed? Unhappy about her current situation?"

"Yeah, it's American for annoying as hell," Joe said, but he kept his voice low. "Admit it, you get tired of the crying, too."

"Sophia cries a lot," Misam said to Dillon. He looked four or five, no older, but his voice held a maturity that didn't match his round cheeks and snub nose.

"We think she is only recently one of us." Nadira pursed her lips, her head turning to watch Sophia and Mona move away. "She will adjust." Despite the confidence of the words, she sounded doubtful.

The man on the bench blew on his hands as if they were chilled. His lips pressed into a thin line.

"He's cold again." Joe jerked his head peremptorily toward the other end of the hall and began walking. "Come on, let's move."

"You worry too much," Nadira complained, but she took Misam's hand and the two of them followed Joe away from the bench, Misam giving a skip and a hop as they went.

Dillon joined them, trailing along as they moved down the hallway. He brushed through one of the wispy white blurs, hearing it whisper, "Slow down, Tom. It's not safe."

When the trio paused, Dillon waved to indicate the random spirits drifting through the hallway, "So if you came back with him, where did all these guys come from? Did they come with you?"

Joe shook his head. "No, it was just the three of us."

"For a long time, it was just us." Misam leaned into Nadira's legs.

"We saw others sometimes," Nadira contributed.

"But they didn't join us," Joe finished for her. He glanced around them. "This started happening a while ago."

The hallway was too packed with both the living and the dead for Dillon to count, but there had to be at least two dozen ghosts mingling with the crowd, even if most of them were merely remnants of their former selves.

"Lately it's everyone." Nadira paused while a cluster of men in dark suits walked through her. "We didn't keep any nice Iraqi ghosts, no, but we come here and all the spirits are sticky. We meet them and they stay with us forever."

"Forever?" Dillon's uneasiness returned. "All of them?"

"So far, yeah." Joe's eyes were sympathetic. He nodded toward the exit. "Give it a try."

Dillon started walking. After fifteen steps or so, he began to feel a pull, a drag on his core tugging him back to the others. He resisted, pushing through it.

The drag felt strong, but not nearly as strong as his tie to his car had once been. He might be able to break away from it.

Maybe Noah Blake was something like a magnet, attracting ghosts the way a magnet attracts iron. If so, if Dillon could get out of the range of his magnetic field, the attraction would end. He'd be free.

But if he managed to break the connection, he'd be leaving all these other ghosts trapped. And meeting them had been the most interesting thing to happen in his afterlife since he'd met his mom. He wasn't sure he was ready to leave yet. He turned to face the other ghosts and let the pull draw him back, as if he were surfing along the tiled floor.

"You, too, yes?" Nadira shook her head.

"Like I said, welcome to the party." Joe sounded apologetic. "But we're a fun bunch. It's not so bad."

The woman in the long dress wandered by them, her melancholy song just slightly off-tune.

"Except for the singing," Nadira said in a fierce whisper.

Joe chuckled. "And the crying," he added with a glance toward the other end of the hallway.

"And the arguing," Misam said with a roll of his eyes.

Dillon bit back a smile. The little boy might look four but his expression was pure teenage disdain.

Nadira flicked Misam's nose with the tip of her finger. "You be careful your face doesn't get stuck that way."

"It never has so far," Misam said cheekily.

"Last couple of months, it's been someone new every few weeks," Joe said. "We found Sophia in Rock Creek Park right after the holidays."

Dillon had once chased his mother on an interminable twenty-mile run through Rock Creek Park. He hadn't noticed any ghosts hanging around, but he could have missed her. It was a big park. Or maybe Sophia had still been alive at the end of November.

"Stop that, Misam," Nadira ordered. The little boy was leaning into the air as if struggling against a strong wind.

"I want to slide. Like he did. It looked fun."

"You'll hurt yourself." His mother tugged at the back of his t-shirt, pulling him closer to her.

"Not really. If you practice, you can get farther away," Dillon said.

"How do you know?" Nadira demanded. "It's painful for us to move too far from Noah."

"For me, it was the car where I died," Dillon said. "I was trapped but I met a girl who knows about ghosts. She told me I could get farther away if I practiced. Do you get snapped back when you go too far?"

Joe winced, a look of remembered pain on his face, and Nadira grimaced as she nodded.

"I won't go that far." Misam straightened, no longer pushing against the air. "It hurts."

"Yeah, it does," Dillon agreed. "But it doesn't do any damage. And the more you do it, the farther you can go."

"In the car where you died?" Joe ducked to avoid one of the floating white lights. "Does that mean you didn't die here?"

Dillon shook his head. He pointed over his shoulder to his mom, still standing across from Noah. "I'm hanging out with my mom."

"Hanging out?" Nadira's eyes crinkled in amusement. "Is that American for haunting?"

Dillon scuffed a foot along the floor. "That makes it sound bad."

Joe snorted. "It's not pretty." He glanced down the hallway in the direction of his friend. "I hate what we're doing to Noah."

"What we're doing to him?" Nadira said. "What about what he's done to us?"

"He didn't..." Joe began.

"No fighting," Misam commanded, raising a small finger in the air.

Nadira wagged hers at him. "No scolding."

He narrowed his eyes at her, pursing his lips. She reached out as if to tickle his stomach and he immediately started to giggle.

"Seriously, though." Joe stepped away from the two of them, closer to Dillon. "If you were trapped, how did you get free? Is it something we can do? Because this—" He waved his hand around at the ghosts in the hallway again. "—isn't doing Noah any good."

Nadira stopped trying to tickle Misam. "As if it's a party for us, being dragged around the world! Misam and I should be in our graves, waiting for the judgement day, and if not there, we should at least be back in Iraq."

"Come on, Nadira, don't start that again," Joe said.

"I like traveling, Mama." Misam slipped his hand into hers again. "It's fun to go to new places."

9

She sniffed with displeasure, but her lips curved as she looked down on him.

"You know we're hurting Noah," Joe continued. "He's changed."

"I..." Nadira tipped her head from side to side, as if trying to decide whether to nod it in agreement or shake it in refusal, and then conceded the point. "Yes. Yes, he's different."

"Back in the day, he was always smiling." Joe's expression was sad as he looked at Noah. "The kind of guy you just wanted to be around, you know? Not a joker, but just... easy. He was real easy. And now, every time another one of us shows up, it's like it pushes him down a little more, a little deeper."

"Does he know we're here?" Dillon asked, surprised. Noah hadn't looked at him or shown any sign of hearing them when they'd been talking.

"No," Nadira said firmly.

"Yes," Joe said equally firmly.

"Maybe," Misam said, with another eye roll.

"It's hard to say for sure." Two living people, their heads bent together, walked through Joe, talking earnestly. He paused and waited until their conversation moved away, then said, "He can feel us. It gets cold around him. And sometimes it seems like he can hear what we say."

"Sometimes?" Nadira scoffed. "Hardly ever."

"I think he's listening sometimes," Joe said, his chin set stubbornly.

"Pfft. You imagine things."

"I don't imagine that he's always cold." Joe's voice began to grow heated.

"There are some people who can sense when we're around," Dillon offered. He'd never met one, at least not that he knew of, but Akira had told him about sensitives, people who got vague impressions when ghosts talked to them. Maybe Noah was one of them. "We can influence them, even though they don't know that we're here."

"It might not be us, anyway," Nadira said. "He might have that thing. What do they call it? The soldier disease. PT something or other."

"I think he is possessed by a jinn." Misam bounced on his toes. "It is in his blood, taking him over."

"That is rude, Misam." Nadira's scolding was gentle, and any effectiveness was probably lost when she shrugged and added, "Although you might be correct."

"Noah is not possessed," Joe said. "But I think we're bad for him. And whatever's causing him to collect all these other ghosts isn't helping. If there's a way to get away from him, we should do it."

"It's not so easy," Dillon warned.

"I'll do whatever it takes," Joe said.

Nadira's mouth twisted. She put a hand on Misam's head, stroking his dark hair. He leaned into her touch. "If it is a jinn, there is nothing we can do without an exorcist."

"It is not a jinn." Joe's voice held a snap.

"You promised, Joe." Misam put up a small finger in warning.

Joe folded his arms across his chest. "I'm not arguing. I'm just... disagreeing."

Dillon stuck his hands in his back pockets and rocked back on his heels, considering the three ghosts before him. He knew of two ways to break the tether holding a ghost to a place. He supposed they'd both work for a tether holding a ghost to a person, too.

But the first method was too dangerous. He'd been ripped free from his car by a vortex ghost, a spirit trapped between the planes of existence. His friend Akira had saved him by sacrificing herself, but if it hadn't been for her, Dillon would have wound up lost in a chaotic sea of nightmarish energy. With no way to escape, he would eventually have been ripped apart, his energy dissolving into nothingness.

It wasn't a risk worth taking. Vortex ghosts were best avoided.

The second method might work, though.

"Have you met any ghosts with a doorway?" he asked.

"A doorway?" Joe raised an eyebrow.

"Not the physical kind. But a passageway, like an opening in the air."

Joe looked skeptical. "I've seen a lot of ghosts, but I've never seen a door."

"Yeah, me neither." Dillon made a face. "We need my friend Rose. She can see them."

"Where is she?" Joe asked.

"Back home," Dillon replied. "In Florida."

Joe snorted. "Might as well be the moon. Noah's not going to Florida anytime soon."

"Then we're just going to have to change that," Dillon said.

Nadira frowned. "And how do you plan to do that?"

Dillon grinned. "I guess I'll start by calling my mom."

2

NOAH

Silence.

Beautiful, peaceful, glorious, golden silence.

It wasn't truly silent, of course, not even close. Noah was sitting in a crowded hallway, men on either side of him, people walking past, footsteps echoing off tiled floors, snippets of conversation floating by. But at least the damn crying had stopped.

His shoulders relaxed and he unzipped his jacket. He'd been burrowed into it, shivering, but it seemed to have gotten warmer. He couldn't get used to how cold it was in the States. Back in Iraq, the guys used to joke that he had built-in AC, but that trait wasn't nearly so handy during Washington's chill gray winter.

"Guardian angels, God will lend thee..."

Noah didn't react. The song was a hallucination, just another one of the voices only he could hear. But he would have liked to grimace. He really hated the singing. Maybe not as much as the crying, but it was close. Fortunately, it drifted away, drowned out by all the other noise.

He let his head rest against the wall behind him, closing his eyes. This business with the grand jury was total bullshit. In the nine months he'd worked for AlecCorp, he hadn't seen or done anything, illegal or otherwise. Most of his time had been spent in training exercises or sitting around an office in Virginia, waiting for an assignment. His testimony was worth five minutes, if that. Meanwhile he'd been waiting for hours. And not with pay.

He needed to start looking for another job. It was a depressing thought.

Maybe he should go home for a while. Visit his family.

That thought was even more depressing.

"Carly? Where are you, Carly?"

"It's not right, it's not right."

"Slow down, Tom. You're driving too fast."

His hallucinations were getting worse. When they started, a decade ago, there had just been three of them: Joe, the little boy, and the Arabic woman. Sometimes other voices came and went, but not so often that it was a problem. Lately, though, the voices started and stayed, more and more of them.

Most of the time, the new ones said the same things, over and over again. It was meaningless, just the static of his subconscious. But there were so many of them. Could he even filter out real voices from the ones his brain conjured up anymore? The clean freak, the crying girl, the singing lady, the angry man, the lost woman, the worrier, the fake Chinese guy... none of them were real.

But what about the husky contralto saying, "Seriously?"

Was she real?

Noah cracked open his eyelids, peering through his lashes. Across the hallway, a redhead stared at her cell phone as if reading a text. He couldn't see the headset she wore but she spoke as if she had a voice connection.

"Good that you're making friends, I guess?"

Noah watched her, his eyes intent on her lips, matching the movements to the murmured words.

"A model? Okay, yeah. I see him."

She caught his gaze. He dropped his lids hastily. Yeah, that voice was real.

"Holy shit. That is so cool." Joe. Not real.

"I want to do that, too. I want to talk to her." The little boy. Not real. But he sounded excited, bouncy, like he was jumping around the hallway.

Noah's mouth twitched, a faint smile curving his lips. The little boy was his favorite of his hallucinations. A psychiatrist would probably say the boy represented his inner child. If so, Noah's inner child had a good sense of humor and a great attitude.

"Allah be praised." The Arabic woman's voice. Not real.

If the boy represented his inner child, maybe the woman represented his inner mom. Noah didn't know why his subconscious would make his mom Arabic, though. He'd love to ask a shrink, although not if it meant admitting to his hallucinations. No way was he ever doing that. They'd lock him up and throw away the key.

"Tell her to be careful." Joe's voice. Not real. *"He knows some of the guys here. She shouldn't say anything that might get him in trouble. Nothing that sounds crazy."*

Joe would be the protector, of course. Ironic, since Noah had so singularly failed to protect Joe. But Noah veered away from that thought just as he had for the past decade.

He straightened, opening his eyes, glancing up and down the corridor, keeping the motion subtle. His fingers itched for the security of a weapon. Not that he was in danger here, of course. But every once in a while, the voices were worth listening to. What kind of trouble had his subconscious spotted?

"We could talk to people, mama," the boy said, still exuberant.

"American people," the Arabic woman answered. *"You'd have to write in English, Misam. Besides, who do you want to talk to, anyway?"*

Noah relaxed. Not this time. They were nonsense words, a nonsense conversation spewed by his overactive brain. No meaning, and definitely not his subconscious alerting his conscious mind to danger he hadn't recognized.

"How are you doing that?" Joe again.

"It took a lot of practice," a teenage boy's voice said. *"I broke a lot of phones."*

Noah let his eyes drift over the crowd of people in the hallway, nodding at a former co-worker he recognized. No teenage boys.

A muscle jumped in his jaw. Another new one. Damn.

He leaned forward, resting his palms on his knees and stared at the floor, trying to shut out the cacophony in his ears. But once they started, they just kept going.

The same damn song, over and over again.

The crying.

"It's not right. It's not right." The angry man.

Again and again and again.

Stress, that's what it was. AlecCorp had been a lousy job for him. He wasn't cut out to be a military contractor. Not that he'd done much, but the waiting around got to him. Now that he was unemployed again, the voices would quiet down.

Yeah, because being unemployed was so relaxing.

But even the fast food joints seemed reluctant to hire someone with only military experience. Apparently being able to hump eighty pounds and field strip an M4 assault rifle in your sleep weren't skills prized by the average American employer. Who knew?

"Excuse me."

Noah started, sitting up.

The redhead stood in front of him, a business card in her outstretched hand.

"Yes?" His voice was wary. Did he know her? She looked vaguely familiar, as if he might have seen her before, in the distance or in some other context, but he couldn't put a name to her face. She had the pale, almost translucent skin of a natural redhead, with minimal makeup and her hair drawn back. She wore a suit, with a loose-fitting jacket and skirt, but the clinging t-shirt underneath it coupled with the control in her movements suggested she was athletic, definitely physically fit.

She smiled at him, but it didn't reach her eyes. "I understand you have a problem."

Noah raised a brow. "Yeah?"

He had several problems that he knew about. Being stuck in this hallway was one. Being unemployed was another. But there was something about her expression, the sympathy in her gray eyes, that sent a tremor of unease down Noah's spine. What did she know?

"It's a problem I'm familiar with." The words were even, but her smile was rueful.

What was she talking about? Noah's voice felt stiff as he said, "I'm not sure what you mean."

"Mmm." She nodded acknowledgement and the sympathy in her eyes deepened. Lowering her voice, she stepped closer to him. "This isn't the time or the place."

Before he could respond, the door to the grand jury room opened. The redhead glanced over her shoulder and Noah straightened, as heads turned and conversations dropped off. All eyes were on the door as a witness exited, relief written on his face, and the door closed again.

The energy in the hall stayed heightened. Lawyers muttered last-minute instructions to their clients and witnesses fidgeted, tugging at suit sleeves and straightening ties.

The redhead turned back, pressing the card upon him. Noah took it, gaze skimming over it.

General Directions, Inc.

Tassamara, FL

555-347-9779

info@generaldirections.com

He flipped it over. No name, no scrawled message. "What is this?"

"You'll have to go there in person."

Before he could ask more questions, the door to the grand jury room opened again. A woman checked a clipboard and called out, "Sylvie Blair?"

The redhead glanced over her shoulder. "My turn, I guess."

Sylvie Blair? Noah had heard that name before.

The redhead turned back to him. "Ask for Akira."

"Akira?" Noah recognized that name, too, but only from the animé. Were real people actually named Akira? He scowled.

The redhead frowned back at him, worried lines appearing between her brows. "Say that Dillon sent you. He wants to help."

"Sylvie Blair?" The woman called out again, louder, her voice impatient.

"Help how?" Noah asked.

The redhead opened her mouth, glanced around, then let out her breath in a controlled sigh. "Not here. I can't explain like this and I don't have the time. But go to Tassamara. You won't regret it."

Turning away from him, she muttered, "Best I can do," almost as if the words weren't directed at him. He watched her go, still frowning, as she crossed to the grand jury room and introduced herself to the woman with the clipboard.

"Sleep my dear..."

"Oh, my, this floor. Carbolic soap, that's what I need."

"You're driving too fast. Slow down..."

"Who's Akira?"

"Ama hina kaychu."

His voices were babbling again, talking one over another. He could even hear the mellifluous mystery language that was his subconscious pretending to speak Chinese. Noah didn't understand Chinese, but he recognized it well enough to know his hallucination was doing it wrong.

"Fraternizing with the enemy?" The question sounded disgruntled.

Noah almost ignored it before realizing it came from the man sitting on the bench next to him. "What?"

The guy nodded toward the doorway. "That's her. The one who killed Chesney."

Noah glanced back but the redhead had already disappeared into the grand jury room. His brows rose. She hadn't looked like a killer.

He looked down at the card in his hand again. General Directions. So many rumors had been flying around in the wake of Alec-Corp's implosion. What had he heard about General Directions? But the story, whatever it was, didn't come back to him.

"You know this place?" He showed his neighbor the card.

The guy grunted. "Sounds like some New Age crap."

The guy on the other side of him craned his neck forward. Noah tilted the card in his direction.

"Think tank," the guy said. "Consultants. And research."

Noah could almost see the invisible quotation marks around the word 'research.' "What sort of research?"

"Spook stuff." The guy leaned back again, falling silent.

Noah considered the card. Spook stuff, huh? He should throw it away. But there was no trash can nearby, so he slipped the card into his pocket. He didn't know what Sylvie Blair wanted from him, but one AlecCorp was enough for a lifetime. No way was he going to Tassamara.

———

A MONTH LATER

The voices were driving him crazy.

Crazier than usual, that was. Technically, Noah knew he'd been insane for years, ever since he woke up in a hospital room to the sound of his best friend's voice. Even in his coma, he'd known that was impossible. The memory of the light draining out of Joe's eyes had been a nightmare he couldn't escape.

But this was today, not back then. Yeah, he was crazy, but why the hell couldn't his hallucinations argue about something reasonable? Basketball, say. Baseball, maybe. But no, his imaginary companions wanted to debate Disney movies.

Worse, they were flat-out wrong. Okay, sure, *Frozen* was decent for a girl movie, but no way did it beat *The Lion King* musically. One impressive song did not stand up to a score that included *Hakuna Matata*, *Circle of Life*, and that one about feeling the love. And *Toy Story* — fine, great movie — but *Toy Story* 2 & 3 were even better, plus sequels. How often did sequels improve on the original? The filmmakers deserved credit for pulling that off.

But if he opened his mouth to argue with his hallucinations... No, he wanted no part of that slippery slope. Talking to them would put him on the fast track to a ratty bathrobe, zombie eyes and a slurred voice, zoned out on whatever antipsychotic the VA was experimenting with.

It was bad enough that he was following their directions. If they started ordering him to assassinate presidents or open fire at a shopping mall, he hoped he'd have the sense to get himself locked up instead.

"Oh, turn right up here," the new guy's voice said. *"We're almost there."*

Almost there? They were in the middle of nowhere, deep dappled light scattered by the trees overhanging the narrow road, no sign of houses or human habitation. But Noah took the right turn as ordered and within a few more minutes, the trees opened up as he entered a small town.

Two minutes later, the trees began closing in again.

"Go back," the voice demanded. *"Go back. You missed it."*

That was it?

Noah wanted to beat his head against the steering wheel. He'd come all this way, driven through the night to get to this tiny spot on the map, and it was nothing. Nothing. One street, maybe two blocks of shops. What the hell?

But he slowed his truck. At a wide spot on the empty road, he made a three-point turn and headed back. His eyes were hot with the burn from a sleepless night. He'd find a cup of coffee, maybe some breakfast, and look around. Maybe he'd ask someone about the business card that sat in his back pocket and maybe not. Either way, he'd made it to the town. Surely the voices that had been nagging him night and day would shut up now.

The town was cute. But strange. Not at all what he'd expected. He'd imagined a place that looked top secret. Concrete walls and big blank buildings, parking lots and fences, that kind of thing. Instead, he'd found a dusty little tourist town. Glass window fronts on cozy shops, wide sidewalks, and street parking with no meters.

As he stepped out of his truck, an impossibly tiny old woman in a brightly-flowered muumuu paused on the sidewalk. She tsk-ed at him, shaking her head. He glanced at the distance between his truck and the curb — the appropriate six inches — and raised his eyebrows.

"Ma'am?" Had he done something wrong?

"Sage, young man," she said. "Sage. Or perhaps juniper." She shook her head again, then toddled away.

Noah blinked. He was tired, but he was pretty sure he was awake. Still, that had felt an awful lot like a moment out of a dream. Surreptitiously — not that anyone was on the street to notice — he pinched his arm.

Definitely awake.

He started walking down the street, checking out the storefronts as he passed. A bookstore, with what looked like a mix of new and used titles. A small drugstore, not one of the chains. Antiques, a gift shop, a window display of fancy rocks and crystals, and finally, a restaurant. Planters of lush blue lobelia bordered the doorway and under an awning, a window with gold lettering spelled out '*Maggie's Place.*'

Noah paused. The restaurant looked nicer than the basic all-American diner he'd been hoping for, but it was the only restaurant he'd seen and he was running out of street.

When he entered, a bell jangled over the door. From behind the counter, a young waitress, her jagged blonde hair tipped with purple, called out, "Sit anywhere you like, I'll be right with you."

A shriek of feminine delight split the air. *"Dillon, Dillon, Dillon,"* a girl's voice chanted. *"You're home! I've missed you so! Where have you been? You missed the wedding."*

Noah took a long, slow glance around the restaurant. It was more crowded than he would have expected for an early mid-week morning, with most of the tables and booths full. But there were seats available at a diner-style counter.

There was not a shrieking girl.

And the only one responding to her delight was his most recent hallucinatory voice, the new guy, saying, *"Hey, Rose."*

Second-most-recent now, Noah supposed. Another hallucination was not what he'd been hoping to find on his long drive to the middle of nowhere. Resigned, he held back his sigh and moved to the counter, sliding into an open seat next to the cash register.

His voices were quieter away from the door, as if he'd left them temporarily across the room. But he could still hear the girl saying, with a southern lilt, *"You could have danced with me. I had to dance with Toby and you should have seen the way people looked at him."* She laughed, the sound contagiously cheerful.

Noah found his lips curving up in an involuntary smile. Huh. This voice wasn't like most of them. She talked like she went places, did things.

"He's a little short for you, isn't he?" the new guy replied.

Noah's smile faded. He hated that voice. It had been badgering him for weeks, pestering him endlessly to go to Tassamara, to find Akira. Apparently his subconscious thought he was living in an anime. It was damn annoying.

"I taught him to jitterbug. He did pretty good for a three-year-old."

"I'm sorry I missed it. I really tried to get back in time."

"What can I get you?" the waitress asked. She couldn't be much out of high school, if that, but she wiped down the counter before him with practiced efficiency.

22

"Coffee, please," Noah responded. He took a deep breath. The air smelled incredible — sweetly spicy, like cinnamon or vanilla. Maybe he didn't want bacon and eggs after all. "And a menu?"

"A menu? Oh, sure." The waitress sounded surprised, but she nodded toward a built-in slot on his side of the cash register. "Grab one from that bin. I'll BRB with your coffee."

Noah leaned to the side. The bin held multiple menus, some large, some small, some colorful, some plain, all different. He grabbed a red one from the middle of the pile and opened it up.

It was in Chinese.

Noah blinked.

It wasn't even the kind of Chinese menu that put English translations or pronunciations under the characters. It was just Chinese.

He stared at it.

"Try the special," a woman said from the seat next to him. "It's a sure thing."

Noah glanced her way.

Time stopped.

And then it started again.

But for a moment, a split second, unnoticeable, he hoped, he'd felt like he'd just taken a hard kick to the gut. Blonde hair, swooping in a graceful curve across her cheeks; green eyes, the color of army drab; a smiling mouth; and the lightest splash of dusty freckles across her nose. He felt a mad desire to count them.

She blinked at him and her smile deepened.

"You must be new in town." Her voice was light, pleasant, nothing special, but he felt the sound of it running down his spine like a shimmer of electricity. She stuck out her hand. "Grace Latimer."

3

GRACE

Whoa.

Hot guy alert.

Grace was just as glad she hadn't looked at the man next to her before telling him to try the special, because she might have stumbled over the words. What in the world was a guy like him doing in Tassamara? He belonged on the cover of a magazine, not on the stool next to her at the local diner.

The pause before he took her hand was noticeable, but not quite rude.

"Noah Blake," he said. His hand was cool in hers, but his grip was perfect, his fingers lightly rough against the smoothness of her own skin.

"So what brings you to Tassamara, Mr. Blake? Just passing through?" she asked. There was no way he was a local. She would have seen him before. Or heard of him. Hell, every single woman in a five-mile radius would be whispering about him, she thought, entertained by the notion.

His eyelashes were unreal. And seriously unfair. The best

mascara on the planet wouldn't make hers that lush and gorgeous. And then there were the stark cheekbones. The stubborn chin. The long, lean fingers.

"Not exactly," he replied.

Plus, there was the stubble. What was it about a guy who was twenty-four hours too far away from a shave? Were pheromones connected to facial hair?

"Oh? Visiting someone in town?" Three days earlier and Grace would have been scrambling to remember the names of the guests Akira had invited to the wedding. But if he was here for the wedding, he was very, very late. Besides, he was much too pretty to be a physicist or an academic. He hadn't gotten those shoulders crouching over a lab table for ten hours a day.

"Sort of."

She waited, head tilted, a welcoming smile on her face, letting the expectant silence stretch. She wasn't going to badger him if he didn't want to talk to her, but the borderline rudeness in his initial hesitation was crossing over into surly asshole territory.

"Looking for a place," he finally said, sounding reluctant.

"Any place I might know?" Grace pushed her empty coffee cup away. She'd already finished eating and she needed to get to work. The wedding had disrupted her schedule and the emails were piling up. She wouldn't have minded chatting with him if he wanted to talk — it wasn't every day that a gorgeous man showed up at Maggie's — but she wasn't going to waste her time if he was a jerk. She reached for the strap of her purse where it was slung over the back of the stool and started to stand, adding, "I grew up here and it's a small town. I know a fair amount about the area."

"Maybe." He sighed. It sounded resigned. Pulling a business card out of his back pocket, he showed it to her, asking, "Have you heard of this place?"

It was a generic General Directions card: no employee name, no direct phone line, stained with brown drops that looked like coffee, and worn around the edges, as if he'd been carrying it around for a while.

Grace relaxed back onto her stool. "I have, yes."

She eyed him with new interest. Gorgeous and now mysterious, too. What was he doing with one of the generic General Directions cards?

He set the card on the counter between them. "What do they do there?"

She raised her eyebrows. "You're looking for them, but you don't know what they do?"

His lips tightened and he looked away from her, glancing down at the countertop.

She didn't wait for him to respond. "It's primarily a holding company, buying and selling stock in other companies," she told him. That was true enough that if she were hooked up to a lie detector, it wouldn't even blip. The vast majority of GD's value and profits came from its holdings and stock transactions.

But the company had two other divisions: Research and Special Affairs, both based in Tassamara. And only the Special Affairs division used the generic cards. One of GD's coterie of unusual talents had given Noah Blake a card. But who? And why?

Did he need someone with their specialized sets of skills? GD's psychics weren't the kind that took walk-ins. Most of their work came through their government connections. But if he was with the FBI or DEA or even the State Department, why wasn't he going through the usual channels?

"Stocks? Like Berkshire Hathaway? Warren Buffett?" Noah said.

"Not in the same league, but yes, the same idea."

He tapped the card with one finger, frowning thoughtfully.

If Grace had to guess... her eyes narrowed, considering him.

Not State Department. He didn't have the right air of arrogance. And his eyes were too shadowed, like he'd seen too much. Maybe the State Department guys had seen just as much, but it didn't usually crack their complacency.

Not FBI. He was wearing blue jeans, a plain black t-shirt, and a worn leather jacket that looked like he'd owned it for years. No FBI guy ever showed up in Tassamara wearing anything other than a white shirt and tie. They were as bad as missionaries that way.

That left DEA, but it didn't feel quite right. Something outdoors, though, and probably in uniform, because his casual t-shirt revealed a line of lighter skin at the base of his neck.

Military? Maybe, although the way his dark hair curled on his nape was decidedly non-regulation.

"Are you looking for someone specific there?" she asked cautiously. That battered card could have been sitting in someone's wallet for years. Maybe someone outside the company had referred him to GD.

He looked as if he was debating his response, before saying, "A guy named Akira."

Okay, that was odd. A guy? The Akira she knew — her brand new sister-in-law — was not a guy. Nor was her ability to talk to ghosts public knowledge. Akira had firmly resisted formalizing any professional arrangement that utilized her gift: she was a research scientist and happy to stay that way.

"I can't say I know a guy named Akira," Grace said slowly. It wasn't a lie. Not really. But she doubted he was listening closely enough to hear the emphasis she placed on the word 'guy.' Keeping her voice casual, she asked, "So why are you looking for him?"

"I was told he might help me."

"Help you with what?" Grace asked the obvious.

Noah's mouth twisted as Emma, the waitress, slid a bright blue mug of coffee in front of him. He blinked down at the steam rising off a milky swirl in the mug, saying, "You put milk in my coffee."

"Cream, actually." Emma looked worried. "Isn't that the way you like it?"

"Yeah, but..." Noah pinched the bridge of his nose, closing his eyes for a second. Then he shut the menu he'd opened and stuck it back into the bin of random restaurant menus that Maggie kept around for the tourists. "I'll take the special."

"Good choice." Emma threw him a cheerful smile, and called over her shoulder into the kitchen behind her, "Another special, Maggie."

As Emma headed away, Grace asked, "Is that not how you take your coffee?"

"I'm used to drinking it black," he said. "On deployment, we usually only have powdered creamer. That stuff makes better fireworks than coffee."

Military. She'd called it right. Grace was on the verge of thanking him for his service, when he shot her a sideways grin.

"I do like it with cream, though. I just didn't remember saying so."

Grace felt a flush of heat run through her, head to toe.

Wow.

She'd been admiring him, but in the abstract, amused by stumbling upon such a beautiful man in such an everyday place. But his smile... it crinkled his eyes and softened his features and warmed his face. Suddenly, he was a different guy. Not just attractive, but appealing.

Really appealing.

It felt like every cell in her body sat up and took notice, and every hormone sprang to life and said, "*Him. That one.*"

Her voice was more breathless than she liked when she said, "So what sort of help are you looking for?"

He picked up the mug. His smile was gone and his voice brusque as he said, "Nothing. It's not important. It's..." His voice drifted off into a mumble, as if he were talking mostly to himself. "... a stupid idea, anyway."

"Well." Grace stood. "I should get to work."

He dipped his head, not looking at her. "Have a good day."

"You, too," Grace replied cordially, but without warmth.

But then she paused.

He was looking for Akira. He clearly wasn't going to share his story with her, but someone had sent him to find a person who talked to ghosts. And he was military, or maybe ex-military.

Maybe she owed him more than the quick brush-off she'd been about to give him. Not because of his smile, not because of the rush of attraction she'd felt, but because maybe he did need help, of the kind that she and her family had also once needed.

Would she scare him away if she started talking about dead people?

She leaned forward, reaching across him to grab a guest check pad sitting next to the cash register. Her awareness of him registered as a tingle of sensation along all the nerves closest to him, her arm, her shoulder, her cheek.

She pulled back, faintly flustered by the feeling and inwardly scolding herself for it. He was just a guy. A guy who maybe needed help. A really hot guy who maybe needed help. She pulled her purse around and began to rummage through it, not looking at Noah. "I'm sure I have a pen here somewhere," she muttered.

He cleared his throat. She looked up. He was holding a pen out to her. He made a tiny motion with his head, gesturing toward a container of pens sitting next to the register and the spare guest check pads. A glimmer of amusement in his eyes made her own lips twitch in response.

Great. Too pretty for his own good, problems in need of solving, and a sense of humor. He might as well be wearing a label with 'Grace's catnip' scrawled on it.

"Thanks." She bent her head to the pad, drawing a quick map. She wrote in the street names, then, frowning, added mileage in parentheses under the names. She wasn't as sure about the distances as she should be, but she'd been driving to the GD offices all her life. The route was too familiar for her to need to know exactly how far one turn was from the next. Ripping the map off the pad, she handed it to Noah. "My distances might be off, but after you eat, you should go check it out."

"Thank you." He didn't look at the map but set it on the counter, his eyes on her. The directness of his gaze held a question, and she felt her cheeks getting warm. Who was this guy?

"Enjoy your breakfast, Mr. Blake." She slid the strap of her purse back over her shoulder. "And welcome to Tassamara."

4

NOAH

Noah's hallucinations were talking over one another again.

"That's your aunt?" Joe whistled.

"Slow down, Tom. It's not safe."

"She's more like a big sister, really," the new guy said. *"She was eight when I was born. I grew up with her."*

"All through the night..."

Why was his subconscious inventing complicated relationships with the woman who'd just left? Big sister? That's wasn't how Noah had felt about her.

Noah's eyes fell on the map she'd drawn for him. Her handwriting was neat but angular, not loopy, and the map was straightforward. It would be easy to find the place, if he wanted to.

He wasn't sure he did.

His hallucinations had latched onto Sylvie Blair's invitation like an alcoholic with a bottle of Jack. They'd been obsessed, relentless, talking about it constantly, especially the newest one.

He'd been curious, too, though. What had Sylvie Blair meant by a problem? Why had she told him to go to General Directions? He'd tried to investigate the company, but the name was so vague that it might as well not exist on the internet, with any relevant results buried somewhere in the midst of millions of maps.

When he'd asked around, all he found were rumors, most of them ridiculous. Noah wasn't gullible enough to believe in a top-secret government agency of super-powered psychics located in the middle of a national forest. He might be crazy, but he wasn't *that* crazy.

But if General Directions was a holding company — stocks, bonds, options — maybe he had his answer. His twin, Niall, worked on Wall Street. Maybe Sylvie Blair thought she recognized him. Maybe Niall was the one with the problem.

Noah could call him. Tease his brother about attractive redheads hitting on him. Find out what his problem was. He knew the number, even though he hadn't used it in awhile.

Before Noah could decide on his next step, the waitress said, "Here you go," and set a plate of food on the counter, next to the map and business card.

"That's the special?" Noah stared at it. Three waffles, streaked with the deep blue and purple of wild blueberries, were topped with a scoop of melting whipped butter. Next to them sat four slices of crispy, thick-cut bacon. The smells rising from the food — salty and sweet, sizzled fat and baked warmth — set his stomach rumbling, his mouth watering. "Blueberry waffles?"

How long had it been since he'd last had a blueberry waffle? Not his last visit home, the one he'd cut short after two strained days. Not the visit before that, either. Christmas, though, whenever he'd last been home for the holidays.

They always had blueberry waffles on Christmas.

It had been years.

"Bacon, too," the waitress said cheerfully, sliding a pitcher of syrup over to him. "Guess you don't have to worry about your cholesterol." She didn't wait for a response but moved off to one of the booths.

"Man, those look tasty," Joe said.

"Ah, they make me wish for kahi. Kahi with geymar and honey." The Arabic woman's voice sounded wistful.

Noah took a bite. The waffles were perfect. Light and crisp, with the tang of blueberries and a hint of vanilla. Abruptly he felt more cheerful. Maybe his long drive hadn't been a total waste of time.

"My mom never made waffles. Never. Sometimes my dad got the freezer kind, though." The crying girl sniffled, then started to weep.

"Come on, Sophia," the little boy's voice said. He sounded like he was coaxing her. Noah could almost imagine a small boy slipping a hand into that of a teenage girl. *"Let's go outside. It's sunny out. You'll like it. There are flowers."*

"It's not right. It's not right." The angry man's voice faded away with the crying girl and the little boy.

"We need your help, Rose."

"He's dreamy." The new girl's voice sounded thoughtful, and like she was right in front of his face, leaning in, not a foot away. *"He looks like he should be in an ad for cologne. Or maybe underwear."*

Noah was not going to react. He was not. But he could feel color rising in his cheeks. He took another bite of waffle and chewed with determination, his eyes on his plate.

"Does he hear us?" the new girl's voice demanded. Rose. That was what the other one had called her. He might as well call her that, too.

"Not really. He might be a little sensitive, though. We tried really hard to get him to come to Tassamara and he finally did."

"Why didn't you just text him?"

"That didn't go so well."

Noah scowled, stabbing his fork into the waffle. His hallucinations were getting worse. More frequent — the voices were almost constant now. More intense — the crying and the sad singing would break his heart if he let them. More detailed — instead of words and phrases, brief snatches of conversation, it was like he was listening in on real people.

And weirder. There had been strange texts and he'd worried about them.

"He thought he'd sent the text to himself in a black-out," Joe said. *"He was afraid he was going crazy. The last thing we want is to end up trapped in some institution somewhere."*

"Mysterious texts are apparently upsetting. Who knew?" The new boy's voice was dry.

The Rose voice said, *"Your mom freaked out, too, didn't she?"*

"Yeah, people don't like getting texts from nowhere."

"Everything okay?"

For a moment, Noah thought the words were still part of his hallucination, but the waitress was refilling his coffee. "Yeah, great," he answered, not looking up.

Hesitantly, the waitress said, "If you're not loving those waffles, Maggie'll make you something else. Maybe an omelette or..."

Pulled back into reality, Noah raised his head and grinned at her.

Her words stuttered to a halt.

"Oh, my," the Rose voice said. *"That smile! He could charm the birds from the trees."*

"They're terrific." Noah set his fork down, determined to pretend his hallucinations didn't exist. "Best food I've eaten in I don't know how long."

"Just like your mom makes, right?" the waitress asked, her answering smile wide with relief.

"Better, I think. Don't tell her I said so."

The waitress mimed zipping her lips. "Our secret." She glanced down at the card and guest check Noah had pushed to the side of his plate. "General Directions?" she asked.

"Yeah. You know the place?"

"Sure, everyone does." The waitress lifted one shoulder. "You picked the right seat, though."

"Oh? How's that?" Noah paused with his refreshed coffee halfway to his mouth. The voices were still talking around him, but he focused on the waitress, trying to let the wash of hallucinated conversation flow over him as if the restaurant was still busy and bustling instead of quieting fast, the breakfast rush over.

The waitress nodded toward the empty stool where Grace had been sitting. "She doesn't act like a big shot, does she? But she runs the company. My cousin's working out there now. She says their cafeteria's not near as good as Maggie's, but the pay's good and they got benefits."

"The company?" Noah set his coffee down without taking a sip. His mind replayed the waitress's words. Runs the company? The woman who'd been sitting next to him?

"General Directions?" The waitress tapped the card. "This place? She's, like, um, CEO or something. The boss. Used to be her mom but when Mrs. Latimer passed, Grace took over. She's real nice." The waitress put the coffee back on the burner and began bustling about behind the counter.

Shit. What had he said to her exactly?

"They all are," the waitress continued. "All the Latimers. My grandma remembers when they moved here and started the business. It was real little back then. They didn't have the researchers or the government work, none of that stuff. Course I don't remember that, I wasn't even born yet."

"Government work?" Noah's fingers jittered against the edge of the counter. She'd said it was a holding company. Stocks. Bonds. Boring stuff. What sort of government work would a holding company do?

"Oh, yeah." The waitress pulled out a textbook and a notebook from the shelf under the cash register and set it down on the counter in the space on the other side of him. "Not that anyone knows much about it." She made an exaggerated wide-eyed face with a shrug and then relaxed into a normal expression as she added, "But once you get used to them, you can kinda tell. They wear suits. In Florida. In the summer."

It sounded like evidence to Noah.

"So the Latimers—?" Noah prompted the waitress.

"Real nice," the waitress replied absently as she flipped open her book. "Max comes in most days. Sometimes he tries to tell Maggie what to make for him." She shook her head. "Never a good idea."

Noah paused. Wasn't that how restaurants worked? Customers ordered the food they wanted? But he was more curious about General Directions and the people who owned it. "Who's Max?"

"Oh, he started the company. Him and his wife. She's gone now, though, so it's just him and the others." She leafed through the pages.

"The others?"

"The kids." She shot him a smile. "Not that they're kids. Grace is the youngest and you saw her, she's all grown-up."

He had. She was. Grown-up and dishonest. Or at least misleading. Why hadn't she told him she worked for the company he was asking about? Why had she claimed it was a holding company?

"Lucas, he's the oldest," the waitress continued. She seemed to have lost interest in her book, pressing a page flat then ignoring it. "We don't see him much. He travels a lot. I think he's the one who mostly does the government work. And then there's Doctor Nat. She's in pretty often, more so now. She and the sheriff, they're getting married and adopting kids. Five of them, can you imagine? They're buying this big house out on one of the lakes. I hear it's got a movie theater inside it."

"Then there's Zane. He just got married this past weekend. Real nice wedding." Her lips pursed into a smothered smile. "The bride... well, I shouldn't say that. Poor Akira."

"Akira?" Noah's tone sharpened. Grace had claimed not to know anyone named Akira. Another lie?

"Yeah, she and Zane got married this weekend. She's a scientist. Some kind of physicist, I think."

"Akira's a scientist? And a woman?" Noah blinked.

"Uh-huh." The waitress gave Noah a curious glance, before flipping open her notebook and pulling out a pencil. "It wasn't like a shotgun wedding or anything, y'know, but they're gonna have a baby real soon now. And poor Akira's been real sick."

The waitress glanced over her shoulder at the kitchen, then leaned in toward Noah. "I probably shouldn't say this, but it's not like everyone in town doesn't know already anyway. She threw up. On the minister. When they were cutting the cake. I can't believe nobody caught it on video. It would've gone viral, put Tassamara on the map. We could've been famous."

She tapped her pencil against her mouth and added thoughtfully, "Although I guess that's kind of a crap reason to be famous. And Akira wouldn't have liked it much."

"Order up, Em," came a sharp call from the kitchen.

The waitress glanced over her shoulder. "Oops, forgot about that one." She gestured at her books in explanation. "Chem test coming up. Maggie swears learning chemistry will make me a better cook. I'm not so sure, but she doesn't mind if I study when we're slow." Leaving her book and notebook where they were, she disappeared into the back.

Noah picked up a slice of bacon and bit into it with a crunch, ignoring the chatter of his hallucinations, stewing in his own thoughts.

Grace Latimer had lied to him.

She'd told him General Directions was a holding company. She didn't mention the mysterious government work. Or the research.

She'd said she didn't know anyone named Akira. According to the waitress, Akira would be, what, her sister-in-law? Not exactly a stranger.

Why had she lied?

And what was she hiding?

Noah wanted to storm into General Directions and demand answers from her. What were they up to?

Paranoid scenarios were swirling around his mind. The rumors he'd heard about psychics were nonsense, of course. Extrasensory powers were a fantasy concocted by the fertile imaginations of the same Victorians who'd turned Atlantis into a mystical advanced civilization.

But technology was another story.

Ten years ago, he'd died. Only for a couple of minutes, but the coma afterward lasted for days and no one had expected him to survive. Ever since then, he'd been hearing voices. Weird voices. Impossible voices.

Had someone decided that a dying soldier was a good subject for experimental surgery? Maybe they'd implanted something in his brain. A transmitter of some kind. Or maybe the first element of a neural communications network. Was he an early stage in an experiment gone unexpectedly wrong when he survived?

The idea that the government — his government, the government he'd served, the government for which he'd almost given his life — would treat him like a useful lab rat was… not quite unthinkable. He could grant the idea the faintest sliver of possibility.

But no. The idea was ludicrous. Delusional, almost.

Still, why had Grace Latimer lied to him? Who was Akira and why had his hallucinations locked on to her name like a guided missile?

He paid his bill, leaving a generous tip for the helpful waitress, and left the restaurant. Outside, he paused by the door, blinking from the bright sunlight. The coffee hadn't done enough. He was awake, but still tired. It felt like his brain was running in circles. If the company had secrets, demanding answers was no way to discover them. He needed a better strategy.

"Slow down. You're driving too fast."

"Do you feel the pull, Rose?"

"Nope, but I'll come along anyway."

"What makes you different?"

"Good morning." The unfamiliar male voice sounded cheerful. Noah glanced to the side, at the stranger approaching him, and automatically stepped away from the door.

"Oh." The man stopped, his expression startled. "Oh. You."

Noah paused. "Do I know you?"

The man was older, dark hair sprinkled with silver, laugh lines around his bright blue eyes. About Noah's height, he was dressed casually, in a rumpled button-down shirt with the sleeves half rolled up and lightweight pants.

"Not yet," the man said cheerfully. "Soon, though." He stuck out his hand. When Noah didn't immediately take it, he grabbed Noah's hand in both of his own, shook it firmly, then let go.

"Do you know that guy?" Joe asked.

"Are you related to him? You have the same eyes," the Arabic woman's voice said.

Noah had no idea what she was talking about. His eyes looked nothing like those of the man in front of him.

"He's my grandpa," the teenage boy's voice said. Sounding doubtful, he added, *"Maybe he could explain to Noah."*

"Your grandpa?" The Rose voice sounded equally doubtful.

Silently, Noah wanted to agree with her. No way was the man in front of him the grandfather of a teenager. He was older, but not that old.

"You know what he's like," the Rose voice continued. *"He confuses people."*

The man in front of him said, "I've been looking forward to meeting you. What took you so long?"

"I think you've mistaken me for someone else," Noah said.

"I don't think so," the man replied.

Noah forced a smile he didn't feel. "I have a twin brother. It happens."

"Maybe, but not this time. No, you're the right one, I'm sure of it." The man gave an unexpected grin. "Not that I don't look forward to meeting your brother, too, of course. But it's you I've been expecting."

"Who told you I was coming?" Noah asked. Who was this guy? Was he connected to the redhead? To the mysterious Akira?

The man looked surprised. "No one. Should someone have?"

"How — why — " Noah shook his head. He was having that sensation of being in a dream again, this time not just a feeling of surreality, but the frustration of an exam that he wasn't ready for or an appointment he couldn't get to on time.

"It's too soon. I shouldn't have said anything." The man reached for the handle of the restaurant door. "I won't bother you any more. But —" He paused.

"But?" Noah asked.

The man looked undecided.

"But?" Noah prompted him again. He hated feeling like this. He wanted answers.

"Too soon," the man muttered, as if to himself. But then he looked directly into Noah's eyes. "It really wasn't your fault, you know. Their deaths. It was a tragedy, but you didn't cause it."

Acid surged in Noah's throat.

It had been hot. Insanely hot, the sweat beading down the back of his neck, dripping into his uniform. God, he hated the desert. The place sucked. Sand everywhere, grit getting into everything, sticking to his skin. It felt like he could never get clean there.

Maybe that was more than just the dirt.

It wasn't regret exactly. He'd wanted to serve. Wanted it badly enough to enlist the day after he graduated from high school, despite his family's dismay. His mom had argued, fought, tried persuasion, but nothing could dissuade Noah. It was only after he'd gotten to the desert, seen some action, that the little niggling idea that maybe he'd screwed up crept into the back of his mind.

The doubt had distracted him. He'd been thinking about an email he'd gotten from his brother. Niall was loving college, having an amazing time, studying laughable stuff like poetry of the Italian renaissance, and partying hard. Noah could have been with him.

Thinking about that had been his first mistake.

The second — reacting too fast. Or maybe not fast enough.

Noah stuffed his hands into his pockets, clenching them into fists, trying to force his brain to shut up.

Shut up, shut up, shut up.

He didn't want to think about Joe's death. Didn't want to

remember the woman walking along the road, the moment her head turned and her eyes met his. The small boy by her side had been almost hidden by her black robes. Had she known about the IED?

She couldn't have. Why would she have been there? He'd seen her, the woman in black, a glimpse of the boy, then all the memories turned into a blur. Bits and pieces, flashes of color and pain. The explosion. The jolting truck. The weapons firing. Flames and smoke, choking on the smells in the air.

Blood.

God, so much blood.

It poured down his head, spilling into stinging eyes. And it spurted between his fingers while Joe's eyes stared up at him, confused, the light in them fading away.

Noah was gone, lost in another place and time, his heart racing, the pounding in his ears drowning out the guns, the screams, the...

"Breathe. Deep breath. Not too fast." It was a woman's voice, calm and even, breaking through the fog. "Stamp your feet. Feel the ground underneath them. Feel the air on your skin."

Noah took a shuddering breath.

Shit.

He dropped his hands to his sides.

A younger, female version of the man who'd been speaking to him had taken his place. Her dark hair held no silver but was tied back in a thick braid. She had the same blue eyes, looking right into Noah's, but her eyes held oceans. Like she'd seen everything and nothing could surprise her.

"Are you all right?" The man peered over her shoulder. "You look like you've seen a ghost."

"Do you need to sit down?" The woman asked Noah, ignoring the man behind her.

"But you don't see them, right? Just hear them," the man said, worry lines creasing his brow.

Noah blinked. Had he heard that right?

"Sound only," the man continued. "It must be so confusing."

"Dad." The woman shot him an exasperated glance. "You've said enough."

"Oh, right, right. Too soon." The man's worried frown didn't change.

Noah's heartbeat was slowing. He could hear again, street sounds, a breeze rustling the leaves of a nearby tree, and voices.

Lots of voices.

"It's not right."

"Is he okay?"

"Guardian angels God will lend thee..."

You look like you've seen a ghost. But you don't see them, just hear them. The words were replaying in Noah's mind. You don't see them, just hear them.

Ghosts.

"Doing better?" the woman said.

Noah felt heat rising, tinting his cheeks. His voice was rough as he said, "I'm fine."

"Exhaustion can be a trigger for flashbacks. You should get some rest," she said calmly.

"I'm fine," he said again. He looked between them, from one to the other. "I don't know who you think I am, but you're wrong. Coming here was a mistake."

"I hope you'll repeat it," the woman said. She held up an envelope, cream-colored, sized like an invitation. "Don't worry about the RSVP. I know you'll be there."

"I — what?" Noah took the envelope as she pushed it toward him.

"Come on, Dad." The woman grabbed the arm of the man behind her and steered him toward the door of the restaurant. "You shouldn't have said that," she scolded him gently.

"But you knew I would." The man followed her.

"Yes, but just think, you could have surprised me." She pulled the door open.

"Is he going to be okay?" The man glanced back at the still motionless Noah.

She glanced back, too, and the smile she cast on Noah was warm. "Of course."

Of course? Noah didn't feel okay. He felt angry and confused and threatened and maybe a little lost. But he knew she was right. Of course he'd be okay.

As soon as he got the hell out of this crazy town.

5

DILLON

"WE JUST GOT HERE," DILLON SAID. "HE CAN'T LEAVE."

Rose patted his knee affectionately. "Your aunt said he'd be back."

She was sitting next to Noah, with Dillon between her and Joe in the cab of Noah's truck. Nadira and Misam were on Joe's other side. Noah had rushed to his truck and taken off like the hounds of hell were after him, so quickly that only the most aware spirits had managed to pile into the truck with him. The others were still being dragged along in the vehicle's wake.

"That's not the point," Dillon grumbled. He supposed it didn't matter one way or another if Noah left now. They'd found Rose and that was the important thing. But he would have liked a chance to see his parents and to spend a little more time with his relatives and Akira. If all went according to his plan, it might be his last chance to say good-bye to them.

"I don't think he should be driving." Joe leaned forward to shoot a worried look at his friend's face. "He's tired. He didn't get any sleep. He shouldn't have stayed up all night."

"You worry like a new mama." Nadira had Misam in her lap.

47

"Or like an old mama?" Misam wiggled, giving her an impish smile.

Nadira pursed her lips in disapproval. She tightened her arms around the little boy, holding him close. "We're going very fast. I don't like it."

The trees on the side of the road were blurs of brown and green, their details lost as the truck whizzed by them. Noah was definitely breaking the speed limit. Dillon angled his head, trying to see the speedometer. Seventy. He was pretty sure the limit on this road was forty.

Movement flickered by the side of the road ahead. Dillon saw Noah start to react and braced himself, grabbing for Joe as Noah slammed on the brakes.

"Whee!" Misam chortled as he and Nadira slid through the windshield and along the hood of the truck. Rose gasped as she tumbled forward and out the door.

Noah lurched against his seatbelt, the tires squealing as he fought the truck to a standstill. But it was too late, too fast, the truck still moving as they skidded past the spot where Dillon had seen motion.

The motion was a deer, Dillon realized. No, two of them, three. Lifting their elegant heads, watching from enormous dark eyes, stepping away on their spindly legs.

Dillon's sigh echoed Noah's. Carefully, Noah pulled over to the side of the road. He put the truck in park and turned the key in the ignition. His head fell back against the headrest and he closed his eyes.

Sophia burst into the cab and the angry man fell through after her.

"I hate this!" Sophia yelled.

"It's not right." The angry man seemed to be agreeing with her. "It's not right."

With the truck at a standstill, the other ghosts began drifting forward, too, bobbing white lights and wisps clustering around Noah.

"Sleep, my love..." the singing woman crooned, her expression as blank as ever.

"Ugh," Joe grunted, waving his arm around his head as if shooing off insects.

Outside the truck, Nadira planted her hands on her hips in disgust. "I told you he was driving too fast," she called to Joe.

"That was fun!" Misam jumped up and down. "I want to do it again. Let's do it again!"

Dillon pushed his way through the truck's door to Rose. "You okay?"

"Of course." She brushed off her pink skirts as if they could have gotten dusty, and shrugged at him, eyes sparkling. "This is so exciting, Dillon. This is the best day ever."

He grinned at her. He liked these new ghosts — the lively ones, anyway — but it was good to be home. He'd missed Rose. Meeting her had made his afterlife so much more interesting.

But she was looking past him, toward Noah. Her smile faded. "Not so great for him, though, is it?"

Joe was climbing out of the truck, too, moving forward to Nadira and Misam. The abrupt stop couldn't hurt the ghosts, of course, but their ties to Noah meant they could be jolted and dragged in ways that weren't exactly comfortable.

"We ought to help him," Rose said.

"Him?" Dillon snorted. He'd spent a month trying to get Noah to come to Tassamara. He'd missed Akira's wedding. He'd had to listen to the damn singing lady's off-key lullaby about a zillion times. And he hadn't done it for Noah. "We need to help us."

"Pfft." Rose brushed off his words. "You could get away if you wanted to. The pull can't be that strong."

"I could, maybe," Dillon agreed. "But what about them?" He nodded toward the other ghosts. "They're stuck and they've been stuck for years."

Rose gave him a sideways glance. "A decade or two is nothing. I spent half a century in my house. And the boys were there even

49

longer. Forty years before I passed, they were there. They're still there, still trapped."

"Not if Noah goes near them," Dillon retorted. Rose's house — the house where Akira and Zane lived — was a big old Victorian with a turret room and a wide front porch. When he'd first been there, it had been haunted by four ghosts: Rose, her friend Henry, and two young boys, faders, perpetually playing in the backyard.

"Ooh, good point." Rose clapped her hands enthusiastically. "We should get him to stop by. If they were out in the world, maybe they'd wake up a little."

Dillon screwed up his nose. "Not likely." He waved toward the faders drifting around Noah. "They'd probably just be like those guys."

Rose pouted, before sighing. "You're probably right. I wish..." She didn't finish the thought, whatever it was. "Well. If wishes were horses."

"If wishes were horses, Noah wouldn't be haunted," Dillon said. Noah was pressing the heels of his hands into his eyes, as if he had a headache. Dillon didn't know what had happened back at the restaurant when Noah had frozen in place, but he didn't think it was good.

"Probably not," Rose agreed cheerfully. "So how were you planning on getting him un-haunted? Akira says that whole unfinished business thing doesn't work, you know."

"I know." Dillon kicked the ground. He'd hoped, more than once, that he'd find some unfinished business of his own and complete it. He'd thought it might have been his grandmother's ghost, waiting for him. And then he thought maybe helping his mom and dad would work. He'd even secretly wondered if getting his dad to smile again would do it. But nothing he'd tried had ever found him a door of his own. If he had unfinished business left, he didn't know what it was.

"I bet it would be pretty hard to find out what she needed to finish." Rose nodded toward the singing lady as she came toward them, her eyes empty, still crooning her lullaby.

"All through the night..."

"Not to mention some of the others," Rose added, giving a doubtful look to the bobbing white lights.

"We don't need to solve everybody's business, though." Dillon eyed Rose cautiously. He hadn't had a chance to explain his plan yet. At Maggie's, they'd been busy with introductions and catching up. He'd barely managed to explain the problem. And he wasn't sure how Rose was going to feel about this part of his plan. "We need a doorway, like the ones you and Henry had, and my gran."

"But you don't have one yet."

"No. But you could find one for us, couldn't you?"

"You should get your own doorway."

"But I haven't. If you found a doorway for us, we could go through it. All of us."

"All of us? What do you want to do that for?" Rose sounded dismayed.

"It's how you got un-stuck," Dillon reminded her. Rose had followed Henry through a passageway to another dimension. Maybe they'd gone to heaven but Rose was vague about the details. When she'd come back, though, she'd no longer been trapped in her house. She could go anywhere, visit any place. She still mostly stuck close to home, but it was her choice, not her fate.

"Well, yeah, but it's awfully permanent. Your way was better."

Dillon snorted. Rose hadn't been there when his grandmother's spirit ripped him loose from his car. It hadn't felt better to him. He'd been terrified and that was before he'd even visited the vortex dimension. Now that he knew what it was like, he wanted no part of it. "A doorway is safer."

"Pfft." Rose waved away the idea. "This is fine."

"Not for him." Dillon pointed to Noah.

Rose sighed. She twirled a lock of blonde hair around her finger, watching Noah.

"And I don't want to turn into one of them." Dillon waved an arm at the wisps.

"You won't." Rose said the words, but she didn't sound entirely sure of herself.

"I might. You might, too."

"I don't know." Rose looked undecided. She opened her mouth, then closed it again as Nadira came around the side of the truck.

"Come on, Nadira, don't be mad," Joe said, following Nadira to where Dillon and Rose were standing by the door.

"We could have been killed," she grumbled.

"We're already dead, Mama." Misam skipped next to her.

"It's the principle of the thing," she said. "He should be more careful."

"He doesn't even know we're here," Joe said.

"That's not the point." Nadira grabbed Misam and boosted him into the truck, ignoring Noah's living presence. Misam scrambled over Noah and she climbed after him.

Joe gave Rose and Dillon a wry smile. "She doesn't like it when Noah takes risks," he said, keeping his voice low. "You should have heard her when we came under fire. You'd think Misam was, you know, really four."

"He is really four," Nadira said, sticking her head out through the window. "He will always be four." She pulled her head back inside, still speaking, but the words incomprehensible.

"What's she saying?" Rose asked.

"It's Arabic," Dillon answered, already familiar with Nadira's habits from the weeks he'd spent with them. "She does that sometimes."

Joe cocked his head, listening. "She's cursing Noah's ancestors." His brows raised. "Ah, and now she's on the government." He stepped up into the truck, saying, "You know, Nadira, bullets can't hurt Misam and a fast stop's just going to bump him around."

In the cab, Noah dropped his hands. His voice was hoarse as he muttered, "Man, I'm tired. I've gotta sleep."

"Come on," Rose said to Dillon, following the others into the truck. "Let's go."

It was like a clown car, he thought. Ghosts on top of ghosts.

She stuck her head back out the window. "Hurry," she said. "You don't want to get left behind."

Dillon wasn't sure that he would get left behind. Rose might say that the pull was nothing, but he hadn't made any serious attempts to get away from the drag. Still, being tugged along would undoubtedly be a lot less pleasant than piling into the cab, so he joined the rest, wedging his way in between Noah and the door, as Noah started the truck.

"The nearest motel is off the highway, about ten miles away, or there's a bed-and-breakfast in town," he told Noah. "It's a lot closer."

"He doesn't hear you," Nadira snapped.

"My grandpa said..." Dillon started.

"I do not care what your grandfather thinks he knows. We have been with him for endless days. Years!" Nadira's voice rose with each word. "He does not hear us."

Rose and Joe and Dillon exchanged glances. Joe gave a tiny shrug, the merest hint of a movement of his shoulders as if to say, "I don't argue with her when she's this mad."

"I saw that." Nadira glared at him.

"Don't be angry, Mama." Misam reached up, putting a small hand on either side of her face, and patting her cheeks. "I liked stopping fast."

For a brief second she held her glare, then she softened. Shaking her head, she said, with affection, "You."

"Me!" he agreed.

"What would I do without you?" She nuzzled Misam's nose with her own, then began tickling him as he giggled furiously.

Noah pulled onto the road. As he headed back into town, he drove at a more reasonable pace.

Rose, sitting mostly on his lap, said, "I hope we stay at the bed-and-breakfast. It has a really nice television. Nothing compared to the one at your aunt's new house, though. She's got a real movie theater."

"Nat?" Dillon asked. He hadn't seen the house his aunt had

bought yet. He'd visited her in the hospital with his parents after she got shot, but he'd been away ever since.

"Uh-huh."

They started talking about the theater in Natalya's new house and the television shows and movies Rose had been watching as Noah drove. Sophia and Joe chimed in, offering their opinions, while the other ghosts sang or muttered or worried, repeating their eternal loops.

Noah evidently had seen the sign for the bed-and-breakfast on the way into town, because he headed almost directly there. The one time he paused, seeming uncertain, Rose leaned toward his ear and whispered, "Turn right."

Nadira rolled her eyes, shaking her head, but Noah turned right. He came to a stop in front of the bed-and-breakfast. It was hidden behind a white picket fence and overgrown hedges with branches arching out into the street, but a small wooden sign, with lettering burnt into the wood, revealed the name. *Sunshine B&B*.

The ghosts flowed out of the truck, the clown car in reverse, as Noah opened the door and got out himself. He grabbed a duffel bag from behind his seat and headed for the gate. Dillon and Rose trailed behind him, still talking, but Misam darted ahead of them.

"I like it," he announced from the other side of the fence.

"Oh, it's nice," Sophia said, sounding surprised.

"Wood floors," muttered Mona. "Beeswax. Or linseed oil."

Behind the hedges was a small farmhouse style building, with two stories, gable windows and a wide front porch. It looked freshly-painted, the trim a polished white. Plants surrounded it, colorful bougainvillea and hibiscus shrubs, sprawling ground cover, beds of early spring flowers.

Avery, the innkeeper, was kneeling in one of the beds, trowel in hand. They rocked back onto their knees. "Good morning," they called out, voice friendly.

Noah didn't react immediately, walking up the brick sidewalk toward the porch.

Avery scrambled to their feet. Their dark hair was short, close-cropped to their head, and they were wearing a plain blue button-down shirt, sleeves casually rolled up, and faded jeans with dirt on the knees. But their eyes were lined with black and their ears held gold stud earrings.

"Checking in?" the innkeeper tried again. They headed to catch up with Noah. "Did you have a reservation?"

Noah swung around, looking startled. "Sorry, what?"

Dillon narrowed his eyes. Sometimes it seemed like Noah didn't hear anyone, not just the ghosts. "Do you think Noah has a hearing problem?"

"Maybe it's a listening problem," Rose murmured. They exchanged glances.

Nadira might be convinced that Noah couldn't hear them, but Dillon wasn't so sure. And it wasn't just because of his grandfather's unexpected words.

Dillon had spent long enough trapped in his car, his words always lost on the people who drove it, to know that living people couldn't hear ghosts. He didn't expect anything he said to reach their ears. But something about Noah — the way he sometimes flinched when they got too loud, the way he stared fixedly into space when they talked about him, the way his jaw clenched when Sophia started crying — was different.

Akira was pretty good at ignoring ghosts. Maybe Noah had had to learn the same skill.

"How did you get him here?" Rose murmured to Dillon. "You said it took a while."

"I said he would listen if we talked to him when he was sleeping." Misam squeezed between them.

"We took turns chanting at him all night long. For days," Dillon said. If Noah was ignoring them, he wasn't just pretty good at it, he was extremely good at it.

"Weeks," Sophia added, pausing next to them.

"Last night it finally worked," Dillon said.

"We were all so happy." Misam bounced.

"Road trip." Sophia rolled her eyes and circled a finger in the air. "Woo-hoo."

"Interesting." Rose tapped a finger against her lips, but let it drop as Avery approached Noah, hand outstretched.

Joe frowned. "Is that a guy?"

"No." Nadira absently brushed a finger against the edge of her eyelashes as if testing that her own dark eyeliner were intact. "That is a woman, of course." But she sounded doubtful.

Saying something incomprehensible, the man in the apron, Chaupi, shoved his way through the other ghosts as if they were insubstantial. The ghosts ignored him.

"Avery doesn't believe in the gender binary," Dillon told the others. "They think it's limiting."

"They're a they," Rose added helpfully. "But they don't get mad if you get it wrong."

Chaupi was gesticulating, pointing at Avery, speaking volubly but still unintelligibly to the other ghosts.

"What's he on about?" Dillon asked Joe, thumb indicating Chaupi.

Joe shrugged. "No idea." He made as if to clap Chaupi on the shoulder, but his hand passed through the other ghost. "If a guy wants to wear make-up, it's his business, dude."

"Or if a girl wants short hair and blue jeans," Sophia corrected him pointedly, tugging at her own feathery locks.

"Right, yeah, whatever," Joe said agreeably.

"They're not a girl or a guy. They're just Avery," Rose said.

Chaupi said something else, speaking more slowly.

"Hey, that's Spanish," Dillon said with interest as he recognized the language. He hadn't interacted much with Chaupi. The older ghost was one of those with little interest in the others, although not nearly as faded as some of them.

"Can you understand him?" Nadira asked.

"Um, no." Dillon had only finished his first year of Spanish in school and it hadn't been his best subject. He could maybe ask the time of day and make change if he concentrated.

Chaupi tried again, his voice louder. Dillon spread his hands and shrugged to indicate his lack of understanding.

Meanwhile, Avery was introducing themself to Noah. They waved a careless hand in the air, then seemed to notice the dirt on it. "Ah, excuse me." They rubbed it roughly along their denim-clad leg and extended it to Noah who took it, looking wary, before following the welcoming Avery down the path and up the porch to the door.

With a sigh, Chaupi turned away, looking dejected. For a moment, Dillon wondered if he should try harder, tell Chaupi to talk slower, something, but Misam was bounding up the steps after Noah, Nadira hurrying after him, so Dillon abandoned the thought. They'd figure out what Chaupi wanted later.

6

GRACE

GRACE PICKED UP THE RINGING TELEPHONE, PRESSING THE button to connect the line. "General Directions," she said in her warmest, silkiest voice. "How may I direct your call?"

Her sister, Natalya, walked in the front door of General Directions just in time to hear her. She paused at the reception desk, shaking her head. When Grace hung up, Nat said, "Practicing your phone sex voice?"

"Why not?" Grace answered, amused. "It's fun. Brightens everyone's day."

"Don't you have better things to do?"

Grace clasped a hand over her heart, widening her eyes. "Better things to do than be the outward-facing front of General Directions, ensuring that our public interactions are smooth and polished—"

"Stop, stop." Natalya put a hand up in protest. "That PR guy really got to you, didn't he?"

Grace wrinkled her nose. "He was a sleaze. We don't need publicity."

"I don't think that was really what he was selling." Natalya perched on the edge of the desk. "We do need to deal with the SEC, like it or not."

"Not," Grace muttered. "Can't we just buy a senator or two?"

"Or ten or fifteen? No, and you probably shouldn't be saying that out loud."

"It's not a crime to be psychic. If the SEC doesn't like it, they should pass a law." Grace leaned back in the comfortable office chair. "It's not as if Max is a hit-and-run day trader, going for the easy scores. We invest in the companies whose stock we purchase. Our profits are based on products, not short-term gains."

"You don't need to argue with me, love." Natalya's smile was sympathetic.

Grace sighed. "I know. It's an informal inquiry. Chances are it will turn into nothing. I'm just annoyed that I have to waste my time with the whole thing."

"So says the CEO who's answering the phones at reception."

Grace laughed. "SEC paperwork is duller than dull. Sitting at the front desk? One never knows what adventures might lie in store."

"About that..." Natalya frowned. She glanced toward the door, opened her mouth, then closed it again, before sliding off the desk. Standing next to it, she said, "I believe I'll leave you to it."

"Hey, wait." Grace half-rose out of the chair but Nat kept moving, waggling her fingers at her, and heading through the door that led to the elevators. Grace sank down again.

Did Nat know something? Her sister could see the future, but she avoided sharing what she knew. Grace had long ago given up on asking her questions, but that frown... what had it meant?

Grace had sent Olivia, the usual receptionist, off to inventory their office supplies. Technically, it wasn't a job that needed to be done — Grace knew they were stocked with all the basics. But it couldn't hurt to be sure.

And Grace was curious. Would Noah Blake use the map she'd given him?

She should look busy, she decided. It would be more professional.

She poised her hands over the computer keyboard. Maybe she should write a memo.

All personnel: Do not send mysterious strangers to lurk at Maggie's. It destroys your boss's productivity.

Ha.,

But she had a better idea. Quickly, before she could overthink her decision, she sent a brief email to the entire Special Affairs division, asking if anyone knew why a guy named Noah Blake was looking for General Directions.

She wasn't going to mention Akira's name. She didn't know whether Zane or Akira were checking email on their honeymoon — she hoped not — but she didn't want to worry them. And she wasn't going to interrupt their honeymoon for anything less than a major disaster. They needed some quiet time together after the challenges of the last few months, and before the baby arrived to take away their quiet time for the next several years.

She turned away from the keyboard. If only the phone would ring again. She'd feel stupid pretending to talk to someone but a real call, that would be okay. And she could rock the phone sex voice, let Mr. Not-so-charming see what he'd missed by blowing her off earlier. She stared at the phone, willing it to ring.

It didn't.

She sighed.

10:30.

Could his car have broken down on the drive to the office? That seemed unlikely. So maybe he wasn't coming. Grace picked up a pencil and tapped it against the desk, wondering how long she should give him. Maybe she should give up and get back to her own desk. Do some of her own work. Damn it, she was usually a lot more decisive than this.

And what was the big deal? Fine, hot guy in Maggie's didn't happen every day, but Grace never had any trouble meeting men. Keeping them, that was another story. But this wasn't that, anyway.

This was just a guy with a business card that might mean nothing at all.

"I'm finished." Olivia's cheerful voice interrupted her reverie. The receptionist waved the tablet Grace had given her earlier in the day. "Office supplies inventoried. I'd say we've got enough post-its to make it through the apocalypse."

"Yeah, the zombie kind." Grace stood and took the offered tablet with a sigh.

"Are post-its useful against zombies?"

"Apparently they'll come in handy for creating watch schedules after we lose power and are holed up in here against the onslaught." Grace quickly skimmed the list Olivia had tabulated. It seemed fine, nothing missing, which meant she either needed to find the receptionist another task to keep her busy or quit waiting for Noah Blake to arrive.

"Is that likely?" Olivia said, uncertain.

Grace smiled at her, moving out from behind the desk so that Olivia could take her place. "No, but it explains why Zane doesn't get to do inventory anymore."

"Gotcha." Olivia's return smile was relieved. "Does that explain the duct tape, too?"

"Apparently there's no such thing as too much duct tape," Grace agreed. She gazed at the door for a moment, mouth twisting. All right, time to give up on the mysterious Mr. Blake.

Turning to Olivia, she said, "We might get a visitor later, a guy named Noah Blake. He'll probably ask for Akira when he arrives, but send him in to me."

"Will do," Olivia said.

As Grace headed down the hallway to her office, her phone rang. She checked the display. Lucas. She frowned. He and Sylvie were on the west coast, doing a job with the FBI in Seattle, so it was early for him to call. She answered the phone, saying, "Good morning."

He didn't bother with the polite response. "What does he look like?"

Grace's brows rose. Was Lucas responding to her email? Already?

"Who?" she asked, just to be sure.

"Noah Blake. Did you see him or did he call? Did Dillon text you?" Lucas's voice held an entirely unexpected urgency.

"Dillon? Isn't he with you?" Grace opened the door to her office and crossed to her desk. She reached down and slid a finger behind the strap of her sandal so she could kick it off.

"Not anymore," Lucas said.

Grace paused, one shoe on, one shoe off. "Not anymore? Since when?"

"We lost him at the AlecCorp hearing."

"The AlecCorp hearing?" Grace's tone sharpened. "That was weeks ago."

"You think I don't know that?"

"How do you lose a ghost?" She sat down abruptly, disregarding her shoes.

"Right. Because it's so easy to keep track of an invisible teenager."

Despite her concern, Grace couldn't resist a snort of laughter at her brother's disgruntled tone.

"This guy you were asking about, Noah Blake. Did you see him?" Lucas continued. "What does he look like?"

"I did, yeah. I ran into him at Maggie's. He had a business card, one of the generics, and was asking about GD." Grace paused. How did she want to describe Noah to her brother? "Dark hair, dark eyes. Ah... a nice smile." Nice wasn't really the word for it. But sexy as hell, meltingly attractive didn't seem like the right description to give to her big brother. "Have you met him?"

"No, I wasn't there. Sylvie —"

Grace could hear Sylvie's voice in the background, asking a question. Lucas must have put his hand over the phone, because his voice was muffled as he answered her.

Grace waited.

Lucas came back. "Sylvie wants to know if he was drop-dead beautiful."

Grace bit back her laugh. Lucas sounded even more disgruntled than he had before. "Yep, that's him."

"Good. Noah Blake, that's got to be a pretty common name. It's probably too late, he's probably gone, but get back to Maggie's. See if he paid with a credit card. Maybe Emma will remember him."

Her brother was delivering orders with a snap-to-it urgency that made Grace's hackles rise. She leaned back in her chair, frowning, amusement gone. "I have a busy day ahead of me, Lucas. Why don't you tell me what this is about first?"

"I'll get someone else then. Who's in town? Is Dave available?"

"Or," Grace said, pretending a patience she didn't feel, "you could tell me what's going on." She hated when Lucas got all authoritarian and bossy on her. Sometimes he acted like she was still the littlest kid, the baby of the family, instead of a competent — some might even say highly competent — adult. "What does Noah Blake have to do with Dillon?"

"Good question." Lucas sounded grim. "He's haunted. Dillon said he was collecting ghosts."

"Collecting them?" The picture that sprang to Grace's mind of a faded basement lined with dusty shelves and spirits trapped in bottles, silently screaming to be set free, had to have come from some old horror movie. The image that followed, of ghosts like Dresden porcelain shepherdesses lined up on white doilies, was hardly more comforting. "What does that mean?"

"Dillon described it as a magnetic attraction, like ghosts were drawn to him."

"Like a ghostly undertow or something? The spiritual equivalent of a rip current?" Grace had never heard of such a thing. And she knew quite a lot about ghosts.

Back when Akira first confirmed that their house was haunted, Grace had hired a researcher to investigate every fact or rumor ever known about ghosts. She'd read hundreds of pages of material covering ghosts through history, from folklore and tradition to modern sightings and technological developments. She couldn't say she'd memorized it all, but she would have remembered reading about a ghostly vacuum cleaner.

"You now know as much as I do."

Grace swiveled in her tall-backed office chair to stare out the window behind her. She'd picked her office for the view. It was on the ground floor in a back corner, looking out on the forest surrounding the General Directions grounds. She loved the serenity of the green and gray and brown, the sense of peaceful timelessness the sight evoked. When her job got stressful — which it did — it reminded her that a world existed beyond her walls and that it would continue on regardless of the decisions she made.

Plus, she liked the squirrels. Her brothers called them rats with tails, but Grace loved their energy and playfulness. Unfortunately, the squirrel show wasn't playing in the middle of the mid-winter morning.

"Has Dillon been collected?"

Lucas sighed. "Maybe. He wanted to help the other ghosts. He thought he could get away if he tried, but..." Lucas paused and his voice was rougher when he continued, "Since then, all we know is that he thinks he's fine and doesn't want us to worry."

"If you're worried about Dillon, why didn't you say something? You should have told us."

"Told Akira?" Lucas replied.

Grace's mouth twisted. Akira's pregnancy, so smooth for the first few months, had taken an unexpected turn after the holidays when she developed late-onset morning sickness. Her doctor said it was stress, nothing to fret about, but that she needed to relax and stop worrying.

As far as Grace could tell, not worrying was not in Akira's nature. But telling her that Dillon might be in trouble right before her wedding would certainly have been more stressful than not.

"Well, maybe not," Grace conceded. "But what did you say to her? She must have noticed that Dillon wasn't with you."

"We said he'd met some other ghosts and was spending some time with them, planning to be home soon. Sylvie showed her his last message and told her he must have lost track of time. She didn't seem totally convinced, but she let it go."

"You should have told me, then," Grace said.

"Nat was in the hospital. Akira was throwing up all the time. You were buying houses and adopting kids and arranging weddings. Not to mention running the company, signing paychecks and sending out those little scheduling memos of yours. You had plenty to do. And enough to worry about."

Grace's brows rose. It was unlike her brother to have noticed that. Her family tended to assume their plans would take care of themselves. They never did, but usually Grace handled the pesky details so unobtrusively that they might as well have.

"Is that you saying that or is it Sylvie?" she asked.

Lucas chuckled. "Sylvie pointed it out to me. I think she might be a little scared of you."

Grace snorted. Her brother's girlfriend was a former Marine, a private security consultant, and not scared of anything or anyone.

"Ow," Lucas said, but with a laugh. "I'm told the proper word is awe."

"Tell Sylvie the feeling's mutual." Grace swiveled back to her desk. "Still, I might have been able to do something."

"Like what?"

"He was in the courthouse that day for a reason."

"Along with several hundred other people."

"We could have gotten an investigator working on it. Put Sylvie with a sketch artist. Run the image through some facial recognition software." Grace thought back to her interaction with Noah. "He's ex-military. We would have gotten a hit on one of the DoD databases, I bet."

"What makes you think that?"

"Ex-military and in the courthouse for the AlecCorp hearings," Grace mused, ignoring her brother's question. "I bet he worked with them." She turned to her computer.

"How do you know he's ex-military?" Lucas asked.

"He told me so." Grace's fingers flew over her keyboard, composing a quick note to one of the investigators she used for routine background checks.

"He told you? You talked to him?"

"Not about ghosts. But yeah, I told him to order the special. We chatted."

"I don't want you talking to him again, Grace. You need to leave this to me." Grace didn't hear Sylvie say anything, but she must have, because Lucas corrected himself quickly. "Me and Sylvie. Leave this to us."

"Don't be ridiculous," Grace replied. She paused in her typing. How deep did she want the investigator to go? A basic background check would be quick, even with just a name and a probable past employer, but a high-level security clearance would net her a lot more information. How much did she need to know about Noah Blake's history?

"It's not ridiculous. Bad enough that Dillon is with him. If he worked for AlecCorp, he's dangerous. I don't want you anywhere near him." Lucas's voice held a crisp, decisive, older brother tone that Grace hated.

"That's not your call."

There was need and there was want, Grace decided. She didn't know what she might need to know, but she wanted to know every-thing. She added another line to her email.

"AlecCorp was into some scary shit. We have no idea who this guy is. Whatever's going on with him, he's not in a good place."

"Probably not." Grace hit Send on her email. "But I care about Dillon, too, you know."

She couldn't say this to her brother — would never say it to him — but she and Dillon had actually been much closer than Lucas and

Dillon. Dillon loved his father, of course, but for much of Dillon's life, Lucas had been away, either at college or working, while their parents raised Dillon.

For her, though, Dillon had been more like a beloved baby brother than a nephew. She'd toted the toddler Dillon around with her like a doll. They'd been together every day. At least until the last few years of his life, when she'd been away at school, too. She felt a twinge of a familiar pain and stuffed it away.

"I know you do," Lucas said. "That's not the point. This guy could be dangerous."

"He's not," Grace replied. "Certainly not to me."

"You don't know that."

Grace had no idea what Lucas was imagining. Did he think Noah would kidnap her? Hold her for ransom? Tie her up and... hmm, that might not be so bad, actually. If he liked whipped cream more than whips, anyway.

She suppressed a laugh. It was a good thing her brother couldn't read her mind over the phone. She didn't think their imaginations were running along the same lines.

"I'll be fine, Lucas."

"I'm serious, Grace."

"As am I."

"He's haunted for a reason."

"Is he?"

"He must be."

"So why were we?"

Lucas didn't answer.

Grace turned back to her window, but this time she barely noticed the beauty of the trees, her gaze far away. All those hours, all that research, all those pages of reading, and the fundamental questions had never been answered. Why was Dillon a ghost? And how could they help him?

Grace's calendar chimed an alert. She had a meeting in five minutes. Reluctantly she turned away from the window. She didn't have time to dwell on the mysteries of the universe: she had a company to run.

But first things first.

"I gave him a map to GD and told him to come by after he finished his breakfast," she told her brother. "I'll let you know how it goes."

7

NOAH

Noah woke up slowly, groggy from sleeping in the daytime. Late afternoon sunlight rimmed the drawn curtains, leaving a line of light on the wooden floor.

The room was silent.

He sat up. He didn't feel rested but he wasn't bleary-eyed tired anymore either.

The room was just as it had been when he'd crashed onto the bed — spartan but spotless, with cream-colored walls and Shaker-style furniture. His duffel bag sat on a luggage rack at the end of the double bed, with the simple coverlet kicked down, almost covering it. A fan spun lazily overhead, creating shadows on the ceiling, a cool breeze, and a faint hum.

The hum was the only sound he could hear.

He lay back against the pillow.

He didn't want to think about what had happened outside the restaurant. Those memories were old, dead, gone. It was the past and it should stay there.

But how had that stranger known him? And what did he know?

He'd mentioned ghosts and that was ridiculous. Noah knew what came after death — nothing.

Human beings were collections of cells powered by a beating heart and electrical impulses jolting around the brain and nervous system. Shut that down and the only thing left was rotting meat, bones, and teeth. And hair. He'd heard that hair supposedly still grew after death, but even that sounded unlikely to him.

Dead was dead.

Oh, maybe if there was such a thing, Joe could be a ghost. Noah could understand why Joe might haunt him. Maybe even the Iraqi woman and the kid. But wouldn't they be ghostly? Moaning and wailing and clanking chains or something? Or demanding that he fulfill their unfinished business, whatever it might be?

Or wanting their revenge?

But Noah pushed that thought away. What about the others?

The singing lady was sort of ghostly. She sang her lullaby over and over again, the tune desperately sad. But why the hell would she be haunting him? The cleaning lady, the fake Chinese guy, all the random phrases and mysterious murmurings... could they really be ghosts?

Noah cleared his throat. Softly, tentatively, a question in the word, he spoke. "Hello?"

He felt like an idiot.

Silence answered him.

Of course it did.

His hallucinations were misfiring synapses in his brain or an excess of dopamine or damage from the hit he'd taken in Iraq, nothing else. And his paranoid ideas about General Directions were fantasies at best. At worst, delusions demonstrating his deepening insanity.

Noah rolled out of bed and headed toward the room's attached bathroom, shaking his head. He should have known better. But as he showered, his thoughts kept straying back to his encounters of the morning. Why did the man at the door seem to recognize him? The woman, his daughter, who had she thought he was? And why had Grace Latimer lied to him?

His brain was running in circles, one absurd idea after the next, as he pulled on his clothes. As far as he could see, he had two choices: leave and forget this whole weird day had ever happened or stay here and try to investigate. The first would be the sensible thing to do. But he couldn't walk away, not yet.

He went down the stairs and paused in the foyer. A hallway led toward the back of the house and he could hear voices coming from that direction.

Familiar voices.

Noah headed toward the sounds. The clean freak was fussing about dust, the way she did, and the crying girl actually sounded cheerful as she said, *"I remember that. Can we watch?"*

The Rose voice said, *"Maybe later. Let's let Misam practice."*

Noah paused in the doorway of a large open room. The walls were lined with shelves overflowing with books and knickknacks — crystal balls, carved wooden boxes, candles in ornate holders, mysterious jars and bottles. It could have been an alchemist's lab in a video game, except for the small kitchen, separated from the rest of the room by a breakfast bar with stools, and the enormous flat-screen television in the middle of the far wall.

The innkeeper was sitting on one of the stools, a bowl in one hand, a spoon in the other, eyes intent on the screen. A sitcom was playing, one Noah vaguely remembered.

"Good show?" Noah ventured when Avery took no notice of him.

"Ah, hello." Avery started, standing and turning to place the bowl and spoon on the counter. "How are you doing? Did you rest well?"

"Yeah, thanks."

The innkeeper had changed his clothes. Or was it her clothes? Noah wasn't sure. He'd thought at first that Avery was male, then, after he spotted the eyeliner, surely female, but even the red jacket and tight black pants the innkeeper now wore were ambiguous. His hallucinations had claimed that the innkeeper was neither, which seemed like a weird way for his subconscious to try to process uncertainty. Still, given that the ambiguity had to be intentional, maybe his subconscious was onto something.

"It's almost time for our cocktail hour," Avery continued. He or she — they — gave Noah a friendly grin. "Well, I call it that, but it's really just wine and cheese. Can I offer you some?"

"*You have to concentrate,*" the Rose voice said.

Good idea, Noah thought. Maybe the innkeeper wouldn't know anything about top-secret experiments, but it was a small town. They must know something about the company and the people involved with it. Some careful questioning could net Noah some useful gossip. Would visiting military types stay at a bed-and-breakfast?

"*Touch the button, then imagine putting all your weight on it.*"

What button? Noah wondered.

"*Like you're doing a handstand on your finger,*" the voice continued.

Noah kept his expression even, but he wanted to roll his eyes. More nonsense, of course. He should have realized.

The innkeeper was looking at him expectantly, so he crossed to the bar. "Uh, a glass of wine would be great, sure."

"*It works better if you try to flow through it,*" the teenage boy's voice said. "*Like when you go through a wall and you get that shivery feeling.*"

Resolutely, Noah forced his attention away from his hallucinations.

"I've got a Chardonnay chilling or a very pleasant Pinot Noir. If you prefer something richer, I could open a Cab."

Noah rubbed the back of his neck. A lot of guys came home and hit the bottle hard, but Noah's fleeting experiences with the same had only made his problems worse. And wine... well, he knew white, he knew red. "Whatever you've got open is fine."

"Pinot Noir it is, then." The innkeeper bustled around the small kitchen.

Noah slid onto a stool seat, wondering where to start, considering and rejecting one opening line after another.

"Nice place you've got here," he finally said as Avery set a glass of red wine on the counter.

"Thank you." Avery glanced around the room with proprietary satisfaction. "I enjoy it."

"Town seems kinda small for the tourist trade." Noah kept his voice casual. "You stay busy?"

"You'd be surprised."

Noah waited, hoping for more, but the innkeeper was digging in the fridge, head obscured.

"Like pushing," the little boy's voice said. *"But with all of me."*

"Yes, just like that," the Rose voice said.

"How so?" Noah prompted Avery.

Avery emerged, hands full. They closed the fridge door with a hip. "Well, Florida," they said vaguely. "Lots of visitors. We get our share."

Noah held back his sigh. Interrogation had never been his forte. At least this one was in English. "Glad you had space available for me, then."

"You had good timing. I was fully booked over the weekend. The last of those guests just left this morning, but I've got a nice young couple staying in the front room and a hiker upstairs taking advantage of the midweek discount." Avery set the cheese on a plate as they spoke, then added some crackers. "And have you decided how long you'll be staying?"

"Not yet." Noah picked up his wine and took a sip, refraining from a grimace with difficulty. Why did people drink grape juice gone bad?

"No rush. But we do have a weekly rate, if you're interested." Avery put the plate on a tray that already held several glasses.

Noah nodded an acknowledgement, but when the voices behind him broke out into cheers and applause, he forced his gaze to drop to the countertop, fighting the temptation to look over his shoulder.

There was nothing behind him. He knew that. How many times had he looked toward a voice only to see nothing? But when he'd controlled his automatic reaction, he looked up to see that Avery was staring past him into the lounge, dark eyes sharp and narrowed.

"Good job, Misam!" Joe said.

"You got it!" The Rose voice sounded delighted.

"I did it, I did it. Did you see, Mama? I did it!"

Noah risked a quick glance. Nothing. "Something to see?" he asked.

"Something's wrong with the television." Avery gave a quick head shake before turning to the refrigerator. "Let's take the wine out to the patio. It's going to be a lovely evening."

Noah leaned back against the counter. The television looked fine to him. The sitcom had ended and some talk show that he didn't recognize was on, but the picture was clear and steady. "What's wrong with it?"

"It's playing itself." Avery had a bottle of white wine in one hand, sparkling water in the other. They gestured toward the television with the wine. "The channel just changed on its own. It's been doing that all afternoon."

"Probably some dust in your remote," Noah offered. He let his gaze skim the room's surfaces, searching for the telltale device. "A short of some kind."

"Oh, yeah, could be." Avery added the bottles to the tray. They lifted it, balancing the weight easily, and started toward a door set in the back wall.

Noah pushed away from the counter and followed. The remote was sitting on an end table next to the couch. He scooped it up. "I'll take a look."

"No, don't do that," the Rose voice said. It was followed by a chorus of other complaints.

Noah paused. Ghosts. That's what the stranger had said, that he was hearing ghosts. But what a bizarre idea. Ghosts were fantasies made up by camp counselors to scare school kids or the wishful thinking of the recently bereaved. They weren't real.

And if they were, what would they want with a television remote?

Noah popped the back of the remote off, shaking out the batteries, searching for signs of dust or damage. The infrared sensor looked clear. He blew a quick short breath into the case, hoping for a hair or bit of fuzz to float away.

"Put it back, please." The Rose voice was right next to his ear, so close that it sounded as if she was peering over his shoulder into the remote, too.

"He cannot hear you," the Arabic woman's voice said, sounding exasperated. *"How many times do I have to tell you that?"*

Noah stared down at the open remote in his hands.

His hallucinations were his own traumas resonating in his mind in ways he didn't understand, he reminded himself. His broken brain picked up on incidents in his life and wove stories around them. That was all that was happening.

But his fingers felt stiff as he put the remote back together, sliding the batteries in, tilting it up to check that the light indicator showed that it had power, pressing the back panel into place, then setting it down on the side table.

"Thank you." The Rose voice sounded triumphant. The television promptly changed channels, once, twice, a third time, a fourth, flickering through stations with scant pauses on each.

Noah pressed his lips together. Then, carefully, he turned the remote so that the infrared sensor was pointing away from the television and toward the kitchen.

It wouldn't prove anything. Some newer television remotes used wireless frequencies to solve line-of-sight problems. But neither the television nor the remote looked like the latest and greatest model.

The channels stopped changing.

"Oh, that is just mean," the Rose voice complained.

Avery paused on their return from outside. "Interesting."

"It's definitely a problem with your remote," Noah said.

With the remote... or with something else?

If he had a chip in his head...

If General Directions had done something to him...

If, if, if.

"*It's not a problem,*" the Rose voice said, sounding indignant. "*We were having fun. Misam wants to learn to change the channels and Sophia wants to watch the Disney channel. Put it back the way it was.*"

Noah shivered with a sudden chill. He tucked his arms against his chest and glanced up, looking for the air-conditioning vent that must be near him.

"I'll take care of it later," Avery said. "Why don't you just turn it off for now?"

As Avery headed toward the kitchen, Noah picked up the remote and pressed the power button, turning the television off. But he paused before setting the remote down again.

"*Come on,*" the Rose voice said, pleadingly. "*Be nice, please. We're not hurting anything. I can turn the volume down if it's too loud.*"

Noah's lips twitched. There was an irony. One of his damn hallucinations offering to turn the volume down. And wouldn't his life be different if it was that simple?

But he set the remote down, pointed toward the television, and showed no reaction when the Rose voice said happily, "*Thank you, thank you.*"

Spoiled grape juice or not, he was ready for that drink.

8

GRACE

He hadn't come.

Grace's disappointment felt irrational, like she was a child who'd been deprived of a treat, instead of a mature professional. But, of course, she was worried about Dillon. Or at least so she told herself.

She turned off her computer with one last glance at the clock on the screen. After seven already. She wouldn't be the last person in the office: some of the researchers routinely worked late into the night. Olivia would be long gone, though, and there was no way Noah would show now.

Her stomach growled and she pressed a hand to it. She should call her brother. He would have had a busy day himself but she knew he'd want to know what she'd found out. He wasn't going to be happy when he learned the answer was absolutely nothing.

She picked up her desk phone, then set it down again at the gentle knock on her office door. Her father didn't wait for an answer but peered around the edge of the door.

"Busy?" he asked her.

"Just wrapping up."

"You work too hard." He came in and took a seat in one of the comfortable chairs in front of her desk.

She gave him an affectionate smile. His words were rote, too familiar to hold any weight. But her smile faded as she took a closer look at him. He looked distracted, almost worried. "What's wrong? Is it Nat?"

Her sister had been shot and nearly killed several weeks ago. She was doing well — out of the hospital and recovering steadily, much faster than all the doctors' predictions — but the sensation of unsettling fear that had gripped Grace at the time hadn't fully faded yet.

"No, no." Her father waved off her concern. "But..."

"But?"

"I may have made a mistake today," he said with a sigh.

"What sort of mistake?"

He didn't answer her right away, so she waited, puzzled. Max's intuition didn't often steer him wrong.

"I think I need you to hire someone." He said the words slowly, as if thinking them out, but then finished with a decisive nod and a real smile. "Yes, that's it. I need you to hire someone."

"Okay." Grace grabbed the pad of paper that always sat on the corner of her desk and a pen. Pen poised, she asked, "Name, job, contact info?"

"Oh, I don't know any of that."

Grace set the pen down and gave him a Look. Her brothers and sister would have winced and apologized immediately, but her father didn't even have the decency to look abashed.

"I'm sure you'll stumble across him somewhere. I just need you to give him a job when you do. Something that will keep him in Tassamara." Her father's smile turned hopeful.

Grace didn't even know where to begin. "Stumble across him? What, am I supposed to start offering jobs to any strange guy I see?" And then a thought struck her. "Wait. What do you know about this guy?"

"Ah..." Her father grimaced. "Nothing. Not really. But I recognized him and..." His words trailed off and he looked away from her, tugging at his earlobe and shifting in his chair.

"And?"

"I just think I may have made a mistake," he muttered. "Scared him off. You know how it goes."

Grace did know how it went, at least for her father. Normal people — the ones who didn't believe in psychic abilities, magical powers, or a world beyond the one their eyes could see and their hands could touch — tended to start giving her father wary looks and hurrying away from him when he got started.

"What did you do?"

"That's not important." He waved off her question, still not meeting her gaze.

"How did you recognize him?"

"Also not important." He looked back at her and gave her a bright smile. It was similar to one Natalya used sometimes, a warning that all further questions were going to be met with noncommittal non-answers.

Grace sighed. "Is this guy, by any chance..." She paused as she thought how to phrase the question. "...good-looking?"

"Absolutely," her father agreed promptly. "Almost too much so. The kind of looks that would make one want to write him off as shallow right away. He's not, though. Shallow, that is."

Noah Blake. It had to be. How had her father met him?

"What do you know about him?" Grace asked.

"Not important." Max stood, apparently feeling that their business was settled. "So you'll do it? Find him and offer him a job?"

Grace picked up her pen again, then set it down. "How am I supposed to find a guy whose name you don't even know?"

"I have faith in you, Gracie."

Grace forbore a roll of her eyes, but with difficulty. It was just like her father to expect her to accomplish the impossible.

Still, she did know Noah's name. Soon enough she'd have contact information for him. Even without more information from her father, she probably could track Noah down, whether or not he ever followed up on her invitation to General Directions.

And since she needed to discover what was happening with Dillon, she would have been looking for Noah anyway, even without Max's prompting. The only thing that had changed was that now she needed to hire Noah, not just talk to him.

"Fine," she said. "I'll take care of it."

———

Three days later, Grace was not so sanguine.

She had Noah Blake's phone number. Unfortunately, he wasn't answering his phone.

She had his address, too. Her father and sister had seen Noah speeding out of Tassamara, but no one had seen him back at his apartment. Wherever he'd gone, it wasn't home.

She had his employment history, his credit rating, and his military records. She knew his birthday, his social security number, and where he'd graduated from high school.

None of that was helping her find him.

Neither was her brother. Gritting her teeth, she did not hang up on Lucas with an effort that deserved a gold star on some invisible karma board somewhere. "We've discussed this," she said into her headset. "There's nothing that you can do here that I can't do just as well. And the FBI needs you where you are."

"I'm worried about my son." Lucas didn't quite growl the words, but it was close.

"I hear that, I do." Grace glanced at her speedometer and lifted her foot off the gas pedal. She wasn't afraid of getting a ticket on the road into GD, but she'd feel like an idiot if she got into an accident because her brother was annoying her. "So am I. But I'm doing everything that can be done."

"Not everything," Lucas muttered.

"We've discussed this, too. Discussed it to death, in fact." With the information she had, Zane could find Noah in minutes — but not from Belize. It was too far away. He'd need to fly back to the U.S. to be close enough for his talent to work.

"I know, but..."

"But nothing," Grace said. "You agreed. We are not disturbing Zane and Akira on their honeymoon. They need this time."

Lucas sighed.

Patiently, Grace said, "I've got an investigator sitting on Noah's apartment, waiting for him to appear."

"Noah? Getting a little familiar, aren't you?"

"I am familiar with him. At this point, I probably know more about him than his mother does." Lucas gave a skeptical huff, but Grace continued. "As soon as Noah shows up at his apartment, I'll fly up there and talk to him. We'll find Dillon."

"I'll fly there," Lucas said. "I don't want you anywhere near him."

Grace rolled her eyes. Her brother could be so damn bossy. Sometimes he acted like he was still a teenager talking to his baby sister. Tapping her fingers against the steering wheel, she slowed for the guard at the security booth and hit the button to roll down her window. "Hi, Bill. How're you doing today?"

"Good, good. Been a quiet morning." The guard nodded at the kayak strapped to the roof of her car. "Heading out later?"

"Looking forward to it," Grace replied. The weather report had been perfect — the late afternoon should be clear, with a light breeze but no rain, the best possible weather for kayaking. Later in the year, afternoons would be muggy with almost daily thunderstorms, and the bugs would be a nightmare. And even though she was starting to think she'd never catch up on her email, she needed the break. It had been a long week. "How about you? Anything going on this weekend?"

"Ah, the wife's got a honey-do list a mile long. She keeps me busy."

"Well, don't let her work you too hard." With a wave, Grace passed through the gate and continued toward the office.

83

"Finished with the small talk?" Lucas asked, his voice dry.

"Yep. And finished with this conversation, too," Grace replied. "You're being ridiculous."

"He could be dangerous."

"He's not." Grace's hands tightened on the steering wheel. She was not going to yell at her brother. They weren't children anymore. They were two adults, having a professional difference of opinion, and she was not going to yell at him.

Maybe if she kept telling herself that...

"Can't you get anything more out of Nat?" Lucas demanded.

Grace snorted. Her sister was being, if possible, even more aggravating than her brother and father. When Grace asked for advice, Natalya just smiled beatifically and said it didn't matter, that everything would be fine in the long run. What good was the long run when Grace needed to know what to do today?

"Feel free to call her yourself," Grace said.

"Maybe I'll do that."

Grace envisioned her brother and sister managing to mutually annoy one another as much as they were annoying her. It was almost as good as counting to ten. "Good. I'll talk to you later."

"The second you learn anything," Lucas ordered.

Grace bit back the sigh that wanted to escape. She was not going to yell at her brother, not, not, not.

"And no offering Blake a job until we get there," he added. "I don't care what Dad says, I want to find out what he knows about these ghosts before you do anything."

Grace bit harder. Fortunately, he said good-bye and hung up before she snapped at him, but she was still fuming as she entered the building.

Olivia wasn't at her desk. Grace frowned and glanced at her watch. "Olivia?" she called.

The young receptionist emerged from the open door behind her desk that led to the security station. "Good morning, ma'am," she said with a bright smile.

"Ma'am?" Jensen, the guard tasked with watching the monitors during the day, stuck his head out of the security station. "Something you should see in here."

Grace raised her eyebrows.

Olivia nodded in confirmation. "You need to check this out."

Grace followed the two of them into the station. The wall of monitors looked almost as innocuous as usual: scene after scene of empty corridors, closed doors, and tall fences. But one of the screens was zoomed in on a close-up of Noah Blake as he raised a pair of binoculars to his eyes.

"Ahhh." Grace released a sigh of satisfaction. She put her hands on her hips. "There you are."

"You know him?" Jensen said, taking a seat.

Grace nodded, eyes intent on Noah. "I was expecting to see him here a few days ago. His name's Noah Blake."

"That's him? The no-show?" Olivia asked.

Grace nodded again. "Damn, but he's pretty," she added under her breath. He'd shaved, so the stubble was gone, but if anything it just made him more appealing.

"He is, isn't he?" Olivia fanned herself. "So hot!"

Grace smothered her chuckle with a cough.

Olivia glanced over her shoulder with an unrepentant grin. She fluttered her fingers at chest-height. "What can I say? He makes my heart go pitter-patter. Other parts, too."

Grace laughed, then sobered. "We shouldn't be talking like this. Sexually suggestive comments create a hostile work environment," she said, quoting from the three-hour sexual harassment seminar she'd made the entire company take after she found out that her brother was sleeping with an employee. "Sorry, Jensen."

"Don't mind me, ma'am," Jensen said, not looking away from the screen. "I'm not blind. I don't swing that way, but if I did, he'd do it for me, too."

Olivia looked like she was trying not to laugh, but she managed an apologetic, "Sorry, Grace, Jensen."

Grace shook her head, her own smile escaping. She looked more closely at the screen. "Where is he?"

Jensen tapped a couple of keys on his keyboard and the screen zoomed out so that Grace could see the forest surrounding Noah. He was outside the fence that enclosed the grounds, in the public lands. Grace recognized the area.

"How did you pick him up out there?" she asked. "That's state land, isn't it?"

"He triggered one of those camera traps the wildlife service asked us to put up," Jensen replied.

"Gotcha." Grace watched Noah set the binoculars down and raise his other hand to his mouth. He took a bite, then tossed something over his shoulder. Grace pointed at the monitor. "What was that?"

"Apple core," Jensen reported. "He's got food out there."

"Yep," Olivia agreed. "He was eating an apple. It was very... tempting." She and Jensen exchanged glances. Olivia muffled her chuckle with her hand, while Jensen's smirk told Grace that whatever commentary she'd missed a few minutes ago would have sent the sexual harassment instructor into hysterics.

She ignored it, frowning. "That's not good."

"Nope. You want I should go out there and run him off?" Jensen sounded eager.

"No, no," Grace said hurriedly. Folding her arms across her chest, she tapped her foot on the floor, and considered her options. She had no idea what Noah thought he was doing out there. What was he going to learn by skulking in the forest?

Theoretically she didn't mind if he spent the next few weeks watching the General Directions parking lot while they waited for Akira to finish her honeymoon. Communicating about his problem would be a lot easier if Akira could tell them what the ghosts had to say.

But it was February and leaving food waste in the forest was a terrible idea. Not to mention illegal.

"All right. I'm going to go talk to him," she said.

"Ma'am?" Jensen spun in his chair, turning to face her so quickly that the coffee in the cup he was holding slurped out and onto his shirt. He jolted to his feet, swiping at his chest.

"I'm going out there," Grace repeated. She glanced down at her clothes. Her outfit was, frankly, adorable. A crisp raspberry power suit with pencil skirt and matching heels, it was sophisticated, bright, daring, but conventional at the same time. Not, however, the best choice for tromping around in the woods. Maybe she should change into the casual clothes she'd brought for kayaking later.

"You shouldn't do that," Jensen said. "I'll go talk to him."

Grace paused. That might be easier. But she didn't want to scare Noah off. He might disappear at the sight of a uniformed guard heading in his direction and she wasn't going to lose him again, not if she could help it. "That's all right," she said. "I'll go."

Jensen's mouth set in a mulish line. "We don't know what he's doing out there or why he's watching the building."

"Well, no."

"He could be a criminal, scoping out the place for a robbery. Or a stalker, after someone at the company. A terrorist, maybe."

"He is not a terrorist." Grace was tempted to tell Jensen some of what she'd learned about Noah: military vet, decorated war hero, surprisingly good financials. But none of that was Jensen's business.

"You don't know that," Jensen said. "Please let me do my job."

For a moment, Grace was unsure of herself. And then Jensen continued, "Besides, Lucas sent out an email. He said you weren't to be alone with this guy."

"Excuse me?"

Jensen flushed, possibly sensing the danger in her tone, but said stubbornly, "It was a direct order, ma'am. I can't disobey."

"Lucas said that I was not to be alone with Noah Blake?"

"I didn't know that's who he was until you said so, but yeah." Jensen shot a glance in Olivia's direction. "He sent out an email."

Grace's voice was absolutely even as she said, "Please forward that email to me."

"Ma'am?"

"Is there something ambiguous about what I said?"

"No, but..."

"I want the recipient list. I'll be sending an email of my own."

"I — yes, ma'am." Jensen stayed on his feet, making no move to obey her.

"Now," Grace said softly.

"Yes, ma'am." Jensen sat down as fast as he'd stood, jostling his coffee again. This time he ignored the splash onto his pants. He spun in his chair and set his coffee down on the desk, pulling the keyboard toward him.

Grace watched over his shoulder as he opened up his email, found the message, and forwarded it to her. The room was silent apart from the tapping of his keys. Olivia shifted beside Grace as if she would say something but fell still when Grace glanced in her direction.

"Done." Jensen didn't turn back around.

"Thank you. I will send out a follow-up email. Meanwhile, you can consider that order revoked." On the last word, Grace's voice finally sharpened into a snap.

She wasn't going to blame Jensen. It wasn't his fault her older brother was a presumptuous, arrogant, over-protective asshole. But how dare Lucas damage her authority with the security team? If he wanted to be CEO, they could fight it out in the boardroom, but the whole family had agreed that the job belonged to Grace six years ago and she did not need their employees second-guessing the company's power structure.

Lucas didn't sign the paychecks. And he didn't give the orders. She did.

9

NOAH

Noah raised his binoculars back to his eyes. Grace Latimer had just arrived at the office, but she was already leaving.

She had a kayak on the roof of her car. Maybe she was going kayaking. It was a perfect day for it — clear, sunny, not too hot, not too cold. The only sound would be the rustling of the trees in the wind and the raucous cries of birds, with an occasional splash as the paddle cut smoothly through the depths and the kayak glided along the surface of the water.

But no, she wasn't dressed for kayaking. She was wearing those spiky heeled shoes that looked so uncomfortable and so hot at the same time, with a form-fitting skirt that barely grazed the top of her knees and a scoop-necked sleeveless top. His fingers itched to graze the edge, to give it the tug that would slide it just a little lower.

"*I am so bored.*" It was the crying girl's voice. Noah's jaw clenched. Complaining was better than crying, but not by much.

"*It could be much worse.*"

"*Yeah, you should try the desert. Sand, sand, and more sand.*"

"*There is nothing wrong with sand. And our skies are beautiful. So big, so open.*"

"Sand. So difficult to clean. It gets everywhere."

"I was thinking vampires. It's a beautiful day. Isn't it nice to be out in the sunlight, Sophia?"

The crying girl began to cry. Noah wanted to swear but he bit back the words, the muscles in his jaw so tense that pain jolted up his cheek into his head. He let the binoculars drop.

"I'll never feel sunshine again," the crying girl's voice said between sobs. *"Never. I hate the sun. I hate it."*

"Ah, shit," Joe said with a sigh.

"Come on, Sophia, let's find a squirrel." That was the little boy's voice. *"They're so weird, with their fluffy tails. Maybe we can find a nest with babies. I want to see a baby squirrel."*

"I hate squirrels," the girl's voice wailed, but it was growing fainter.

Noah closed his eyes. The other voices were talking over one another again, the words confusing, chaotic. The fake Chinese was loudest, the voice lilting incomprehensibly, so close it sounded next to his ear. He wanted to bash his head against the trunk of the nearest tree. Maybe he could pound the voices out of it.

"I didn't mean to do that," the Rose voice said. *"She's very sensitive, isn't she?"*

"That's one word for it," Joe grumbled.

Noah wanted to suggest a few others. Pain in the ass worked for him. He also wanted to roll his eyes and demand to know what they were talking about. Vampires?

Instead, he set the binoculars down next to his backpack and rubbed his hands against his knees, feeling the denim of his jeans against his palms.

Reality.

This was reality. The light warmth of the sun falling through the tree leaves above him, the hint of a breeze carrying scents of decaying leaves and fresh growth toward him, they were real.

The voices were not.

Maybe they were insanity, maybe they were something else, but either way, listening to them, trying to understand them, was a dead-end street. He needed to ignore them.

He stood, stretching out the kinks in his neck, trying to relax his jaw, and paced forward. He wasn't entirely sure what he was doing. Putting General Directions under surveillance had seemed like a decent idea. He'd watch the company, track deliveries, observe the employees and see what he could learn. He still had a few contacts in DC. With license plates and photographs, he ought to be able to discover some names. Names could lead him to educational backgrounds and areas of interest, information that might provide clues to the research being conducted inside General Directions' closed doors.

Solo surveillance sucked, though. The crying girl wasn't wrong—watching cars drive in and out of a parking lot was insanely boring. Plus, he had no way of knowing what was important or what he might be missing. What if the key deliveries arrived at midnight? He didn't have the gear to spend the night in the woods.

And the lines of sight were horrible. The ground was flatter than flat, so he couldn't hide himself on a hillside and watch from above. Instead, he was barely outside the fences, peering through undergrowth with a limited range of view. At least the brush was dense enough to give him some cover.

A short distance away, the landscape was almost bleak, with tall, skinny, gray-trunked pine trees, as widely spaced as if they'd been planted, growing on sandy dirt coated with dry brown pine needles. But the closer he got to General Directions, the lusher the forest became. The area around the buildings was green and gorgeous, with palm trees and ferns fighting for space and elegant oaks draped with Spanish moss arching into the sky.

There was motion in the parking lot. A dark green sedan was pulling in. Noah moved closer, brushing the sharp leaves of a palmetto out of his way with one arm, grateful for his jacket's protection despite the warmth of the day.

He leaned against an oak tree, watching as the man who'd spoken to him the other morning stepped out of the car. He shot a glance in Noah's direction and Noah stilled. He should be reasonably camouflaged in the trees, but he wasn't making much effort to hide. But the man smiled, his expression neither suspicious nor wary, so Noah relaxed. The guy must have seen one of the blue jays that fluttered through the forest or maybe a woodpecker with its bright red head.

"Uh-oh, dude, you are so busted." Joe sounded so close to his ear and his voice was so filled with laughter that Noah flinched.

"She looks kind of pissed. She doesn't get mad much." The Dillon voice sounded thoughtful.

Noah couldn't help himself. Even though he knew better than to respond to his hallucinations, he looked in the direction of the voices.

Damn.

Grace Latimer was marching toward him, hair disheveled as if it had gotten caught in some hanging branch, lips compressed in a tight line. She looked entirely out of place. With every step, the heels on her shoes sank into the soft ground.

Noah wanted to disappear into the trees, fade away like the professional soldier he used to be, but it was obviously too late for that. He didn't know how she'd spotted him, but he didn't imagine that she was out walking in the woods for the scenic view. He lifted his chin and straightened his shoulders, not speaking as she strode in his direction.

She stopped about ten feet away. Her cheeks were dotted with color, and from this close, he could see sweat beading at her temples.

"Fancy running into you here," Grace said. Her smile didn't reach her snapping eyes.

Noah felt a real smile tugging at his lips. "Nice day for a walk."

She glanced down at her feet. Her shoes were a deep pink color with overlapping straps, three-inch stiletto heels, and open toes. They matched her outfit, or they had before she'd stepped in mud. Now they were smeared with dirt, sticky with plant debris. "Oh, yeah, fabulous."

Noah didn't laugh, even though he wanted to. "Am I trespassing?" he asked, keeping it casual. He hadn't expected to be seen, but he hadn't made that much effort to hide either.

"You're on public land." The words were unfriendly.

He waited.

She took a deep breath, then exhaled. Her smile looked more genuine when she said, "Sorry." She pushed her hair back, tucking it behind her ear. "I'm annoyed at my brother, not you."

Noah lifted a brow.

She came closer, stopping next to him, and peered through the trees. "Not much of a view."

He gave a noncommittal murmur.

"I'd be happy to give you a tour if you like."

His eyes narrowed. She acted like they had nothing to hide. Was that pretense? "Tours usually only show the highlights."

She glanced at him and then back at the parking lot, in a way that made it clear she knew exactly what he'd been doing. "And this is better, how?"

Noah scowled. So maybe he'd been thinking his surveillance was pointless, but she didn't have to rub it in.

She put a hand on his arm and leaned closer to him. "Look, I understand..." But before she could finish her sentence, an alarm began ringing from the building, an urgent *wheep-wheep-wheep* blaring through the trees.

"Oh, that is ridiculous." She glared in the direction of the building. "You haven't done a thing."

He'd like to, Noah thought. She was standing so close to him that he could smell her shampoo, or maybe it was her soap. Or maybe it was just her. She smelled like girl, like jasmine flowers and vanilla, mixed with something just a little spicy. His brain was ordering him to step away from her, to break the spell her scent created, but his body refused to listen.

She looked up at him and her eyes met his. Her lips parted as if she were about to say something, but the words didn't escape. The sensation he'd felt before, of getting lost in her gaze, returned, deeper and more intense. He raised his hand to touch her cheek.

"*Oh, they like each other,*" the Rose voice said. "*How sweet.*"

Noah let his hand drop. What was he doing? He should move away. But he stayed motionless, frozen under her gaze.

Grace caught her lower lip between her teeth for one long moment, then she smiled and put a hand on his chest. "My big brother doesn't get to tell me what to do."

What did her brother have to do with anything? Noah frowned, puzzled, but Grace lifted her face to his, swaying in to him.

Maybe she intended a quick brush of her lips against his, the slightest taste of forbidden fruit, but she fit next to him perfectly. Noah could almost hear the satisfying click of a jigsaw puzzle piece finding its place. His unruly hand slid around her, coming to rest on the small of her back, as his lips deepened the kiss.

Her fingers on his chest closed, fisting into his t-shirt. He could feel their warmth through the cotton, but it didn't match the heat of her mouth. All of his senses were caught up in her — taste, touch, scent — until the noise from his hallucinations finally penetrated his consciousness.

The clean freak was screaming. At least Noah thought that scream was her voice. Angry man's rant had lost a word. He was saying, "*It's not... it's not...*" over and over again.

"*Mama, mama, what is it?*" the little boy's voice was squealing with excitement.

The crying girl was no longer crying. "*Holy shit, it's big.*" She sounded awed.

"*Oh my goodness, it looks so soft. I wish I could pet it,*" the Rose voice said.

"*Noah, man, hate to interrupt, but now ain't a good time for that.*" Joe's voice in Noah's ear was matched by a cold chill against his back.

"*Aunt Grace, stop kissing him! Why don't you have your phone? Damn it, damn it.*"

Noah lifted his head. Grace's eyelashes fluttered open and she stared up at him. She looked as dazed as he felt. He wanted nothing more than to go back to kissing her, to take long, slow, sweet minutes exploring her mouth, but he turned his head in the direction of his hallucinations.

He sucked in a breath.

Holy shit.

Crying girl was right. It was huge.

Huge and black and furry, with ears that stuck up like a corgi, and a muzzle like a cocker spaniel, but with eyes tiny and beady like no dog he'd ever seen. It pawed at his backpack with one immense furry paw.

Bear.

For a second, Noah felt frozen, immobilized by the sheer size of the creature, but then he swung sideways, pushing Grace behind him.

"Hey," she protested.

The bear lifted its head. Its eyes met Noah's. It tilted back on its hind legs, not quite standing, but lifting its forepaws off the ground.

"What in the world do they think they're doing?" Grace sounded mystified. Noah risked a quick glance over his shoulder. Uniformed guards were bursting out of the building, running toward the forest.

The bear rumbled. Even through the blaring siren and the cacophony of his hallucinations all talking at once, Noah could hear it, a deep, raspy sound like a chair scraping across a tiled floor.

Grace heard it, too. She gave a muffled "eep," as if she were choking back a scream.

"Run," Noah ordered, keeping his voice low. "Get away. Go."

"No, no, no," Grace said breathlessly. She pressed up close against him. He could feel her warmth, sense her face peering around his shoulder. "Never run from a bear. Don't make eye contact. Are you making eye contact? Don't make eye contact."

Now she told him. It took a remarkable effort and Noah's lips wanted to pull themselves into a snarl, but he let his eyes drop to the bear's midsection.

"Yeah, so, that's what I came out to tell you." Grace's words tumbled over one another. "Throwing apple cores. Bad idea. Against the law, actually, to leave food waste in the forest. Big fine if you get caught, but, well, bigger problem if you attract a hungry bear. Obviously."

The last word came out on a squeak as the bear rose to a standing position.

"It's February. Don't bears hibernate?" Noah bit out the words through clenched teeth, a growl that wasn't nearly as deep or as foreboding as that of the bear.

"It's Florida. Not exactly freezing."

Good point. The bear's head swiveled, its nose lifting into the air, and then it dropped to the ground again and began backing away, dragging Noah's backpack with it.

Noah swore and took a step in the bear's direction.

Grace grabbed his arm. "Don't be stupid."

"It's got my pack."

"Do you have more food in there?"

"My lunch, yeah."

"Then it's not your pack anymore."

The bear was disappearing into the trees, Noah's backpack bumping along beside it.

Noah tried to tug free of Grace's hold, but her fingers tightened on his upper arm.

"If you get close enough that the bear feels threatened, it'll hurt you. And then my security team will have to shoot it. Are you really going to kill a bear over a sandwich?"

Noah stopped trying to pull away. An irrepressible grin stole across his face. "Nice priorities. Not worried how much damage it could do to me?"

"It's the bear's forest. We're the trespassers."

"My cell phone, my wallet..." Noah patted the leg of his jeans, feeling for his truck key. At least he'd kept that on him. But the key to his room at the B&B was tucked neatly into the front pocket of the pack. It was going to be damn embarrassing to explain to Avery that a bear ate it.

"Replaceable. And the bear will abandon what it can't eat. We can come back and look for your stuff later."

"Ma'am! Ma'am!" One of the guards bellowed. Noah glanced back. A guard on the inside held a rifle over his head, passing it up to another, who was halfway over the fence. The third was on the ground already, reaching up to retrieve the weapon.

"Time for me to go, I think."

Grace's gaze followed his. "They're not going to shoot you."

"Let's not test them."

"I need to talk to you."

He'd just kissed her and it had been a damn good kiss. The connection between them felt deeper than chemistry. Talk? No, Noah needed to run. Far and fast and right away. "Maybe some other time."

"No, really. It's important."

She hadn't let go of his arm, but he gently peeled her grip off. Was there a tactful way to say that he was the kind of walking disaster area smart women steered clear of? Probably not, but he squeezed her fingers before releasing them and saying, "This was a mistake. I shouldn't be here."

The guards were crashing through the trees now, almost on them.

"Yes, you should be. I need to — I want to—" She looked adorably flustered, her cheeks flushed, lips full, but he could see her pulling herself together, straightening her shoulders, lifting her chin. "I have a job for you if you want it."

He paused for a second. A job? He'd been looking for months. But his hesitation was brief as the sounds got closer.

"Not sure this is the place for me." Before she could argue further, he touched a finger to his temple in a wry half-salute, and started walking. He didn't break into a run but he moved as quickly as he could. Within seconds, Grace and the guards were out of sight behind him.

10

DILLON

"He kissed my aunt. I can't believe he kissed my aunt," Dillon said. He was trailing along behind Noah with the other ghosts as Noah strode through the forest, at a pace not quite a jog, but fast enough that the ghosts were falling farther and farther behind him.

"It was a lovely kiss, too." Rose clutched a hand to her heart. "So romantic. And then the way he stood in front of her with the bear." She gave a shiver of delight. "It was almost as good as when Spider-Man rescued Mary Jane from those bad guys in the rain."

"But he kissed her! My aunt."

"I am fairly sure that technically she kissed him. It was quite forward of her." Despite her words, Nadira didn't sound disapproving. A small smile played around her lips.

"That bear! It was so cool!" Misam gave a skip and a hop, trying to keep up with the others' longer strides.

"Kissing my aunt is not cool," Dillon muttered. He kicked at a pine cone on the ground, his foot passing through it. Grace had had boyfriends before, of course. There'd been that dweeb she'd gone out with for a while in high school and then a revolving cast of professor-types who'd come to visit her on summer vacations. They hadn't all been horrible but none of them were nearly good enough for her.

And neither was Noah. He glared at Noah's back.

"Don't be silly, Dillon." Rose clasped her hands together. "Just think how convenient it would be. They can fall in love and get married and buy a house and live down the street from Akira and Zane. And we can all stay in Tassamara together. Maybe they'll come to movie nights at your other aunt's house. And eat at Maggie's, of course. It'll be just like always, only with lots of company." On her last words, she flung her arms wide and then spun in a circle, bright with happiness.

"He is not gonna marry my aunt," Dillon said.

"Think what beautiful babies they'd have," Rose said encouragingly. "His eyes, her hair. Or maybe her eyes, his eyelashes. Can you imagine? On a little baby girl? Oh, she'd be adorable." She tucked her hand into his arm and leaned into him.

Dillon rolled his eyes, but his expression softened. Grace would make a really great mom. She deserved pretty babies, if she wanted them.

"He heard us," Joe said abruptly. "Did you notice?"

"What?" Surprised, Dillon turned toward Joe.

"He heard us," Joe repeated. He let his steps slow, falling farther behind Noah. "Twice. Did you see it?"

Dillon thought back.

"You always think that," Nadira scoffed.

"He's right, though," Sophia said unexpectedly. "Joe's right. Misam and me, we saw her when we were hunting for squirrels. We were coming back with her. He wasn't looking toward us until Dillon said she was mad and then he did. I saw him."

Nadira snorted. "Nonsense. So he looked around, so what? Perhaps he heard Dillon's aunt approaching."

"But that's what happened with the bear, too." Joe stopped walking. "I don't know who saw it first. Mona, maybe? She was screaming."

Mona drew herself up. "It startled me," she said with dignity, in one of her rare moments of non-cleaning-related speech.

"It's not right," muttered the angry man. "It's not right."

"Well, maybe you saw it first," Joe said to him. "It doesn't matter who did, because it wasn't Noah. He didn't see it at all. He was busy kissing your aunt, Dillon." The balls of light and shades were drifting around them as Noah continued moving away and Joe shifted to avoid one, waving at it irritably. "But when he stopped kissing her, he looked over his shoulder. He must have heard us. Why else would he have looked behind him instead of at her?"

"Perhaps he heard the bear," Nadira suggested.

"Did you?" Joe asked her. All of the ghosts had stopped walking and were gathering around him, including Chaupi and the angry man. The remnants started to collect around them, too.

"I..." She paused, considering. "Not until it growled. It was surprisingly quiet for such a large beast." She gave a shudder. "That growl, though. It made my blood run cold."

"Do you have blood, Mama?" Misam asked her. He looked down at himself. "Do I have blood?"

Nadira patted his cheek. "It's just an expression, dear one."

"I don't think I have blood anymore," he said decidedly. "I would know."

"Of course you don't have blood." Sophia hugged herself. "If you had blood, you could die and we can't die. We're stuck."

Joe ignored the byplay between the younger ghosts, looking troubled. "I don't think he heard the bear. I think he heard us."

"Does it matter?" Nadira asked.

"Yes, of course it does," Joe said with surprising vehemence.

"But you always said he could hear us."

"I know, but... Can't you imagine what that would be like for him? If he knows we're here? To feel like there are invisible eyes on him constantly? That he's never alone? It's creepy as hell." Joe leaned in Noah's direction, tense lines appearing in his brow and around his mouth, as if he were fighting something unseen.

101

"Oh, come on," Dillon said. "We're not so bad."

Misam began rubbing his stomach and Nadira shifted uncomfortably.

"We need to keep moving." Nadira nodded toward Noah's disappearing back. "This shall soon become uncomfortable."

"Oh?" Rose glanced at Dillon.

He shrugged. He didn't feel it, but the pull wasn't as strong for him as it was for the others.

"We have to talk about this, though," Joe said. "And not where Noah can hear us."

"Why not?" Dillon asked.

If Noah could hear them, really hear them, not just vaguely sense them, they needed to talk to him. They could explain who they were, how they'd wound up with him, how he could help them. If Noah could hear them, maybe he could take them to a place where they could find a ghost with a doorway — a hospital, say, or a retirement community. A place where people died because death was inevitable, not because they'd been stupid or unlucky. Rose could point out the doorway, the ghosts could go through... Dillon gave a bounce, almost like one of Misam's.

Joe started sliding forward, his feet not lifting off the ground. "Walk, but slowly," he said, beginning to move his feet.

Nadira gave a grunt of discomfort and began moving, too, nudging Misam along in front of her.

"I hate this," Sophia said bitterly. "Hate it, hate it, hate it." She stomped off after Noah, her steps silent but her body language eloquent. Mona began hurrying through the brush, passing through bushes and tangled undergrowth in a straight line toward Noah. Chaupi and the angry man followed suit.

"What are you worrying about now?" Nadira asked Joe as the wisps and remnants began drifting after Noah, too.

"If he knows we're here, if he knows we're us..." Joe's lips pressed together. "I don't know how he'd react."

Nadira's lip curled. "Perhaps we should be afraid of what he might do, should he come to believe in our presence."

"What do you mean?" Joe asked.

She shrugged and didn't answer, but her glance at the top of Misam's head was worried.

"Maybe he would think we are jinns. Instead of an exorcist to fix the jinn inside him, the one that traps us, the exorcist would get rid of us." Misam looked up at his mother's face. "What do you think would happen, Mama, if an exorcist tried to cast us out?"

"You are too clever by half, my boy." Nadira paused, just long enough to scoop him up.

He wrapped his legs around her waist and leaned into her, his head peering out over her shoulder. "I do not think I would like to be exorcised," he said, his expression thoughtful.

"Exorcism doesn't work," Dillon said with conviction, but he couldn't help frowning. Misam's words hit a little too close to his own experience with another dimension.

"How do you know?" Nadira asked.

"Akira said. Her parents tried it with her when she was little."

"Perhaps they didn't find a good exorcist. Perhaps it worked on the spirits around her but not on the jinn inside her. Perhaps..." Nadira tightened her grasp on Misam, but she didn't finish her thought, adding brusquely. "We must hurry. If Noah starts his truck..."

Dillon grimaced. He remembered what it had been like when Akira had driven his car away without him. The pain had been agonizing. He didn't know whether it would be the same for him with Noah: it was possible that the distance would simply break a tie that had never seemed too powerful. The ghosts with stronger ties to Noah would suffer, though.

"Do you want me to take Misam?" Joe asked her. "You want a piggyback, kiddo?"

"It's all right. I have him." Nadira broke into a trot, jiggling Misam and singing him a song in lilting Arabic.

"Noah wouldn't exorcise us," Dillon said as he and Joe and Rose fell behind the others. "Would he?"

"No, of course not," Joe replied. "At least I don't think he would."

"What do you think he'd do?" Rose asked.

"I don't know. But he'd try to help us, I'm sure of that," Joe said.

"We're not so easy to help," Dillon stuffed his hands in his pockets, hunching his shoulders.

In their first conversation after he'd learned that Dillon was a ghost, his dad had asked, his voice rough with emotion, "How can I help you? What do you need?"

Dillon hadn't had an answer for him. He didn't know what he needed, why he was still hanging around.

Akira, though, had been brisk, telling his father about her past experiences, all her failed attempts to find the mysterious white light of lore. She'd finished with, "Ghosts simply are. They're not a problem that needs fixing. They're people, usually ones who died untimely deaths, still working out their time here. That's all."

But Dillon had known from the expression on his dad's face that he found her answer profoundly unsatisfying. He felt that way about it himself. Yeah, maybe he'd died too young, but why did that leave him trapped?

"Noah wouldn't do anything that would hurt us," Joe said, but his voice was grim. Dillon wondered if he was trying to convince himself, but Joe continued, "But if he can hear us..." He shook his head and then took an angry, wild swing at a tree trunk ahead of him, his fist sliding right through it and then his body following suit. He wasn't making any attempt to go around the plants, just shoving through them as if they didn't exist.

"If he can hear us?" Rose prompted.

"It explains so much," Joe burst out. He glanced at Dillon. "I know I said he could hear us, but that was mostly just to annoy Nadira."

Rose's eyes went wide. "To annoy her? On purpose?"

Dillon had spent enough time with the other ghosts that he

wasn't surprised. "She probably claimed he couldn't hear you just to annoy you," he said dryly.

"You know how it is." Joe's dimples flashed. "Being dead is boring. Arguing with Nadira makes life — uh, afterlife — a lot more interesting."

Dillon rolled his eyes, but Rose laughed.

But Joe's face sobered. "But if he can hear us, then—" He waved an arm wide to indicate the wisps scattered ahead of them in the forest. "No wonder his life sucks. He should be in school, getting a degree. But how would he study if we're always talking around him? He should have a girlfriend. But if he can hear the kid asking questions every time things start heating up, of course his hook-ups are never going to turn into anything real. He should have a life, damn it. He's still alive. But he doesn't and it's because of us. It's because he knows we're here, even if he's never admitted it."

Dillon skirted a tree as Joe marched through it. Maybe Joe was right. But if so, they needed to talk to Noah. They needed to explain. "We should tell him we're here. Who we are."

"No." The easygoing joker in Joe had disappeared, leaving a hard-eyed soldier adamant in his place. "Not you, but Nadira, Misam, and me? He'd blame himself. We need to be quiet around him. Dead quiet. And somehow we've got to get the rest of these ghosts away from him. We need to find one of those doors you talked about and soon."

Dillon exchanged glances with Rose. She frowned and opened her mouth, as if to say something, but at that moment, Noah must have started his truck. Joe gave a startled yell and disappeared in a whoosh of wind as the gentle pull that Dillon had previously felt tugging at his core turned into a yank that had him tumbling into the air.

The last thing he saw as he was drawn away was Rose cupping both hands around her mouth and calling out, "I'll catch up with you!"

11

GRACE

OLIVIA WAS STANDING BEHIND THE RECEPTION DESK, HER cheeks pink with excitement. "That was amazing! Are you all right? That was—" She let the words drop off and spread her hands wide as if to say that she couldn't encompass all that she'd just seen.

Amazing. Yeah, that was a good word for it, Grace thought.

"It looked huge," Olivia continued. "How close were you? On the screen, it looked like it was right there next to you, like you could almost touch it. And when you didn't notice it and it was getting closer and closer, oh my God, it was like a horror movie." She clapped a melodramatic hand over her heart.

Oh, right. Olivia was talking about the bear. Grace had been thinking about that kiss.

"It was pretty big," Grace replied.

Noah Blake's kiss was like hot chocolate on a cold day, the kind made with real milk and good chocolate. Except plain hot chocolate didn't have the right sizzle. No, Noah's kiss was like Mexican hot chocolate, with chili peppers and maybe topped with whipped cream and scrapings of dark chocolate.

"Were you scared? You didn't look scared. You looked…" Olivia stopped talking. She pressed her lips together in a smirk.

Grace arched a brow and waited.

"Sorry, ma'am. Just remembering what you said earlier. You know, about creating a hostile work environment and all," Olivia said. She took her seat behind the reception desk, her expression demure, her eyes dropped.

Grace choked back a chuckle. Olivia didn't do demure well. Grace could still see the mischief hiding behind her half-smile.

Olivia's gaze flickered up to Grace. She must have seen Grace's amusement, because she added, "But does he kiss as good as he looks? Because that was…" She fanned herself.

Grace laughed. Then she tried to make her expression repressive. "That was inappropriate of me."

"Hey, he doesn't work here. You should go for it."

Grace sobered. Her father had told her to hire Noah. Instead she'd chased him off.

"So who saw that?" she asked. Her hand drifted to her mouth, her pinkie nail slipping between her lips.

Olivia didn't meet her gaze. "Oh, just me and Jensen. And, ah, well, your dad had just come in. He'd stopped by. And then the other guys came running when the alarm went off, of course, and so…"

"The company, in other words?" Grace realized she was biting her fingernail and pulled it out of her mouth.

"I won't say anything, not if you want it kept quiet, but you should probably tell the guys to keep their mouths shut, too."

"I think I can survive a little gossip," Grace said. But could Noah? If she could somehow convince him to take a job with General Directions, how would his co-workers react? Would he get hassled for having kissed the boss?

Damn it. Kissing him had been an impulse, driven as much by her annoyance at her brother as attraction. Not that she regretted it, not really, but it might have been a mistake.

Olivia's smile was sympathetic. She picked up the paper on the top of her in-box, "I'll just get back to work. On, um..." Her brow furrowed. "A purchase order for the quantum teleportation guys. Why do they want us to buy them cats?"

"No cats." Grace snatched the paper away from Olivia. "They're trying to sneak that one by you because I already said no. I'll talk to them." She glanced down at the paper and shook her head. "Why couldn't Schrödinger have theorized about goldfish?"

She crumpled the purchase order as she headed to the door. She needed to get to work. She had too much to do to obsess about Noah Blake. But her father met her at the door to her office.

"Did you hire him?"

"Not exactly, no."

Grace opened her door. Her father followed her into the room.

"No? But you looked—"

Grace raised a finger. "Do not start with me, Dad." Reaching her chair, she looked down at her shoes. They were toast. There was no way she'd ever get them clean. With a sigh, she slipped them off and dropped them into the trash can under her desk. Barefoot, she sat down in her chair.

Her father crossed to the front of her desk.

She looked up at him. "Something you need?"

"I need you to hire Noah Blake." His tone was the patient parent-to-small-child tone that she remembered well from her childhood. He might have been telling her to clean her room.

"He has to want to be hired." She turned away and hit the power button on her computer with more force than it needed.

"He seemed to like you."

Grace's lips twitched with the beginning of a smile. Despite her worries about the consequences, the glow of a really good kiss was still warming her. Noah might come with warning signs and flashing neon lights of danger, but she wasn't sure she could muster the right amount of regret for kissing him.

"Possibly not as much as I liked him," she muttered to her keyboard.

"Oh, no, just as much," her father said cheerfully. "Trust me, I know."

"What do you know, Dad?" Grace demanded, turning back to him. So far he'd refused to say more than that he wanted her to hire Noah. "Is this about Dillon?"

Her father's cheer faded. He turned away from her, walking to the shelves that lined one wall of her office. Although he ran a hand across a line of book spines, she didn't imagine he was looking at their titles when he paused by a shelf of framed family photographs.

"Do you remember the day he died?" he asked.

"I wasn't here." Grace's reply felt automatic, although the memories immediately leaped up to engulf her. The phone call, the pause after her mother said her name. Grace had known that something was terribly wrong before any more words were spoken.

In those few brief seconds, she'd imagined what she thought was the worst. Car accident, heart attack, cancer.

She hadn't even come close to the reality.

She would never forget — could never forget — the image tied to the memory. She'd left dirty dishes in her sink from the day before. A red Fiestaware cereal bowl, a single spoon, a glass flecked with dried orange juice pulp. She'd been thinking she should have rinsed her glass when she answered the phone, and still looking at it when her mother said the words that changed the world.

Something about the incongruity burned, as if the universe had punished her for her carelessness. But she knew that thought was silly. Life didn't work that way.

"I was so angry at your mother," Max said, his back still turned to Grace. "She refused to help me. It wouldn't have made a difference, of course. I know that now. But at the time..."

"What wouldn't have made a difference?" Grace asked. She didn't remember her father being angry. There'd been no yelling, no arguing. But then she'd barely gotten home before her mother was gone, too.

Max picked up a photograph. She couldn't see which one he held. "I gave him CPR until the ambulance came. She told me it was too late, that he was gone, but I refused to listen. I didn't want to believe her." He set the photograph back down and picked up another one.

Grace didn't know what to say. She hadn't known that. She'd never asked for more details after the bare harsh truth of the fact of Dillon's death. But she'd been the one to find her mother's body. She understood how someone could persist in trying to change an unbearable reality long past the point of reason.

Max glanced over his shoulder. "You did the same, didn't you?" He gave her a wry, tired grin. "More like me than your mother, after all."

"I couldn't believe it was real," she said. "It felt like a nightmare. An impossible nightmare. I kept thinking it had to be a bad dream, but I couldn't wake myself up."

"I didn't want to let go," her father said.

"I know just what you mean." Grace placed her hands on her desk, spreading her fingers wide, staring down at them as if the sight would block the memories. She hated thinking about that day. That week, that month.

She hadn't known before that grief came in waves, that the pain of loss would batter her and then recede, and then return, again and again and again. But time did heal. The space between the waves grew, until entire days went by when she didn't think about her mother or Dillon. Maybe even weeks. Not yet months, though.

"I wonder sometimes if it's my fault," her father said.

Grace made a noise, somewhere between a snort and a chuckle. "Survivor's guilt," she said briskly, closing her hands into fists. "Natalya says it's natural and to get over it."

She'd blamed herself, too. So many times, so many ways.

If only she'd come home for the summer. If only she'd been there to talk to Dillon. If only she'd set a better example, made him see that living without a psychic gift was nothing to be ashamed of, nothing to dread. If only she'd known what he was thinking about doing.

If only she'd gone upstairs a few minutes earlier. Found her mother sooner. Done more to help her, been a better daughter.

Washed that damn juice glass instead of leaving it in the sink.

If only.

"Not their deaths," her father said, again looking at the photograph he held. "I don't blame myself for that. But maybe Dillon's still here because I refused to let him go."

"That's not..." Grace began an automatic denial, but paused before she finished. "That's... hmm... I'm sure you're wrong."

Akira claimed that ghosts weren't stuck between worlds because they had unfinished business. She said she'd tried to help them, more than once, without success. But what if the business wasn't theirs? What if some ghosts were trapped, not because of what they still needed to do, but because someone living still needed something from them?

But no. Max had to be wrong. If he was right, the world would be filled with ghosts. No one wanted to say good-bye to their loved ones. No parent would let a child go. No mother would leave her children. Sure, some people died reasonable deaths — timely, appropriate, after loving farewells to their relatives and friends — but wouldn't everyone else wind up stuck between the planes of existence?

"I suppose you're right," Max said. He didn't sound convinced.

Grace wasn't sure she was either. She needed to think more about it, but meanwhile, a rush of affection for her father pushed her to her feet. She came around her desk and joined him at the shelves, leaning into his side. He slid an arm around her shoulders and set the picture down.

The photographs were all older. Most of them had belonged to her mother. Vacation shots, college graduations, a single family portrait with Cinderella's castle as a backdrop, taken when they were young. No Dillon in that one.

But there was one of three-year old Dillon, seated in Santa's lap, his expression dubious. Grace remembered him bursting into tears seconds after the photo was taken. Her fault: she'd been eleven, too old for Santa, and Dillon had been sensitive enough to catch on to her disdain.

And another — a kayak with Grace in the front, Max in the rear, Dillon in the middle, when Dillon must have been about ten. That was the last picture she had of him.

Teenage Dillon had never wanted his picture taken, ducking out of shots when he could. And they'd all been so busy — Lucas mostly away, working on establishing GD's government business, medical school for Nat, college for Zane and Grace — that they'd never gotten together for an updated family portrait. It must have seemed like there'd be plenty of time for that someday.

"I should frame one of the group photos from the wedding," Grace said. "Add it to the set."

"And one from Nat's wedding, too. One with all the kids," her father said. "And another with the baby, when he gets here."

"Definitely." Grace took a sideways peek at her father's face. He was still looking at the photos, but his expression seemed more resolute than sad. "Something to look forward to?"

"Absolutely." He gave a quick squeeze and let his arm drop. "First we have to help Dillon, though."

"And how do we do that?" Grace tried to keep the question light.

"I wish I knew." Max sighed.

"Will hiring Noah Blake help Dillon?" Grace asked.

"Oh, I don't know," Max said. He seemed surprised by the question.

"You don't know?" Grace wanted to stamp a foot in exasperation. What were they talking about if not Dillon's connection to Noah?

"No." Her father blinked at her. "Why would it?"

"Dad!" Grace rolled her eyes. "Why do you want me to hire Noah?"

"I recognized him," her father said. "He belongs here. You just need to make sure he stays until he realizes that."

Grace snorted. "He lost his stuff to a bear. That might keep him here for a while." But she frowned. It wouldn't take him long to replace whatever he'd lost, but it did give her a window of opportunity.

Time to take advantage of it.

1 2

NOAH

Deciding it was time to get the hell out of Dodge was easy.

Acting on that decision? Not so much.

Noah hated the idea of calling for help, but what else could he do? No wallet meant no ID, no cash, no credit cards, no driver's license. No way to fill his truck's gas tank. He wasn't going to make it back to DC on half a tank.

He stared at the phone in his hand, trying to nerve himself up to press the buttons.

"Everything okay?" Avery asked. The innkeeper had generously and without prompting offered Noah the use of a cell phone when he'd explained about the bear, his backpack, and the lost key to his room. "You need me to look up a number for you?"

"No, I'm good." Noah held up the phone and gestured toward the door to the patio. "You mind if I take your phone outside?"

"Feel free." Avery continued wiping down the counters in the small kitchen.

Noah stepped outside. The day was warm, the aromas of the flowering plants lifting into the air and saturating the breeze. He sat on the nearest bench, hand closing around the phone. He had two choices, the only two numbers he knew by heart, but the decision was obvious. And it could be worse. At least he had the choice.

He tapped the number. It rang once, cut off in the midst when his brother picked up.

"Yeah?"

"Yo." Noah's tone was more brusque than polite. But he was fighting unexpected emotion.

What the hell. It was just his brother. But how long had it been? Six months? More?

"Noah?" Niall breathed out the name. Noah could hear that he was in a crowd, background chaos hammering away. "Hang on."

Noah rubbed the back of his neck and waited. Shit. He shouldn't have called. Or he should have called sooner, a couple of days ago, that imagined friendly call to ask about hot redheads. That would have been infinitely better than this plea for help.

Niall must have shut a door because the sound fell away. "Dude, where are you?"

"Um, Florida."

"Florida? Seriously? Uh, okay."

Noah wanted to laugh. His brother sounded so surprised. Maybe he should have told his family when he came back to the States. Well, yeah, he should have. But he hadn't.

"I need some help."

"Yeah? Anything, you know it. You've got it. What do you want? Money? A lawyer? Dancing girls? Tell me, dude."

"Dancing girls?"

Niall chuckled. "Whatever, man. If that's what you need, you know I'd make it work."

Noah's smile seeped into his tone when he said, "No dancing girls. But — long story — I lost my ID. And my cash, credit cards."

"Drunken binge?" Niall said the words lightly, but Noah could hear the undercurrents.

He tilted his head back and stared up into the clear blue sky. The muscles in his neck had tied themselves into knots already. Dealing with his family always did that to him these days. It's not that he didn't love them. It's not that they didn't love him. But finding common ground felt like shooting in the dark. He wanted to defend himself — he hardly ever drank, he didn't even like alcohol — but it wouldn't help.

"Bear, actually."

"Bear?"

"Yeah, the big furry kind. Growly? Annoying? Big. Seriously, way bigger than you'd imagine."

"Okay. Could be worse. Crocodiles, right? You got lucky, dude, good thing you didn't get snapped up by a crocodile."

Noah rolled his eyes, but a smile stole across his face as his brother started humming, then half mumbling, half singing, the lyrics to the old *Peter Pan* song about smiling at the crocodile.

"Pretty sure it's alligators in Florida," Noah said.

"Oh, right." Niall stopped singing. "Disney, though. Hey, how close are you to Orlando? I could hop a plane, we could hit a theme park or two. Ride Space Mountain?"

"Don't you have a job?"

"Friday afternoon, bro. I could be there by midnight. We could play all weekend and I'd be back at work by the time the market opens Monday morning. Easy."

Noah took a deep breath. "Maybe next time. Right now, I want out of Florida."

"You got it." Niall sounded more resigned than disappointed.

"Not after we tried so hard to get him here!" the kid's voice protested. *"We have to stop him."*

"Stop him? We can't do anything. We're totally and completely helpless." The crying girl sounded bitter, but at least she wasn't crying.

"Hush. Not around him, remember?" Joe said, sounding annoyed.

"I'm sorry. I wish I..." Noah covered his eyes. The damn voices. They were driving him crazy. Surprising himself with an abrupt decision, Noah added, "I'm gonna get help. I'll call the VA. Make an appointment, see a shrink."

The hallucinations had been bad enough. But the idea that General Directions had done something to his brain, as tempting as it had been, as hopeful as he'd found it, had to be delusional. As much as he didn't want to admit it, his problems were growing into more than he could ignore away.

"Noah, if you're ready for help, you don't have to wait for the VA. Come on." His brother sounded impatient. "Come to New York. I'll get you into the best doctor in the city in 24 hours. It's just fucking money. EMDR, that's how they're treating PTSD now. It's some eye motion thing. You stare at a light or something."

Noah gave a puff of laughter. He shouldn't be surprised that Niall had researched treatments for post-traumatic stress. His whole family had been trying to fix him for a long time. "Did you look that one up or did Mom?"

"Dude." Niall sighed. For a moment, a burst of noise came through the phone as if someone had opened the door. "You didn't even call on Christmas."

"Yeah, I was…" Noah let the sentence trail off. He didn't want to lie to his brother. He hadn't been busy or away or any of the other excuses that came to mind: he'd been newly laid-off, sitting in his barren apartment, staring at the walls, and wishing something, anything, was different. Calling home had crossed his mind a hundred times, maybe more.

But he hadn't done it.

Silence. It stretched. Painful and awkward and miserable.

And then one of his voices broke it. It was the kid, asking, in a piercing whisper, *"That's the holiday with the fat man in the red suit, right? I like him."*

"Shush," Joe said.

"He should have called his mother. She gave him life. A phone call is the least she deserves." The Arabic woman was whispering, too.

"It was right after AlecCorp lost their contracts, remember? He

118

was laid off. He didn't want to worry them." That was Joe, also low-voiced.

Noah didn't need to hear any more of his voices chime in. He knew already that the clean freak would complain about dust, the crying girl would cry, the angry guy would say it wasn't right and the fake Chinese guy would make no sense.

Right on cue, the singing lady's voice drifted into his ear, crooning, *"Sleep my love, and peace attend thee..."*

"Can't we get her away from him?"

"It's not right."

"Look, can you help me?" Noah stood, feeling the urge to move, to escape.

"Of course," his brother answered. "Money? Where do you want me to send it?"

"I'm in this little town called Tassamara. Florida, obviously." Noah walked across the patio and into the yard, eyeing the overgrown bougainvillea draped along the back fence.

"Tassamara." Niall sounded thoughtful, before his voice burst into excitement. "Holy shit, seriously? What the hell are you doing there?"

"I'm... I... it's... what do you know about this place?"

"Hot babe alert," Niall muttered. "Man, I would like a piece of that action."

"What?" Noah snapped. His brother might be part of a Wall Street culture that Noah didn't love, but he wasn't crass. At least, not usually.

"Not the blonde," Niall said hastily, before adding with a chuckle, "Although, I gotta admit, she's quite something. You know who I'm talking about?"

"Grace Latimer?" Noah asked reluctantly.

"Yeah. Gorgeous, smart, oblivious. But the company — they're golden, my man. They buy crap. Shit you'd steer your worst enemy away from. And then it turns out the company they've bought holds some obscure patent that everyone working in solar power needs, or has some no-name technician who turns out to be a super genius, or whatever. They've got the Midas touch. And the blonde — butter wouldn't melt. Cool as can be as she walks into a boardroom to announce that they've just scarfed up majority interest and she's the new owner."

"It sounds like you've seen her in action."

"Yeah, there was a deal a couple years ago. A subsidiary of Davis Corp. We had an option on..." Niall started talking stocks, percentages, shares — jargon that made Noah's eyes glaze over. But he got the general point. His brother knew of General Directions and not as a top-secret research facility working on military experiments.

He interrupted Niall to ask, "Do you know anything about the research they do?"

Niall chuckled. "Eh, rumors only. I've got the impression that it's whatever strikes Latimer's fancy — teleportation, I heard. Like that's going to go anywhere. But you never know, I guess. I wouldn't rule it out."

"Military work?"

"DoD stuff? Nope, definitely not. Government funding is public info. I'd know."

"Why? Aren't there thousands of companies doing military work?"

"Yeah, but that one's got the Midas touch," his brother repeated. "You know me. Any edge, bro."

Noah's lips curved up. Yeah, he did know his twin. He didn't know how they'd come out of the same womb, though. How had he gotten every idealistic gene and his brother every pragmatic one? But if Niall thought profit could be made by watching General Directions, he'd have the company under a microscope. "So, no shady medical experiments?"

"Huh." Niall snorted. "No shady anything, as far as I know. Some SEC investigations into their stock trades, but that's just because their luck is unreal. None have ever gone anywhere. Have you heard something? I think one kid is a doc, but she's maybe a radiologist? Something to do with imaging, anyway. Nothing creepy. What do you know?"

"Not a thing. I've met a few people who work there, that's all."

"The blonde?"

"Yeah."

"She's a babe, isn't she?"

Noah ran his tongue over his teeth, half amused, half annoyed. He probably shouldn't tell his asshole brother that he was an asshole, not when he needed Niall's help.

"Yeah, don't answer that. Twin telepathy, I know what you're thinking."

Noah chuckled. It had been so long. Years since he and Niall spent real time together. But in the moment, they could be back in high school, bickering over who'd called dibs on Niall's hot lab partner first.

"Man, it's good to hear your voice," Niall said, sobering.

"Yours, too." The words caught in Noah's throat. Who was he to call his brother an asshole when he was the one who'd let his family down?

"So, money," Niall said brusquely. "Wire transfer? Or Fedex. That's easier. Yeah, I can overnight you a debit card and a cell phone. I'm assuming this number's not yours?"

"Borrowed it from the guy — uh, person — who runs the place I'm staying, yeah." Noah still hadn't decided whether Avery was male or female.

"Give me the address. I'll get you what you need by tomorrow midday."

Noah closed his eyes, but recited the address to his brother. He didn't deserve Niall. He was a crap brother. But his litany of self-reproach was nothing he hadn't thought before.

"One condition. Call Mom."

Noah shoved the heel of his hand into a closed eye, his other fist clenching on the phone.

"She'll be happy just to know you're breathing."

121

"No, she won't." Noah sighed. "Nothing I do can make her happy."

"She's a mom. She worries. She can't help it."

"Yeah, but... it's better this way."

"For you, maybe."

"Are you going to call her when we hang up?" Noah asked.

"Yes," Niall snapped. "Of course I am. Dude, she worries about you every single day. It was bad enough when you were in the Army. At least then she knew she'd get a phone call. It would almost be easier if you were—" His heated words stopped, as dead as the word he hadn't said.

"Yeah." Noah's eyes burned, but his voice stayed steady as he said, "I know the feeling."

"*Shit*," Joe said.

"*If he dies, what happens to us?*" The crying girl sounded more thoughtful than worried.

"You know I didn't mean that." Niall's voice was rough. "It's just... we miss you."

His family missed the old him, Noah knew. The him who laughed. The him who let people in. The him who could be honest.

He missed that guy, too.

"*No, seriously,*" the crying girl said. "*If he dies, what happens to us? Do we get to stop following him around all the time? Because that might not be so bad.*"

Great, now his subconscious wanted to kill him.

"It's okay," Noah reassured his brother. "I miss you, too. I'll..." He paused. He didn't want to lie. But he dreaded calling home with a passion most people reserved for root canals. He'd rather have a root canal. At least a dentist would give him good drugs.

"Compromise?" Niall suggested.

Noah felt a smile creeping up his face. "Go."

"Postcards. Five of them. And you call on our birthday. I'll be there, so I can, you know, take the phone away if it gets too much."

Their birthday wasn't until July. "One postcard a month or can I send them all tomorrow?"

"One a month," Niall said firmly, but his voice softened when he added, "First one to Mom, but you can mix it up on the next four. I wouldn't mind getting the occasional postcard myself."

"All right." They chatted for a few more minutes, but the noise level on Niall's side rose and lowered as if a door kept opening and closing, and he finally said he had to get back to work. Noah let him go with relief, grateful his brother hadn't asked more hard questions.

He stood, phone in hand, planning his next moves. He should have been smarter about stashing some cash in a safe spot in his truck, but it was too late for regrets. Damn, but he was hungry. He could seriously go for a Big Mac, but Avery's cocktail hour cheese and crackers would have to do for the night. At least breakfast was covered. He wouldn't starve before Fedex arrived. He headed into the house, head down.

"Bad news?" Avery asked from the kitchen area.

Noah looked up, shaking his head. "No, it's..."

But his words trailed off when he met the even gaze of Grace Latimer. She was perched on one of the stools at the breakfast bar. He swallowed, his mouth instantly dry. She'd changed her clothes. The fashion-plate suit was gone, leaving her in jeans and a black fleece pullover. She'd looked good in the heels and skirt, but she looked just as good, maybe even better, dressed for the outdoors.

Noah crossed toward the bar, holding the phone out to Avery. "Thanks for letting me use your phone."

"No problem," Avery replied. "Let me know if there's anything else I can do."

"I appreciate that." Noah gave a brief nod.

He was standing close enough to Grace that he could feel her warmth, a shimmer of heat that radiated from her like one of those heat lamps at a fancy restaurant with an outdoor patio.

"I don't have your wallet," she said.

He looked directly at her for the first time since crossing the room. "I didn't think you did."

"I do have people looking for it." One corner of her lips rose. "My staff was surprisingly enthusiastic about taking the afternoon to stomp around the forest, scaring off the bears. I think they'll find it."

"I'm okay if they don't." He tipped his chin toward Avery and the phone he'd returned. "I have a... friend, sending money."

"In the meantime, can I buy you that lunch you missed? Maggie's Place? She does a great meal. As you know."

Noah wanted to say no. The last thing he needed was to spend time with the woman next to him. She was disaster, looming like a pile of drugs laid before a junkie. He figured she was somewhere between pot and heroin — maybe a casual painkiller addiction?

But his mouth formed the word, "Sure," entirely against his will.

"Terrific." She grabbed his hand, folding her fingers around his own. They felt warm against his skin. He wondered how long he'd been cold without noticing, but let himself be tugged along as the phone he'd handed back to Avery rang.

"Hello, Sunshine Bed-and-Breakfast," Avery said into the phone, before letting it drop and adding, "Enjoy your lunch."

Grace waggled the fingers of her free hand at Avery, saying, "See you later, Ave," and Noah nodded with a quick glance over his shoulder.

As they entered the hallway, Avery started talking, words fluid and completely unintelligible to Noah, but somehow familiar. He pulled Grace to a stop, listening. One of his voices — the one that spoke in fake Chinese — burst into speech, the sound drowning out Avery's voice.

"Something wrong?" Grace asked. She let go of his hand.

"What language is that?" Noah asked.

She cocked her head back toward the kitchen and then said, "Quechua. Avery's family still lives in Peru."

"Does it sound like Chinese to you?"

She looked surprised. She paused, listening. "I could see that," she said with a nod. "Something about the rhythm? And maybe some of the sounds."

He had to be imagining the similarity. No way could his subconscious speak in a language he'd never even heard of. It was impossible. Unless...

"I don't know much about languages, though," Grace said. Her clear gaze met his.

Noah's suspicions faded. He was being paranoid again. General Directions hadn't put a transmitter in his brain. He wasn't the victim of some illicit experimentation. Grace Latimer ran a legitimate holding company with a solid reputation. His brother had told him so and if there was anyone on the planet Noah could trust, it was his twin.

His fake Chinese voice fell silent. In the kitchen, Avery continued speaking.

Noah listened for a moment longer.

It was impossible. Absolutely impossible. But the words sure sounded like those of the voice he'd been listening to for months.

13

GRACE

SHE SHOULDN'T HAVE KISSED HIM.

She also should have thought to check the bed-and-breakfast days ago. Grace was annoyed at herself for skipping the obvious. If she'd realized Noah was still in Tassamara, she would have called Avery right away. But at least she'd found him there this afternoon.

She slid into one of the bench seats of a booth at Maggie's, giving Noah a bright smile as he did the same on the opposite side.

Possibly she should have thought a little more about how to approach this conversation, too. True, she thought she'd have the entire flight to DC to figure it out, but still, she'd been so focused on finding Noah that she hadn't considered what she was going to say to him.

She took her phone out of her bag, opened the cover so she could see the screen, and set it on the table. She straightened it, lining it up so the edge of the phone was precisely parallel to the edge of the table, then folded her hands in front of her, leaving the phone to the side. If Dillon was watching, he could hardly fail to notice his cue. What did he want her to do? This was his opportunity to tell her.

But when she glanced up, Noah's eyes were on her. Did he think she was being rude, paying more attention to her phone than to him? She should explain.

But maybe not by telling him that she was hoping her ghostly nephew would send her a text.

She gestured at the phone. "I'm expecting a text. From the office. When they find your pack." It felt like a stupid excuse, but at least it had the virtue of being true. Or partially true, anyway.

He nodded, but before he could say anything more, Emma arrived at the table. "Good afternoon," she said breezily. "Late lunch, early dinner, or just a snack?"

"Lunch for me," Grace responded. She hadn't eaten yet. She raised her eyebrows at Noah, inviting his response.

"Uh, lunch is fine, I guess." His frown deepened, though, as if he were unsure of his answer.

"Two specials?" Emma asked the question, but didn't wait for an answer as the bell jangled over the door and two more customers entered. She moved away from the table, calling out, "Good afternoon, Mrs. Mulcahey, Mr. Voigt. Good to see you both."

Mr. Voigt wasn't using his cane and Mrs. Mulcahey wasn't in her wheelchair, Grace noticed, lips curving in satisfaction. Not that the improvements in their respective healths had anything to do with her, but it was nice to see that the effects of Akira and Zane's wedding hadn't worn off yet.

Emma didn't return. She was fussing over the two older people, helping to get them settled into a table by the window.

"Friends of yours?" Noah asked, following the direction of her smile.

"Oh..." Grace thought about explaining.

She could tell him the truth: that Kaye Mulcahey had multiple sclerosis and seldom left her house and that when she did it was in a wheelchair, and that Abe Voigt used a cane, had for years. But that at Grace's brother's wedding to Akira — the person Noah was looking for who Grace had denied knowing — Akira's dead father appeared to escort her down the aisle, apparently opening something like a dimensional portal to do so. And that Rose, a ghost who might have gotten promoted to angel by moving on and then returning, had absorbed energy from the portal and shared it with Kenzi, Grace's adopted niece, who'd used it to heal the older people, possibly only temporarily.

Yeah, maybe not.

Her father would have leaped into the explanation, but Grace was far more cautious.

"It's a small town," she replied. She adjusted the spacing of her phone, moving it a smidgen closer to her. Why wasn't Dillon texting her?

"So you mentioned." Noah glanced over his shoulder again. Emma had disappeared into the kitchen. "Looks like we've lost our waitress."

"She'll be back." Probably bearing food, if Grace knew anything about it. Maggie might have started preparing their meals before Grace and Noah even walked in the door. Emma's questions were often a formality, one that Maggie considered proper restaurant etiquette.

"What's the difference between lunch and dinner?" Noah asked.

Grace blinked at him. Was it a riddle? "What?"

He tilted his head toward the kitchen. "Why'd she ask that? What's the difference?"

"Lunch is lunch food and dinner is dinner?" Grace hazarded a guess, not sure what he was looking for.

He gave a slight shake of the head, implicit negation, but didn't continue his line of questioning. "Thanks for looking for my stuff. You didn't have to do that. It's all replaceable."

"They might not find it," Grace replied. "It's a big forest."

"Yeah. Interesting location for a holding company." The emphasis he placed on the last two words was unmistakeable, and his tone was dry as he added, "That is what you called General Directions, right?"

"Primarily a holding company," Grace corrected him, wondering what he'd learned about the company since she'd last spoken with him.

"And the research and government business?"

"If I'd known that was what you were interested in…" Grace lifted a shoulder. "I might have gotten more detailed in my explanation."

"Does that include an explanation of someone named Akira? Your sister-in-law, I believe?" he asked.

Grace winced. Oops. She hadn't expected that half-truth to come back to haunt her. "Not a guy?" she offered.

His look in response held the sorrow of a betrayed puppy — reproach, disappointment, the merest trace of pain. It was something about the eyelashes, she thought, feeling a laugh rising. He might not even realize he was doing it.

"Our dog used to look at me like that," she said. "Every morning when I went to school. Like I was breaking her heart."

He gave a spurt of surprised laughter and the heat of attraction stirred within her. She tried to ignore it, giving him a conciliatory smile. "I'm sure you can understand why I might not be more forth-coming to a total stranger looking for my sister-in-law. You obviously don't know her and I didn't know why you were asking about her."

"Fair enough," he replied, but he seemed distracted.

Grace glanced at her phone. Still no word from Dillon.

Did Noah know he was haunted?

If Dillon wanted her to talk to Noah about ghosts, surely he'd be telling her what to say. The fact that he wasn't was mystifying. And a little worrying. Grace wished she could talk to him and demand some answers, but she didn't want to risk scaring Noah away.

"As you might know by now, Akira's on her honeymoon," she said. "She'll be back in a couple of weeks."

"Long honeymoon."

"She's having a baby in May. This is likely to be their last chance for a vacation for a while, so they wanted it to be a good one."

"Makes sense." Noah's eyes flickered to the left, as if he was listening to a conversation happening in the aisle.

Grace sensed an opportunity. He hadn't exactly responded positively to her earlier offer of a job, but maybe she could just slide it by him while he wasn't paying attention. Take his acceptance for granted, make saying no more difficult than going along with her. "I understand you'd like to talk with her."

"Yeah." The frown between Noah's eyes deepened. He wasn't looking at her, his narrowed gaze aimed at the floor next to the table.

"Long-term, of course, Special Affairs is the right department for you," Grace said smoothly. "You'd be working with Akira and Zane. Zane would be your manager."

"Uh-huh," Noah muttered.

Grace bit back her smile. Whatever he was listening to, it wasn't her. "In the short-term, until they get back from Belize, I'll add you to the security team. It seems like a good fit for your skillset."

"Uh, what?" Noah's eyes lifted to her.

"You can start Monday." Grace shot him a bright smile as Emma arrived at the table, carrying two plates of food.

"Wait, what?" Noah said to Grace, ignoring the food.

But Emma slid the plates onto the table before them, saying, "I'm guessing whose is whose." She glanced over her shoulder and added in a whisper. "You haven't been hitting up the Mickey D's, have you, Grace? Maggie was grumbling."

"Not me." Grace spread her fingers to indicate her innocence. Her plate held her favorite chicken salad with grapes on a poppy-seed roll, sliced in half, with a side of coleslaw.

But Noah's plate was piled high with golden fries, thin-cut and glistening, plus a double-patty burger topped with lettuce and melted cheese on a sesame-seed bun.

"She thinks those skinny fries are an abomination." Emma heaved a sigh. "But if that's what you like, it's what you like." She pushed the plate with the burger on it closer to Noah, ran an expert eye over the table checking for ketchup, condiments and silverware, before snapping her fingers. "Drinks. BRB."

"We didn't order," Noah said, frowning at his plate.

"That never bothers Maggie."

Noah lifted the top off of his burger, revealing two sliced pickles, diced onions, and a coating of tangy orange Thousand Island dressing mixed with mayo. "This is a Big Mac."

"I think McDonald's would object to you calling it that. Trademarks, you know. It's a burger. With, perhaps, similar qualities."

Noah stared at his plate.

"Let me guess. Exactly what you wanted for lunch?"

"Yeah." Noah sounded grim.

"Maggie's good." Grace kept her voice mild. She reached out and filched one of his fries, nibbling it as he contemplated his food. "Mmm, hot grease and salt. Delicious."

"Help yourself."

"I did." She picked up her sandwich as he looked at her.

Emma whisked by their table. "Coke," she announced, placing an icy glass in front of Noah, "and sweet tea." She set the second glass by Grace. "Right?"

Grace nodded at her and the young waitress grinned. She looked the same question at Noah as he set the bun back on top of his burger.

"Yeah, great." He picked up the Coke and took a swallow as Emma breezed away.

Was this the moment to talk to Noah about psychic gifts? Unusual intuitions? Abilities that science couldn't explain or understand? Before Grace could decide, the bell jangled over the door and Natalya entered, followed by three of the kids. Grace leaned back in her seat, setting down her sandwich.

Kenzi was talking a mile a minute as she followed Natalya to the counter. "And Mrs. Joshi said that I could bring cupcakes to school on my birthday, too, but I want my cupcakes to be the yellow kind. With lots of colors in the icing. Or maybe blue icing but sprinkles. Can I have sprinkles on my cupcakes? I like sprinkles." She gave a skip to catch up to Natalya.

Grace smiled. Her new niece's selective mutism was long gone. In fact, Kenzi seemed to be making up for lost time with her chatter.

"It's not your birthday, silly," said Michael, trailing behind them. Or maybe that was Mitchell. Grace wasn't quite sure which twin was which.

"Sprinkles look like mouse turds. You want your cupcakes to have mouse turds on them?" Mitchell — or possibly Michael — sounded disgusted.

"I don't want those sprinkles, I want the pretty sprinkles. Rainbow sprinkles," Kenzi replied.

"Chocolate tastes better, though," one of the boys objected. "Chocolate cupcakes are the best."

"No chocolate. Yellow cupcakes. That's what I want. And rainbows."

"But—" the other boy started, but Kenzi interrupted him when she spotted Grace.

"Aunt Grace, Aunt Grace!" Kenzi dashed over to the booth. Grace was already sliding out, ready to catch her hug. The little girl wrapped her arms around Grace's torso, pressing against her. The boys followed more slowly.

"Hey, Grace," said Mitchell. Grace identified him easily now. Mitchell was always the first to approach, always the first to speak.

"Hi, Grace," Michael said, hanging back behind his brother.

"Hey, guys." Grace stroked a hand down Kenzi's hair. "How's it going?"

"It's Friday. We don't have to go to school for two whole days." Mitchell held two fingers up in emphasis.

"I love school now," Kenzi said, releasing Grace. "My teacher is nice. And we had cupcakes today, because it was Talia's birthday, and I get to have cupcakes on my birthday, too."

"I heard," Grace said. "Sounds like you've got big plans. Maybe you can bake them with your mom. Then you get to decorate them yourself."

"That would be good. Not with my mama, though, because she's in heaven now, but with Mom."

"Exactly." Grace cupped Kenzi's cheek for a quick second.

The little girl's eyes flickered to Noah and she gave him an open smile. "Hello. Are you friends with my Aunt Grace?"

"This is Noah Blake," Grace answered before Noah had a chance to. "He's going to come work with us."

"For the comp'ny," Kenzi said with a nod. "'Cept not like people visiting, like a place you go to learn things when you're too grown-up to go to school anymore. What are you going to learn?"

Noah opened his mouth, closed it, then opened it again and said, "I guess I don't know yet."

"Mom has a big machine." Mitchell spread his arms wide. "It takes pictures, so she can see what's inside people. That's what she learns about."

"Grandpa Max says he learns something new every day," Michael offered.

"Grandpa Max is funny," Kenzi said. "He says things that don't make any sense, but not like my other grandpa. Good things. And he tells good stories."

Grace chuckled as her eyes met those of her sister.

"A nice summary of our father if I've ever heard one," Natalya murmured as she joined them.

"He bought all of us bikes. Two bikes." Kenzi held her two fingers up to show Noah. "One to have at his house and one for our house. Travis and Jamie, too. He said they were good for the 'vironment but mostly he likes going fast."

"We all have to wear helmets, though," Michael volunteered. "All of us. Even Jamie and Jamie says he's too old and shouldn't have to."

"Jamie was persuaded by the pictures of bike accidents that I showed him." Natalya put a hand on each boy's back. "Maybe too persuaded. He's being very cautious now." She smiled at Noah. "Hello. It's nice to see you again."

He dipped his chin in wordless acknowledgement.

"We didn't really have a chance for introductions the other day. I'm Natalya Latimer and these are my kids, Kenzi, Mitchell, Michael." She nodded at each kid in turn.

Grace was pleased to see that she'd gotten the twins' names right.

"And Travis and Jamie. They're her kids, too. She's 'dopting us. All of us," Kenzi piped in. "But they're not here yet. They're still at school."

"We're picking them up and then heading over to your place for dinner, Grace. Dad's decided that all the kids need to learn how to change a bike tire."

Knowing their father, that meant that at least one of the kids would need that skill in the future.

"I'm not feeding you, am I?" Grace asked.

Grace was as capable as her father of dumping a box of spaghetti in a pot of boiling water and opening a jar of sauce, but Natalya had a thing about the children eating actual vegetables for dinner and it was the end of the week. The fridge would be pretty bare.

Natalya tilted her head toward the cash register. "Maggie's taking care of that. But there'll be enough for you if you'd like to join us. Both of you," she added, with a nod directed toward Noah.

"I'm set, thanks." Noah indicated his plate.

"Offer's open if you're hungry again in a few hours," Natalya replied. She let her hands drop from the twins' backs and gestured toward the counter. "Maggie's going to give you guys an after-school snack until it's time to pick up your brothers. I think Emma said something about chocolate chip cookies."

"Yum." Grace wasn't sure which boy said it, but they both bolted for the counter.

"Gotta work on the manners," Natalya said under her breath, but she let the boys go, giving a rueful shrug.

Kenzi paused to say, "Bye, Aunt Grace, see you later. Bye, Mr. Blake," before she darted after the twins.

Natalya turned back to Noah. "I don't know what you've learned about me, Mr. Blake, but I'm a radiologist."

She paused.

It was an expectant pause. And then it turned into a waiting pause, like the kind a teacher leaves when she's expecting a student to admit that he hasn't done the homework.

Grace frowned. It felt like Natalya was deliberately making Noah uncomfortable. She wasn't sure whether to interject and take him off the hook — were they playing good cop, bad cop? — or wait and see where Nat was going.

"I heard something like that," Noah finally admitted, sounding reluctant.

"I thought you might have." Natalya's voice held amused approval, like he'd given her the right answer. "My imaging equipment is top-of-the-line. The best in the state of Florida, truly cutting-edge. If you ever want a look at your brain, I'd be happy to scan it for you. I can either explain the resulting image set to you directly or send it to another radiologist for interpretation. And if you want a witness, someone who can confirm that you're seeing your own results, I'm happy to oblige. I'm available anytime."

She glanced back at the counter, and corrected herself with a chuckle. "Almost anytime. Still getting used to the five kids thing. It's not like having a cat, that's for sure." She gave Noah a warm smile, then fluttered her fingers in farewell to both of them and strolled away.

Grace sat down again. Noah was motionless, sitting so still he might have been frozen.

"Okay, that was odd," she said to him. "Are you, do you..." She couldn't think how to phrase her question tactfully, so she went with blunt. "Are you worried about your brain? Do you think you have a tumor or something?"

136

He looked back at her. For a long moment, their eyes met. He wasn't smiling.

Grace felt the same frisson of attraction she'd had the first time he'd smiled at her, but deeper, stronger. She wanted to help him. She wanted to tell him everything would be okay. But mostly, she wanted to lean across the table and kiss him. Instead she held his gaze until his eyes dropped and he picked up his burger.

"Or something," he said and took a bite. He couldn't have conveyed his Keep Out message more clearly without posting No Trespassing signs. But then he finished chewing and nodded toward her sister. "What does she think is wrong with me?"

14

DILLON

"I think he is possessed by a jinn," Misam insisted.

"Maybe he's a necromancer. Or a warlock. He's stealing our souls so he can use them to power his evil magic." Sophia shot a sulky glare in Noah's direction.

Dillon had to bite the inside of his cheeks to keep from laughing.

"Noah is not possessed. And he doesn't have evil magic." Joe folded his arms across his chest, his hands curling into fists. He didn't sit but stood, wide-legged, at the end of the table. At his insistence, the ghosts were gathering at a booth at the far end of the bistro from Noah and Grace, far enough away from Noah that he wouldn't hear them.

Dillon thought Joe's efforts were pointless. The faders were congregating at the booth, too, but slowly. Many of them were still drifting around. Noah might not be listening to their conversation, but if he could hear ghosts, he'd be hearing other ghostly voices, too: the woman calling for Carly, the guy worried about driving too fast, the kid with the peanut allergy, all the random phrases the wisps whispered and cried and sang.

"There's no such thing as jinn. Or magic," Joe continued, voice firm.

"I bet you didn't use to believe in ghosts, either," Sophia said bitterly. "Back when you were alive."

Joe opened his mouth as if to retort, then closed it again.

"It doesn't matter why Noah's caught us," Dillon said, sliding into the booth next to Sophia as Misam clambered up and over his mom, perching on the back of the bench, his feet on the seat. "We need to decide what to do. If Noah leaves Tassamara tomorrow and Rose hasn't found us yet, she won't be able to show us a door and we'll never escape."

"How come he didn't capture her, too?" Sophia demanded. "Why didn't she get pulled along with the rest of us?"

Dillon lifted a shoulder. "I told you she was special. She went through a doorway and came back. It made her... different." Rose wouldn't like it if he told the others what Akira thought about what had happened to her, but even she couldn't deny that coming back had given her unexpected abilities.

"A doorway like the one you want us to go through," Nadira said with a frown. "I am still not sure about this plan."

"Let's worry about that later, when we find one," Dillon said. He'd been trying to reassure Nadira for weeks, ever since he first met the other ghosts. Eventually they'd have to convince her, he knew, but he'd cross that bridge when he came to it. "Right now we have to decide what to do about Noah. If he can hear us, shouldn't we tell him who we are? What we are?"

"No," Joe and Nadira said in unison.

"We cannot know how he will react," Nadira said.

"Badly," said Joe. "That's how he'll react. Badly. We don't tell him."

"I think we should kill him," Sophia said unexpectedly.

"Sophia!" Nadira protested, eyes widening with shock.

"Oh dear, oh dear." Mona raised a hand, sketching the sign of the cross on her chest hurriedly.

"You heard him," Sophia defended herself. "He wouldn't care. He thinks it'd be easier to be dead." She snorted. "Boy, I bet he'd be surprised."

"We are not killing Noah." Joe's tone was even, but Dillon could hear the annoyance under his words.

"We could, I bet." Sophia pursed her lips thoughtfully. "Maybe we could electrocute him. Like in the shower or something. Do that energy surge thing to the water. Maybe he'd fry."

"Sophia!" Nadira snapped. She reached up to put her hands over Misam's ears. "Don't talk like that."

"Stop, Mama." Misam pushed her hands away. Earnestly, he said, "I do not think we should kill Noah, Sophia. We might get sent to hell."

"We're in hell," Sophia muttered, but she slumped down against the bench and fell silent.

One of the wisps floated across the table. Dillon could hear it complaining. "You promised. You promised we'd go."

"You know, even if Noah was possessed by a jinn, that's probably not the problem," Dillon said.

"Why do you think not?" Nadira sounded surprised.

"The jinn would have had to take him over in Iraq, right? We don't have jinn here." Dillon didn't think he believed in jinn. But Nadira and Misam did and he didn't think Joe should rule out the possibility with such vehemence. Necromancers, on the other hand... well, he was pretty sure Sophia hadn't been serious. He nodded toward the wisp. "You said this didn't start until you came back to the States."

"That's right," Joe said. He relaxed his hostile stance. "He had us, but this stuff—" He waved his hand around at the shades and floating balls of light. "—this stuff didn't start happening until we came home."

"We'd met other ghosts, but Mona was the first to join us," Nadira added.

The cleaning woman was standing on an empty chair, dusting a

141

hanging light fixture, but she glanced in their direction at the sound of her name.

"What was different about her?" Dillon asked. They'd talked about the other ghosts before, but they'd never gone into detail about how they'd wound up together.

Nadira snorted and Joe laughed.

"That place!" Nadira drew her scarf across her face, then dropped it as she added, "Any decent woman would have wished to leave."

Joe's grin was wide as he explained, "The guys from AlecCorp took Noah out when he first started with them. To a strip club. Nadira was madder 'n a wet hen."

He added appreciatively, "I'd never heard some of those words before."

"Pfft." Nadira's eyes crinkled in amusement. "It was disgusting."

"I liked it," Misam said with a cheeky smile. "I liked the ladies' sparkly clothes."

"It wasn't a dive, but it was no Vegas joint," Joe said. "We think Mona might have been there since before it became a club."

"Oh, dear. Oh, dear." Mona stepped off the chair. "That floor. It will never come clean. My husband will be here soon. It has to be spotless. I have to try harder." She dropped onto her knees, a bristle brush in her hand instead of the feather duster she'd been holding, and began scrubbing. "Carbolic soap, that's what I need."

"Poor Mona was trying to clean the floors." Nadira shook her head.

"Mama made all the lights pop," Misam said. "Pop, pop, pop. All of them! It was very dark."

Nadira patted Misam's leg. "I'm sorry, love. I know you didn't like it."

"They had to shut down and when we left, Mona came with us," Joe said. "She was the first."

"Had she been trapped there?" Dillon asked. Mona's long skirt and blouse were drab and shapeless. They could have been from any part of the early twentieth century, but he thought her hairstyle, rolled back and off her face, might have been from around the second World War.

"Yes, she'd been there many years," Nadira said. "Decades spent cleaning a den of iniquity, poor girl." Nadira leaned across the table and added in a whisper, "She says she doesn't remember her death but I think her husband might have killed her there. Sometimes the things she says..."

"She's still worrying about him." Sophia took in a deep, shuddering breath. "Even dying didn't let her escape. It's so sad."

"Cut it out, Sophia." Dillon poked her. "Mona's fine."

Sophia's lower lip quivered, but she didn't say anything more.

"So if she'd been trapped, how did she leave with you?" Dillon asked the others.

"Nadira helped her. I think Mona wanted to come with us." Joe looked back at Nadira. "Right?"

She nodded. "I pulled her out of there." Her voice held a hint of triumphant pleasure. "She didn't want to be in that sinful place any more than I did, so I took her by the hand and didn't let go when Noah finally left."

"Chaupi was next." Joe gestured toward the older man. Chaupi had gone into the kitchen and was investigating the pots on the stove and peering over Maggie's shoulder as she flipped a burger on the grill. "We found him in the kitchen of a take-out Chinese place."

"Why did he come with you?" Dillon asked.

The other ghosts exchanged glances. Joe was the first to shrug. "He just did."

"Do you remember how upset Mona was, Mama?" Misam kicked his feet against the back of the bench.

"When you took her away from the strip club?" Dillon asked in surprise.

"No, no, she was happy to leave there," Nadira replied. "It was with Chaupi, at the Chinese place. The kitchen had bugs. Big ugly brown things, scurrying on the walls."

"Roaches," Joe interjected. "Way gross. A couple bugs ain't gonna hurt anybody, but that place had a problem."

"Interesting," Dillon said. Had Chaupi hated the place where he was trapped? Maybe the ghosts wanting to leave had something to do with why they'd been attracted to the others.

Of course, that hadn't worked for Dillon. He'd still been stuck with his car after meeting Rose and Henry. He'd wanted to escape, but until his grandma's spirit had ripped him free, he'd only managed to extend his reach a few hundred feet.

"I don't know when the first glow ball showed up," Joe continued. "I don't think I even noticed them at first. They're like the bugs, one or two's no big deal, but once you start to get a lot of them, they're a pain."

"And then the singing lady," Misam said.

As if prompted, she wandered by the table where they sat. As always, her eyes were unfocused or perhaps focused on something none of them could see, as she crooned her low, melancholy melody. "*All through the night.*"

"We picked her up at this training Noah went to in Virginia. She was wandering around the grounds," Joe said.

"Virginia was nice. That place was fun," Misam said.

Nadira opened her hands. "Fun, I don't know, but pleasant enough."

"Pleasant enough." Sophia snorted. She folded her arms across her chest, wrapping her hands around to her shoulders as if she were hugging herself.

"You weren't with us yet, Sophia. It was back in autumn, when the leaves were just changing color," Misam told her.

"Autumn." Sophia sounded wistful. "I was in school. I hated school. I wish..." She let the words trail off.

"You were still alive in autumn?" Dillon asked. "This past autumn?"

"Yes." Sophia pulled her knees up, huddling into a ball. "I didn't know..."

Dillon had suspected that Sophia hadn't been dead for long. He hadn't wanted to ask — death felt like a sensitive subject and he didn't much want to talk about the stupid way he'd died — but from things she'd said before, he thought she might have killed herself. Still, traipsing around with Noah was a lot more interesting than being stuck in one place for years.

He patted her shoulder, feeling awkward. "It could be a lot worse."

She looked at him, with her too big eyes and her hair that looked like she'd chopped it off herself, and said, "It could be a lot better, too."

"Were you expecting heaven?" He'd never thought much about his own death, but becoming a ghost had been a pretty unpleasant surprise.

She snorted. "I was expecting nothing." Her eyes started to well up. "I thought it would be all over. Like being asleep, only not having to ever wake up again."

"You wanted that?"

"Yes," she said vehemently, tears disappearing. "Yes, I wanted that."

On the other side of the restaurant, Rose popped through the door. She glanced around, spotted the other ghosts, and headed in their direction.

"Hey, look," Dillon said, relieved by the interruption. "Rose is here."

"That's what supposed to happen," Sophia said, ignoring the interruption. "That's what my mom said when my grandpa died. She said he'd be at peace, no more suffering, and we should be glad for him. I wasn't glad."

"Here you are," Rose said cheerfully as she joined them, squeezing in next to Dillon.

"I'm glad you found us," Dillon replied. "Noah's talking about dragging us back to DC. Or somewhere else. Turns out he's got a brother in New York City. We could wind up there."

"New York City?" Rose's eyes widened. "I wonder if there'd be snow. I've never seen it in real life."

"This is not life," Sophia said bitterly. "You wouldn't be able to touch it. You wouldn't be able to feel it. It would just be white stuff on the ground."

"We saw snow in Baghdad once," Misam said. "It was very exciting."

"What did it feel like?" Rose asked.

"We were already dead." Misam scrunched up his nose. "I did not feel it. But it was very beautiful."

"It hurts," Sophia said. She was staring into space again. "Snow hurts. It burns like fire against your skin."

"That doesn't sound very pleasant," Rose said doubtfully. "It looks so pretty in the pictures."

"It snowed the day I died. For a little while, anyway. And then it turned into rain. It was the day after Thanksgiving. My mom wanted to know what I wanted for Christmas. I told her I wanted to die. She got so angry at me." Sophia laughed, a harsh, scraping sound. "She grounded me. Grounded! Can you believe it?"

Dillon blinked. Something was going wrong with his vision. It was turning fuzzy. Blurry, almost. He blinked again, looking around the restaurant. The walls and surfaces looked oddly reflective, as if the light was changing, as if his sight was shifting.

"I snuck out," Sophia continued. "It wasn't like they'd notice. I walked to the park. It was such a long walk. I don't think I ever walked that far before. My feet hurt but I didn't care because I'd stolen all my grandpa's leftover pills. It didn't matter to him. They didn't do him any good. He died anyway. That's when it started to rain."

"Rose," Dillon said, his voice hushed. "Do you see that? Is that what it looked like to you when I... before, I mean? When Chesney was here?" He'd been so angry. Furious, frustrated, devastated by the collapse of all his plans, and it had all happened so quickly.

"Oh, dear." Rose put her fingers over her mouth.

146

Nadira was staring at the light fixture above their table. "What is it?" she asked, curling a hand around Misam's leg.

"What's happening?" Misam reached out and touched the wall next to him, stroking it as if he expected to feel texture under his fingertips. "Why does everything look so soft?"

"Rain!" Sophia burst out. Her voice began rising and she scrambled to her feet, standing up on the bench next to Rose. She kicked out, her foot flying through the table's surface. "It was rain, like the universe was crying with me. But the universe doesn't care. It's all just a horrible joke."

One of the floating balls of light drifted toward their table. A transparent wisp followed. And then another.

"Akira's trying to find a way to measure spirit energy," Rose said. It sounded like a non sequitur but her eyes met Dillon's.

He knew she was thinking the same thing as him. "I don't think we need a ruler to decide that maybe this is too much."

Too much spirit energy created a vortex, a portal to another dimension that dragged in passing spirits. He'd been to that other dimension once. He never wanted to go back.

But he knew how to get out.

The others would be trapped.

"What do you mean?" Joe asked. He was staring around the room, too. "Why does everything look so weird?"

"I've seen this before," Nadira said. "At that place where we found Mona. Before all the lights went out. Remember?"

Joe chuckled uneasily. "I was watching the dancers. I didn't notice."

"I came and sat in your lap," Misam said. His actions followed his words as he slid off his perch on the back of the bench and onto his mother's lap. Her eyes were wide, but her arms closed around him. "After the lights went out. What is it, Mama?"

"Oh, dear," Rose muttered. "Dillon?"

"Sophia. You need to stop what you're doing." Dillon kept his voice calm, but his stomach churned with fear.

"Doing? I'm not doing anything." She threw out her arms. She'd stopped crying. She looked too angry to cry. "I can't do anything, because I'm dead. Dead and gone and nothing. I'm nothing."

"When you get upset, you pull in energy from the air," Dillon said. "It's why it gets cold around us. But too much energy is dangerous."

"Dangerous? How can anything be dangerous? We're dead! Dead, dead, dead! And it's horrible. It's worse than being alive." Sophia swung out with her arm. It passed harmlessly through the hanging lamp and into the wall. "Nothing can hurt us. We don't exist!"

The light bulb crackled and popped, broken glass scattering across the table.

The living people noticed. Behind the counter, the waitress, Emma, put a hand on her hip. "Oh, no. Not this again."

Dillon swallowed, looking at Rose. Was his fear making their danger greater? The last time he'd crossed to the energy plane, his anger and frustration had combined with the fury of the recently dead — and, technically, murdered — Raymond Chesney. If they all stayed very calm, could they stop Sophia from breaking the boundary between the dimensions?

"You should run, Dillon." Rose gestured to Nadira and Misam, hand sweeping through the air as if to brush them along. "You, too. Go. Get as far away as you can."

"What is happening?" Nadira asked. "Dangerous how?"

"We can't get far enough away. We're tied to Noah," Dillon said to Rose. He could feel the energy in the air now, tingling against his skin. The room was turning foggy. In moments, he knew, it would disappear entirely, leaving them in an endless sea of darkness and churning power.

The other spirits would be there with him, but they didn't know how to project energy. Only Misam had managed to change the channels. With no way out, they'd be lost, trapped until the sizzling currents of power ripped them apart and they dissolved into noth-ingness.

"Run," Rose repeated. "I'll try to absorb some of her energy."

"Can you do that?"

"Akira does."

"And it killed her!"

Rose gave a breathless chuckle. "Well, it's decades too late to kill me. You go. Let me hold Sophia here while you get Noah to leave. Quickly now."

"He can't hear us." Nadira was wide-eyed and uncertain, but her voice reflected the tension in the air and her arms had closed around Misam.

"I'll text Grace and ask her to tell Noah to run." Dillon scrambled out of the booth.

Sophia's fists were clenched, her face screwed up in a grimace, fury locking her tears away. The wisps and floating balls of light were congregating around her, but she ignored them, her eyes distant, unseeing. "Nothing matters. Nothing. We're not real. We don't exist."

"Come on." Joe reached toward Nadira, not touching her but gesturing as if he wanted to put his arm around her shoulders and hurry her away.

"Hurry." Dillon moved toward Noah. He could feel the pull getting stronger, tugging him back toward Sophia, but he resisted it, fighting his way toward the door.

Maybe vortexes were just nature at work. Like lightning in a thunderstorm. A build-up of energy and then zap, a crackling bolt of electricity, discharging power safely into the ground. Of course, safe was relative. Lightning could be deadly to those who got in its way.

Misam, Nadira and Joe were following Dillon, but some of the others were floating toward Sophia.

"Mona, Chaupi," Dillon called urgently. "Come this way." He tried to grab the angry man, but the other ghost wasn't solid enough. Dillon's hand passed right through him.

"It's not right," the man muttered, but his eyes were wide, his face touched with panic as he slid inexorably toward Sophia and Rose. The singing lady was almost to the booth, drifting through the chairs between her and it.

A wisp faded with a crackle and sizzle like water hitting a hot grill.

"Keep moving. Faster!" Dillon concentrated, trying to text Grace.

Rose stepped up onto the bench next to Sophia and put her hands on the younger girl's shoulders. "You're real, Sophia. Real as anything."

"I can't feel anything. Nothing hurts."

With a gasp and one last uncertain note, the singing lady disappeared.

"That's not true," Rose said calmly. "Everything hurts. I know. It gets better." She put her arms around Sophia and pulled her into a tight hug. Rose's face contorted into a grimace and she shivered.

"I don't understand." Nadira clutched Misam to her, but he was peering over her shoulder, trying to see what was happening. "Explain, please. What is this?"

"Sophia's turning into a vortex ghost and opening a portal to another plane of existence." Dillon wanted to shove his way past Noah and out the door, but the pull was too strong. He leaned into it, like fighting against a fierce wind, but he could feel his feet slipping against the floor, drawing him back.

"She's doing what?" Joe gave a disbelieving chuckle.

"She's going to Hell and taking us with her. So run!"

15

NOAH

Noah's mind replayed the words he'd just heard. *She's going to Hell and taking us with her.*

Great. His hallucinations had found religion. That was just what he needed. He was going to turn into a religious crazy, one of the ones who believed they were Jesus, he just knew it.

Ignoring his voices, he tried to focus on Grace. She was frowning, craning her neck to see across the room behind him. There'd been a pop and a tinkle of breaking glass from that direction.

One of the twins stood up, perching on the foot rail of his stool and peering around the cash register to look toward the back of the room. "Wow, cool! Didja see that?"

"Stay in your seat, please," his mother said with a worried frown.

"What happened?" Noah asked Grace.

"Just a light bulb breaking." Grace tried to dismiss it, turning her attention back to him, but she was biting her lower lip and her brow was creased.

"Noah, my man, it is time to get the hell out of here," Joe said right next to his ear.

Noah straightened automatically, eyes doing a fast, surreptitious scan of the room. What had his subconscious noticed? What was he missing?

"*Quickly, quickly,*" the Arabic woman's voice said urgently.

"*I don't want to go to hell.*" That was the little boy's voice, just two notches above a whimper.

"Are you okay?" Grace asked.

Noah tried to smile, but his face felt stiff. It probably looked more like a grimace. "Fine."

Her phone chimed. She put a hand over it, but didn't pull it toward her, her eyes still intent on his.

"*Check your phone, Grace. Check your phone!*"

Noah nodded toward her phone. "You can get that," he said, trying to sound casual. "I don't mind."

"It might be the office. They might have found your stuff."

"That'd be great." Noah scanned the room again. Nothing. The older couple were smiling, laughing, not paying attention to anything but their own conversation. The waitress was heading toward the back table where the light bulb had blown, a dustpan and brush in hand.

"*Now would be a good time to hear me, Noah. A real good time.*" Joe laughed. It was a reckless, breathless, desperate laugh. The laugh of a man on the edge.

The laugh he'd given the first time they drove into a firefight instead of away from one.

Noah stood, pushing away from the table in an abrupt movement just as Grace looked at her phone.

"I've got to go. Sorry." Noah glanced over at the counter. The kids were eating, the boys still chattering about the light bulb. One of them, Noah didn't know which, was up on his knees on his stool, following the letter of his mom's injunction to stay in his seat, if not the spirit.

Noah paused. Were the kids in danger? Despite the waitress sweeping broken glass off the table, he still couldn't see anything that would tell him why his subconscious was freaking out.

Feeling like an idiot, he muttered the question under his breath. "Are the kids in danger?"

"No, just us," Joe responded, as if he and Noah had been having these conversations for the past decade.

A decade during which Joe was dead, Noah reminded himself. For a moment, he felt torn. He knew he shouldn't do what his hallucinations told him to do.

"You need to leave." Grace stood, too. The crease on her brow had turned into a scowl. Her phone in one hand, she put the other on his arm, as if she would force him out the door. "Now."

Noah froze. Why was she saying that? If she'd heard him talking to himself, she should be asking what he meant by danger. If she hadn't, what did she know?

If all the things that had happened to him since he'd met Sylvie Blair in a DC hallway were pieces of a jigsaw puzzle, surely he had enough information to see the bigger picture.

The conversations, as if he was overhearing real people instead of snippets of sound. The strange encounters with people who acted like they knew him. The remote control, changing channels on its own. The innkeeper, speaking a language he'd been hallucinating for months.

Brain scans and job offers, blueberry waffles and burgers like Big Macs.

That kiss in the forest.

None of it added up to anything that made sense.

His voices were all babbling at once and behind them, he could hear the agonizing sound of the crying girl, sobbing as if her heart were breaking.

"Go on." Grace tugged at his arm. "Get out of here. Quickly."

With a confused shake of his head, Noah started toward the door as a woman came out of the kitchen. He kept moving but his eyes widened in instinctive appreciation.

That was the cook?

Wow.

And she could cook.

She stood in the kitchen doorway, hands on her hips. A wide, colorfully-printed headband held back long dark waves of hair, and a clean apron covered casual clothes. Her eyes snapped as she pointed toward the broken light, directing her words to the woman at the counter. "Is that your father's fault?"

"He's not even here," the doctor objected with a laugh.

"The last time we lost a lightbulb, it was because he was inviting ghosts to live here. I am not interested in running a haunted restaurant."

Noah paused, his hand on the door. Last time... ghosts... What?

"Ghosts?" The boy kneeling on the stool clapped his hands, his balance perfect. "We have a ghost who watches tv with us. She's nice but she doesn't like football. Jamie got mad at her 'cause she kept changing the channel, but then him and Dad went and watched tv downstairs, 'stead of in the movie room."

Noah stopped moving, the door to the restaurant half open.

"Rose," the cook agreed with a nod. "She's all right." Raising her voice, Maggie added in the direction of the back table, "At least she doesn't make a mess."

The doctor was watching him, Noah realized, with a small smile playing over her lips. She didn't look worried, not like she thought he was going to freak out again. She wasn't rushing over to talk him down from some kind of psychotic break. She just looked calmly interested, like she was waiting for his response with amusement and a sort of warm affection that he had done nothing to deserve.

"Don't try to take the base out while the power's on, Em," the cook said. "We can put a new bulb in when we close." Shaking her head, the cook returned to the kitchen.

Grace had followed Noah to the door. "You need to go," she said, her voice urgent. "Leave. I'll take care of this and catch up with you."

"Yeah, all right." He nodded. But he didn't move. His brain felt like it was spinning in circles. Dead was dead. Ghosts did not exist.

Or did they?

16

DILLON

"Go, go, go," Dillon chanted. He'd herded the other ghosts — at least the ones he could touch — outside the door ahead of him, but Noah had stopped in the doorway. Why was he just standing there? They needed to leave!

Dillon started to form another text message to Grace, but before he could complete it, the pressure that he'd been fighting against began to ease off. He stumbled forward, almost falling on top of Joe. Nadira and Misam were beyond Joe, Mona with them.

Dillon glanced over his shoulder. Rose was holding a sobbing Sophia and she looked different. She'd never been a fader, but the pink of her sweater looked deeper, the gold of her hair brighter. She seemed denser, more solid, and almost glowing, as if she was lit from within.

Dillon stopped pushing away from them. No answering tug began drawing him back.

Nadira kept going, carrying Misam out into the street and down it. Dillon could see when she hit the edge of her range, because she leaned into the pull, bracing Misam's head with one hand. It looked to him, though, to be about the usual distance that she could get away from Noah, not a response to the vortex.

"Are we okay? I can't feel it anymore." Joe had his arms extended, as if to shelter the others from the pull, but he let them drop to his sides.

"I think so," Dillon replied. He looked back into the restaurant. The angry man was standing near Rose and Sophia, his mouth moving as if he were muttering his usual phrase. Some of the wisps and faders were also clustered around them. Chaupi was emerging from the kitchen, his expression mildly questioning, as if he had just noticed that something unusual was happening.

"You need to leave," Grace repeated, clutching her phone.

Exhaling with relief, Dillon sent her another text.

Her phone chimed. Grace blinked at her screen. "Oh. Okay. Maybe not."

"Okay?" Noah stared at her.

Still staring at her phone, she asked, "Are you all right?"

"I'm fine," Noah replied.

Grace's gaze flickered to him, then returned to her phone.

She wasn't asking about Noah, but about the ghosts, Dillon realized. She was waiting for him to answer. But he didn't get a chance to send her a message before Joe grabbed his upper arm and hauled him out the door and into the street.

"We need to talk," Joe said, towing him toward Nadira.

She'd turned to look back in their direction, but she wasn't coming any closer. Her arms were wrapped around Misam, clutching him to her in a fierce hug. He wasn't kicking to be let down, but his head was craned to look their way, too.

Mona turned to the glass window at the front of the restaurant. "Vinegar," she said. "I can get rid of these smudges." With frantic energy, she began polishing the window.

Dillon didn't resist Joe's pull, although he shot one last glance at Rose. She was patting Sophia's back soothingly. Sophia's sobs looked like they were slowing down, her body shuddering with gulping, shaky gasps.

"What was that?" Joe asked.

"How could Sophia open a gateway to Hell?" Nadira demanded as soon as they were close enough. "Is she a demon?"

"No, no." Dillon shook his head. "I don't think there's any such thing as a demon. Or at least I've never met any."

"Hell has demons," Nadira said, her voice rising. "Pits of fire, scalding water, black smoke, burning wind. And demons!"

Dillon patted the air with his hands, fingers widespread, trying to soothe her. It would be just his luck if he upset her so much that she turned into a vortex ghost herself. "It's not exactly hell then."

"What exactly is it then?" Nadira asked, her dark eyes shooting daggers at him.

"It's..." Dillon didn't know where to start. He should have told the other ghosts about the vortex weeks ago. But it wasn't something he liked thinking about. Every time he remembered Chesney's ghost — the feeling of his energy, that grimy chemical burn enveloping him — he felt both guilty and revolted.

He'd hated Chesney, he really had. But he was pretty sure he'd destroyed Chesney's soul and he didn't much like having that on his conscience. Knowing that Chesney would have happily destroyed him and his parents didn't make him feel any better about it.

"It's what?" Nadira snapped.

"It's another dimension, I think. An energy dimension. It's not burning, but it's..." Dillon bit his lip. He didn't want to scare them. Or did he? They needed to be warned. "It's very unpleasant," he finally finished.

"Hell is more than unpleasant." Nadira's grip on Misam started to relax as if Dillon's words were reassuring her.

"Yes." Dillon sighed. "Akira used to think vortex ghosts destroyed other ghosts. But it's not the ghosts so much as it is the energy. Too much spirit energy creates a hole that opens into..." Dillon spread his hands, searching for the right words. "It's like an ocean. Of energy. It feels like chaos, but it's a place of... of unbecoming."

"Of unbecoming?" Joe repeated, inching closer to Nadira and Misam.

Dillon lifted his shoulder in a shrug, trying for a nonchalance that wouldn't reveal his fear. "Maybe it's the universe's way of cleaning up leftover spirit energy. But we get sucked in and then, well, souls dissolve into nothingness there. Or get..." He swallowed. "Shredded."

Should he tell them that he'd been the one doing the shredding? But if they got more upset, they'd create more energy, and the more energy they created, the more danger they'd be in.

Misam whimpered. "I don't want to be shredded."

"Nobody's getting shredded," Joe said. He and Nadira exchanged glances.

Dillon couldn't tell from their expressions what they were thinking. Did they just not believe him? They'd felt the pull, the same as he had, but Noah had been dragging them around for years. Maybe the vortex hadn't felt different enough for them to appreciate the danger. He didn't want to frighten Misam, but he had to make them understand the risks.

"Ripped apart," he said. "Broken down into component bits."
He paused.
They didn't say anything.

"Dead," he added. "Really dead. Gone for good, no longer existing in any form. That kind of dead."

Joe put a hand on Nadira's shoulder. "Okay, that doesn't sound good."

Nadira snorted. Her grip on Misam had tightened again. "No. That sounds very bad."

Dillon nodded. "You guys must never have gotten really angry at one another."

"They argue all the time." Misam wiggled to get free. Nadira set him down, but kept a careful grip on his hand. "All the time!"

Nadira glanced at Joe. He seemed to realize he was still touching her shoulder and removed his hand, stuffing it into his pocket self-consciously. Nadira's lips twitched as if she didn't know whether she wanted to smile or scowl.

"It's not the same," Dillon said. "My gran turned into a vortex ghost. When she died, she was... upset. Grieving and angry and lost. She couldn't find me and she got stuck between the dimensions. And then later, I met this other ghost and he was threatening my mom. He made me mad."

Dillon dropped his gaze, staring at the sidewalk. He'd known better. He'd been aware of the danger. But his feelings had over-whelmed him and he hadn't been able to control them.

Softly, he said, "Despair is very powerful. And very dangerous."

"Okay," Joe said briskly. "No despair. Got it."

"No despair," Nadira agreed. She sniffed. "It is a great sin and I am not inclined to it, anyway. But if you have been to this other dimension, Dillon, why are you not—" She opened her fingers wide.

"Disintegrated," Misam finished for her.

"I didn't get trapped there," Dillon said. "I started texting my mom and I sort of gradually faded back into this dimension."

Nadira's eyebrows shot up, her expression dubious. "So to save ourselves from this place that is not-quite-hell, we must learn to text?"

It was partly relief — that they believed him, that they weren't asking harder questions, that Nadira was looking for solutions instead of getting upset — but Dillon gave a snort of laughter.

"I suppose. But it would be better not to wind up there. We need to find a doorway. The other kind of doorway."

And they needed to find it soon. Dillon had wanted to help the other ghosts since the day he'd met them, but he hadn't felt any urgency about it. They'd been trapped with Noah for years. What difference did another few weeks or months make?

But if a vortex was a build-up of spirit energy being discharged into another dimension, maybe Noah wasn't responsible for the accumulation of ghosts around him. Maybe the ghosts were forming their own whirlpool of spirit energy — enough to attract other spirits, but not enough to break through into the energy dimension.

At least not until now.

And if that was the case, even if Rose had managed to save them for the moment, one more ghost — or one more burst of intense emotion — could become the tipping point, the last straw that plunged them all into the void.

17

GRACE

Dillon wasn't answering. Grace stared at the screen of her phone, feeling her breath tight in her throat. Was he all right? The last text — *Nvm, it's ok*— stayed steady on the screen, no new letters forming. It certainly implied that he was fine, but damn it, why couldn't he share a few more details?

"Are you okay?" Noah asked.

Grace glanced up to meet his frown. She'd been staring at her phone for too long, she supposed. Long enough that he'd realized something was wrong.

"I'm fine." She stuffed her phone in the side pocket of her bag. She could try talking to Dillon again but she was reluctant to do so in front of Noah. The guy was a skeptic. He wanted a logical explanation for everything, including Maggie's ability to know what people wanted to eat before they even walked in the door. He didn't believe in auras and when she'd hinted at her sister's gift, he'd practically rolled his eyes at her.

Okay, maybe he hadn't been quite that bad, but he'd definitely made his distrust clear.

And it was more than doubt, it was distrust. Grace almost wished

Lucas were here so that he could read Noah's mind and tell her what was going through his head. If she was going to fulfill her father's wishes and hire him, though, she couldn't afford to scare him off by having conversations with the empty air.

She gave him a bright smile. "Let me just pay."

Noah nodded and stepped outside.

Grace paused for a moment until she was sure that he was waiting by the door for her, then headed back to the counter.

Maggie came out of the kitchen carrying a bag. She passed the bag to Nat. "Here you go. Irish stew, side salad, soda bread, and a caramel apple crisp. You might want to pick up some vanilla ice cream to go with the dessert."

"Yum!" Mitchell had been sitting obediently on his stool, but he jumped down and reached for the bag. "I love stew."

Maggie winked at him as she stepped to the cash register. "Must have been your night."

At the counter, Kenzi gave a sudden shiver. "Ooh, sizzles," she chirped. She spun her stool around. "I have sizzles again."

"Sizzles?" Natalya shot a sharp glance at her daughter. "What kind of sizzles?"

Kenzi was jittering, almost dancing in her seat. "Good sizzles," the little girl said, sliding off her stool.

Grace put a hand over her phone, feeling its reassuring solidity, the angles under the soft leather of her purse. Were those good sizzles similar to the ones Kenzi had felt at the wedding?

Natalya passed her credit card to Maggie, but both of them were watching Kenzi. The little girl looked around the restaurant, and then, like a homing beacon, headed straight to the booth holding Kaye Mulcahey and Abe Voigt.

Natalya frowned. Grace slipped her phone out of her purse, thumbed it on, found the text messages she'd received from Dillon, and tilted it so Nat could see the screen.

Her sister's brows raised and then she nodded. "I should have guessed."

162

Grace's answering smile was wry. Natalya could see her own future in as much detail as most people remembered their own pasts, but ghosts threw off her ability. According to one of the mathematicians in GD's materials-modeling department, ghosts were a random variable introducing chaos into a dynamic system.

Life might be predictable, at least as much as the weather was predictable — not necessarily from moment to moment, but in general strokes — but ghosts were the equivalent of the unstable air in a thunderstorm forming a tornado or the tectonic shifts that created tsunamis. If Natalya was surprised by Kenzi's behavior, it was because ghosts were influencing the material world in unexpected ways.

"He reacted," Grace said softly. "He said he had to leave, got up to go."

"He? Oh." Natalya shot a quick glance at the door. Grace was tempted to turn and look herself, but if Noah was watching, she didn't want him to think they were talking about him, even though they so clearly were. "Yes, I suppose that could be."

"Could he feel it, do you think?" Grace asked. Akira could feel the vortexes. In fact, she'd been killed, albeit temporarily, when she'd encountered one. If the same was true for Noah, he might be in as much danger as Dillon could be.

"Hmmm." Natalya took her credit card back from Maggie. Her murmur didn't sound like a yes or a no, just a noncommittal acknowledgement.

Grace held back the sigh that wanted to escape. Why must her family be so frustrating? Was a straight answer really too much to ask for?

She pulled her own credit card out and handed it to Maggie.

"Everything okay?" Maggie asked as she slid the card through the reader.

Grace couldn't tell from her expression whether the question was a pro forma courtesy or a worried acknowledgement of the shattered lightbulb and her hushed conversation with her sister.

163

"Lunch was delicious, as always," she replied. "As for anything else..." She shrugged. "Your guess is as good as mine."

Maggie shook her head. "I swear this is your father's fault," she muttered. "As if a haunted restaurant is nothing. No one wants to be thinking about death while they eat dinner. Not to mention the implications. I don't want my customers wondering whether my cooking kills people."

"If it did, they'd die happy," Grace offered.

Maggie did not smile. "Lima beans. And..." She paused, head tipped to one side, face screwing up with vague disgust. "Cod with cheese sauce? Who would do that?"

"Oh, yuck." Grace put a hand up in protest. "My college dorm cafeteria. Every Friday. Please, no."

"Baked, maybe." Maggie stopped in the act of handing Grace's credit card back to her, eyes unfocused. "With goat cheese. Chives. Maybe some lemon zest."

"That sounds delicious," Natalya said.

"Which would defeat the point." Maggie pushed Grace's card the rest of the way in her direction.

"No ghosts, I promise," Grace said quickly. "Not that I have anything to do with it. Them. Ghosts. I don't know anything. About anything." She took her card, lifted her shoulders in a shrug, and offered Maggie a conciliatory smile.

Natalya's gaze was on Kenzi as the little girl patted Kaye Mulcahey's hand. "I don't think you need to worry about losing customers. Not today, anyway." She glanced back at Maggie and added, "And Dad was miserable when you were angry with him. I'm sure he's learned his lesson."

Maggie pursed her lips, but her eyes were amused. "Good." She nodded toward the bag that Mitchell still held. "Enjoy your dinner."

"Always." With a wave, Natalya rounded up the boys, called to Kenzi, and headed for the door.

Grace was about to follow suit, but as she started to say good-bye,

164

Maggie indicated Noah with a tilt of her chin. "And enjoy the rest of your date. He's quite something."

"It's not a date," Grace said quickly. "He's not — we're not — I'm going to hire him. For GD."

"A scientist?" Maggie's brows shot up.

"Security, probably. Or Special Affairs."

Maggie frowned in Noah's direction. "Special Affairs? Huh." She gave a snort, followed by a sigh and a glance back in the direction of the broken light bulb. "Ah, well, I guess Max is off the hook, then. He's like Akira, is he?"

"Something like that," Grace replied vaguely. Inwardly, though, she winced. Maggie was no gossip, but information flowed through Tassamara like water through a sieve. It was like osmosis: what one person knew, the whole town knew within days. Grace suspected it was an inevitable side-effect of living in a town of psychics, but maybe it was just a small-town thing. Either way, she still had no idea what Noah knew about his situation, if anything. It seemed a bit unfair that in the very near future, the entire town would know more than he did.

She said good-bye and followed her sister to the door. Noah was waiting for her outside. Natalya and the kids had already disappeared down the street.

"Thanks for lunch," Noah said, unsmiling. His expression was opaque. Grace had no idea what he was thinking.

"Time for your tour of GD?" She intended the words as a statement, definitive and assured, but somehow an interrogative lilt escaped, turning them into a question.

"I don't think—" he started.

She interrupted him. "You want to meet Akira. You really do."

"So I've heard," he responded dryly. A corner of his mouth lifted.

He had a really nice mouth, Grace noticed, not for the first time. She smiled back at him. "First step. Visit the company, let me show you around, see how you like the place. It can't hurt."

She waited, holding her breath, as he considered. "We don't bite," she finally added, a hint of exasperation in her tone. After all, how many job offers came with no questions asked? Plenty of people would be delighted to get this kind of welcome from General Directions.

"No?" he responded with a flash of humor in his eyes.

A flush of heat ran through her veins as she raised a hand in solemn promise. "Never." She should stop there. She shouldn't say another word. But his eyes were holding hers, and she had to add, "Not at work, anyway."

Damn it. She shouldn't be flirting with him. This was not a date. She was helping her nephew and that was it. But his lightning grin raised her temperature another few degrees as he dipped his head in her direction.

"A tour," he conceded. "We'll see how it goes."

18

NOAH

Noah rubbed a hand over his eyes. He wasn't imagining what he was looking at, was he? He opened his eyes again.

A tennis ball floated before him.

He ran his hand above it, below it, around it, searching for the hidden forces keeping it in the air. Could it be held up by an air current, a fan with enough force to keep the lightweight ball elevated? Not if he couldn't feel a draft. Magnets? Maybe the tennis ball wasn't really a tennis ball. But he couldn't see anything that looked like a magnet, either on the ball or in the rather plain, mostly empty room in which they stood.

Maybe the ball had an engine in it, a tiny, soundless jet-propelled engine, working like a helicopter. Without blades. But drones floated in the air, right?

Of course, that had to be it.

"You guys working on drone technology?" he asked Grace.

She gave him a look. The look said something along the lines of, "Are you blind?" but her verbal response was a much more delicate, "Something like that."

He eyed the ball again. Floating, it was definitely floating. And he couldn't hear a thing.

"Why is he such a skeptic?"

"He's logical, that's not a crime."

"He watches the wrong kind of television shows. He should watch more science fiction."

Well, he couldn't hear a thing except his usual repertoire of hallucinatory voices. Right on cue, Joe chimed in with a grumpy, *"Shush. All of you."*

Grace — the only person who was truly present — was talking, too. "On night shift, you'd be expected to patrol. Our scientists often work late, sometimes through the night, although they're not expected to. But inspiration doesn't always arrive during normal business hours. You'd need to learn the names and faces of the people who work here. I realize some security jobs don't require that, but we can't rely on ID cards and thumbprints."

"I've got a pretty good memory," Noah said, still staring at the ball. He'd seen drones. They usually had propellers of some sort. If it was solar-powered... no, that made no sense. Some kind of anti-gravity?

"It might not be for long, anyway. Once Akira and Zane get back..." Grace let the words trail off, opening the door across the room from the ball. "Looking good, Dr. Winkler."

"Thank you," the small woman in the adjacent room said. Sounding apologetic, she added. "We're still not managing much in terms of weight yet, and the energy expenditure makes no economic sense. I can't say that this will ever be practical in terms of—"

Grace interrupted her. "No worries, I'm just showing a new employee around."

New employee? Noah still wasn't sure how he'd gone from planning to get out of town as fast as possible to starting work on Monday, but it was beginning to feel like a done deal.

"Oh, of course." The woman peeked around Grace and shot Noah a quick smile. "Welcome to the company. You're going to love it here."

"Thanks." He ducked his head in a nod.

"We'll leave you to it." Grace led the way back to the hallway and toward the elevator.

The floor plan wasn't complicated, nothing Noah would have trouble remembering, but the place was much bigger on the inside than it looked. From the outside, the parking lot led to several independent buildings resembling the small town versions of modern office suites. The kind of places that ought to have a dentist on the first floor, an orthodontist on the second, maybe a lawyer on the top. But as soon as they'd entered, Grace had taken him into an elevator that dropped down and opened into a sprawling complex of underground labs with tunnels connecting the buildings.

"So I wanted to show you some of the projects we're working on, give you an idea of the kind of things that we're doing." Grace shot him a look. "Any questions?"

Noah couldn't interpret the look. Did she want him to ask if they were magic? Because he was tempted, but the words were so incongruous in the setting of sleek walls, tiled floor, that there was no way they were escaping from his mouth. He'd spent a lot of years hiding his insanity from everyone he knew. He wasn't giving in to it now.

"I'm good," he said.

"Okay." She took a deep breath, inhaling as if she were girding up for some unknown battle. She didn't fuss with her hair or pull at her clothes, but she lifted her chin and straightened her shoulders before pressing the button to summon the elevator. "Let's visit the security station and meet some of your future co-workers."

"Would these be the same guys who, ah, came running this morning?"

"The very ones." She didn't meet his eyes as the door slid open and she stepped inside.

He followed her, trying to bite back his smile. It probably wasn't funny to her. No CO wanted to get caught in a compromising position. But she saw it on his face and her own relaxed.

"You might hear about it," she warned him. "Our morning, um, adventure."

"I'd expect so," he replied comfortably. The ribbing would probably start the minute she wasn't in hearing distance. If it didn't, it would mean they hated him on sight. Either way, he'd manage.

"Bear jokes forever," she said with a sigh.

"What do you call a wet bear?" he asked her.

"Seriously?"

He kept his face straight. "A drizzly bear."

She gave a pained grimace, but she laughed, too, and the tension in her shoulders disappeared.

"Dad jokes. He tells Dad jokes," the Dillon voice said, sounding disgusted.

Noah wanted to laugh, but he didn't. But he did stop trying to hide his smile as Grace led him past the reception desk and into the small office behind it.

"This is the security station," Grace said, stating the obvious. The room held a wall of monitors, showing scenes inside and outside of the facility. As he watched, the scenes shifted.

The guard at the desk jumped to his feet. Young, clean-cut and muscular, his eyes raked over Noah in a comprehensive sweep that looked less than welcoming. "Afternoon, ma'am."

"Jensen." Grace nodded at him. She gestured toward Noah. "Noah Blake. He'll be coming to work for us. With you. At least for a few weeks."

The temperature of her voice had dropped by about ten degrees. Not hostile, not cold, but edged with a fine chill that said, 'Fuck with me and you'll regret it.'

"Yes, ma'am." Jensen didn't quite snap to attention, but it was damn close.

Noah was torn between sympathy for the guy and a rush of unexpected lust for Grace. He wanted to melt the frost from her tone, bring back the warmth in her eyes, even turn it into heat.

But then Jensen offered him a friendly smile and said, "You're going to love it here."

Hadn't that scientist, Dr. Winkler, said the same thing?

"So I hear," Noah replied warily.

Grace shot him a smile over her shoulder. The chill was entirely gone from her voice when she confided, "I pay them to say that."

His brows rose and he blinked, before he said, "What?"

"Not big bucks or anything. Just a gift certificate for the local spa. Who doesn't like a massage or a manicure, right? And the extra business is good for the spa."

Jensen guffawed, his moment of intimidation clearly over. "The look on your face."

"I don't ask them to lie," Grace elaborated. "But when I give a tour, it's usually for a scientist I'm trying to recruit. Tassamara is remote and General Directions doesn't have the academic credibility some of them want. We pay well, but I like to make a good impression, so when an employee says something positive during the tour..." She lifted a shoulder in a shrug. "Gift certificate."

"So someone else already said you were going to love it here?" Jensen shook his head. "I'll have to come up with a new line. But it is a great place to work. We get gift certificates." He laughed.

"And terrific employee benefits. Good health insurance, the usual vacation time, a 401K, contributions to continuing education... although that last." Grace tipped her hand back-and-forth in an equivocating gesture. "We haven't had too many employees take us up on that. We hire a lot of PhDs and they're not usually interested in more school. Plus, it's a long drive to the nearest university. We've got a couple people doing online programs, though."

"Cafeteria's good," Jensen contributed. "And the people are friendly." He cast a sideways look at Grace, before adding in a tone almost neutral enough to hide the mischief, "Real friendly."

Grace looked amused. She let it go, nodding toward the monitors. "Any luck out there?"

"Yeah." Jensen sounded disgusted. "Smithson found it."

"Really? I wouldn't think wandering around the forest was Derek's speed." She glanced at Noah. "He's the head of research. Not the outdoorsy type."

"I think he cheated. He had these weird glasses on, and he had his head down staring at a screen most of the time."

"Hmm." Grace tapped her lips. "Had the bear already abandoned the pack?"

"Yeah, but he found the bear first. Then he backtracked."

"Thermal imaging to find the bear, I bet. We've got some glasses left over from Akira's..." Grace paused and glanced at Noah. He could see her considering her words, before she finished, "...project. And I bet he used the variable threshold modeling AI we've been working on to look for its trail. I didn't think that project was far enough along to be useful yet. I'll have to ask him about it."

"Like I said," Jensen muttered. "He cheated."

Grace chuckled. "Next time I send y'all out on a treasure hunt, I'll make sure to make up some rules first. Do you know where he left it?"

"In your office, I think."

"Great, thanks."

Noah followed as Grace led the way to her office, but he paused at the door when she crossed to her desk, taking it in.

He wasn't sure whether to be intimidated or impressed. Her desk was a work of art. Made of curved stainless steel with panels of stained glass in shades of pink and purple on the front and sides, it belonged in a museum of design. Or at the very least an office in Milan or Madison Avenue, not a sleepy small town in Florida.

Behind it, she had a desk chair of pink leather: tall and imposing, but pastel. In front of the desk sat two over-stuffed lavender armchairs, positioned side-by-side at an angle for easy conversation whether she was sitting behind the desk or in one of the chairs. One wall was lined with bookshelves, filled with books and photos. The windows on the other two walls looked out into tangled forest.

It was simultaneously ultra-feminine and imposing, comfortable and dramatically unconventional. In her casual jeans and fleece, she could have looked out of place. But she didn't.

The neat pile of his possessions on her desk did, though. She made a face as she looked down at it and picked up his phone, which sat on top.

She held it out to him, her expression apologetic. "Apparently the bear didn't like your phone."

"Wow." Noah came forward and took the remains out of her hand. It was crushed, the screen shattered, the circuits inside visible through the broken plastic of the case. "I'm guessing there's no Verizon store in town?" His lip curved at the look she gave him. "Yeah, I didn't think so."

"Small town, middle of a national forest," she said. "We're happy to get a signal."

His wallet was undamaged, Noah saw as he picked it up, but his pack was a lost cause. The bear had managed to tear the zippers out of their seams in its quest to eat his sandwich. He checked it for any other contents, retrieved the key to his room, and held the pack up. "Trash?" he asked.

Grace bent and fished out a can from under her desk. His pack wasn't the first casualty of the day, Noah saw. Her pink shoes were sitting in the can, mud spread halfway up their sides.

"Sorry about your shoes," he said.

She shrugged. "My own fault. I should have changed before I went out there. I knew better."

Her eyes met his. The hum of attraction between them flared into heat. He knew they were both thinking about their encounter in the forest, about the feel of lips touching, bodies pressed together, the spark of desire.

"*Tsk, tsk.*" The clean freak sounded disapproving. "*A soft-bristled brush, that's what she needs. Let the mud dry, then a good scrub.*"

Noah didn't repeat her words to Grace. Instead he dropped the pack on top of the shoes and took a step back.

19

GRACE

G RACE SAT IN HER CHAIR AND GESTURED TO NOAH TO TAKE A
seat in one of the chairs in front of her desk. She'd been as professional as she could be on their tour of the company, talking about the
facilities and the job responsibilities, but the sight of her muddy shoes
stirred up all her feelings again.

She'd had crushes before. For a solid three weeks in sixth grade,
she'd drawn hearts around Charlie Kilpatrick's initials in the margins
of her notebooks, before he tried to convince her that Megadeth was
musically superior to Alanis Morrisette. Crush over.

Then there'd been the usual high school and college stuff. Infatu-
ation that came and went, attraction that mysteriously appeared and
then disappeared when the guy in question turned out not to be The
One. Not that she knew who The One was, or even who she wanted
him to be.

And it would be ridiculous to think that the man sitting across
from her was it. Him. The One.

But there was something about him. Not just his looks. Sure, he
was pretty, but she wasn't that shallow. She'd met plenty of good-
looking guys, and gone out with her fair share. He was different.

Not that she knew him, not really. Oh, sure, she knew every detail a solid background report could pull up. She knew he responded well to surprise bear encounters. She knew he had a sense of humor. And she knew that he was a really good kisser.

She wished she didn't know that. It made talking about paperwork and W4s and insurance policies all the more difficult. But she persevered, only losing her train of thought once or twice along the way when his eyelashes distracted her.

She finished with, "So, any questions?"

His eyes met hers. "No, I..." His lips pressed together like he was holding back words.

She folded her hands in front of her and waited.

"A few," he finally finished.

"Go for it."

He did not leap into speech, but watched her. She couldn't read his expression. Wary, maybe. Or skeptical?

"Go ahead. Ask me anything. I promise I'll answer."

He tilted his head in the direction of the door. "What were you going to say back there?"

Grace frowned. "When?"

"You were talking about thermal imaging glasses. You were going to say something and then you changed your mind."

Grace bit the inside of her lip. How perceptive of him. How unfortunately perceptive of him. But it wasn't as if she was hiding some deep, unsavory secret. Her lips twitched.

"What was it?" he asked again.

"Honestly?" Grace opened her hand in amused self-deprecation. "Experiments. I was going to say 'Akira's experiments,' but it sounded so creepy. Experiments. Like she's a mad scientist or something. She's really not."

He didn't look convinced. He was watching her with a narrow-eyed intensity that made Grace think of a cat. Not a house cat. More like a panther. She didn't shift in her seat, but it took an effort.

"Next?" she asked.

176

Would he ask more about Akira's project? She'd been trying to determine where ghostly energy might fall on the electromagnetic spectrum. Modern ghost hunters used electromagnetic field readers, but Akira scoffed at them. She said they were better at picking up cell phones and microwaves than ghosts.

So far all of her results had been negative, though. The thermal imaging glasses couldn't reveal a ghost even from a few feet away. According to Akira that proved ghosts didn't emit radiation in the infrared range of the electromagnetic spectrum. She'd started muttering about wave-particle interactions instead.

"Back in the restaurant," he said. "You got a text."

"A couple of them," she agreed.

"Who were they from?"

"My nephew," she answered easily, but with a little inner trepidation.

"Will you tell me what they said?" Noah asked after a long pause.

Grace considered him. She could do that. It wouldn't leave him less confused, she suspected. He wouldn't know what they meant. Instead of answering, she pulled her phone out, called up the texts and passed it across the desk. "Go ahead."

He picked it up. She wasn't surprised when he started to frown. "*Vortex opening, plz get away,*" he read aloud. "*Nvm, it's ok.* What does that mean?"

"Nvm? Shorthand for never mind, I expect." Grace hid her smile. She bet he was a good poker player. He controlled his expressions well. But she could see the exasperation in the line of his mouth.

"What's a vortex?"

Grace leaned back in her chair. Choosing her words carefully, she said, "In this context, I think it refers to an accumulation of energy. A certain type of energy. But Akira would be better at explaining. If you can just wait a couple of weeks until she gets back, I'm sure she'll be able to answer all your questions."

"My questions about what? What is she supposed to be the big expert in? The redhead, she said I needed to talk to Akira, too." His frustration wasn't subtle anymore.

"Sylvie, yeah." Grace picked up a pen and tapped it against the side of her desk as she thought. She didn't know what to do and she hated feeling uncertain. But she wasn't going to lie to him, not again. "Ghosts."

Noah scowled. "What?"

"Akira. She's an expert on ghosts. She wouldn't appreciate me telling you that. She'd want me to tell you about her thesis, her physics research, the work she's done on sonoluminescence. But really, it's ghosts."

"You believe in ghosts?"

Grace couldn't tell whether he was taking her seriously or not. He looked skeptical and he sounded skeptical but she thought she could hear something else in his voice, too. Could it be hope?

She kept her words light when she answered. "I believe in everything."

His mouth twisted wryly, as if he thought she was kidding. "Right."

"No, really." Grace set the pen down. "I believe in ghosts. I believe in psychic phenomena. I believe in angels and auras and energy, and that there's infinitely more to the universe than we understand or are even capable of perceiving."

Noah did not seem convinced. "Werewolves?"

Grace laughed. "Okay, maybe not everything. Shape-shifting is probably biologically impossible. Converting functioning cells into another form — at speed, while maintaining life — would take a tremendous amount of energy. It would explain, of course, why werewolves are always depicted as ravenously hungry. Unless they were in an area of incredibly abundant protein sources, they'd starve to death. The law of conservation of energy means the math would never be on their side. If a virus caused shape-shifting, it would kill the host really quickly. Evolutionarily speaking, it's tough to see how it could survive."

Noah blinked.

"Vampires, now, I wouldn't rule them out," Grace said with enthusiasm. "We're not working on life-extension technologies, but there's some interesting research being done on coenzymes that could reverse cellular aging processes. And, of course, parasites and bacteria are already known to cause food cravings. Yeast wants sugar. Maybe some other bacteria wants something in blood. Iron, maybe, or a protein."

She shrugged. "Immortality through human blood consumption is unlikely, but maybe not the unlikeliest thing ever. Changing into a bat, though, that's gotta be wrong. And the fear of crosses, also implausible. But garlic — now, that's cool. Garlic contains a chemical compound, allicin, that's got anti-everything properties — anti-microbes, anti-fungi, anti-bacteria. So if a bacteria both caused a craving for human blood and regenerated dying cells, garlic might actually kill it."

"You think vampires are caused by bacteria?" Noah was looking at her as if he still wasn't sure whether she was joking. "You seem to have put a lot of thought into this."

"Well, yeah," Grace admitted. "Once you accept that ghosts are real, you do start wondering about the rest of the things that you don't believe in. And I say 'you', but I really mean me. Once I accepted that ghosts were real, I took a long hard look at everything else on my list of impossibilities." She gave him a sympathetic smile.

"Okay, so..." He rubbed his hands over his face like he was trying to wake himself up. Abruptly, he stood. "I should go."

Grace jumped to her feet. Damn. She'd screwed up. She'd chased him away with her talk of ghosts and she didn't want him to leave. Not just because of Dillon and not because her dad and her brother, in their own separate ways, were going to annoy her to death if she lost Noah again.

But there was something between them, a chemistry she'd never felt before, and she wasn't ready to let him walk away from it.

"Give me a chance to prove it," she said, with no idea of how she could do so. She'd heard Akira grumble about how hard it was to convince family members that their loved ones were still around and Akira could communicate with the ghosts. Grace had no such ability.

But her eyes fell on her phone, still sitting at the edge of her desk where Noah had placed it.

There was one ghost she could communicate with. If he was willing to help her out, maybe between them they could make Noah believe.

"How are you going to do that?" Noah shook his head.

Before he could continue rejecting her outright, Grace put up a hand. "Come kayaking with me."

"What?"

"Kayaking," Grace repeated. "I was planning to go later, after work. But we can go now. Guaranteed privacy. Only some birds and maybe a turtle or two to hear what we have to say."

He hesitated.

"It's a beautiful day for it," Grace coaxed. "And come on, you can't come to Florida and not do anything fun. The tourist board would be devastated."

He didn't smile, but she thought she could see amusement in his eyes.

"Neutral territory," she continued. "A place of your choosing. I'll shift the seats in the kayak. I'll even let you have the rear."

"Control freak, huh?"

She lifted a shoulder. She wouldn't call herself a control freak. True, the world ran more smoothly when she was in charge, but she didn't mind letting someone else steer now and then. But she could see that he was wavering. "You came all this way. Aren't you curious to hear what I'm going to say?"

If he wasn't, she was. How was she going to persuade him that ghosts existed?

He obviously knew something. But he couldn't see ghosts the way Akira did, because if he did, Dillon would be talking to him directly. Still, he'd stood up in the restaurant, been about to leave. Maybe ghostly messages came through to him like intuition, a sensation of dread or a premonition of danger.

He nodded slowly. "I guess I am at that. Lead the way."

NOAH HAD DRIVEN HIS OWN TRUCK TO GD, BUT WHEN HE started toward it, she stopped him.

"Not a lot of parking where we're headed," she said. "Let's take my car."

"Where are we headed?" he asked, but he followed her without waiting for her answer.

"I was going to go to Sweet Springs," Grace said as she hit the button to unlock the doors. "It's nice. Sort of a winding stream under live oak trees. Very peaceful. But since you're coming, we should go out on the St. Johns."

"Why's that?" he said, taking his seat.

"It's wider. More scenic. More birds. And this time of year, with the weather not too cold, we've got a chance of seeing manatees."

"Manatees? Aren't they hard to find? I thought they were endangered," Noah said.

"They are," she agreed. "Endangered, that is. Hard to find?" She tilted a hand side-to-side in an equivocal gesture. "No guarantees on the river. If we had more time, though, we could head down to Blue Springs. The water's warm year-round there, so they're practically a sure thing this time of year. On the river, the water's a little cooler, so you never know." She shot him a glance. "Have you ever seen one?"

"Not a lot of manatees in Maine. Or in the Middle East. Those are pretty much the only places I've ever been," he replied.

Grace frowned. "Your apartment's in DC. AlecCorp was based in Virginia. And Army basic training, that'd be what, Georgia? Then there was the hospital. That was in Germany, wasn't it?"

She could feel Noah's eyes on her so she glanced his way again. He was staring at her.

"You going to tell me that a ghost told you all that?"

"Tempting." She laughed. "Seriously tempting. But no. I ran a background check on you."

She kept her hands in the perfect nine and three positions on the wheel, waiting for him to react. Would he be annoyed?

"A background check?" He sounded more surprised than annoyed.

"Well..." Grace cleared her throat. Should she admit this? "Actually, more of a high-level security clearance investigation. It's a little more in-depth than the average background check. By this time next week — well, or maybe the week after — I'll know what you ate for breakfast. In kindergarten."

"What? Why?" The surprise had become shock. Still no annoyance, though.

Grace kept her eyes on the road. "We run background checks on everyone we hire," she finally answered. It was true, but disingenuous. But she wasn't going to tell him about Dillon, not yet, and she didn't want to admit to her own curiosity, either.

"I didn't apply for a job."

"And yet..." Grace turned onto the narrow, one-lane dirt road leading to the river. Her car rumbled along it, bumping over uneven ground. "Here we are."

The distraction was nicely timed.

"Where's here?" Noah asked as the road opened onto a small clearing with enough room for three or four cars to park on the graveled dirt.

"An access point for the river," Grace said with satisfaction.

She did a three-point turn to back into the parking space closest to the wide downward slope at the river's edge, glad that she wouldn't have to back all the way down the forest service road and look for a different spot instead. On a day as nice as this one, the parking spaces could easily have been taken.

She hopped out of the car and began undoing the tie-downs that held the kayak to the roof, whipping the straps free with practiced ease. As Noah emerged, she tossed the straps into the car and then headed to the back of the car to begin tugging the kayak free from the saddle.

"Let me help," he said, joining her and reaching for the kayak.

"Sure." Grace stepped to the side and let him take the stern of the boat, picking up the bow as it slid off the rack. With two of them, shifting the kayak to the water was easy. Grace left Noah at the water's edge and went back to the car, opening the back door and pulling out the paddles and a waterproof dry bag.

Rejoining Noah, she placed the paddles on the sandy ground next to her and held open the bag. "Anything you want to keep dry?"

He tilted his head toward the car. "I stuck my wallet in the glove compartment. It seemed safer. Wouldn't want to lose it to a hungry 'gator." His smile invited her to share the joke.

For a moment, Grace couldn't breathe. The heat of attraction surged through her veins. She wanted to step closer, to lean up to him, to wrap her arms around his neck — and maybe he could see that on her face, because his eyes darkened and his gaze dropped to her lips.

But then he flinched and glanced to the side before dropping his gaze to the ground. "Want me to adjust the seats?" he asked, voice brusque.

"Yeah, okay," she said, wondering about his reaction. He'd done that in the restaurant, too, she remembered, but she'd thought nothing of it at the time. There'd been other people around and she'd assumed he was paying attention to something she hadn't noticed.

But they were alone in the clearing. Could he be responding to the ghosts?

With quick competence, he moved the back seat from its usual center spot to the rear of the kayak and slid the front seat back to a more usable position.

"I take it you've kayaked before," she said, bending to pick up the paddles.

"Yeah. When I was a kid, our house was on a lake. We had

canoes, kayaks, row boats, sail boats. During summers, my brother and I practically lived on the water."

Damn it. The last thing she needed was another reason to like him. But she loved the water. She could pretend to be a city girl when she needed to, but most of the time, her kayaking trips were the high-light of her week.

"All right, then," she said briskly, passing Noah his paddle. "You get the rear. You get to decide where we go."

"Upstream, downstream?" he asked. "What are the currents like?"

"The St. Johns is the slowest-flowing river in the entire United States. It flows north, so head south if you want the easier ride back, but it doesn't matter much. More chance of manatees to the south, though." She glanced at his sneakered feet. "You worried about getting wet?"

"In this weather? No." He wasn't laughing at her but his chuckle was rueful. "This could be August in Maine." He glanced around and added, "Well, except for the trees. The colors. The humidity."

Grace followed his look. The colors were mostly muted shades of tans and browns and amber, with streaks of gray Spanish moss and splashes of deep green brush. Sprinkled light green marked new leaves just sprouting. It looked like mid-winter to her. And the air held a hint of moisture, but also the brush of a light breeze off the water and the prickling warmth of strong sunshine. It was definitely not humid.

Noah inhaled. "It smells wrong, too. Good, but wrong."

Damp earth, rotting leaves, growing plants, and the fresh scent of flowing water all smelled exactly right to Grace. "What should it smell like?"

He inhaled again, his chest rising. "More pine, I guess. Crisper, somehow."

Grace pointed to the nearby scrub pines. "Pine trees," she said, feeling defensive for her forest.

Noah grinned at her and shook his head. "Not the same. You'll have to come to Maine sometime."

"I've never been there," Grace admitted, stepping into the kayak and taking her seat, her paddle propped across the boat in front of her. "In fact, all I know about Maine is lobsters and L.L. Bean. Or is that Ben & Jerry's?"

"Ben & Jerry's is Vermont. Not actually the same state." Noah lifted the stern of the kayak and slid it forward a couple more feet, until it was almost entirely in the water, then climbed aboard with a splash or two.

"Proving my lack of knowledge." Grace waited until she heard the sound of his paddle sliding into the water before lifting her own. "Do you miss it?"

"I..." Noah hesitated. "I do, yeah. It's been a long time, but it was a great place to grow up. Can't say I miss the winters much, though. We used to cross-country ski and snowboard, of course, and that was fun, but most of the time, during school and all, it was just dark. Dark in the mornings, dark by the time we got home from school."

In the bright Florida day, with the sun glimmering off the water and the sky the purest shade of blue, it was hard to imagine. "I got my master's degree in Virginia, but that's as far north as I've ever lived."

They were gliding through the water, stroking in unison, their paddles pulling together in a rhythm they hadn't had to coordinate. Noah's stroke gave the kayak more power, so it felt like they were almost flying over the river's surface, but Grace didn't feel any push to compete.

They talked inconsequentially — about places, sports, childhood activities — until Grace caught sight of movement in the plants at the edge of the river.

She lifted her paddle out of the water, holding it chest-high. Noah caught her signal and stopped paddling. She indicated the motion she'd seen. "Slowly."

She let him steer the kayak, even though her fingers itched to control their direction, and they drifted closer. The plants were

185

disappearing, strands of leafy water hyacinth being pulled under the dark water.

"Do you see it?" she asked, voice hushed.

"See what?"

"The plants?"

"Something's eating them," Noah realized. "Holy shit."

"Yeah." Grace smiled, pleased by the incredulousness in his voice.

"That's—"

"A manatee," she supplied as the gray sea cow floated to the surface.

"It's huge." He sounded appropriately awed.

"They're pretty big," she agreed. The manatee drifted toward them, almost brushing the kayak, then dropped down into the depths, becoming invisible in the dark water. The leaves of a nearby plant began rustling as the manatee began chewing its roots.

"Wow. Okay, that's cool."

Grace looked over her shoulder at him. He looked lighter on the water, easier, as if the sun was chasing away his demons.

It was time to talk.

20

DILLON

"We need to talk," Rose said.

"Yeah," Dillon agreed, but he was watching Grace. She was turning around to face Noah, tucking her legs up before swiveling on the seat, her paddle braced behind her. The kayak rocked precariously and Dillon held his breath, but Noah compensated perfectly, leaning forward and shifting until they were balanced again.

Grace laughed. "Not up for a swim?"

Noah grinned at her. "Not sure I need to meet any alligators today."

Dillon wanted to tell him how unlikely that was. Not that there weren't alligators in the St. Johns — there definitely were, loads of them. Any body of water larger than a puddle in Florida could have an alligator in it. But most of them were small and they avoided people and they weren't likely to be leisurely swimming near a kayak in the middle of the day in February. Maybe in May, when it was warmer. Or at dusk, when they typically hunted.

Instead, he stuffed his hands in his pockets. It was weird being out on the water like this, no boat involved. It felt familiar yet wrong. When he was a kid, he and Grace and his grandfather had come

187

kayaking most weekends in the winter. He wished he could tease her right now, reminding her of all the times they'd overturned kayaks when he was little. Sometimes Max had dumped them out on purpose to teach them how to recover, but sometimes they'd tried to bounce one another out.

And then sometimes they'd gone in the water completely by accident. One time they'd been eating lunch while floating along one of the local springs. He and Grace had spotted a turtle at the same moment and they'd both leaned too far. He still remembered the shock of hitting the cold water before coming up to see Max calmly treading water while taking a bite out of his peanut-butter sandwich. He wondered if Grace remembered that day.

"What did you tell them?" Rose asked.

"Not to talk about it," Dillon answered her.

With the exception of Rose, the ghosts had all gotten dragged along to General Directions with Noah. Dillon wasn't sure whether that meant his theory about the accumulation of spirit energy creating the attraction was wrong or not. Some of the ghosts — the singing lady, the guy with the peanut allergy, a few of the white balls of light — were gone, lost to the vortex, but enough were left that the pull might still be caused by having too much spirit energy in one place. Or maybe it was something about Noah, as they'd been thinking before.

Either way, Dillon had strongly suggested that they stop talking about it, at least until they'd all had a chance to calm down. The last thing any of them needed was for emotional conversations about their imminent permanent destruction to lead to exactly that.

Rose had finally caught up with them at GD just as Grace and Noah were leaving to go kayaking. They'd all stayed quiet in the car, but now some of the ghosts were exploring, others floating along the surface of the water.

"Mama, Mama, look." Misam popped up in the midst of the water hyacinths. "There's another sea cow under here."

"You can swim right through them," Joe reported, appearing next to Misam. "Just like people. They don't even notice. I guess it's not exactly swimming, though."

Nadira was kneeling on the water's surface, her long black robe draped around her, peering into the depths. "They are quite ugly. Their faces look squashed. Sort of like a camel's face, only much bigger."

"Come under, Mama," Misam said. "You can see better from under."

"I'm happy here, dear," Nadira said decidedly. "I don't like how dark it is down there." She gave a delicate shudder.

"Speaking of that..." Joe rose up out of the water, drifting through it as if walking up an invisible slope. He looked toward Rose and Dillon and the kayak. "We all good?"

He wasn't really looking at them, Dillon realized, but beyond them to where Sophia and Mona drifted. If a ghost could be exhausted, Sophia looked exhausted. She wasn't crying anymore, but she was lying flat on the surface of the water, face down. Mona hovered near her, feather duster in hand.

Before Dillon could answer him, Grace finally responded to Noah. "How do you feel about meeting some ghosts?"

Dillon winced.

Joe swore under his breath.

"Oh, dear." Rose twirled a curl of hair around her finger.

Noah's mouth twisted. "Is that what we're doing?"

"I hope so, yeah." Grace fumbled with the bag at her waist, pulling out her cell phone.

"Ghosts don't exist," Noah said flatly.

"We need to decide what to do." Dillon wasn't going to ignore Grace, not again. He hadn't had a chance to answer her when she'd talked to him in the diner, because Joe had dragged him away, but he'd spent so long unable to communicate with his family that he never took the moments when they reached out to him for granted. "Do you want to let Noah know that we're here?"

Joe looked torn. He folded his arms across his chest. But Noah turned his head and looked in Dillon's direction.

Dillon stepped back. Noah's eyes were looking straight through him, no sign of recognition, but it still felt like he was responding to Dillon's words.

"Ghosts don't exist," Noah repeated. Maybe he was still talking to Grace, but he wasn't looking at her.

"Yeah, that's what you think, dude," Dillon replied. "Decision time, Joe. Come on."

Joe sighed.

Sophia rolled over, staring up at the sky. "You're never going to prove it to him. He doesn't believe in anything."

"Grace will have a plan. Grace always has a plan," Dillon said confidently.

Grace had been thumbing on the screen of her phone, but now she handed it to Noah.

He took it. "What am I doing with this?"

She spread her arm to indicate the scene around them. They weren't entirely alone — no one was ever alone on the St. Johns. There were other kayakers downstream and a bigger tour boat trundling along upstream. A rowboat held a couple of men fishing. But no one was close to them. Grace gestured toward the spot where they'd seen the manatee. "Our location is as random as nature can make it. I couldn't have known where we'd find a manatee."

She turned her head from side to side, pushing back her hair so that Noah could see her ears. "No mysterious ear pieces, no way someone could talk to me remotely."

Noah didn't look convinced.

"What?" she asked, letting her hair drop.

"If I, hypothetically, had a transmitter in my head, you could have one in yours, too," Noah pointed out.

"Seriously?" Grace rolled her eyes.

Sophia snorted. "What are we supposed to be, some stupid radio play?"

Rose clapped her hands. "Ooh, I used to love those when I was little. My mother always listened to one about this family in San Francisco. We could act it out!"

"We are not going to pretend that we're a radio play," Dillon said.

Grace tilted her head to one side. "A transmitter in your head? Is that what you're worried about?"

Noah's chin rose. "I'm not worried about anything. I'm just trying to figure out what's going on down here and why people I've never met think I'm involved with it."

Grace didn't look convinced. Her eyes narrowed. "Can you hear them?"

"Hear what?" Noah didn't blink but color rose in his cheeks.

"He's lying," Dillon said. "Look at him. He can hear us."

"I think you're right." Joe sighed again.

Nadira and Misam had joined the cluster of ghosts now surrounding the kayak. Nadira folded her arms across her chest. "All these years."

"Maybe he only started hearing us recently," Joe suggested.

Grace shook her head. "If you had a broken transmitter in your head, why would I put one in mine? And if I had a working transmitter in my head, why wouldn't I just offer to fix yours? I'm not asking you to believe in elves and fairies. Or even aliens."

"Neural networks," Noah muttered. "Sound bouncing off wi-fi signals somehow."

"I don't know much about sound, but I'm sure it's possible to create a technology that could cause you, and only you, to hear voices. Some sort of electrical nerve stimulation, maybe?" Grace leaned back in the kayak, one hand on the paddle next to her. "Sound waves cause vibrations in the cells of our ears that turn into signals that travel along the auditory nerves. Maybe an implant of some sort could skip the sound wave step and just vibrate inside your head."

"That's not knowing much about it?"

Grace lifted a shoulder. "I read a lot. We don't have anyone working on anything like that, but it doesn't seem impossible."

Noah didn't respond.

Grace gave him a bright smile. "Of course, the question you have to ask yourself then is why? Why would we do something like that to you? What do we get out of it?"

Noah grimaced. "Nothing. Which should always have been obvious. People who hear voices are crazy. That's all there is to it." He nodded toward her paddle. "Let's head back."

Grace put up a hand. "Not yet. You promised me a chance."

"To prove that ghosts are real?" He gave a skeptical laugh. "That was a mistake. It's not gonna happen. I might be crazy, but I'm not that crazy."

"Have a little faith." Grace nodded toward the phone he still held. "Dillon, you're here, aren't you? Please say hi."

"What do you think?" Dillon asked the others. "We ready to try talking to him?"

"Which is better, ghosts or insanity?" Joe asked, but the question sounded rhetorical as he nodded toward the phone.

Sophia answered anyway. "Insanity," she yelled, smacking the surface of the water with her hand.

"Oh, dear," Mona murmured.

"It's not right," the angry man said.

"Ghosts," Nadira said with a frown.

"Ghosts." Misam nodded.

"Oh, ghosts, definitely," Rose said.

"And the ghosts win." Dillon closed his eyes, concentrating on texting a message to the phone Noah held. *Hi, Noah. My name is Dillon.*

Noah stared at the screen, his expression grim. "Big deal, so you got someone to text me at a certain time."

"Right, because I knew exactly when we'd find a manatee," Grace said, voice dry.

"If it wasn't the manatee, it could have been something else. Maybe you point out that big black bird over there," Noah said, pointing to an anhinga sitting on a low branch, its wings outspread.

"Maybe even that boat going by. It looks like a tour boat, so it's probably on a schedule, right?"

"Excellent critical thinking skills," Grace said, sounding amused. "But we're not done yet. Ask me a question."

"How does a ghost send texts?" Noah asked.

She laughed. "Not the kind of question I had in mind. But they're beings of energy, capable of manipulating electronic signals. It's not easy. It took Dillon a lot of practice and quite a few phones to figure it out. If Akira hadn't helped him, he probably couldn't have done it."

"And I suppose that's why everyone's not getting text messages from the dead," Noah said sarcastically.

Grace's smile didn't change. "Cell phones haven't been around that long and ghosts don't get a handbook. Or even usually meet many other ghosts. Often they're trapped where they died."

"You sound like an expert."

"I've read all the research. And I've got a personal involvement, of course."

Noah stared at her. "All right. Tell me about that."

Her smile faded. "Still not the kind of question I meant," she said, looking away from him, out across the water. "But you're right, it matters."

Dillon hated seeing the sadness in her eyes, hated hearing it in her voice. And he didn't want to listen to her tell the story of how he'd screwed up. But if Noah could hear them, hear him, then this was an opportunity. Dillon could add details as Grace spoke, details that Noah would have no way of knowing. He'd have to believe her when she confirmed that the details were true.

"My parents came to Tassamara before I was born," Grace began. "Their car broke down while they were on their way to Disneyworld, stranding them here, but they fell in love with the place. They went home. Virginia, at the time. My dad was in a doctorate program at the University of Virginia in biochemistry. He'd already had some — well, you might call it luck — with investments. But my mother didn't think it was luck. He joked about serendipity and intuition, but she believed he could see the future."

"He doesn't really see it," Dillon said. "It's more like he just knows stuff that hasn't happened yet. Like the way he recognized you, even though you'd never met him before."

"They moved here and started the company, General Directions. At the time, it was my dad working out of a home office, buying and selling stocks. Again, it was before I was born. I don't remember it. But he did well. The company grew, expanded, hired people, started the research division. And, whether you believe it or not, it became clear to both of my parents that some psychic abilities are real and that Tassamara is a place that, for whatever reason, strengthens people's natural abilities."

"Not everyone, though," Dillon said with a sigh. "Only if you've got the power to begin with."

"Psychics. You're serious," Noah said.

"I am." Grace paused, as if waiting for more of a reaction.

"She is," Dillon confirmed. "Lots of people here are psychic. My dad, my other aunt, my uncle, people in town. Akira. Everyone who works for the Special Affairs division, pretty much."

"Are you claiming to be psychic?" Noah asked Grace.

Grace spread her hands. "Not me. Normal as they come."

"Not me, either." Dillon stepped closer to the kayak, his voice getting soft. He hated talking about his death, hated thinking about it. He'd been so stupid. "I really wanted to be psychic. My dad and my uncle were always gone, always busy doing cool stuff. Working for the FBI and shit. And I was just the kid, stuck at home. Curfew, 11PM, even on weekends."

"Six years ago," Grace started. She hesitated, biting her lip.

"I stole some pills," Dillon said. "A lot of them. I'd read about hallucinations maybe kick-starting psychic abilities. I figured it was worth a try."

"My nephew died," Grace finally said.

"She's skipping the hard part." Dillon wasn't looking at the other

194

ghosts, wished they weren't listening although he knew they were. "I guess the pills did make me hallucinate. I felt like I was floating. Levitating would have been a cool psychic ability, but I wanted more. I wanted to fly. So I kept taking the pills. Finished off my grandma's Ambien, started on her high blood pressure medication."

"And then my mother died, three days later." Grace stared down at her own hands.

"She had a stroke. You know what causes strokes? High blood pressure," Dillon said. "I guess maybe she didn't have a chance to get her prescription refilled."

"Oh, Dillon," Rose murmured.

Dillon didn't look at her. He could hear the sympathy in her voice, but he knew he didn't deserve it. "Go ahead," he said to Noah. "Ask her. You know you want to."

But Noah didn't say a word, just sat in the kayak with his lips pressed together.

"My father insisted that their spirits weren't gone." Grace lifted her chin, her eyes meeting Noah's steady gaze. "We... well, I, at least, took it for his grief talking. It's one thing to believe that my sister knows her own future and another to accept life after death and ghosts walking among us."

Noah opened his mouth, then closed it again without speaking, giving his head a minute shake.

"He started searching for someone who could communicate with spirits. Last year, he found Akira. She's not a medium. She doesn't speak to the dead. For some reason, that distinction is really important to her. But she does see ghosts. And she can talk to them. One of the ghosts that she met in Tassamara was my nephew, Dillon."

"You believe you're haunted by the ghost of your dead nephew?" Noah asked.

"Not me." Grace's smile was wry. "Not anymore, anyway. I think he's haunting you, now."

Noah's grip on his paddle tightened, but he looked as if he wanted to thrust the phone back at her.

"Akira hates trying to convince people that ghosts are real, whether they believe her or not," Grace said. "Skeptics accuse her of being a con artist, doing her research, that kind of thing, but believers... well, no one's ever happy to learn that the person they lost is a ghost."

21

NOAH

Noah had heard every word the Dillon voice had said to him.

He would still rather believe that there was a transmitter in his head. Long-distance cameras recording his every move. Maybe some kind of mini-satellite following him, with a crew of artificial intelligences responding to his actions.

Because if ghosts were real...

"So let's get started," Grace said. "I need you to ask me a personal question, one that my baby brother would know the answer to."

"Baby brother?" Noah asked.

Grace lifted a shoulder, just as the Dillon voice said, *"I grew up with her. My dad was just a kid when I was born and my mom wasn't around. Grace is more like a sister than an aunt."*

It wasn't the first time the voice had said something of the sort. Noah rubbed his forehead, feeling the pinch of an incipient headache as he remembered the day he'd arrived in Tassamara. What had the voice said then? Not really an aunt? Something like that, anyway.

"Close enough. My parents raised Dillon," Grace replied.

Eight years older, that's what the voice had said.

"I think the traditional approach is for a ghost to tell me something that only you and he would know," Grace went on. "But the only ghost I know how to communicate with is Dillon. I don't know whether there's anything he'd know about you that I might not have been able to find out other ways, and I did tell you I'd run a background check. I want this to be fair. I don't want you to think I'm tricking you. So you ask a question, we wait for Dillon to answer via text, and then I'll answer, too. If our answers match — when our answers match — you'll know that I'm telling you the truth."

She looked so honest, her green gaze meeting his without hesitation. She'd looked away when she was telling him about their deaths, but not as if she was lying, more like it still hurt to talk about.

Noah could understand that. He never mentioned the friends he'd lost, not to anyone. He remembered them, but what good would talking about them do?

"Come on," Grace coaxed him. "Something simple. What's my favorite color?"

A corner of Noah's mouth lifted. It was too obvious. Her office, her shoes — his subconscious was smart enough to know she liked pink.

"*Easy one,*" the Dillon voice said. "*Purple.*"

"*Really? But she never wears purple,*" the Rose voice said.

"*Purple is not her color,*" the Arabic woman's voice said. "*She should wear warm colors. Peach, moss green.*"

The phone dinged and he glanced at the screen. *Purple*, it said.

All right, so his voices and whoever was sending him texts were in agreement. He couldn't decide if he was surprised by that or not. If his voices were hallucinations, how could the person on the other end of the phone line know what they were saying?

So they weren't hallucinations. They were computer-generated. He was overhearing transmissions of some kind. Maybe the voices saying the same things over and over again were code. Maybe the fake Chinese guy was using a very complex code.

"Purple," Grace said. "Always has been."

198

Noah paused. That made it three for three: the voices, the phone, and Grace herself. Yeah, that was weird. "You don't wear much purple."

She flashed a smile at him, quick, amused. "I'm too vain. It doesn't look good on me. I still like it, though."

Apparently his hallucinations agreed with her aesthetic sense, or at least the Arabic woman's voice did. Noah looked down at the phone again. It still said *Purple*. Then it dinged again as a new message showed up. *Can you hear us?*

Hallucinations.

Or some mysterious technology that had people commenting on his life as if they were present, as if they were watching him constantly.

Or ghosts.

He could ask her how her nephew died. Was it pills? Had her mother had a stroke? But he didn't want to bring the look of pain back to her eyes. And if this was an elaborate con — begging the question, of course, of what possible reason she had to set him up this way — he needed to ask a question no one could have anticipated. It couldn't be too obvious: no birthday or favorite food, nothing some stranger sitting on the other end of a transmitter might have on a list.

"Childhood pet?" he asked. It wasn't the best question. She'd mentioned a dog in the restaurant. But it was the first thing that had come to mind. He'd have to try for something more obscure on his next question.

Grace clapped a hand to her heart and opened her mouth, then stopped herself. She opened her hand, indicated the phone he held and waited.

"*Uh-oh,*" the Dillon voice said. "*This is a hard one.*"

"*You don't know the name of your childhood pet?*" the Rose voice asked.

"*My gran was allergic, so we didn't have any. But she only found that out after Grace got a puppy. It had some stupid name, Snuggles or something like that. Grace was really sad when they had to find it a new home. They gave it to a friend of hers so she could still visit it, but then the friend moved away. And I only know that because I've heard the story — it was before I was born."*

"Snuggles?" The laugh in Joe's voice had Noah fighting to hold back his own smile.

"That wasn't it, though. It was Sniffles or... I can't remember." The Dillon voice sighed.

"Can you text that to him?" the Rose voice asked.

"It's too long, I'd run out of energy."

"You'll have to guess," the little boy's voice said. *"Maybe it was Snuffles."*

"Sweetums, maybe. I think it had sweet in the name."

"Come on, Dillon." Grace closed her fingers and shook her head. "You've got to remember this."

"I do remember," the Dillon voice protested. *"Just not the details."*

"My mom had allergies. We had a dog for a while, but it was before Dillon. I loved her, though." Grace brought her hand back to her chest. "Broke my heart when we had to give her away."

Noah had to ask. "What was her name?"

"Sparkle Sunshine Sweet Girl," Grace replied without hesitation. "Yes, I named her myself. Yes, I was six years old. She was a great dog, though. Part Jack Russell terrier and part chihuahua, so small, but loads of personality."

Sparkle Sunshine Sweet Girl was not Snuggles. But the stories were so much alike.

Noah had been listening to voices no one else could hear for ten years.

An entire decade of trying to hide his insanity from everyone around him, even from himself.

An entire decade of pretending his life had a soundtrack only he could hear.

An entire decade of believing that his injuries had damaged him so profoundly that he would never be normal again.

Maybe he'd been right about that last.

Hearing ghosts, after all, was not exactly normal.

But the crying girl was wrong: ghosts were better than insanity.

Except that if his voices were ghosts... His hand tightened around the cell phone. Then Joe was a ghost. His best friend had spent the past ten years stuck following him around, instead of moving on to wherever spirits were supposed to move on to.

That was not cool.

"One more question," Noah said.

"As many more as you need," Grace replied.

His eyes met hers and a shiver of awareness passed between them. Her gaze didn't drop, but a hint of pink rose in her cheeks. A slew of questions sprang to mind: first kiss, first boyfriend, favorite position, most intriguing fantasy...

"Baby brother friendly," Noah said, keeping it light.

She gave a breath of laughter. "Please."

The label inspired him. "Best Disney movie."

Her eyebrows rose.

"*Oh, this is a good question,*" the Rose voice said.

"*Aladdin,*" the little boy's voice said, sounding jubilant. "*It's the best one!*"

"*Frozen!*" The crying girl's voice was closer, as if instead of calling from a distance, she'd joined the others around the kayak.

"*The Jungle Book,*" Joe said. "*Best Disney song ever: I Wan'na Be Like You. Second best, Bare Necessities.*" He started humming the latter.

"*Piffle.*" The Arabic woman sounded annoyed. "*Finding Nemo.*"

"*Nemo's Pixar, that doesn't count. And before you say it, Dillon, neither does Toy Story. Best Disney movie has to be a musical,*" Joe said firmly.

"*Oh, my. Y'all have strong opinions about this, don't you?*" Rose said.

Softly, in a voice that sounded surprisingly determined, the clean freak said, "*Beauty and the Beast. Be Our Guest.*"

201

"Dancing dishes and an enormous library, yes, yes," the Arabic woman said. *"Those are good qualities. But Nemo has the turtles and they are the best. The dancing dishes do not compare."*

"The turtles don't sing," Joe said. *"They can't win."*

"Aladdin has a genie and a tiger and a monkey. And songs! It is the best." The little boy sounded as if he was dancing around. Noah could almost picture him swinging off his mother's hand and bouncing back and forth between the others.

What did they look like, he wondered. His ghosts. Were they transparent? Did they look like they had in life or in death? He hoped they weren't creepy *Sixth Sense* style ghosts.

The memory of the blood streaming down Joe's face had him swallowing hard for a second before he pushed the thought away, instead envisioning Joe grinning at him as they bonded over the proper making of a bed, Army-style. That was Joe, the real Joe. Not the other Joe, dying in his arms. That other Joe was a moment in time, not a presence.

"Aladdin is so problematic," the crying girl said. *"You should hate it."*

"I don't, though," the little boy said. *"I love it."*

"It doesn't matter what any of us think," the Dillon voice said. *"It only matters what Grace thinks."*

Not the Dillon voice, Noah realized. A teenager named Dillon. Dead six years. Was he still a teenager? But he still sounded like a teenager. And the kid was still a kid after all this time. So ghosts didn't keep growing up. They were stuck.

Grace had a small smile playing around her lips but she was waiting, eyes on the phone.

"Do you know what she likes?" Joe asked.

"Yep," Dillon responded, as the phone dinged.

"The Little Mermaid," Grace said without waiting for Noah to look.

He looked. Her phone agreed with her. *The Little Mermaid.*

He made a face. "Really? It's such a terrible message. Give up your voice for a guy? How can you like that?"

"No, no, no, that's not the message." Grace laughed. "Ariel wants to see the world before she ever sees Eric. She trades her voice for legs and freedom, plus the girl has confidence. She believes in herself. She knows she's going to get her voice back. And she would have if Ursula hadn't cheated. Kiss the Girl? He was totally gonna kiss her."

"*It's a good movie, but it's no Finding Nemo,*" the Arabic woman said.

"*Nemo doesn't count. It's not a musical,*" Joe said.

"*She must not have seen Frozen,*" the crying girl said. "*It's way better than the mermaid movie.*"

"*Who said the only good movies were musicals?*" the Arabic woman demanded.

"*Aladdin is better,*" the little boy said, sounding sulky.

"*Noah should kiss the girl,*" Rose said. "*He couldn't possibly have a better cue. It would be so romantic.*"

"No, he shouldn't," Dillon objected. "*That's my aunt. There should be no kissing.*"

"*Oh, don't be so stodgy, Dillon. They like each other. How does the song go again?*" Rose hummed a line.

Obediently, the little boy began to sing, complete with the full *sha-la-la-la* and Jamaican accent.

Long habit had Noah trying to hide his reaction, but Grace must have spotted some flicker of expression, because she raised her eyebrows. He could see the moment she made the connection when her eyes widened. She glanced around her at the water, the boat, the plants, the overhanging branches, and caught her lower lip in her teeth.

"All we're missing is the chorus." Her eyes were bright with laughter.

"All you're missing is the chorus," he corrected her.

It took her barely more than a breath to realize the implication. "You can hear them?"

He dipped his chin in a minimalist nod. So many years of keeping his secret: it felt wrong to let go of it so easily. And yet, how could he deny the evidence? Sure, ghosts were implausible, but apparently less so than any of the crazy theories he'd come up with. And the sensible, logical explanation — that he was insane — just didn't fit the facts, not anymore.

"*He can hear us?*"

"*Did he say yes?*"

"*What did he say? Did he do something?*"

"*Did you see him? He nodded, didn't he? Did you see?*"

Deliberately, Noah turned his head so that his gaze was directed toward the sound of Joe's voice. He couldn't see anything except water and wilderness, the tangled branches of trees, spiky water grasses and weeds, but he said, "Hey, Joe," just as if he truly believed his old friend was standing in the water next to him.

He did believe it. Mostly.

But the tiny skeptical inner voice that expected his hallucinations to respond with nonsense, with a spew of disconnected phrases and random sentences, was silenced when Joe laughed, and sounding delighted, said, "*Noah, my man!*"

The other ghosts burst into a cacophony of conversation and exclamations. Noah could even hear the angry man in the mix, saying, "*It's not right, it's not right,*" in a tone of wonder.

"You believe me?" Grace said. Of all of them, she seemed the most surprised.

Noah nodded. "Yeah."

"Wow. I thought convincing you would be much harder," she said. "Akira says it's really difficult to persuade people that ghosts are real."

"The cell phone helped. Plus, well..." The words felt trapped in Noah's throat, but he forced them out. "I'm not just taking your word for it. I've been listening to them for a long time."

"How long has it been?"

"Ten years."

"And — how many?" she asked tentatively. "Dillon told his mom that you were collecting ghosts, but I wasn't sure what that meant."

He gave a chuckle without humor. "No idea. There's a buddy of mine, Joe, my best friend from Basic. An Arabic woman and a kid. Another woman — she likes to clean things. A girl." He paused. Maybe he wouldn't mention that the girl cried a lot. He didn't want to set her off again. "A dude that's allergic to peanuts. A lady that sings. A guy who's kind of pissed off all the time. A woman who wants some guy named Tom to stop driving so fast." He tried to remember some of the others, but her mouth had already fallen open.

"Wow." She mouthed the word, rather than saying it aloud.

He shrugged and forced a smile. "I tried to ignore them. Until recently, most of them didn't stick around. Joe and the woman and the kid did, but apart from them... I heard things, words here and there, bits of conversations. They didn't usually make sense. Hallucinations, I thought."

"That must have been difficult," Grace replied.

"I can't say I got used to it, but I got used to ignoring them. Most of the time, anyway."

"Really difficult."

The sympathy in Grace's expression nearly undid him. Keeping his voice light, he quickly changed the subject. "But you have lousy taste in movies. *The Lion King* is clearly the best Disney movie of all time."

It was like pointing out a squirrel to a dog. All his voices — his ghosts, he corrected himself — immediately took up the argument again as Grace's eyes widened indignantly.

"So wrong." She held up a hand, ticking off songs on her fingers. "*Part of Your World, Under the Sea*, the fish song. Not to mention Ursula's song, the one about the poor unfortunate souls. How can you not love that? And she is such a great villain, way better than what's his name, the evil uncle. Evil uncles are such a cliché."

Noah grinned at her. "I'll have to watch it again sometime. It's been long enough that I've forgotten the details."

"Please tell Grace I'm sorry I couldn't answer her before. I was a little busy," Dillon said in his ear as the others continued to argue.

Noah stopped smiling. "Yeah. About that…" He had so many questions he didn't know where to begin, but he relayed Dillon's message to Grace.

She nodded. "Vortex, he said. Like the one he survived before? That's not good."

"What do you know about them?" Noah asked.

"I've talked to Akira about her theories. She believes we — meaning spirits or souls or whatever you want to call our essential energy, the part of us that lasts after our material selves are gone — that we exist in at least two dimensions beyond this one. A vortex is an opening into one of those dimensions. Not a pleasant place, as I understand it."

"All right. So we avoid vortexes. No more diner." The food was great, but Noah wasn't going to risk Joe's existence for a good meal.

"It's not so easy." Grace looked troubled.

"The vortex opens when there's too much spirit energy in one place. We're not safe anywhere," Dillon said.

"We're dead," the crying girl said bitterly. *"Dead ought to be safe. This is so wrong."*

"It's not right," the angry man piped in, in seeming agreement.

The air around Noah suddenly seemed colder. He shivered, glancing at the sky. Had a cloud covered the sun? It was getting later, the sun dropping toward the horizon, but the sky was clear.

"I do not like this," the Arabic woman muttered.

"Oh, dear," the clean freak said. *"I should be scrubbing. What am I doing?"*

"It's water, Mona. It's as clean as it's going to get," Joe said, but even he sounded worried.

"We don't know why ghosts exist," Grace said. "Some of them, like Dillon, seem to be trapped. Whatever's supposed to happen after you die just didn't happen for them. Others apparently choose to stay. My mom..." She gestured as if erasing a chalkboard. "Long story. But eventually, after Akira helped her, my mom left. Moved on."

"Is that what I'm supposed to do? Help them so they can move on?" Noah asked skeptically. He felt like a character in a bad Lifetime movie. He didn't want to be an asshole about it, but believing in ghosts was hard enough. If they were going to try to convince him that heaven and hell were real, he was going back to bed until he woke up from this weird dream.

"Maybe. If you can figure out how," Grace said, her wry smile not reaching her eyes. "It's not as easy as you might expect."

"How tough can it be? They're supposed to look for a white light, right?"

Grace's smile turned real. "Akira would roll her eyes at you and start ranting about the 1970s. She says some guy made up the whole white light thing back then and it wasn't even a white light. It was gold. But no, they don't need a white light. They don't even need to move on. We just have to discover why you're attracting them and make it stop. Simple enough."

"Simple?" She made it sound easy, but Noah wasn't convinced.

"When Akira gets back, we'll ask her. She'll run some experiments." Grace waved her hand, fluttering her fingers up through the air as if playing a scale. "She'll figure it out."

"*She never figured out how to get me free from my car,*" Dillon said. "*Or Rose from her house.*"

"*And a vortex is as bad for her as it is for y'all,*" Rose said. "*The last time she found one, it killed her.*"

What? Noah frowned, turning his head toward Rose's voice and trying to hear what she was saying through the chaos of his other voices all asking questions at once.

22

GRACE

He believed her.

And damn it, Grace wished he'd kissed her. She wanted to feel his lips against hers again, wanted to touch him. Wanted to see if the magic of the morning had been a fluke, a one-time thing, or whether they really fit together as perfectly as it seemed.

But the moment was long gone.

Noah was scowling, not looking at her, his brows drawn down.

Why had he decided to trust her? She'd been so prepared for a long, arduous attempt at persuasion that her success left her feeling off-balance.

Or maybe that was just Noah.

A snowy egret spread its wings and took flight, its ungainly legs tucking back against its body. Grace watched it, following its path up into the air, and realized the sun was brushing the tops of the trees. Her kayak had reflective tape, but no lights, so they needed to start back before it got much darker. She gestured toward Noah's paddle. "We should get moving. It'll be getting dark soon."

He nodded, still frowning and clearly listening to the ghosts, but leaned forward, passing her the cell phone he'd been holding. She picked up the dry bag from the floor of the kayak and put the phone away, then grabbed her own paddle. She held it out to him. "Can you hang on to this while I turn around?"

He answered with a seemingly unrelated question: "Akira died?"

Grace drew the paddle back. Why was he asking that? "Technically, I guess so. Yeah. But my sister resuscitated her. It wasn't, you know, fatal. It was a very temporary death."

"Ghosts are dangerous for her, though. She's been hurt by them in the past?" It was half a question, half a statement.

Grace stared at him. How could that not have occurred to her? She was used to thinking of ghosts as people. As friendly text messages and helpful energy; as relatives and congenial visitors; as Dillon, as Rose. But Akira hated her ability for a reason.

"Shit," she said. "You're her worst nightmare."

Noah grimaced.

"Sorry," she said quickly. "Not you, but—" She gestured with the paddle, rocking the kayak. "Them. Ghosts. Lots of ghosts." She pressed her free hand to her temple, wanting to bang it against her head.

How stupid of her not to have considered the risk to Akira. And to the baby, too. At the best of times, Akira was reluctant to get involved with ghosts. At six months pregnant, she'd be horrified at the possibility of running into a dozen ghosts, maybe more. The energy could be deadly to her.

"I should have thought of that. That's not good."

"Your nephew is beating himself up enough for both of you." Noah reached for her paddle. "Let's go while he rants."

She passed it to him and he braced both paddles across the kayak and waited while she turned around. He handed her paddle back to her and she dipped it into the water. The current was with them, so in no time they were flying across the water, but Grace barely paid attention to the rhythm of their strokes while she worried.

Would the ghosts harm Akira? Ghosts in the vortex, the ones who were unable to perceive the physical world but fighting to survive, were dangerous. They could use Akira's body to pull themselves back onto the material plane. Could and did. She'd been fending off their attacks since childhood.

If she'd been in the bistro when the vortex started to open, what would have happened? Neither Max nor Nat seemed to think that Noah's presence was dangerous, but ghosts interfered with their ability to see the future. Or rather, ghosts could change the future they saw, surprising them with the unexpected.

But Rose had been in the bistro.

She'd saved Akira once before. And she'd saved Dillon when he'd gotten lost in the vortex. As long as Rose was around, Akira should be fine. At least Grace hoped so.

"Rose was there, wasn't she?" she asked, her stroke splashing deep into the water. "In the bistro, with the vortex. Could she have kept Akira safe?"

Noah paused, listening. Then he started to nod and began paddling again. "Rose says yes. She says she knows how to stop a vortex from opening now, but that it's not fun and she'd really rather not." He paused again, then made an amused noise. "Sorry."

"For?" Grace asked.

"She'd also like me to stop leaving her behind, because she's got better things to do than search for us all over town," Noah answered.

Grace smiled, too, feeling reassured. The breeze was getting cooler, the sun drifting lower in the sky. In the quiet, she could hear the chirping and calling of birds, getting noisier as they finished feeding and started settling for the night. She wondered what Noah was hearing.

"That is not your unfinished business," Noah said.

"What is it?" she asked.

"The kid — Misam," Noah corrected himself, "wants to go to Disneyworld."

Grace laughed. "That sounds fun."

"Apparently, he saw a commercial. He wants to go on the safari ride at Animal Kingdom." He paused, and then added, "And Rose wants to go to the Magic Kingdom."

"How about Universal Studios?" Grace suggested. "Dillon's never been to any of the Harry Potter stuff, has he?"

"Don't you get in on this." His tone held underlying laughter.

"Oh, come on. Harry Potter? Diagon Alley? Magic wands? Doesn't it sound cool?" It had been years since Grace had gone to one of the Orlando-area theme parks. She could go any time, of course — they were only a couple of hours away, close enough for a long day trip or a fun-packed weekend. But without her mom and Dillon... well, she just hadn't been interested. "I hear there's a huge dragon that breathes fire."

"Crowds, lines, screaming kids." Despite his words, Noah's voice was amused.

"Fireworks, parades, roller coasters. Don't tell me you don't like theme parks."

"Been a long time since I've been to one. I'm sure it'd be fun. But..." The splash as Noah dipped his paddle into the water was louder, as if he was putting more energy behind his stroke.

"But what?"

"What's the chance we run into more ghosts there? Any place with a lot of people wandering around is going to have had its share of unexpected deaths."

It sounded like he was directing his words to the ghosts, so Grace didn't respond, but she pulled harder, digging her paddle deep into the water as if shifting dirt.

She couldn't argue with Noah's attitude. She didn't want Dillon taking any unnecessary chances. But if Noah was going to restrict his movements based on the risk to the ghosts, how soon would he become as trapped as they were? The fear of believing he was halluci-nating might be as nothing compared to the frustration of knowing he was haunted.

They'd almost reached their embarkation point, so Grace lifted her paddle out of the water, letting it rest across her lap while Noah steered them in. The kayak bumped the shore and Grace scrambled forward, climbing out with a single splash into the shallow water. She grabbed the fore end of the kayak with her free hand and tugged, leading it toward the muddy beach.

She didn't want Dillon to leave. She wasn't ready to say good-bye.

But the ghosts couldn't keep haunting Noah. It was no way for him to live.

Something would have to be done.

23

DILLON

"WE'VE GOT TO DO SOMETHING," DILLON SAID. "WE NEED TO find a door."

"About that…" Rose started.

"You are obsessed with these doorways." Nadira walked along the water's surface and onto the dry land, before turning and saying, "I do not like a plan that requires venturing into the unknown."

Misam scrambled after her. "We might like the unknown."

"It would have to be better than this." Sophia waved an arm at the surrounding trees, tone scornful."

"Hey, don't diss the river," Dillon objected. "This place is great."

"This place is great," Joe agreed. "But you're right. We need to leave. We can't keep following Noah around."

Noah made a gentle leap out of the kayak onto dry land. He managed it perfectly, not even getting his feet wet.

"I'm not insulting your stupid river." Sophia kicked at the surface of the water. "I just meant this whole thing. Being invisible. Being helpless."

"It's not right," the angry man muttered, head down. "It's not right."

"You are too impatient, Sophia. You will never prosper if you do not learn inner calm." Nadira waggled her finger as if scolding, but her tone was gentle.

Joe choked. Misam laughed. Dillon put his hand over his mouth to hide his own smile. Even Mona looked away and then around and up as if wondering who was speaking.

Sophia sent Nadira an exasperated look.

Nadira shrugged. "Well, I never said I was good at it."

"Anything would be better than this," Sophia said. "Does it really matter where the door goes?"

"Of course it matters, you silly girl." Nadira put her hands on her hips. "You are not in pain here, you are not suffering, you are not hungry. You would like the flames of hell much less than this tranquility, I dare say."

"Tranquility." Sophia snorted. "You mean endless boredom, right?"

"Here, let me," Noah said to Grace, gesturing toward the prow of the boat and extending his paddle in her direction. She took the paddle and he grabbed the kayak and pulled it out of the water and up the gentle slope toward the car.

Dillon didn't know whether Noah was ignoring them or listening to every word that they said. He seemed focused on the kayak, but he'd definitely been paying attention earlier.

"We do not know where these doorways lead," Nadira repeated.

"It doesn't matter if we can't find one," Joe said, following Noah out of the water.

"Right. About that..." Rose stood at the water's edge, her eyes on the wisps and blobs of ghosts that were drifting after them.

"Rose knows where they go," Dillon interrupted her to explain. "She went through one before."

"Why is she still here then?" Sophia demanded of him, before turning to Rose and asking her the same question directly. "Why are you still here?"

"I came back," Rose answered.

"See?" Dillon added. "It's not a big deal. You can come back if you don't like it."

"Not easily," Rose objected. "It takes a lot of energy. If Akira hadn't died, I wouldn't have been able to."

"You need a death to power these doorways?" Nadia said. She shook her head. "That is unsettling. And rather distasteful."

"Oh, dear," Mona murmured. She moved away, beginning to flutter her feather duster over the trees at the edge of the clearing.

"No, it's not," Rose said. "It's just a doorway. It opens both ways."

"And where does it lead?" Nadira said. Misam paused next to her and she put her hands on his shoulders, tugging him close. He leaned against her legs. "You must explain if you wish us to go."

"I'm not trying to make you go." Rose spun in a circle, her pink skirt flaring out around her, her arms outstretched, her face lifted to the sky. She came to a stop and said, "I like it fine here."

"Rose!" Dillon glared at her. She wasn't helping. They were all in danger as long as they stayed. She needed to convince the others that it was okay to move on.

"What?" She widened her eyes at him.

"We need to go," he said, trying to keep his voice patient. "Remember the vortex? What if you hadn't been there? What if Akira had been there instead?"

She wrinkled her nose. "There is that. But..." She looked around at the ghosts gathered around her and at Grace and Noah, who were paused, standing by the car, Noah listening and Grace watching him. Even the angry man was waiting to hear what Rose had to say, although Mona was fluttering her feather duster along the bushes at the edge of the road. "Could you describe color to a blind person? Or music to someone who can't hear? I don't have words for it."

"Try," Nadira said again.

Rose heaved a sigh. "How?" She raised her hands to her head as if she were going to tug at her curls but then inspiration seemed to strike. Quickly she said, "Like this. Imagine you're a chick. A baby chick, inside a shell. Before you've hatched, you don't know what's outside your shell. It's like that."

"That makes no sense," Nadira said scornfully.

"It does so. If you're a baby chick inside a shell, how could you possibly picture everything that exists outside your shell?" Rose waved an arm wide, indicating the world around them. "Plants and trees and birds and bugs?"

"Heaven has bugs?" Nadira gave a skeptical frown, but her hands relaxed on Misam's shoulders.

"Don't tell Mona," Joe said under his breath, giving Nadira's arm a gentle nudge with his elbow. Nadira gave a muffled snort of laughter.

"If we were chicks, we would love bugs," Misam said cheerfully. "They would be yum-yum delicious."

"Exactly!" Rose said in triumph. "Not that there are really bugs. I meant that, whatchamacallit, metaphorically."

"Humph," Nadira snorted. "None of this sounds right. This must be some American thing. Misam and I should be in our graves right now. And on judgement day, we'll be taken into paradise, a most beautiful garden with delicious foods and all our loved ones. No bugs."

"There's not real bugs," Rose protested. "I mean maybe there are, but I didn't mean them that way."

"Bugs or no bugs, we need to go," Dillon repeated.

Joe stuffed his hands into his pockets. "I think we should go, too."

Noah turned away and began busying himself around the car, opening the door, grabbing the tie-down straps, beginning to fasten the kayak to the roof.

"What was that about?" Grace crossed to the other side of the car.

"Moving on," he said, passing her a strap. "Heaven apparently has bugs."

"Bugs? Like spiders and mosquitoes?" Grace tossed the strap over the kayak.

Rose stamped a foot against the ground. "Not like that."

"Not exactly," Noah told Grace.

"Forget the bugs," Dillon said, exasperated. "I've been to the other place. I don't want to go back there. And trust me, none of you would like it, either."

"You've been to one other place." Nadira held up a single finger. "As has she." She gestured toward Rose. "But perhaps what you call a doorway is really a gate to one of the levels of hell. Or heaven, I suppose. There are many levels of both and no way to be sure which one some random door will lead to."

"Not that it matters," Joe said. "We've never even seen one of these doors."

Rose sighed. "Well..."

"We haven't looked for one," Dillon said. "We need to start. We need to get Noah to take us places. Maybe a hospital or a nursing home, some place where people die a lot."

"Okay, that's creepy." Sophia sounded pleased. "You want to go hang out with dead people? Maybe Noah could take us to a morgue."

"We are hanging out with dead people," Misam said. "We are dead people."

"Misam, don't say that." Nadira stroked his hair back, away from his face. "It sounds so unpleasant."

"I've been trying to tell you," Rose started.

"No morgues." Noah finished buckling the tie-down strap and picked up the paddles. "I'm not visiting any morgues."

"A hospital then, maybe," Dillon suggested.

"And if we find one, what then? How can we know whether this doorway is a gateway to hell or not?" Nadira said.

"It doesn't matter, because we haven't found one." Joe folded his arms across his chest. "Until we do, arguing about it is pointless."

"That's never bothered you before," Nadira replied, half acid, half amused.

"Point to Mama," Misam chirped, drawing an imaginary line in the air.

Noah chuckled as he stuffed the paddles into the backseat of the car.

Grace sent him a questioning look.

"Arguing again," he responded briefly.

"They do that a lot, don't they?"

He dipped his head. "Pretty sure it's what being dead is all about."

Dillon snorted as a bunch of the other ghosts responded at once: Misam with a clap of his hands in resigned agreement; Joe with a wry, "Sorry, man,"; Nadira with a huff; Sophia with a muttered, "When you're in hell,"; and even the angry man with his usual complaints.

"What's the conclusion?" Grace asked.

Noah shrugged.

"We can't just go looking for more ghosts," Joe said. "Odds are they won't have a doorway, either. None of the ghosts we've picked up have had one of these doorways."

"That's not actually—" Rose started.

"And more ghosts might create the vortex, which is definitely a gateway to hell, correct?" Nadira said. "We should not take that chance. We should stay right here until the ghost expert returns."

"We can't wait that long," Dillon said. "And it's too dangerous for Akira. We have to find a doorway and go." Looking for a doorway would be a risk but it was one they had to take.

"If it was so easy, we'd have found one of them already," Joe said.

"I've been trying and trying to tell you." Rose flung her arms wide dramatically. "You have one."

"What?" The surprise came from several voices at once.

Rose pointed. Dillon followed the line of her arm. Chaupi was wandering toward them along the river's surface with a few of the trailing wisps.

"You've had one. All along. You didn't need me at all," Rose said, sounding exasperated. "You just needed to talk to Chaupi."

2 4

GRACE

"Who's Chaupi?" Noah asked.

The surprise in his voice had Grace raising her brows. Something had obviously startled him. She paused on the verge of getting into the car, looking at him over the roof.

"That guy?" He was frowning, but making no move to get into the car himself. When he caught her eye, he told her, "One of them has a way to move on. A doorway. Or maybe it's a gate. But apparently they could all use it, if they wanted to."

"What? Who?" she demanded.

It couldn't be Dillon. Not yet. It was too soon.

"Not sure whether I mentioned him before, but he doesn't speak English. I..." He rubbed his head, looking sheepish. "I used to call him the fake Chinese guy. But I don't think he's really Chinese."

He listened for a moment, then shook his head. "Yeah. Not Chinese." He pulled open his door and got into the car. Grace followed suit.

"He might be speaking the same language as the innkeeper," Noah said, frowning.

"Really? As Avery?" Grace started the car. "Quechua?"

"I think so. It'd be a pretty big coincidence."

"My dad would say there's no such thing, just lines of fate intersecting."

"Fate?" Noah scoffed. "I don't believe in..."

He paused.

Grace sent him an inquiring glance as she put on her seatbelt.

He lifted a shoulder. "Well, I don't believe in ghosts, either."

She smiled, checking the view in the rear view mirror, before asking, "Ah, are we all present and accounted for?"

Noah listened, head tilted to one side, then nodded. "Close enough, anyway."

Grace backed up, then began to drive. The quiet in the car felt natural but she could tell from casting quick sideways glances at Noah that he wasn't sitting in silence. It was interesting to see him react — blinking, lips twisting, eyebrows subtly lifting and falling. He'd had a lack of expression before, a stillness, that must have been carefully cultivated. Relaxed, his face held a lively warmth.

After a few moments, Grace had to ask. "What are they saying?"

Noah's voice was dry as he responded. "Your nephew is practicing his Spanish, trying to find out why Chaupi hasn't moved on."

"Oh." Grace frowned. Did Dillon speak Spanish? "When did he learn Spanish?"

"Not sure he did," Noah muttered.

Grace chuckled, feeling more cheerful. While Noah listened to the ghosts, she'd been trying to strategize, to come up with a solution to the problem posed by too much spirit energy in Tassamara. Helping them move on was the obvious answer, of course.

But she had to admit, if only to herself, that she hated that possibility.

Dillon had been gone for such a long time. She'd never stopped missing him, but she' d gotten used to his absence. The empty space he left in her life wasn't filled and never would be, but she'd adjusted. They all had.

Only then she'd learned he'd never really been gone at all.

On Christmas, he'd texted her reminders of holidays long past, like the year her mom had accidentally melted the candy in their stockings by leaving them too close to the fire, and the time they'd both had the stomach flu and she'd thrown up on his presents.

For the first time in a long time, it had felt almost like a real Christmas.

And for him to leave now... it would be like losing him all over again.

Besides, if it was time for Dillon to go, surely he would have his own doorway. There had to be a better answer.

"What? No." Noah shook his head. "That's... no. Not gonna happen."

"What is it?" Grace asked.

"They want me to get Avery to translate."

Grace turned onto the road that led to General Directions. "That makes sense, I guess."

Noah made a scoffing noise. "How does that conversation go? By the way, could you tell me what a ghost is saying? It's not like asking for extra towels or the location of the nearest ATM."

"Avery would be thrilled," Grace said confidently. She liked Avery. The innkeeper was opinionated, sarcastic, interesting, and always up for hosting a fun local evening. The B&B's weekly movie nights sometimes overflowed the sitting room, with Avery the first to throw popcorn at the screen when a character did something stupid. And Avery was a true believer, willing to accept every passing stranger's stories of kything, nensha and retrocognition.

But if Avery translated, and they convinced this ghost to move on, would Dillon insist on going too? If he did, he'd miss Natalya's wedding. He'd miss Akira's baby being born. He'd miss... everything.

And she'd miss him.

"I'd have to explain about the ghosts. About hearing voices."

"So?"

Noah didn't answer right away. He was staring out the window.

"A problem?" Grace asked.

He didn't say anything for a moment and then he looked her way, with a rueful smile. "You're the first person I've ever told. First time I've ever talked about it."

"Seriously? You didn't—" She took a hand off the steering wheel to gesture. "I don't know. Look for help? Talk to your family? Your brother?"

He looked out the window again.

"Not a good subject?"

He sighed. "I figured I knew what would happen. They'd tell me I was crazy and send me to a shrink."

"Maybe," she conceded. "But a therapist might have helped you cope."

"I coped just fine."

"Just fine and happily are not the same."

"I'm not sure happy is an option for someone who hallucinates. Or is haunted." He winced, closing his eyes and raising one hand to an ear. "Guys. Sorry."

"The chorus kibitzing?"

"The chorus?" Noah snorted. "Yeah, you could say that."

"What's the consensus?"

He grinned at her. "Strong opinions on whether it's worse to be haunted or to be the one doing the haunting and one dissenting voice from Rose, who thinks happy is always an option."

His grin did interesting things to her stomach. Or maybe it was her bloodstream, sending a hormonal cocktail of delight hurtling through her veins. A little breathless, she said, "I like her attitude."

His lips quirked but he didn't answer.

Returning her attention to the road, she tapped her fingers on the steering wheel. She didn't want Dillon to move on. But these other ghosts, maybe it could be time for them to go. The question was, why were they stuck?

"Avery won't mind helping you. They believe in ghosts. But there's no rush, right? If the ghosts don't have doors of their own, maybe there's something they should be doing here."

"That unfinished business thing?"

"Akira says it doesn't work, but maybe she's wrong. Or maybe it works for some ghosts and not others. Or maybe..." She fell silent, thinking. Maybe it wasn't the ghosts' business that was the problem. Her father's words to her earlier in the day still had her feeling uneasy.

Could the business belong to the living? Could spirits be trapped by the people they'd left behind?

She slowed for the security booth. It was late enough that the guard had gone home, but the sticker on her car's window lifted the automated gate and let her drive through.

"I wonder," she started slowly, knowing she was probably interrupting some ghostly voice.

"Yeah?" he prompted.

"I wonder if knowing why you're haunted might help to, well, get you un-haunted." She pulled into her usual parking space.

Would he throw the question back to her, the way she had done to her brother? He wasn't the only one who'd been haunted. Dillon might be wandering freely now, but he'd started out as trapped as any other ghost.

But Noah's situation was different. His ghosts weren't trapped where they'd died, the way most of the ghosts Akira had told them about were. They were tied to Noah. There had to be some reason for that.

Every hint of amusement in his voice was gone as he said quietly, "Isn't it obvious?"

Grace glanced at him. He was looking away, staring out the window, not moving to get out of the car.

"No," she answered, puzzled. "Should it be?"

"I think so." He looked back toward her. His face had shut down again, his expression grim, lips firmed, but he shrugged as if resigned. "It's because I killed them."

Grace froze as he got out of the car.

Killed them?

225

He couldn't be talking about all of them — he obviously hadn't killed Dillon or Rose and somehow she didn't think he'd killed some dude with a peanut allergy or a woman telling a guy named Tom to stop driving so fast.

So... the first three. His friend from Basic. The woman and the kid.

Shit.

How did you tell a soldier that the things he'd done in a war zone were not his fault?

And what if they were?

NOAH

"YOU DIDN'T PLANT THAT *IED*," JOE SAID.

The Arabic woman snorted.

She knew, Noah thought. She knew.

He wanted to walk away. He didn't want to see the shock or the disgust or even the pity that would be in Grace's eyes.

But his throat felt tight. He was going to have to talk to them. To Joe, the woman, the kid. And what could he say? How could he apologize for everything he'd done and failed to do?

First things first, though. Like it or not, he needed to say good-bye to Grace. No stomping straight off to his truck like a surly teenager, no matter how much he wished to.

As he rested one hand on the car roof, waiting for her to get out, a dark blue sedan drove into the parking lot and pulled into a parking spot a few spaces down. Two people emerged: a man that he'd never seen before and a familiar copper-haired woman. Sylvie Blair.

"*Hey, my mom and dad are here,*" Dillon said.

Grace stepped out of the car. She turned toward Noah, opening her mouth, and spotted the new arrivals. A multitude of emotions flurried across her face — recognition, exasperation, annoyance — before she replaced them with a polite neutrality.

"It appears my brother has reprioritized his workload," she said, adding quietly, "We'll talk later."

Noah appreciated the reprieve. But at the same time, he wanted to tell her that there was nothing to talk about. If he was haunted because of his guilt, no words would ever change that reality. He couldn't go back and fix the past.

Meanwhile, her brother was striding toward him, hand outstretched, Sylvie following a few steps behind.

"You must be Noah Blake," he said. "Lucas Latimer."

Warily, Noah shook hands, nodding in acknowledgement. What had Dillon said about his father? That he was some kind of psychic, Noah knew, but he couldn't remember if Dillon had mentioned specifics.

"What are you doing here, Lucas?" Grace demanded, before nodding toward his partner in politer greeting. "Sylvie."

"Grace," Sylvie murmured back, a Mona Lisa smile on her lips. "And Mr. Blake. It's a pleasure to finally see you again." She put the faintest emphasis on the word "finally."

He raised an eyebrow at her. If she'd told him more, maybe he'd have arrived sooner. Or not. Maybe if she'd told him more, he would have rolled his eyes and stayed far away.

Maybe that would have been better.

"*Your mom is really young,*" Sophia said. "*And your dad is hot.*" She sounded disapproving.

"*Ew,*" Dillon said. "*That's my dad.*"

"*He is pretty dreamy,*" Rose said cheerfully. "*Such luscious hair.*"

"*He is a very attractive man,*" Nadira agreed. "*You have his eyes.*"

"*You should like that, though. You would have looked just like him when you grew up,*" Rose added.

Noah bit back his sigh. Really? Did he seriously have to listen to a bunch of invisible girls crushing on a hot guy? At least they weren't talking about him this time.

Lucas blinked at him, a tint of color rising in his tanned cheeks. He cleared his throat, looking uncomfortable.

"Did you finish the job you were working on?" Grace asked pointedly.

Lucas turned his attention to her. "Not exactly, no."

"What exactly does 'not exactly' mean?"

Noah put his hand over his mouth, rubbing his chin to hide his smile. It was the same voice she'd used earlier with the guy at the security station, Jensen. It had the same frosty edge, composed of two parts perfect enunciation and one part southern belle, and he liked it. It made him want to kiss her until she melted, until she was disheveled and laughing and breathless, and pulling him closer and kissing him harder.

Lucas looked pained. He opened his mouth, then closed it again, shook his head, then put his hand over his eyes.

Sylvie stepped forward. She looked like she was smothering a smile, but she said, "Is Dillon here?"

"He is, yes," Grace replied. "Is that why you're here?"

Sylvie stole a look at Lucas who still had his hand over his eyes. "More or less."

"Is it more or is it less?" Grace said. She turned her attention to her brother. "You have responsibilities, Lucas. It was your choice to take those responsibilities on. We have a reputation to uphold. We don't walk away from jobs half-done. Isn't that your policy?"

Damn, but she was pretty when she was pissed off.

Noah shifted, feeling a stirring that he was just as glad she was in no position to see. It was more than a little awkward to be lusting after a gorgeous woman in front of her brother, no matter how much the feeling was reciprocated.

And he knew it was reciprocated. That moment in the kayak, when their eyes had met... if there hadn't been a crowd of ghosts around them... In a split-second flash of imagination, he saw himself leaning forward, taking her lips, her enthusiastic response, the kayak spilling, the two of them in the water. She'd wrap her legs around him...

"Oh, God," Lucas muttered.

Sylvie was quivering, her lips tucked together as if she were holding her breath. Noah frowned at her. Was she trying not to laugh?

"We need to talk," Lucas said.

Noah wasn't sure who the words were directed to. Lucas wasn't looking at anyone in particular, his eyes fixed on a point somewhere over the kayak. Could he be talking to Dillon?

"No," Lucas said, eyes shifting to Noah.

"*My dad reads minds,*" Dillon volunteered. "*He knows what you're thinking. My mom's an empath. She can tell what people are feeling. But when they're together, they're both stronger. It's like they've got a double super-power when the other one is around.*"

Great.

That was just great.

"*That would suck,*" Sophia said, sounding horrified. "*You could never get away with anything.*"

"*Man, that would be hard,*" Joe agreed. He sounded more awed than appalled. "*No little white lies. No claiming traffic was bad when really you were just goofing off.*"

"*Lying is the source of all sin,*" Nadira said. "*You shouldn't do it anyway. All the same, I would not like to live with someone who knew my every thought.*"

"*Nah, you get used to it,*" Dillon said. "*It's not so bad. And it's really fun sometimes, too. I used to try to make him laugh at the wrong places when we were at the movies.*"

Deliberately, Noah forced his attention away from the ghostly voices. Maybe he should mentally start reciting the alphabet or the Military Code of Conduct. Or maybe he should sing.

"You'll have plenty of chances to talk to Noah," Grace said, moving around to the front of the car. "He starts work on Monday."

Not "Kiss the Girl," though. That wouldn't be a good choice. The reminder of the kid singing *sha-la-la-la* had Noah fighting to maintain a straight face. Out of the corner of his eye, he could see Sylvie losing her struggle not to giggle.

Lucas, however, wasn't laughing. "What?" he said to Grace.

Her smile was not friendly. "Noah starts work on Monday. With the security team, for the moment."

Noah stuffed his hand in his pocket, wrapping his fingers around his truck key. He didn't want to disagree with Grace and he didn't want her brother reading his mind. But he wasn't so sure...

Sha-la-la-la, he thought, as loudly as he could.

Sylvie snorted.

"We discussed that," Lucas said to Grace. "I told you my position."

"Your position is an opinion." Grace folded her arms across her chest. "And your opinion is irrelevant."

Lucas took a deep breath. Maybe he was counting to ten.

Sylvie put a hand on his arm. "Maybe we should all go inside and talk. We can hit up one of the vending machines for a snack along the way. It's been a long day."

"It's been a long week." Lucas glared at his sister as if he blamed her for that.

"Dillon was missing for weeks, plural." Grace moved her hands to her hips. "Shouldn't that have meant for some long months?"

"Oh, don't you start with—" Lucas's tone was heated.

"Nope." Sylvie's gentle touch turned into a firm grasp.

"*Uh-oh,*" Dillon said, sounding guilty. "*Are they fighting about me?*"

"*Did you let them know where you were?*" Rose asked him.

Sylvie began tugging Lucas toward the door of the building. "You are not doing this. Not like this. We're going to get a snack and maybe a drink, hit the restroom, and then we'll sit down and talk like civilized people. No saying things you'll regret later just because you're tired and hungry and worried."

Lucas let himself be towed along.

"I sent them some texts while I was away," Dillon said. *"Told them I was fine."*

"Parents like to know more about their children than that," Nadira said. *"You're as bad as Noah. Never calling his mother. Hmph."*

Ouch. Noah winced. Over the years, Nadira had commented caustically on his behavior more than once. More than a few times, in fact. He'd thought of her as the voice of his conscience sometimes. But it was different now that he knew she was another person, not just his subconscious.

"I'll text them," Dillon said. *"Right now."*

Grace let her hands drop, eyes searching Noah's face. "Don't worry about Lucas. He likes to think he's in charge, but he's not."

"I'm not worrying." He needed to tell her that he wasn't sure about working here, about working for her. It would be a mistake.

And it should feel like a mistake to her, too, he thought, closing his hand around his truck key. He'd just told her that he'd killed three people. Shouldn't she be rescinding that job offer right about now?

"He's over-protective," she went on. "It's not personal, really. He just thinks that anyone who worked for AlecCorp is... well..." She shrugged.

"A killer?" Noah said gently. It was not untrue. "Or traumatized? The returning vet as ticking time bomb?" He didn't blame her brother, but a hint of the bitterness he felt at life post-Iraq seeped through. People were quick enough to thank him for his service, but it didn't help him fit in any better.

"It's not the military he has issues with," Grace said. "He was investigating AlecCorp for months. He's not a fan."

"He's not the only one," Nadira said. *"Those people..."*

He could imagine the disapproving shake of her head and her pursed lips, and his own lips twisted into a wry smile.

"Eh, they weren't so bad," Joe said, before adding a reflective, *"Well..."*

Noah knew exactly what he meant. AlecCorp had been a mixed bag. There'd been some guys there that he'd want to keep his little

232

sister away from, too, if he had one. "It's not a problem. I understand. But..." He should tell her he didn't want the job. Instead he found himself saying, "I should go."

"Are you sure?"

"Things to do, places to be." He kept the words light, but the key was digging into his palm. He forced his fingers to relax.

"Are you going to talk to Avery?"

"The sooner the better, I guess."

"Well, don't... don't do anything drastic, okay?" Grace's eyes shifted around the parking lot. Maybe she was addressing Dillon.

"*I'll send a text,*" Dillon replied. He sounded quite cheerful.

"He'll text you," Noah told Grace.

"That's..." She sighed. "Yeah. Okay." She glanced back at the door to the offices. "I should go deal with my brother. Unless you want me to come talk to Avery with you?"

"I think I can manage a conversation."

"Right." She looked at him, eyes searching his face. "Everything's going to be okay."

Was she trying to convince him or herself? Noah couldn't tell, but he gave her a nod that he hoped was reassuring.

BACK AT THE BED-AND-BREAKFAST, NOAH FOUND AVERY SITTING on the back patio, with a sadly depleted plate of cheese and crackers on the table before them and a glass of wine in their hand. Empty glasses and crumpled napkins gave evidence that at least some of the guests had enjoyed the cocktail hour, but Noah was grateful to find Avery alone.

Grace had assured him that Avery would be perfectly comfortable talking about ghosts, but Noah wasn't sure he was comfortable bringing the subject up.

Ghosts.

Was he living in the Matrix?

But if he was, there was a computer-simulated voice that very much wanted to be heard talking over his shoulder. The stream of words that were probably not Chinese had continued almost non-stop ever since the other ghosts had started trying to communicate with Chaupi. Noah might as well give in to the construct.

"Ah, welcome." Avery stood. "Tail end of the snacks, I'm afraid, but I can still offer you a drink. Wine? Beer?"

"I'm good, thanks." Noah waved off the invitation. "Sorry to disturb you."

"Oh, no, no, not at all." Avery set their glass down on a side table and began gathering up the used glasses, setting them on a tray.

"I would like to talk to you, though." Noah dropped down onto the bench. "Do you have a minute?"

Avery paused. "Of course."

"So, Grace tells me..." Noah started. Then he stopped. How exactly was he going to ask this question?

"Just say it," Nadira said encouragingly.

"Spit it out," Sophia added.

"Do you want me to send a text?" Dillon asked. *"Avery knows about me. Everyone does in Tassamara, pretty much."*

"Guys, if you could maybe just let Noah talk," Joe said.

"Yes?" Avery repositioned the ice bucket, shooting a glance at Noah.

"I have to ask you..." Noah ran a hand through his hair, shifting his gaze away. "I'm sorry. This is uncomfortable for me."

"Yes?" Avery repeated, but their tone was warier.

Noah blew out a breath. Why was this so damn hard? But the idea was so absurd. And he'd hidden his secret for so long. He'd rather go on a thirty-mile forced march than tell a stranger that he heard voices. But finally he said flatly, "Grace tells me that you believe in ghosts."

"Oh!" Avery's eyebrows arched in surprise. They tilted their head to the side. "That was not what I was expecting."

For a second, Noah was confused. Then he realized Avery must have been anticipating a more personal question. A corner of Noah's mouth lifted in wry acknowledgement. Everyone had secrets, didn't they? And of course, their own secrets were always the ones they cared about the most.

Obscurely comforted, he said, "I hear voices. I'm told they belong to ghosts."

"They do belong to ghosts."

"We are ghosts."

"Told?"

"Do you still not believe in us?"

"Right. Yeah, I heard about that," Avery said casually.

Noah stared at them. "You heard about what?"

"Oh, not the details." Avery continued clearing up desultorily, picking up a napkin, moving a small plate to the tray with the glasses. "Just, you know, that you had a gift."

"I wouldn't call it that," Noah muttered. How the hell could Avery have learned about the ghosts? Not even Grace had known until he admitted it to her and he'd been with her until he'd left her at General Directions. Had she called while he was driving here, trying to smooth the way for him? He supposed he shouldn't be annoyed with her if she had — she must have meant well — but he didn't like it. "Did Grace call you?"

"No." Avery must have heard the annoyance in his voice because they shot him a doubtful look. "My next-door neighbor told me. She works at the spa."

"The spa?"

"Sure, down the street." Avery gestured vaguely toward the fence.

"It's hard to keep a secret in a town of psychics," Dillon said.

"It's hard to keep a secret in Tassamara," Rose corrected him. *"Always has been."*

"Small towns. Alike the world over," Nadira said, voice dry.

Noah leaned back against the bench.

Okay, weirdest day ever.

His deep dark secret, the burden he'd been carrying for what felt like forever, was now gossip. Not even very interesting gossip, if Avery's calm reaction was anything to go by.

"Were these ghosts messing with my television yesterday?" Avery perched on the edge of the bench across from Noah.

"Yeah." Noah braced for their reaction.

"That is so cool." The innkeeper clenched a fist over their heart. "I have a haunted inn. Oh my heavens, it's like a dream come true. Can you stay? Can they stay?"

Noah blinked.

"*I like this guy,*" Joe said.

"*She is not a guy,*" Nadira said.

"*They aren't a guy,*" Dillon corrected her. "*They aren't a she, either.*"

"*Right, right. Whatever. I like them,*" Joe said.

"Actually, that's not what I'm hoping for," Noah replied. Behind him, Chaupi began speaking again, a fast blur of words that Noah couldn't understand.

"I'm working on it," Noah said. The voice — the ghost — didn't slow down. Noah raised his hand, palm up and open, in a stop sign directed over his shoulder. "Give it a rest, man."

"A ghost? Really?" Avery gave a shiver of delight.

For a moment, Noah thought about telling them exactly how many ghosts seemed to be following him around, but then he shook his head slightly. Even someone as excited about ghosts as Avery might not want to know that their home was currently infested with the spirits of the dead.

Instead, he said, "One of the ghosts haunting me doesn't speak English. Do you think you could help me talk to him?"

"I would be delighted." Avery clasped their hands together in front of them. "It would be an honor."

Noah wanted to object. An honor? More like a nightmare. But he wasn't going to argue with Avery's willingness to help. With a nod, he said, "In your language, could you—"

"Which one?" Avery interrupted. "I know several."

Carefully, trying to get each syllable correct, Noah repeated what Chaupi was saying.

"Quechua," Avery said, and then rattled off several sentences at a speed that Noah had no chance of following. Chaupi obviously had no such trouble, responding eagerly. And far too quickly.

Noah sighed. This might be harder than he'd anticipated. "Maybe start by asking him to slow down."

"*Ari.*" Avery nodded. "I mean, yes," they added, before returning to Quechua for a quick couple of sentences. Finished, they waited expectantly for Noah's next words.

"One of the other ghosts, Rose, says that you have a doorway, a path to the next plane of existence." Noah felt like an idiot saying those words aloud, but Avery didn't seem fazed. They translated eagerly.

"The other ghosts wonder why you haven't used it and would like to join you when you do," Noah continued.

Avery's brows rose, but they spoke again.

For the next several minutes, Avery and Noah went back and forth, exchanging phrases. It wasn't simple: the language was so unfamiliar to Noah that more than once he stumbled over Chaupi's words while trying to repeat them for Avery, and had to ask the ghost to slow down and try again.

But finally he said, "I think that's it."

Avery waved a cocktail napkin where they'd scrawled a few notes. "So is this what you do? You find out what they need and help them move on?"

"I wish." Noah took the napkin from Avery and smoothed it over his knee. He stared at the name and the address, the first things Avery had written. "They never do seem to move on. But..." He looked up and shot a quick grin at Avery. "I also didn't know they were ghosts until I got here. This could be a first."

"That is so cool. You could travel the world, helping spirits. You could be like that guy on television, the medium. The one who tells people how their relatives died." Avery shook their head. "Like they need to know that. It would be so much more interesting if sometimes he could tell them things they don't know, instead of just the things they do."

Noah didn't have the slightest desire to be on television. And he was not going to wander around the world looking for ghosts to help. But it would be nice if he could help this one specific ghost. He lifted the napkin. "How do you suppose I can find her?"

"Not a problem." Avery whisked the napkin out of his hand. "I'll call Grace."

"Grace?" Noah wanted to grab the napkin back. If anyone was calling Grace, it should be him. But he resisted the impulse. Over the course of the past twelve hours — or maybe it was the past four days — his entire life had been upended. From the moment he'd seen Grace's green eyes in the restaurant, the world had stopped being a place he understood.

And maybe he'd stopped being someone he understood, too. For so long, he'd felt trapped. Somehow his choices had turned him into a person that he'd never wanted to be, someone who couldn't let go of the past, couldn't move on.

He'd thought he knew what the world was. He didn't believe in magic, he didn't believe in miracles. And he knew himself, too — damaged beyond repair by what had happened to him, by what he'd done.

But now... it was like the world was a kaleidoscope and Grace Latimer had given it a good hard spin. All the pieces — everything he understand about reality, about existence, about who he was — they were spinning and shifting and he didn't know yet where they were going to wind up, what the world would look like when the spinning stopped.

26

DILLON

"Dang it." Dillon had been pacing behind Noah as he listened in to the three-way conversation between Noah, Avery, and Chaupi, but now he took himself off to the far end of the patio, dropping into one of the empty chairs with a sigh. Most of the other ghosts followed him, leaving Chaupi and some of the wisps hovering by Noah and Avery.

The news wasn't good. Chaupi had left behind a pregnant girlfriend in Peru. He wanted her to know his fate, that he hadn't abandoned her intentionally. But it had been thirty years, maybe more, and all he had was the address where she had once lived.

"Hmph," Nadira snorted. "A man who conceived a child outside of marriage? This is the gate you would have us go through? Surely it must lead to a particularly dark corner of hell."

"No, it won't," Rose said absently, watching Chaupi with a frown.

"Tell me that after you have gone through a dozen of these doorways, not just one," Nadira said smartly.

"Maybe we could go through his door without him," Dillon suggested. "Rose, if you can show us where..."

Rose interrupted him, shaking her head. "If that worked, one of you would have popped out of here by now. You've walked right past the door more than once."

Dillon scowled. It seemed unfair that Rose could see it and he couldn't. "You could take us through, couldn't you?"

Rose wrinkled her nose. "What if using it closes it? I'm not stealing Chaupi's afterlife from him."

"Maybe we could convince him to go without waiting." Dillon eyed the older ghost. Chaupi was standing by Noah and Avery, head cocked to one side, as if he was trying to understand their conversation. He'd been a ghost long enough to have started fading, the colors in his plain t-shirt, white apron, and khaki pants beginning to wash out as if they'd been out in the sun for too long.

Nadira followed his gaze. "Can we not find another doorway? One that does not belong to an adulterer?"

"How can he be an adulterer if he wasn't married?" Joe took a seat in the chair next to Dillon, leaning back and extending his legs.

"You know nothing about sin." Nadira rolled her eyes.

"What's an adulterer?" Misam asked.

"Never you mind," his mother said. She waved him toward the grassy lawn. "You go and play."

He ignored her.

Unexpectedly, Sophia spoke up. "Why don't we have doors of our own? If he gets one, how come we don't?"

"I think it's because we shouldn't have died when we did," Rose responded. "We're like the unripe fruit of souls, not ready to be picked."

"Ew," Nadira protested. "I am not fruit. Or a chicken."

"You had a door, though, didn't you?" Dillon asked Rose.

"Yes, but only after Henry came back. If I'd lived, I would have been pretty old by then, so maybe that's when I would have died if I hadn't... well, made a mistake," Rose said.

"What was your mistake?" Misam asked Rose.

Dillon opened his mouth to say something, anything. He knew

how Rose had died. Akira had told him the whole story after Rose had moved on the first time. He didn't want her to have to share it if she didn't want to.

But before he could think of what to say, Rose, quite calmly, said, "I conceived a child outside of marriage. And then I tried to stop it from being born."

Nadira drew in a sharp breath as Misam asked, in a tone of innocent curiosity, "How did you do that?"

"Never you mind," Nadira snapped at him. "Go and play. Now." He ignored her again.

Rose smiled at him. "It's not important." She looked at Nadira and said, "My doorway didn't take me to hell, and Chaupi's is probably safer than mine was. Less of a sin." She lifted her shoulders in a shrug.

Nadira bit her lip, looking troubled, then put a hand out to Rose. "I am sorry for your loss. And for any offense I might have given."

"None taken," Rose assured her.

Sophia said, "If we're unripe fruit, shouldn't we wait? Until we get our own doors? Until we're ripe?"

Dillon wanted to bang his head against the nearest brick wall. "It's not an invitation-only party. We're dead. That means we're ready."

"Hey, I hate this as much as you do." Sophia folded her arms across her chest.

"More, probably," Dillon admitted. He hadn't managed to create a vortex until he'd been sure he'd totally screwed up his mother's life.

"But maybe we're supposed to resolve our unfinished business." Sophia hunched her shoulders. "I could probably talk to my parents."

"What and then you'll get a white light? And your grandparents waving at you from the other side? I've talked to my parents. I've seen my grandma. It didn't help." Dillon jumped up from the chair so he could start pacing again.

Calm, he told himself. Calm. He didn't want to open a vortex just

241

because he was so desperate to avoid one. He took a deep breath and let it out in a quick exhale. "Sorry."

At the other end of the patio, Noah nodded at something Avery was saying and then started talking, his expression serious.

"If we have unfinished business, Misam and I, it would be in Iraq." Nadira pursed her lips.

"Do you think we need to see Papa?" Misam sounded doubtful. He slipped his hand into hers.

"I don't know what there would be to say to him. And..." Nadira glanced at Joe, then looked away. "Well. No."

Joe studied his toes, but his dimple flashed in a quick smile.

"It's not right," the angry man muttered.

"Oh, dear. Oh, dear. I'll never get this clean." Mona dropped to her knees and began scrubbing the paving stones of the path.

"That's for sure," Sophia said. She crouched next to Mona and pointed at the moss and grass flourishing in the tiny gaps between the stones. "They need the dirt to survive, Mona. Leave it alone. Unless you want to be a plant-killer." She said the last word with an emphasis that made it sound equivalent to serial killer.

"Oh, dear." Mona sat back on her heels, eyes wide and perturbed.

"Mona's unfinished business seems to be cleaning something she didn't get clean enough the first time," Joe said.

"Trying to get it perfect for her husband, yes," Nadira agreed.

"Even if we could find her husband, she should tell him to get lost instead of trying to clean for him," Dillon said firmly.

Sophia stood and turned to Joe. "What about you?"

"Me?" Joe looked surprised.

"You. What's your unfinished business?"

"It doesn't work that way," Dillon grumbled. He'd done the unfinished business thing. His business was done, as complete as he could get it, but he still didn't have a door. At least they weren't arguing about whether to go, though. That was progress.

"I don't know." Joe shrugged. "I mean, my whole life is unfinished, isn't it? I was twenty years old. I don't think there's some magical thing I needed to accomplish to make my life complete."

At the other end of the patio, Avery began to talk, using their hands freely. They arched a doorway and spiraled a finger around in a twisting circular motion.

"What's Avery doing?" Dillon said. He headed back toward Noah, the other ghosts joining him. He'd moved away so he could talk without disturbing Noah and Avery, but now he wanted to know what Avery was saying.

Avery kept speaking. They drew their hands toward them as if dragging something heavy, flickered their fingers, pausing now and again as if searching for the vocabulary they needed.

Chaupi looked startled and drew back. He responded so quickly that Noah had to put up his hand in another slow-down motion, before repeating his words to Avery.

Avery nodded in satisfaction. They spoke some more, without bothering to translate for Noah. This time a wide arm gesture indicated the world and Dillon distinctly heard his Uncle Zane's name.

"What's he saying?" Misam whispered.

"Shush, love," Nadira answered in an equally hushed voice. "Let him listen."

Chaupi looked torn. He glanced around at the watching ghosts, then dropped his gaze to the ground. He walked a few steps away and stared at the garden wall, then turned back. He folded his arms, considering.

"What's he saying?" Avery asked Noah.

Noah shook his head. "Nothing. It's quiet."

Avery stood and started speaking again. This time their words seemed more earnest than passionate. They patted their chest with an open palm, then turned the hand outward.

"You promising him something?" Noah asked, leaning back.

"Sure." Avery gave a shrug. "I go home every year. I've told him we'll find his girlfriend and that I will personally visit his village and tell them what happened to him." He added another sentence or two in Quechua, sounding more caustic, and sat back down, crossing his legs in a defiantly relaxed motion. "And now I've told him that if I say his soul has been eaten by a qosqo, I'm sure they'll be saddened to hear it."

"A what?" Noah asked.

"Your vortex," Avery said. "An energy center that eats living energy. We have them in Peru, too."

Chaupi gave a sharp nod. He didn't look entirely pleased, but he stepped closer to Noah and said a few words. Then he looked around at all the other ghosts and gave an almost beatific smile. He made a wide, sweeping motion with his arm, the motion seeming to encompass all of them, even the bobbing lights and the faded wisps.

"Oh, dear," Nadira said.

"Oh, yes!" Dillon punched the air. "He's going to take us, isn't he?"

Noah repeated Chaupi's words and Avery gave a smug nod. "He'll help."

Finally.

If Dillon's heart still beat, it would have been racing. When his gran left, she'd asked him if he wanted to join her, but he hadn't been in a hurry to leave the rest of his family. Being able to communicate with them was new to him. He'd wanted to spend some time with his dad, and getting to know his parents better had been great.

But now he was ready. No more risk of the vortex, no more chance of being trapped by some ghostly power he didn't understand. Metaphor or not, it was time to learn to fly.

Nadira buried her hands in the arms of her robe. "I don't know about this."

"Me, neither," Sophia said.

"What?" Dillon turned to them. "But we have to go. It's too dangerous to stay."

"This door could be dangerous, too," Nadira said.

"It's an adventure, Mama," Misam piped up. "You like adventures."

"Noah should take us to New Zealand," Nadira said. "That would be a nice adventure. I'd like to see Middle Earth."

"That other place." Sophia held her chin high. She wasn't crying. "That thing that was dragging me. You said it was nothingness. Unbecoming. Maybe I want that instead."

"Oh, Sophia, no." Dillon didn't know whether he should hug her or shake her. The memory of the grimy ammonia sensation, the swallowing gray poison oozing over him, came back to him and he shuddered. Sophia's soul wouldn't be like that. She was unhappy, but he'd seen her sparks of humor, her sarcastic rejoinders, her moments of enthusiasm. She didn't belong in the crushing emptiness of the energy ocean. "No way."

"Nothingness sounds good," Sophia insisted, but her voice was softer.

"I've been there. You don't want to go there."

"If I deserved a door, I'd have a door."

"Well, you don't have one. And if you stay, if you don't wind up in the vortex, you'll turn into one of them." Dillon waved his arm toward the faders and wisps. "Is that what you want? To spend decades fading away until you're just a single memory? One last remnant of who you once were, floating around, saying the same thing over and over again?"

"I... no," Sophia said in a smaller voice. "No, I don't want that."

"We need to move on," Joe said.

Nadira sighed. She let her eyes drop to Misam and put a hand on his head. Then she gave a single nod, pressing her lips together.

Sophia sniffled and wiped a hand irritably against her cheek. She didn't say anything more.

Dillon looked around at the others. Most of the wisps seemed as oblivious as always. How were they going to get them through Chaupi's door? "But how are we going to make this work?"

He reached out for Chaupi's hand. The older man held his hand out willingly, but it drifted right through Dillon's, only a mild tingling buzz to indicate where their essences met.

Joe gave a bark of laughter. "Damn it. Not so easy, after all."

"Well," said Nadira cheerfully, "that was a good idea, Dillon, but we'll have to try something else."

"I'm not giving up." Dillon scowled.

Energy, that's what ghosts were. Energy, still trapped on this plane of existence. Chaupi just needed more energy to become solid again.

New ghosts, fresh from their deaths, emotional or angry, could generate energy, but the older they became, the longer they existed in an incorporeal state, the more their energy dissipated and the less able they were to renew it. Even if somehow he could frustrate Chaupi, the older ghost probably couldn't make himself solid again.

But Rose knew how to absorb the energy from other ghosts. That's what she'd done with Sophia.

"Rose," Dillon said. "That thing you did with Sophia. Can you do the opposite to Chaupi?"

"Hmm." Rose folded her hands in front of her face in thoughtful speculation, then shrugged. "Maybe." She reached for Chaupi's hand. Her hand passed through him, like Dillon's had, but instead of pulling back, she kept it there.

"It's not just Chaupi, though." Joe waved an arm around the yard. "We can't leave all the crazy ghosts to haunt Noah. That would suck."

"It's not right," the angry man said, stepping closer to them.

"Hey, no offense, man," Joe said to the angry man. "But come on, no one wants to listen to that for the rest of their life. You gotta go, too."

But slowly, almost imperceptibly, the colors in Chaupi's clothing, his skin, his hair, were starting to darken and deepen, until he was no longer transparent. He gripped Rose's hand and lifted it to his lips, bowing his head over it, and said, "Gracias."

"It's not right. It's not right." The angry man turned to Rose.

"What's going on?" Noah asked.

"It's okay," Rose replied to Noah. "I can make this work."

"Make what work?" Noah asked. "What are you doing?"

"What's happening?" Avery asked, their eyes intent on Noah's face. "This is so wild."

Rose placed a finger on the center of the angry man's chest, the tip passing through a button on his white shirt. He waited, his eyes on her. Like Chaupi, he slowly began to solidify, the colors draining into his clothes and hair until he was fully present.

"The numbers were wrong," he said to Rose earnestly. "There was an error in our calculations. It wasn't safe."

She smiled at him before saying, "It's over now. It's time to go."

"Yes." He lifted a hand, turning it as if admiring it, then reached toward Chaupi. Their hands met and clasped. "Thank you," he said. "Thank you."

"You're welcome." Rose glanced around the garden, at the wisps and balls of light, and seemed to brace herself. "This might take a while."

"Are you sure you can do this, Rose?" Dillon looked around the garden, too. Restoring Chaupi was one thing, but there were a lot of ghosts. Did she really have enough energy?

"Sure thing." Rose waved off his concern and put her finger into the nearest wisp. Under her touch, it gradually began to take shape, becoming a young man in a old-fashioned baseball uniform, his expression surprised.

"Time to move on," she said to him, patting his arm. She gestured toward the angry man, who reached out to take the baseball player's hand.

In a quiet voice, Joe began telling Noah what she was doing. Noah relayed the news to Avery as Rose went around the garden, rejuvenating ghosts.

Not every ghost solidified. The balls of light drifted away from her hands, unchanged, and a few of the wisps seemed to turn away from her, too. Most, though, reformed into people. And it must have been obvious what they should do, because one ghost after another joined hands.

The noise level in the garden was going up as wisps reclaimed their voices. Noah was frowning, listening to Joe and the chaos, and telling Avery what he was hearing.

"Are you going to say good-bye to your parents?" Sophia asked Dillon.

"Good idea." Dillon should have thought of it himself, but no matter. He closed his eyes and concentrated. *Moving on. Love, D.* That would do for his mom, his dad, his grandpa.

But Akira needed more. He paused, then texted her, *Moving on. Thanks for everything. Take care of H. Love, D.* There was so much more he wished he could say. She'd changed everything for him. He would be forever grateful. And he hoped he'd see her again, one way or another. But if he tried to express all that... well, he'd be a fader himself before he finished saying everything he wished he could say.

He ought to message some other people, too — his aunts, his uncle. But they'd get the news from his parents or his grandpa.

"You're lucky." Sophia stared at the ground as if she could learn something from the patterns in the paving stones on the patio.

"I guess. Do you want me to..." He let the words trail off, not sure what he was offering. He didn't know Sophia's parents.

She lifted a shoulder. "What, send them a text? It would just confuse them."

"You'll see them again," Dillon tried to reassure her.

She made a scoffing noise. "In forty years, maybe. My mom's not that old."

"It'll feel fast, I bet. Time probably moves differently over there."

"My mom's here, though. It won't feel fast to her." Sophia looked away.

Dillon didn't know what to say. He wished he could help, but he didn't know how. At least she wasn't talking about wanting nothingness anymore.

Nadira was fussing over Misam, smoothing down his hair and dabbing at his cheek as if cleaning imaginary dirt. He stood patiently under her touch, his face wearing a grin a mile wide. His eyes met

Dillon's and Dillon grinned back at him, seeing excitement to match his own.

"Ready?" he asked Misam, reaching out for the little boy's hand.

"Yes!" Misam grabbed Dillon's hand. Behind him, Nadira was shaking her head, her lips shaping words that looked like a prayer.

The line trailed through the garden now, doubling back around the hedges and bougainvillea.

And Rose was finished.

"It's not all of them," she said. "But I think it's enough."

Joe straightened from where he'd been leaning over Noah. He nodded. "The balls, they don't make noise. They're okay. And those other ones..."

"They don't want to come back. I could feel them pushing me away." Rose curled her arms around herself, huddling into them with a shudder as if she were cold.

"But they'll be quiet," Joe said with satisfaction. "Good enough." He dropped his hand on Noah's shoulder. For a second it looked like Joe wanted to say something more, but then he nodded. His expression was resolute as he turned and walked back to the others.

He hesitated as if unsure whose hand to take, but Nadira waggled her fingers at him peremptorily. His lips curved into a smile as he grabbed her hand.

"If we wind up burning in hell, I want to be sure I am close enough to hit you," she told him. "Hard."

He laughed, but his eyes were affectionate.

"Oh, dear. Oh, dear." Mona's feather duster appeared in her hand. She began dusting the plants.

"Stop doing that." Sophia reached for the feather duster. "You don't have to clean anymore. Everything's clean enough."

Mona stared at her, then at the duster in her hand. She drew it in to her chest, clutching it possessively, then looked around at the other ghosts. For a moment, Dillon wasn't sure what she'd do, but she took a deep breath and nodded at Sophia.

The feather duster disappeared and Mona took a place at the end of the line, holding onto the hand of a girl in a pinafore, who was looking around her with wide eyes. She held out her other hand to Sophia.

Sophia paused for a moment, then took Mona's hand. Dillon grabbed Sophia's free hand. Rose reached for Joe's hand. Her fingers slid right through.

"Oh!" She gave a startled laugh and stepped away from him.

The long chain of ghosts rambled around the garden, Chaupi at one end, Joe at the other. Only Rose wasn't a part of it.

"Rose?" Dillon's voice cracked on the word.

"Go on, Chaupi." Rose motioned with both hands, the backs of her fingers toward Chaupi, as if pushing him along. "Time to go."

Chaupi inclined his head to her and said something, adding in English, "Good-bye." Holding tightly to the hand of the ghost next to him, he turned and stepped away, disappearing into nothingness.

"Rose?" Dillon said again.

She turned toward him. He could see the bougainvillea through her body, he realized, as the ghostly conga line began to move. The deep peachy colors of her skirt and sweater had faded to a pastel pink and her skin no longer held even a trace of healthy golden glow.

She'd become a fader.

She'd given too much of her energy to the other ghosts. It had drained her, past the point where she herself was substantial enough to touch another. Had she gone too far? Would she be able to regain the energy she'd lost?

"Are you coming?" he demanded.

"Don't worry about me, Dillon. You go on now."

"But, Rose, you've faded. You'll turn into one of them." He indicated the nearest revivified ghost with his chin, unwilling to let go of his grip on Sophia's and Misam's hands.

"I'll be all right. I'm sure I'll catch up to you someday. We'll meet again." Her smile was encouraging.

The line was moving, one ghost after the next popping out of existence.

"How?" Dillon demanded. "That's not what happens and you know it. Faders just fade away."

Rose lifted a hand, fluttering insouciant fingers. "I'll be fine." She wrinkled her nose at him. "You know I like it here."

"Yes, but..." Dillon looked at the line ahead of him as the baseball player disappeared into emptiness.

Could he go? Without Rose?

Could he really leave her behind?

A woman called, "Carly?" in a soft voice as she stepped away and disappeared.

Rose was wrong. She wouldn't be fine. If the vortex was the destruction of self, fading was the extinguishing of self. It was slow oblivion. But what he could do about it? If he stayed, could he help her?

The girl in the pinafore was gone.

Dillon's hand tightened on Sophia's, his fingers clutching hers as hard as he could. He wanted so badly to go.

He swallowed hard. He had to decide.

And he had to decide now.

27

NOAH

Noah listened to the chaos around him, aware of Avery's gaze on his face. The ghostly voices had gotten louder and louder, until he felt like he was sitting in a crowded bus station, but they were gradually falling silent, one after another.

He should have talked to Joe.

Their brief good-bye had barely even been that.

He should have said something more. He should have told him all the things he didn't know how to say. How sorry he was. How much he missed him. How desperately he wished that it could have been different, that he had been paying more attention that godawful day, that he'd spotted the bump in the sand that must have been there, that somehow he'd shoved Joe out of the way...

The crying girl burst into tears.

"*Sophia, no,*" the kid cried out.

"*What? Sophia!*" Joe's voice, raised in protest.

"*I'm sorry, I'm sorry,*" the crying girl wept. "*I'm sorry.*"

Noah straightened, sitting upright and listening intently.

"*Mashallah.*" The Arabic woman. She didn't sound upset. More like relieved. *"Praise be to God. Thank you, Sophia. Thank you a thousand times."*

"What is it?" Noah asked. "What did she do?"

"I'm not ready. I'm not. My parents. I was so mad, but..." The crying girl spoke between gasping sobs.

"Damn it." Despite the words, Dillon sounded more resigned than angry.

"Sophia let go of Mona's hand," Rose said, next to Noah's ear. *"She didn't follow her through the door. It's gone now, closed after Chaupi and the others."*

Noah was conscious of an odd sensation. Relief? Was that what he was feeling? It wasn't that he didn't want his voices gone. The thought of life without them, of waking up to silence every day, of never needing to pretend he couldn't hear them again, was wonderful. It would be a dream come true.

But maybe he and Sophia had something in common, because he didn't think he was ready either.

"Most of them are gone," Joe said. *"I'm sorry, man. I know you'd like to be rid of us."*

"Hey, that's not — I'm not — I don't —" The words tangled on Noah's tongue. He wanted to tell Joe how he really felt, but he wasn't even sure how that was.

"The suspense is killing me." Avery leaned forward, uncrossing their legs. "What's going on?"

Noah welcomed the interruption. "Some of the ghosts are gone. But not all of them."

"I, for one, am glad," Nadira said. *"If Misam and I must go through some random doorway into the next world, it should be a Muslim door."*

"Oh, because some random Muslim door would be so much better? I've heard about your Hell. It doesn't sound pretty," Joe said.

"What Hell is pretty? Eternal torment isn't supposed to be fun."

"Don't start, Mama, Joe," the kid said. *"Bad enough that we are still stuck without making us listen to you argue. All you do is argue.*

254

Fight, fight, fight. All day long. Hell is an eternity spent listening to the two of you."

"*Misam!*" Nadira sounded shocked.

"*Don't be mean to your mother,*" Joe said sternly.

Noah gave a rueful shake of his head, resisting the temptation to laugh. The kid sounded pissed. But his amusement faded quickly when the kid burst into tears.

"*I don't want to be a ghost anymore. I wanted to go.*" The little boy wept.

"*I'm s-s-sorry.*" The crying girl's words were muffled, as if she cried alongside him. "*I'm sorry.*"

"*We shall go, my darling boy, we shall,*" his mother comforted him.

"*We'll find another doorway,*" Dillon said. "*A better one.*"

"*Not yet.*" The crying girl spoke through her sobs. "*We need to go talk to my parents first. I need to go talk to them.*"

Uh-oh. Noah wasn't sure he liked the sound of that.

It wasn't that Noah didn't want to be helpful. He was willing to do what he could for his voices. But telling some bereaved parents that he could hear their dead teenage daughter's voice sounded... uncomfortable. Really uncomfortable.

"*Um, Sophia, it might not be that easy. They might not react the way you think they will,*" Dillon said.

The crying girl took a deep shaky breath and said, sounding determined, "*They never listened to me while I was alive. But I'm going to make them listen to me now.*"

How exactly was she going to do that when Noah was the only one who could hear her?

"*Maybe you could send them a letter?*" Dillon suggested. "*You could get Noah to write it for you.*"

Okay, that sounded like a horrible idea. Those poor people. Getting letters from their dead kid? No way. Noah could imagine how his mom would feel in like circumstances.

Nope, never going to happen.

"Your parents aren't going to believe Noah if he writes to them," Joe said. *"They'll just think he's crazy. Anyone would."*

Exactly. Noah would have high-fived Joe if he could.

"I want to talk to them," Sophia said. *"See them. A letter's not good enough. I need to say good-bye."*

Avery's eyes were intent on Noah's face. "What is it?"

Before Noah could explain, the door to the house burst open, the screen flying so fast that it banged into the wall. Grace emerged, followed by Lucas and Sylvie. Her color was heightened, as if she'd been moving fast, but her eyes met Noah's and she came to an abrupt stop a few feet into the backyard.

She planted her hands on her hips. "Don't do anything drastic. Isn't that what I said?"

Her brother moved around her. "Dillon?"

"Uh-oh," Rose said. *"I think your family might be a little upset about this."*

"I sent them texts," Dillon protested.

"Is he gone?" Sylvie asked Noah directly. She didn't look as upset as Grace, but she was unsmiling.

Noah shook his head.

"Not yet?" Lucas stepped forward. "Can we, we'd like to, would it be okay if..." He raked a hand through his hair and muttered, "I wish Akira were here. We should have called her days ago."

"She is on her honeymoon," Grace snapped. "We are not interrupting her. We are not worrying her." Her eyes narrowed. "Did you text her, Dillon?" She directed the words to the air, glancing around the patio as if she might spot him somewhere among the shadowed greenery lit by strings of fairy lights.

"Yes?" Dillon's answer was tentative.

Grace glared at Noah. "Well?"

"He did, yeah," Noah answered for Dillon.

She threw up her hands. "Unbelievable. So damn selfish." She clenched her hands into fists and pressed her lips together. For a moment, she trembled on the verge of an explosion, but then she turned on her heel and walked out the same way she'd come in.

"Whoa." Sylvie's tone was hushed. She put a hand on Lucas's arm and they exchanged glances. She shook her head slightly. The two of them seemed to be communicating without words.

Noah stood. He wanted to follow Grace. She was pissed, he could see, but he could reassure her and let her know what had happened. And that Dillon wouldn't be leaving, at least not this evening.

Avery jumped to their feet, too. "Isn't this exciting? Can I offer you a drink? Some wine, beer?"

"*You have upset your aunt,*" Nadira said.

"*Didn't you say she didn't get angry much?*" Joe sounded amused.

"*I didn't mean to be selfish. I wasn't — I'm a ghost! I'm supposed to move on if I can! Akira would understand. I mean, I think she would. Rose?*"

"*Akira knows ghosts disappear. She'd be glad to know you hadn't been caught in a vortex again. But I bet she would have liked to say good-bye in person. And, well...*" Rose let her words trail off.

Sophia still hadn't stopped crying, but with a sniff and a gulp, she said, "*Just say it. She's on her honeymoon. You're not supposed to make people sad on their honeymoons.*"

"*I didn't mean... oh, damn.*"

Sylvie turned to Avery. "A drink would be great. Some sparkling water for me, if you have it? And Lucas will take a beer. And then we'd like to talk to Dillon for a couple minutes. I assume you know what's going on, since you don't seem confused."

"Oh, yes, it's been quite something." Avery picked up the tray of empty glasses, then paused as if considering the plate with its remnants of cheese and crackers.

"Let me help you with that." Sylvie took the plate and a few stray napkins and followed Avery into the house.

Lucas stepped closer to Noah. "You said Dillon's not leaving tonight?"

Noah hadn't said that. He'd thought it.

Lucas grimaced. "Sorry. I usually try to be more discreet."

"How does that work?" Noah asked. "You hear everything people think? Doesn't that get noisy?"

Lucas dipped his head, accepting the change of subject. "It can, yeah. Mostly it's just ambient sound, though, unless I'm focused on someone. Crowds are a lot louder to me than they are to most people, but it's still just crowd noise. I tune it out."

Like I do, Noah thought. With my voices.

"Yeah, probably."

Okay, that was just weird.

Lucas lifted his shoulders in a shrug, smile wry. "Yeah. Sorry. About Dillon..."

"Yeah," Noah said. "Things went sorta wrong, I guess. I'm not sure how much you know, but one of the ghosts had a gate to another dimension. I'm not voting on whether it's heaven or hell or someplace entirely different. Some of the ghosts I've been dragging around used it, but at least a few missed the boat. I'm not entirely sure who's still here, but I've heard Dillon's voice, so I know he is."

Lucas nodded. "No rush, then, I guess." He glanced around the patio the same way Grace had a few moments earlier.

Noah angled a thumb in the direction he'd last heard Dillon's voice. Not that it really mattered, he supposed — neither of them could see Dillon — but he understood the desire to talk toward the right person.

Lucas acknowledged the gesture with a minuscule nod and turned in the indicated direction. But he didn't speak right away. Maybe he was gathering his thoughts, maybe he just didn't know what he wanted to say.

Or maybe he was uncomfortably aware of the audience. Noah was definitely uncomfortably aware of being an audience. What did you say to the kid you'd lost?

For that matter, what did you say to the kid you'd killed? The friend you'd failed? He had some conversations of his own that he wanted to have, but he definitely didn't want company for them. Bad enough that the other ghosts might be there, unseen listeners to every word he wanted to share.

Lucas shot him a glance.

And worse, of course, to have someone listening to every thought that you didn't want to share.

Sha-la-la-la, Noah thought.

Lucas chuckled.

"*I hope he's not mad at me,*" Dillon said.

"*Would you like some privacy, Dillon?*" Nadira asked. "*Should we walk away?*"

"*Yeah, we could go in the house,*" Joe added.

Noah cleared his throat. "I can probably make it into the house without dragging Dillon along, if you'd like to be alone."

"It's okay." Lucas sent a quick flash of a smile in his direction. "We said the important stuff a few months ago, I think."

Sylvie rejoined them. She slipped her hand into Lucas's and said briskly, "Ya gotta do what ya gotta do, Dillon. If you're ready to move on... well, you know that's what I've wanted for you. This whole being a ghost business just doesn't seem healthy to me. But—" She glanced at Lucas, her smile loving, maybe a little rueful. "Your dad asked me to marry him and I said yes."

"*Your parents aren't married?*" Nadira sounded shocked.

"*Oh, another wedding, yay! You'll have to dance with me this time, Dillon,*" Rose said.

"*If we're still here, I'll dance with you,*" Joe offered. "*Been a long time since I've been to a good party.*"

"*We'll have such fun!*" Rose clapped her hands.

"We haven't gotten into the details yet," Sylvie said, "so we don't know where or when. We were waiting..."

"Until we found you again," Lucas finished for her. "We've been..."

He and Sylvie exchanged looks and Sylvie continued, "...concerned."

259

Nadira snorted. "*I don't think that was the word they were looking for.*"

"*I think your mama means scared,*" Misam said.

Sylvie's phone started ringing. She pulled it out, sharing the screen with Lucas, and nodding in acknowledgement. "Thanks. We wanted you to be the first to know." Her eyes were bright. There was a sheen to them that might have been tears, but her voice was steady as she said, "It's okay if you can't make it to the wedding. We want what's best for you and if moving on is the right thing for you, you do it."

2 8

GRACE

RAGE BOILED IN GRACE'S THROAT, HOT TEARS BURNING BEHIND her eyes.

She was over-reacting she knew, but the knowledge only made her anger stronger.

Damn Dillon. How selfish could he be?

Her feet had propelled her down the hallway, out the front door, past the gate. She was on the sidewalk in a heartbeat, headed anywhere. Her stomach churned. Her face felt stiff, the skin around her eyes tight. Without conscious thought, her legs sent her along Millard Street, past the shops and houses, to the little park at the end of town.

In the deepening twilight, Mrs. Swanson was scattering birdseed by the pond, an assortment of ducks gathered before her. Automatically, Grace catalogued them. Four Muscovy, with their mottled black and white feathers and red backs. Three mallards, one male with his iridescent green head and two subdued brown females. A couple of smaller wood ducks, both male with crested heads and brightly patterned feathers, hung back, away from the bigger birds.

Grace took a deep breath. The brush of the cool air on her hot cheeks was bringing her back to herself.

Dillon was an idiot. But he'd been fifteen years old when he died. It was a selfish age.

She should really tell Mrs. Swanson not to feed the birds. The Muscovys were a nuisance species, big, aggressive, crowding out the native birds.

Instead she came to a silent stop by the water's edge.

Mrs Swanson glanced in her direction. Her hand stilled in the bag of seed. "Well. That's not right."

The ducks began squawking in protest at the pause in their food service, the Muscovys jostling one another, but the old woman twisted the top of the bag closed, saying sternly, "None of that. You've had enough for today."

Turning, she put a hand on Grace's lower arm. "Come along, dear."

The tiny woman's head didn't even reach Grace's shoulder, but Grace let Mrs. Swanson lead her back up the slope to the street and down the sidewalk.

"You've had a shock, I expect. Some tea will help. Chamomile, I think, or maybe skullcap. It's very calming. Eases the soul." Mrs. Swanson paused on the sidewalk outside her front porch. The sign in the window saying 'Auras Read Here' was as discreet as pink neon could be.

She studied Grace. "That red's fading a bit. Not so angry? But that muddy blue, so close to the heart. That's sorrow. Yes, definitely skullcap." She patted Grace's arm. "You wait here, dear, I'll be right back with a nice herbal mix for you." She disappeared into her house.

Grace sat down on the porch steps. Lights were starting to come on as full night settled over the town and the breeze was turning chill.

If Dillon wanted to move on, that was surely his business. His choice.

She might not be ready, but was she ever going to be ready? She blinked back the tears that wanted to escape.

She wished she could talk to her mom. Just for half an hour. To hear her mom's voice, to let herself be folded into her mother's hug. She could imagine the sharp, searching look her mother would give her, followed by the, "Chin up, darlin'. That's my girl," words of approval.

But she'd managed to let her mother go. The loss hurt, sometimes with a sharp burst of pain, sometimes with a deep ache, but she'd learned to live with it.

Dillon, though...

The screen door banged open and Mrs. Swanson rejoined her on the porch, a plastic baggie filled with dry leaves in her hand. "Here you go." The old woman thrust the baggie in her direction as Grace stood. "One tablespoon or thereabouts, steeped in water that's almost boiling for three minutes. You'll find it very relaxing — skullcap makes a peaceful blend. But add sweetener because it tastes like cow manure."

Grace's lips twitched into a smile as she took the baggie. "Thanks, Mrs. Swanson."

"You're welcome." The old woman cocked her head to one side, her eyes serious as she regarded Grace. "I hope it's nothing too worrisome? You and your family, you've had some exciting times lately. Your sister's taken on a big job. Five children? Bad enough when they come one at a time. I remember thinking when I had my third I'd never get a wink of sleep again. 'Course, she's got it easier since they're all housebroke, so to speak. But you got a lot on your shoulders, too, filling your mama's shoes at that company and all."

"The company's doing fine."

Mrs. Swanson snorted. "I'm sure it is. Don't mean it's easy."

Down the street, Noah emerged from the gate of the bed-and-breakfast. He looked in both directions, searching, but not spotting Grace tucked away on Mrs. Swanson's porch. Was he looking for her? She moved, stepping onto the lowest of the porch steps into his line of view. He saw her and started heading their way.

263

Mrs. Swanson followed her gaze. "Oh, honey, no." She shook her head. "No, no, no."

"What is it?"

Every line on Mrs. Swanson's wrinkled face deepened with her scowl. "Good girls, they always like the bad boys. But that boy's aura is a mess. Did he upset you?"

"It wasn't his fault. I'm not upset at him."

"He's got secrets. Hard secrets, the kind with weight."

Grace knew that already, but she did wonder how Mrs. Swanson could tell that from his aura. What color were secrets? "I know his secrets. Some of them, at least."

"I'm not blind, you know." Mrs. Swanson leaned over her porch railing, craning to look at Noah. He was at the corner of the street, waiting patiently while a car turned in front of him. "That gray is... oh. Huh."

"What huh?"

"The gray's gone silvery." Mrs. Swanson peered at Noah. "With some of that sparkle your new sister-in-law's got. Not so much of it, not like her, but the silver glimmers. That's strange."

Grace's hand tightened on the baggie, the leaves crinkling under her fingers. "Strange good? Or strange bad?"

"Not sure I can say. It's right pretty. That's good, I suppose." Mrs. Swanson regarded Noah with a puzzled look as he walked toward them. "I saw him the other day. Told him to burn some sage. For the cleansing, you know. Never seen sage do so much good so quick."

Noah had almost reached them. Mrs. Swanson, both hands grasping the porch railing, appraised him before shaking her head and saying, "You must have found some high-powered sage, young man."

He looked startled and then his face relaxed into a wry smile. "Something like that. Good evening, ma'am."

"Indeed it is." Mrs. Swanson considered him for a moment before giving him a brisk nod. "And I'll let you two get on with enjoying it. You take good care of her, you hear?"

As Mrs. Swanson retreated into her house, Noah shot a glance at the baggie in Grace's hand. "You rushed right off to your dealer?"

"Ha." Grace couldn't help smiling at him. She held the baggie up. "Herbal tea. Made with something that sounds poisonous but apparently will be good for my shattered nerves." She tried to say the words lightly, as if she wasn't serious, but a trace of her real feelings leaked through.

"I'm sorry. I guess I should have stopped them."

"Not at all. It must be a great relief to you."

"You'd think so, wouldn't you?"

The extra few inches provided by the porch step had them almost eye-to-eye. Grace searched his, trying to understand the doubt she heard in his voice. "Not so much?"

"Barely had time to get used to the idea of ghosts before they were headed off." He smiled, but his eyes stayed serious. "But you left before I had a chance to say — the door closed and not all of them made it through. Dillon's still here."

"Oh." Grace wasn't going to lie and say she was sorry. She wasn't. "Is he — are they disappointed?"

His smile turned real. "Mixed opinions. Some are, some aren't."

"Dillon?"

"A little of both, I'd say. I don't mean to spoil the surprise but your brother's getting married."

"Another wedding!" Grace's eyes widened before she laughed. "I guess that's no surprise. Maybe it's contagious."

"Like a virus?"

"The bubonic plague. Get bit by a flea and the next thing you know..." Grace snapped her fingers. "It's all white lace and champagne."

"Don't forget the dancing. Rose and Joe are already planning their takeover of the dance floor."

Grace felt a rush of pleasure. "So you think you'll be here? They'll be here?"

"I need to talk to them, I guess. The ghosts, I mean. First, though..." He thrust a slip of paper in her direction.

Grace took it, glancing at it automatically, then holding it up to see it better in the dim light. A name, an address. "What's this?"

"Avery said you'd help. We promised Chaupi, the ghost with the door, that we'd find his girlfriend and tell her what happened to him. That's where she was thirty years ago."

"Thirty years?" Grace arched her brows.

"Avery managed to convince him that you could do it. That's why he was willing to leave."

Grace frowned at the paper. Some basic legwork might find her and if not, she could put Zane on the job. She might have to send him to Peru, but they'd manage. Not until after the honeymoon, though.

"All right." She folded the paper and slipped it into her pocket. "I'll take care of it."

"Just like that?"

"I'll put the investigator who's currently watching your apartment on it. She'll probably be thrilled to move on to a more interesting job."

"You have someone watching my apartment?"

She shrugged. "My nephew's with you. We wanted to find him. That meant finding you." She started walking back toward the bed-and-breakfast.

Noah fell into step beside her. "He says he's sorry, by the way."

Grace didn't look at him. "It's okay."

It wasn't really okay.

But her feelings were such a complex mishmash of anger and grief and regret and relief that she didn't want to try to untangle them. Not right now, and not with Noah. He had his own ghosts to worry about.

And his own guilt.

"You said some of them are gone," she said. "Who's still with you?"

"Does it matter?"

"Maybe."

She would have said more, but a jogger came up behind them, passing them with a quick, "On your left. Hi, Grace."

"Hi..." Grace scrambled for a name, then let it go. He was probably an employee, but he'd gone by too quickly for her to place him. Another employee, one of the biochemists, was walking toward them, pushing a stroller.

Maybe a public street wasn't the right place for this conversation.

"Evening, Grace," the scientist said as he neared them.

"Hey, Leo. How's the baby doing?" Grace answered.

The baby answered with a fretful cry.

"They call it the witching hour," the scientist answered with a yawn. The cry turned into a wail and he shook his head, hurrying past, saying, "Gotta keep moving."

"Good luck," Grace called after him.

"Do you know everyone in this town?"

"Hmm. Tourists wander through. Sometimes new people come to town. But pretty much, yeah."

They'd reached the gate to the bed-and-breakfast, so Grace paused.

"Does it feel like living in a fish bowl?"

She chuckled. "I suppose I'm used to it."

"Avery knew about the ghosts before I said anything."

"Ah." She grimaced, trying to read his expression in the twilight. "Is that a problem? It's hard to keep secrets in a town of psychics."

He shrugged. "Just strange, I guess."

He didn't make any move to open the gate, so Grace stood with him on the sidewalk, searching his face. In the fading light, his eyes looked darker, a deeper brown, more chocolate than caramel.

"Your eyes change color." As soon as she said the words, she felt heat rushing into her cheeks. What a stupid thing to say. But she wasn't thinking, she was just looking at him.

Seeing him.

"Yours don't." He lifted a hand as if he'd touch her cheek. "Prettiest Army green I've ever seen."

Grace's skin felt awake, aware of him in a way she'd never felt before, as if her cells were a compass and he magnetic north. She wanted him to touch her. She wanted to feel his fingers on her skin, turn her face into his hand, let her lips brush against his warm palm.

But instead of touching her, he took a step back.

2 9

DILLON

"It's all right," Dillon said gloomily. "Go ahead, kiss her, I don't mind."

"Shut up, man," Joe said. "He's not going to kiss her when he knows we're all standing around watching them."

"We'll turn our backs," Nadira offered, sounding amused.

"It's so romantic." Rose sighed with satisfaction. The streetlight behind her shone through her body. Dillon could see the hedges and fence behind her almost more clearly than he could see her.

He should never have asked her to help the other ghosts. She'd saved them but at what cost?

"They're such a pretty couple." Rose tilted her head to one side, admiring them.

At least she was still talking. Maybe she wouldn't fade out entirely.

"He's a guy, he's not pretty," Joe objected. "Good-looking. He's good-looking."

"Oh, come on," Sophia scoffed. "He is so pretty. He's like the definition of pretty."

"You never saw him in the desert," Misam said. He'd stopped

crying, but he wasn't yet back to his usual cheerful self. "Dirty and sunburned and with those lines on his face from the goggles they wore. He wasn't so pretty then."

"I don't know." Nadira considered Noah, tilting her head to one side, and scrutinizing his features. "Even when he was dirty, he had that—"

"Guys, really?" Noah took another step away from Grace, letting his hand drop and stuffing it into his back pocket as if he regretted its initiative. "Sorry," he said to her. "We're…"

"Not alone, right," she finished for him. "And you were worried about my fish bowl."

She sounded more amused than upset, but to Dillon it felt like one more mark against him on an ever-growing list.

"Tell her I'm sorry," he said impulsively. "Tell her… ah, damn it." He'd already asked Noah to tell her that he was sorry and she'd brushed it off. But he'd seen in the way she turned away from Noah that it wasn't okay, that she was still mad. "Never mind."

"We'll leave," Joe said. "We'll go inside. Or maybe you should go inside. We can stay outside."

"What are we going to do out here?" Sophia complained. "We should go inside. We can watch television in there, and he can stay outside."

"Hey, wait." Dillon looked around at the other ghosts. They'd left his parents and Avery in the B&B's backyard, talking about weddings, but Noah had excused himself to come find Grace, saying he wanted to ask her about searching for Chaupi's loved ones. The ghosts had automatically traipsed along after him.

But where were the glowies? The white balls of light weren't with them and neither were the few faded wisps that had refused to form into people again. They must have remained in the garden.

"The other ghosts didn't come with us," Dillon said.

"Look at that. The innkeeper might have a haunted garden, after all." Joe sounded delighted.

"Maybe we're free," Misam said. "Free!" He burst into a run, charging full tilt at the hedges that surrounded the yard. He disappeared into them and was gone, for a second, two, three...

Dillon only made it to six before Misam was gliding back to them, his lower lip stuck out in glum disappointment.

"No luck?" Joe said.

Misam shook his head and let his glide take him to his mother's side. She hoisted him up and let him wrap his arms around her neck. He melted into her, mumbling, "Not free," before burying his face in her shoulder.

Nadira rubbed Misam's back. Her gaze met Joe's.

"We'll find a door," Joe said to her. "A good door, one you're happy with."

"Maybe you and Sophia should try, Dillon," Rose said. "With so many fewer ghosts, the attraction might be easier to fight."

"I'll try," Sophia said, "But I'm not leaving until Noah helps me. And I will be mean about it." She stomped off, down the street and away from the house.

"I'm not sure being mean to Noah is the best way to get him to help," Dillon said, following her.

Sophia sniffled. "I need him."

"What do you want to tell your parents?" Dillon asked. He thought back to that first awkward conversation with his dad. Akira had helped, but it had been the worst experience of his life and afterlife.

Worse than when his grandma had found his body. He'd still been so confused then. Worse than when Grace had driven his car, her sobs so hard he worried she'd crash it. Worse than watching his grandpa turn old overnight.

Sitting with Akira and his dad, trying to tell his dad that it wasn't his fault...

That was the worst thing about being dead. Everyone you left behind blamed themselves.

Sophia hadn't answered his question. They'd made it to the corner and were walking toward the park at the end of the street.

"I was good in school," she finally said. "I always got straight As. And I was good at violin. And I was… I was good. My parents, they expected me to be good and I always was. I was good at killing myself, too. I guess I just want to tell them I'm sorry I was so good at that."

"It's not going to make them less sad."

"It might."

"It won't."

"They think I'm gone," she said. "Gone forever. Not gone for a while, not someday going to meet again, but kablooey. Zapped. Nothingness."

"You nearly were," he told her.

"But I'm not," she said. "And I think they'll feel better if they know that."

Dillon sighed. He wasn't sure she was right, but she might be. And he understood how she felt. For the first few years after his death, he'd wanted so badly to talk to any of his relatives. Well, not to talk to them — he'd done that every time one of them used his car — but to be heard. To have them listen. To know that they understood how much he regretted what he'd done.

"Have you seen them since?"

"They came and saw the place. Both of them. And then my dad came back once." Sophia kicked at a stone on the sidewalk. "He cried. I never saw him cry before. But my mom never came back."

"It probably wasn't where she wanted to think of you," Dillon suggested.

"Yeah, probably not." She flashed him a quick, unexpected smile. "It was a nice tree, but I didn't mind so much when Noah and all of them walked by."

Dillon laughed — and then he paused, looking at the pond. They'd reached the park. "Hey. We kept walking."

Sophia spun in a slow circle. "We're free. We can go anywhere."

"Yeah." Dillon waited.

Sophia's chin firmed. "But we should go back. I need Noah's help."

He nodded, and they turned back.

At the B&B, Noah and Grace had returned to the patio. They were seated with his mom and dad and Avery, the other ghosts scattered around them.

"If Dillon and Sophia aren't caught anymore, these other ones probably aren't either. They might stay here when you go," Rose was saying. "Avery can have a haunted inn."

"Maybe we should leave then," Noah replied, frowning. "Before something happens and they get caught again."

Grace sat up straighter in her chair, and opened her mouth as if she wanted to say something, then shut it.

"Something? Avoid strippers and cockroaches and we should be fine." Nadira was still holding Misam, but he lifted his head and smiled as Joe snorted with laughter.

"When you go, can you take me home?" Sophia asked.

"You're back?" Noah said with surprise, glancing in their direction.

"I need you to talk to my parents for me." Sophia sat down on the table across from Noah, staring at his face as if she could will him into helping her.

"Talk to your parents?" Noah shook his head. He sounded regretful but firm as he added, "No."

"But you have to," Sophia insisted. "I need to talk to them. I need to let them know that I'm okay."

"You're dead. That's not going to seem okay to them, and talking to me is not going to change that."

"They think I'm gone forever, like never-coming-back gone."

"And they'll never believe me when I tell you you're not. What am I going to do, knock on their door and say, 'Hi, you've never met me, but your dead daughter is talking to me?'" Come on, that door is going to get slammed so fast, I'll be lucky if it doesn't knock me out."

"I'll help you," Sophia said. "I'll tell you things that only I know."

"You should talk to Akira." Grace leaned back in her seat.

"Her again," Noah muttered.

"She is the subject matter expert," Grace said. "She's knocked on those doors before."

"Please?" Sophia said, both plaintive and determined. Dillon could see that she wasn't going to give up. But she didn't threaten Noah or start to cry, she just waited.

"It would be a kindness." Nadira was looking at the top of Misam's head, not Noah, her voice soft. "I'm sure Sophia's parents would be grateful."

"Only if they believe me," Noah said. He looked up at the sky as if hoping to find an answer written there, then exhaled audibly. "All right, I'll talk to your parents, Sophia. But first, we'll stick around and meet Akira. I'm gonna need her help."

30

NOAH

Noah wished he'd kissed Grace.

It was probably good that he hadn't, of course. The invisible audience was off-putting enough, but the older brother who could read minds — and was currently looking pained — was equally discomfiting.

On the other hand, she was looking severe, frown lines between her brows, lips turned down, and he didn't want to see her that way. He wanted her smile, the tilt of her chin as she laughed, the light in her eyes.

But the moment was long gone.

And during the next few weeks, it didn't come again. Noah stayed in Tassamara. He showed up to work at General Directions on Monday morning, and spent his time getting to know the place and its people.

It was not quite as weird as he'd imagined it to be. The experiment he'd seen on his first visit was, in fact, psycho-electrostatic levitation, triggered by an employee with telekinetic abilities. Although the explanation sounded like "blah-blah-blah something, blah-blah-blah psychic," to Noah, he got the general idea — magic. But most of the other offices and labs seemed much more ordinary: people sat at computers, in office chairs, and if what they were doing was magical, it sure looked like business as usual from the outside.

The job was not exactly exciting. Sometimes he watched the monitors, sometimes he paced the halls, sometimes he sat at the guardhouse checking people's IDs when they entered the grounds. It was not thrilling. But the paycheck was nice, and he felt like maybe he was over the adrenaline stage of life, anyway. It was good to know that no one was going to shoot at him and that a moment of distraction from a hallucinated voice wouldn't risk the health of a friend. Or even a co-worker. Hell, even an enemy.

He liked having a job where death wasn't on the table.

He saw Grace almost every day.

It wasn't nearly often enough.

Their conversations at General Directions were always brief and usually interrupted. Sometimes she seemed like she wanted to talk to him more seriously, but someone always needed her attention, her signature, or her presence at a meeting. Or her phone would ring.

On the weekends, she came to movie night at the bed-and-breakfast and cheerfully threw popcorn at the large screen television with the rest of them, but there was always a crowd, people overflowing the room, sitting on the floor. No chance for any private moments.

Noah told himself that was okay. The job was temporary and he wasn't staying. He was only waiting for Akira to get back from her honeymoon, and then he'd be moving on, ghosts or no ghosts.

On the Saturday almost three weeks after his arrival, Noah was trimming the hedges in the garden of the bed-and-breakfast. He'd bartered some weekend work on the yard in exchange for a reduced rate on his room, but he should have guessed from Avery's smirk that there was a reason the innkeeper had avoided trimming the overgrown shrubbery.

He raised an arm and wiped sweat from his forehead. Damn, but it was hot. Avery had warned him that the weather was going to be unseasonably warm, but it had to be in the mid-80s, maybe hotter. In

March. He didn't want to know what working outside in August would be like.

His injudicious move was enough to make the bougainvillea branch he'd been holding twist in his other hand. He swore again, dropping it as its harsh thorns drew another line of blood along his bare skin.

"*I think the plant is winning,*" Rose said. The other ghosts were watching Peruvian soccer — or, as Avery insisted it be called, football — inside, but Rose had said she'd rather watch plants grow than grown men chase a ball around, and was keeping him company outside.

"If I didn't know better, I'd swear it was intelligent," Noah muttered. "And out to get me."

"*You started it. You're the one chopping its branches off.*"

Noah glowered at the plant. "It's not intelligent, is it? Self-aware? Attacking me on purpose?" Plants didn't have brains. It couldn't be conscious. But he'd promised himself not to be surprised by anything this town threw at him. Maybe they had their own breed of special evil plants?

Rose bubbled with laughter. "*No, of course not. It's just a plant.*"

Noah eyed the bougainvillea branch before lopping it off just above one of the thorns. Trimming the plant was bad enough but dragging the big branches of thorny viciousness to the curb for yard waste pickup had taught him more than he wanted to know about safely handling it.

"You never know around here." He took a step back and admired his work, then grimaced as sweat stung his fresh scratch, burning with an intensity out of proportion to the trivial injury.

"*Hmm, I can use that,*" Rose said thoughtfully.

A cool breeze danced across his skin. Surprised, Noah glanced at the bougainvillea and then farther away, into the nearby trees. The air was still, the leaves motionless. Where had that breeze come from?

"Nice, huh?" Rose sounded satisfied. "*Built-in AC. Being haunted's not all bad, right?*"

Noah chuckled, realizing what she'd done. "I thought you had to get upset to make it cold. Mad or miserable or something."

"*Blood works, too.*"

Noah's mouth twisted. "Ew. Really?"

"*Yes. So don't bleed around any hostile ghosts.*"

"What would happen?" Noah tossed a branch into the pile by his feet.

"*Oh, you could wind up with a poltergeist. Or a ghost might try to possess you.*"

"Possess me?" Noah lowered the hedge shears. "That sounds uncool."

"*Don't worry. We won't let anyone do that.*"

"Glad to hear it." Noah set the hedge shears on the ground next to the plant and retreated to the patio. He picked up the bottle of water he'd left on the low table and took a swig.

"*I hope it didn't happen to Akira while she was on her honeymoon,*" Rose said.

"We'll find out soon." Noah picked up his cell phone and glanced at the time. Akira and Zane were supposed to be arriving in Tassamara today, but they were traveling by private plane, so their timing was indefinite.

He was looking forward to meeting the mysterious Akira. It was impossible for him not to believe in the ghosts now. Between texts, Avery's ability to speak a language that was manifestly not Chinese, and the Latimers' easy acceptance of Dillon, he knew he couldn't be hallucinating. But the tiny part of him that wondered about transmitters and neural networks and conspiracies wanted to watch Akira respond to the voices he heard, to know for sure that his voices weren't just his.

"Three weeks is a long honeymoon."

"*It does feel like they've been gone for a while. The sweet olive is already blooming.*"

"The sweet olive?"

"The tree with the shiny green leaves and little white flowers."

"The one that smells like summer?" Noah knew exactly which tree Rose meant. He hadn't seen it before — it definitely didn't grow around his home in Maine — but he'd stopped dead in his tracks trying to identify the fragrance the first time he walked past the one down the street.

Rose sounded wistful when she answered, *"It's been a long time since I could smell it. My mama used to say it smelled like apricots. But when it's flowering, it means winter's either over or about to begin."*

Noah wiped sweat from the back of his neck, feeling the way his t-shirt clung to him. Winter definitely felt over to him.

"It was going to be their last chance to have a vacation for a good long time, though. The baby's due at the end of May, you know."

"And she went to Belize?" He'd known Akira was pregnant but he hadn't realized she was so far along. "Isn't that dangerous?"

"Her doctor said she'd be fine. Although it probably was Natalya telling her that she'd be fine that convinced them to go."

"I thought the doctor never told people about the future?"

Before Rose could answer him, the door to the house opened and Grace walked out onto the patio. She was squinting against the late afternoon sunshine, but when she saw Noah, her eyes widened.

Noah felt a rush of awareness. He was hot and dirty, his skin prickling with sun and sweat, while she looked cool and crisp, her casual clothes still worn with her ineffable air of elegance. But when she bit her lower lip, his mouth went dry.

The air between them felt charged with electricity. Without taking his eyes off her, he lifted his water bottle to his mouth and drank again.

She sounded breathless when she said, "Zane just called."

"Yeah?" He set the water bottle down.

"Akira wants to meet you here, in the garden."

"Here?" Dillon protested immediately. He must have followed Grace outside. *"It's the most haunted place in Tassamara now!"*

"Here?" Noah repeated after him. "Is she sure that's a good idea? Aren't there supposed to be a bunch of old ghosts floating around still?"

Grace lifted a shoulder. "If she senses that the energy is dangerous, she won't come in. But she said she'd rather get it over with than have to worry about whether she was going to be the starring attraction at Avery's next scary movie night."

"All right." Noah nodded. "Do I have time to clean up?"

Her lips twitched with amusement, and he could see mischief in her eyes, but she said, "If you're in the middle of something, she won't want to interrupt. Feel free to continue."

Noah glanced at the pile of bougainvillea branches and the hedge clippers. He'd made good progress but the job wasn't done. He'd like to finish, rather than starting over later, so he shrugged.

"I did want to talk to you, though," she continued.

"About?"

"Your job, General Directions, the future."

The future. Now there was something Noah had been carefully avoiding thinking about.

"You firing me?" he asked, keeping the words light. It might be better if she did. There couldn't be anything here for him, not long-term. He didn't know what he wanted, but it wasn't to watch a wall of monitors all day long. Not unless she was on every screen, anyway.

In their two weeks of fleeting meetings, casual hellos, and interrupted conversations, his sense of connection with her had only deepened. He wanted her. He liked her, too. And he wasn't blind: he knew the feeling was mutual. But she was a millionaire CEO and he was a messed-up, haunted vet. What future could there possibly be for the two of them?

"Not at all." Her eyebrows arched. "I was thinking that with Zane back, you might like to start working for Special Affairs."

"Special Affairs?" He knew the people she was talking about, of course. They were the magic ones. There weren't a lot of them — maybe ten or twelve that he could recognize — but most of them seemed to be out of the office more often than they were in.

"I think you could be an asset to the team. Lucas agrees."

"How so?"

"Oh, the possibilities are unprecedented." She spread her hands, then brought them back together again. "Imagine how useful ghosts could be."

"*Useful, huh? Wonder what she has in mind?*" Joe asked.

"Picture, say, a hostage situation. You could have eyes inside with absolutely no risk of discovery," Grace said enthusiastically.

"*That sounds fun. I mean, not fun exactly. Not for the hostages, anyway. But it could be cool,*" Sophia said.

"*I want to help the hostages! Like in the movies!*" The sound of Misam's voice moved as if he were jumping around the garden in excitement.

Noah ignored them. "They're hoping to move on. Soon, I think."

Grace shrugged. "Until they do..."

"Wandering around to crime scenes could be dangerous for them if there are other ghosts there. Maybe one of those vortexes?" Noah did not want his ghosts destroyed. A nice door, a friendly new plane of existence, that sounded great to him.

He still hadn't talked to them, not the way he wanted to, but he would. Soon. And then they could move on. But not to a place that involved the eternal destruction of self.

Grace grimaced. "Okay. Good point. But — what's wrong?"

He followed her gaze and realized that he was pressing the scratch on his arm with his other hand. It burned, out of proportion to the depth of the minor injury. "It's nothing," he said, letting his hand drop as if he'd been caught with it in the till. He was not going to lose all guy credibility by making a big deal over a trivial injury.

"Bougainvillea," Grace said, not asking a question. "Avery should have told you to wear gloves, long sleeves, a hat, maybe a veil, some mosquito netting. That stuff is nasty. And there's a toxin on the thorns, as if long spikes weren't sufficient self-defense."

"Toxin?" He put his hand back over the scratch.

"Not fatal. Just annoying. But it's an evil plant."

"Ha." Noah chuckled. He'd thought so, too.

"I'll be right back." Grace turned and disappeared into the house.

Noah picked up his water bottle, took one last swallow, then poured the remainder over the scratch. It might not help but it couldn't hurt to try to rinse off any poison that might be on him.

Grace returned, carrying a small first aid kit. "Antiseptic wipe, antibiotic ointment," she said, holding it up. "And a Band-Aid."

"No Band-Aid."

Grace laughed. "We'll negotiate."

31

DILLON

As Grace opened the first aid kit, standing close to Noah, Dillon paced the garden nervously.

Most of the ghosts were gone. The number left were a fraction of those in the courthouse — some of the glowing balls of light, a few wisps, and the six that he thought of as real ghosts. But still, he hadn't been thinking when he brought them here. He'd been so sure that Akira would help that he hadn't considered the potential danger to her and the baby.

"Dude, relax," Joe said. "None of us are going to kill your friend."

"It's not like my grandma meant to kill her," Dillon said under his breath, glancing at Sophia.

"I'm not gonna kill some pregnant lady," she snapped at him, making a face.

"You wanted to kill Noah." Misam jumped for a branch of one of the magnolia trees, but it was too high for him to reach.

"That was different." Sophia stepped behind him and hoisted him up. "Oof, you're kicking," she complained, as Misam grabbed the branch and half-pulled, half-wiggled himself over it.

Astride the branch, he beamed down at her. "Sorry for kicking, but thank you for helping!"

"No problem." She eyed him in the tree. "Move over, I'm coming up, too."

"I'm going higher," he told her, scrambling to his feet and reaching for the branch above him. "To the very top."

"Sounds like a plan," Sophia said, pulling herself into the tree after him.

"I'm just worried," Dillon said. He'd brought the ghosts here, after all. If anything bad happened to Akira, it would be his fault.

"You should stop," Rose said brightly. "You'll feel really silly if you worry so much you go red."

"That's not going to happen." Dillon kicked at a tuft of grass. He gave her a sideways glance. "Maybe you should worry some?"

"Oh, pshaw." Rose brushed off that idea with a wave of her hand.

Dillon frowned, attention caught by the solidity of her hand. Her fading hadn't grown worse since the other ghosts left — her skirt was still pastel, her hair a lighter gold — but it hadn't gotten much better either. She was still translucent. Although maybe not quite as translucent as she had been earlier in the day. Was it the light?

"Are you worrying about Akira?" he asked, wondering if she could be getting stronger, hoping she was.

"Akira? No." Rose patted his shoulder, but he couldn't feel her touch. "She'll get over it. You know she will."

"Get over what?" Dillon asked.

"Get over being mad at you." Rose gave him a sweet smile. "It's probably good that you're already dead, though."

Joe laughed and Nadira's lips twitched as the door to the house opened, and Avery emerged, followed by Akira and Zane.

Akira paused at the threshold, one hand curving around her very pregnant stomach. Dillon couldn't believe the change. He hadn't seen her in weeks, but she looked like she'd swallowed a basketball. She stood in the doorway, eyes flickering over the garden, lifting to the balls of light drifting around the patio.

Grace had been bent over Noah's arm, wiping on the antibiotic, but she pulled away, and the two of them turned to look at Akira and Zane.

Rose danced to Akira's side, delighted questions spilling out like water flowing from a wide-open faucet. "Welcome home! How was your trip? Did you like Belize? Did you see the howler monkeys? Were they as loud as you thought they'd be? Did they howl at you?"

"Is it okay?" Dillon asked Akira hurriedly. "Are you okay?"

Akira shook her head, but not as if she was saying no, more as if she couldn't believe what she was seeing. "At least Rose only brings me one ghost at a time."

Dillon grinned with relief. It was fine.

She'd be fine.

He hurried over to her, but paused before hugging her the way he would have liked to. She hated the feel of ghostly energy passing through her body. But she stepped closer to him and leaned over to let her lips drift across his cheek in a kiss neither of them could feel.

"It's good to see you. I've missed you. But what the hell was that message? Thanks for everything?"

"I meant it!" Dillon said.

"Not much of a good-bye. And after missing the wedding, too."

Dillon hung his head. "It was a chance to move on."

"Didn't I tell you not to be in such a hurry?" Rose sounded smug.

Dillon snorted. Maybe he felt bad, but he wasn't going to let Rose get away with that. "You should talk. Look at her, Akira. She's all faded. At least I was going someplace, not just melting away."

"She's... oh, Rose." Akira's expression became one of startled dismay. "Dillon's right. What did you do?"

"I'm fine." Rose brushed off Akira's worry. "I want to hear about your honeymoon."

"What's wrong with her?" Noah asked. He and Grace had approached the house and were standing near them, but not in what must seem to them to be the empty spaces Akira was talking to.

"You must be Noah." Akira tipped her head, eyeing him skeptically, "So you can hear ghosts?"

"So they tell me," Noah replied.

"You sound like you don't believe him," Dillon said, surprised.

"Well." Akira shrugged. "I have to admit, I'd like some proof."

Noah's eyebrows shot up and he gave a bark of laughter. "You want me to prove that I hear them?"

"Uh-huh."

He laughed, shaking his head. "I think that's my line."

She shrugged again. "I've never met anyone else who can truly communicate with the ghosts I see. There are a lot of ghosts here, so that's evidence of something. But maybe you're just a sensitive."

"I wish," Noah said ruefully. He grinned. "Rose asked you about howler monkeys. Dillon says Rose is faded. But I can't see them, so I don't know what that means. Is that proof enough?"

Akira nodded, looking pleased. She extended a hand. "Akira Malone. Uh, Latimer."

He shook her hand. "It's a pleasure."

"You are truly haunted," she told him. "That must suck."

"Apparently this is nothing," he said. "Most of them left a couple weeks ago."

Her eyebrows raised and she looked around the garden again, as if counting balls of light. "Seriously?"

"Yeah, there's really only the six of us left," Dillon replied for Noah. He waved for Nadira and Joe to come closer, introducing them as they did. "And Misam and Sophia are in the tree."

Akira glanced up as Misam called out, "Coming down!" and launched himself from the highest branch.

"Misam!" Nadira protested, but Misam only laughed as he floated, arms spread wide, down to the ground. Sophia peered out from between the dark green leaves. She shook her head, then stepped off the tree herself, descending at the same speed.

"You're not counting the glowies as ghosts? Or those faders?" Akira asked after the introductions.

"Nah," Dillon shrugged. "They don't talk, they stay in the garden now, they're just sort of here."

"Hmm." Akira frowned, her eyes narrowing as she gazed at one of the balls of light hovering over the bougainvillea.

"What are you thinking?" Grace asked her.

"Oh." Akira shook her head, turning her attention back to the others. "Experiments. You know I'm trying to find ways to measure spirit energy." She shot a worried frown in Rose's direction. "Although maybe I should start researching ghostly medicine, too."

"I'm fine," Rose repeated.

"You don't look fine," Akira said.

"She absorbed energy from Sophia before," Dillon said. "When Sophia was, um, upset. I think she should do it again."

"I'm not upset." Sophia scowled at him.

"Not from you." Dillon waved at a wisp. "Maybe from them? They wouldn't care."

"You know, they were all people, too. Once." Rose twisted a curl of hair around her finger.

"Now they're just leftover energy," Dillon said. "Leftover energy that you could use."

Rose made a face. "That's creepy."

Akira folded her arms over her mound of belly. "You need a doorway. Like the one you had before."

"They all do," Noah said. "Can you help them?"

Akira grimaced. "I haven't had much luck with the doorways. It's surprisingly difficult to open a portal to another plane of existence. I've never been willing to resort to Satanic rituals."

"Satanic rituals?" Zane asked with a half-laugh, putting his arm around Akira's shoulders.

"Kidding," Akira said, bumping her head against his chest affectionately. "I'm pretty sure they wouldn't work."

"Let's not try," Zane said.

"Yeah, I'm with him on that one." Noah frowned, glancing at the long, bloody scratch on his arm.

287

"Ditto," Grace said dryly. "But if you can't help with the doorway, Akira, maybe you can still help Noah. Sophia wants to talk her parents. I said you'd give them some advice."

Akira grimaced. "Relatives. And parents are just about the worst." But she looked at Sophia and unfolded her arms, moving her hands down and lacing her fingers together protectively over her abdomen.

"I need to talk to them," Sophia said.

"Yeah, yeah." Akira nodded. "No worries, I'll help. But while we're at it, maybe you could help me with my research, too."

32

GRACE

GRACE CLOSED THE FILE ON HER COMPUTER WITH A SIGH. SHE stared at the background image on the screen without really seeing it, wondering what she should do. The military jargon was dense, but not unclear, and the detailed incident report was thorough. Plus, there were the award recommendation forms. Not just Noah's, but those of other members of his unit.

Of course, maybe they were wrong.

Or a pack of lies.

She needed to talk to him.

She'd felt like she needed to talk to him for weeks now, but it wasn't the kind of conversation that lent itself to casual moments. It was tough to follow up, "Enjoying the weather?" with "By the way, I've been doing some research and I think you're all wrong about your life."

Plus, they were never alone. She didn't mind the small town element of never being alone. As far as she was concerned, people gossiping about her was an inevitable byproduct of running the town's largest employer. And she was in the privileged position of not needing to care. Nothing people said could affect her career or family, and she wasn't one to read more into an insult than envy or jealousy.

But the ghosts were another story. She didn't know them. She didn't know how they'd react and she didn't know what they could do. Maybe they couldn't hurt her, but Akira had plenty of reasons to fear angry ghosts. Maybe Noah would, too.

She glanced at the time. Almost 11:30. It was a Saturday but Noah and Akira were in one of the downstairs labs, trying out the latest equipment Akira had ordered, a realtime hybrid superheterodyne-FFT spectrum analyzer that she hoped would recognize and record ghostly energy.

Grace could go visit them, but ostensibly she was in the office to catch up on some of her own work. She had a backlog of over two hundred emails. She had budget reports, project updates, and acquisition assessments piling up faster than she could read them, not to mention a dozen meetings to schedule. She should be on the road right now, preparing to attend a board meeting of one of their subsidiaries in Arizona, before flying to New York City to meet with their lawyers and a representative from the SEC, and then traveling to South Carolina to evaluate a real estate deal her father had recommended.

At the very least, she should take care of the paperwork in her inbox.

She picked up the top sheet. A purchase order for goldfish? She chuckled. The quantum teleportation team had taken her suggestion. Grabbing a pen, she signed the order, then paused before dropping it into her outbox.

Maybe she should run down to their lab and find out what they planned to do with the goldfish first. It might just be a goldfish, but she didn't want them torturing the poor thing.

And if that meant she wandered right by the lab where Noah and Akira were working, well, so be it.

She took the elevator to the lower level, her heels clicking along the echoing floors as she strode through the deserted hallways. The quantum teleportation guys were unlikely to be in, so her excuse was transparent. But it was her company. She could go where she wanted, do what she wanted. Interrupting Akira and Noah was perfectly reasonable if she was passing by anyway.

Perfectly reasonable if you were obsessed, she admitted to herself with another inward sigh.

For the past few weeks, Noah and Akira had been working together. Noah had learned everything Akira had to teach him about the difficulties of talking to the living about their deceased relatives. He was as prepared to meet Sophia's family as he was ever going to get. Meanwhile he and Akira were running all the experiments that Akira could invent.

But any day now, he was going to give up. He'd hop in his truck and drive north, taking his ghosts with him.

Before he did, she had to talk to him. She had to tell him... what, exactly?

She'd had a picture in her head of the guy she'd find someday. Maybe it had been a little vague, amorphous, but she'd known she'd never go for one of the smooth-talking business-types she so often met. And the law enforcement guys were all too controlling.

She'd thought — when she'd had time to spare a thought for her romantic future at all — that someday she'd stumble across an acade-mic. Not in the offices of General Directions, of course: she couldn't date an employee. But somewhere, somehow...

Instead, there was Noah.

When he looked at her, it felt like he saw her. Which was silly, of course. Didn't everyone looking at her see her? But no. People looked at her and saw brisk competence. Problems solved. Dollar signs, sometimes. Polish and poise, she hoped, at least most of the time.

She didn't know exactly what Noah saw. But she knew what she saw in him. It wasn't just that he was attractive, although he was. It wasn't the darkness that shadowed his eyes sometimes — despite Mrs. Swanson's fear, Grace knew better than to fall for a troubled guy believing she could fix him. But when she was with him, she felt...

connected. Like he was the best friend she hadn't known she was missing.

Her footsteps slowed as she reached the open door to the lab where Akira and Noah were talking.

"Like a Faraday cage," Akira was saying. She looked off into space for a moment before shrugging. "It's just a name. And an idea. Not like I'm looking for a ghost prison, Dillon."

"Hey." Grace paused in the doorway. "How go the experiments?"

Noah was leaning against a lab table, but he straightened at Grace's approach.

From a chair across the room, Akira tilted her hand in a so-so gesture. "We've collected plenty of data. The spectrum analyzer is giving us some interesting results. But I'm not at all sure I know what to do with them."

"Short version," Noah said. "Joe, Misam, and Nadira are still trapped."

"And the possibility exists that Noah's previous problem of attracting every passing spirit could recur," Akira added.

Grace opened her mouth. She should tell Noah what she'd learned.

Akira had always been adamant that ghosts existed not because of anything done or undone in their lives, but because of the tragic, untimely nature of their deaths. She didn't believe people or places were haunted for any reasons more profound than an accident of nature, a freak occurrence like a rogue wave.

Grace wasn't so sure. She knew that Akira had never had any luck trying to resolve ghostly unfinished business, but what if...

Before she could find the words she needed, Akira glanced to the side and said, voice dry, "I don't think a long-term plan that relies on none of you ever getting angry or upset again is a real solution."

Grace closed her mouth again. On the other hand, how would the ghosts react? She looked at Noah. He was looking back at her. Their eyes met, tangled, for a long second. Grace didn't want to look away. She could feel heat rising in her cheeks, a tingle of warmth beginning to flow.

Akira cleared her throat.

Grace pulled her gaze away from Noah.

Akira was watching her, a faint, amused smile curving her lips, but then she grimaced, wrapping her lower arm around her belly and letting her chin drop to her chest. "Ow..."

"Are you okay?" Grace stepped into the room.

Akira waved her free hand in the air, before lifting her head and exhaling. "Braxton-Hicks."

Was that supposed to mean something?

"It's nothing," Akira said. "Just contractions."

"Contractions?" Grace blinked, counting dates in her head. "That's... no. You've got two months to go. We haven't had your shower. You can't have the baby yet."

Akira laughed. "No, no," she said. She shoved her chair back, rolling along the floor toward her desk. "Braxton-Hicks are just early contractions. My body getting ready, I guess. They can start any time in the third trimester. They don't mean Henry's on his way." She wrinkled her nose. "Although I'm totally rethinking the natural child-birth thing. If these are little contractions, the real thing must be serious hell."

She glanced toward a filing cabinet in the back of the room. "Dates? The fruit, you mean?" She paused, listening, her expression dubious. "I'm not a fan. Especially since moving to Florida. They look too much like the gigantic roaches they have here."

A puff of laughter escaped Grace. "We call those palmetto bugs."

Akira shuddered. "Yeah, that's to make yourself feel better when you turn the light on in the bathroom and one scampers across the floor. They're gigantic roaches." Talking to the file cabinet again, she said, "Is there any scientific evidence for that?"

"For what?" Grace asked.

"Nadira's telling her that eating dates will make her labor easier," Noah answered as Akira reached for her keyboard and started typing.

"I think that's what they have epidurals for," Grace replied.

"Nadira disapproves," Noah said.

"Disapproves? Of pain relief?" Grace hoped Akira didn't plan on taking medical advice from a ghost.

Noah raised a hand in a stop signal. Speaking to the same file cabinet as Akira, he ordered, "No more details. I do not need to know this."

"Well, look at that," Akira said, sounding pleased. "Dates. The research backs you up, Nadira."

"Dates?" Grace crossed the room to look over Akira's shoulder. She was browsing some sort of scientific database.

Grace leaned closer and read "US National Library of Medicine" as Akira said, "510 minutes versus 906 minutes — that's over six hours less time in labor. I'd probably be willing to eat real roaches for that."

"Ew." Grace straightened without reading the rest of the article.

"Well, dead ones. They're just protein."

"Double ew. Dead or alive." Grace made a face.

"Yeah, you've never felt a contraction," Akira said darkly, resting a hand on her belly. She cocked her head, listening. "You'll have to tell me all about it."

Grace heard Noah give a pained, but barely audible, grunt of objection, but some of the other ghosts must have protested as well, because Akira responded with a laugh and a wave of her hand as if erasing the suggestion. "All right, all right. No labor and delivery stories with impressionable young ears in the room. Later." She turned back to Grace. "What were you about to say when I interrupted you?"

"Oh, ah..." Grace hesitated. She'd like to talk to Akira about what she'd been thinking, but maybe not in front of the ghosts, not yet. "What were you saying about a Faraday cage?"

"Right, a Faraday cage." Akira shrugged. "It's an enclosure designed to block electromagnetic fields. An elevator can work like a Faraday cage — the metal interferes with electromagnetic signals, which is why cell phones sometimes lose connection when you're between floors."

"There's not much signal down here, anyway." Grace patted her pocket automatically, but she'd left her cell phone upstairs. All the offices had landlines for just that reason.

"Yep, being underground can block cell signals, too. But apparently not ghosts. We tried using the elevators, but the effect wasn't strong enough to disrupt the bond between the ghosts and Noah. A Faraday cage might do it. With the ghosts on one side, Noah on the other, increasing the distance between them might snap the bond, the way Dillon's bond to his car was snapped when he got caught in the first vortex. It's just an idea."

Grace didn't hesitate. Maybe it was a dumb question, but the only way to find out was to ask. "Did you try Nat's scanner room?"

"Nat's scanner room?" Akira batted her forehead with the heel of her hand, grimacing. "Duh. Pregnancy brain, I swear."

"What about it?" Noah asked.

"We had to make a special room for it," Grace explained. "Total pain. It was after…" She paused, wondering how to explain.

After Dillon and her mom had died, Grace had come home to step into her mother's impossibly big shoes. Her dad had tried to maintain a facade of normal in public, but in private, he went silent and gray, like a ghost himself. Lucas had become stone-cold and obsessive, determined to save the world. Even Zane, the most easygoing of them all, stopped laughing.

When he hadn't bothered to pre-order the latest video game console, Grace had known she had to do something. Spending several million dollars on a high-end scanning system so Natalya would come home and work in Tassamara had felt like a bargain. Remodeling the building had been a drop in the bucket after that.

"The room is shielded, right?" Akira said. "To protect the scanner from any electromagnetic interference."

"Yep," Grace said, realizing she didn't need to explain, not really. "I don't remember the exact specs," she added apologetically. "Although I'm sure I could track them down if you need to know."

The corner of Akira's mouth lifted. "A good scientist establishes all the variables in her experiments. Accurate data is important. But I'm probably not going to be writing a research paper on this, and it certainly wouldn't get published if I did, so let's not worry about it for now."

She pushed herself up out of the chair. "Let's control the experiment. One ghost in the scanner room, the others can walk away with Noah. Nadira, why don't you come to the scanner room with Grace and me? We'll talk girl stuff. Noah, you can take Dillon, Joe, and Misam, and head down the hall."

Grace would rather go with Noah. She didn't need to hear one-sided pregnancy stories. But Akira wouldn't be able to get into Nat's lab without a passcode, so Grace obligingly followed her down the hall.

She opened the door and waved Akira inside, leaving a pause for Nadira to follow her, before saying, "You don't really need me for this. I'll just—" She waved the goldfish purchase order to indicate that she should continue running her errand. Maybe she could catch up to Noah.

"Yes, I do." Akira grabbed her arm and tugged her through the door. The room was almost empty, dominated by the giant piece of machinery in the middle, with no chairs or furniture beyond the table that slid into the scanner.

"You do?"

"Girl talk." Akira closed the door and leaned against it, blocking Grace's exit.

"I don't know anything about pregnancy. Or babies."

"Yeah, that's not what I'm interested in." Akira was smiling. "Are you sleeping with him?"

Grace felt her cheeks heating. "Of course not."

"Why not? He's hot as hell and the chemistry is obvious."

"I thought you wanted to talk about babies."

"I'll get to that, but come on, sex is far more interesting." Akira glanced over Grace's shoulder, toward the scanner, then turned her attention back to Grace. "Only the one kiss? In all these weeks?"

"How do you — oh." Grace's flush deepened. Of course the ghosts knew every move Noah made. They were invisible observers of his every act. "Anything more would be inappropriate. I can't get involved with an employee."

"But, Grace, if you rule out employees, who's left?" Akira was still leaning against the door, barring the only avenue of escape.

Grace opened her mouth and closed it again. "Guys from other places?"

Akira made a scoffing noise. "Don't tell me you don't like Noah. I wouldn't believe you for a minute."

"That's not... I can't... he isn't..." Grace lifted her chin and stopped talking. She wasn't going to let Akira fluster her. Not any more than she already had, anyway.

"Oh, you do like him." Akira gave an approving smile. "You shouldn't wait for him to make the first move. He's probably intimidated. You're beautiful, smart, rich, even nice." She added a shake of her head to the last word. "Any guy would be intimidated."

"I'm not—" Grace started to object before pausing. Of course she was intimidating. If she wanted people to take her seriously, she had to be. Noah didn't exactly seem intimidated, though. If anything, she had the feeling he was quietly amused by her efficiency.

"You should seduce him," Akira went on.

Grace should end this conversation. Swiftly and decisively, the way she'd shut Jensen down the day she'd kissed Noah in the woods. Instead she found herself saying, "How am I supposed to do that?"

"I've always been a fan of the direct approach. Try saying, 'I'm very attracted to you. Is the feeling mutual?' And then when he says 'yes,' you say, 'terrific, my place or yours?'"

Grace choked out a laugh. "And if he says 'no'?"

Akira shrugged. "I can't see that happening. I saw the way he was looking at you. But if he doesn't manage an unequivocal yes, you just say 'well, let me know if your feelings change,' smile sweetly and move on. No big deal."

"I don't think I can do that."

"Well, if it's too soon for seduction, you should ask him out. On a date. A real date." Akira spoke briskly, but then she paused. She frowned, nose wrinkling, and directed her words over Grace's shoulder. "No go?"

Grace glanced behind her, even though she knew she wouldn't see anything. "What is it?"

Akira lifted her chin toward the center of the room. "Nadira's feeling the pull." She sighed. "The shielding on the room must not be strong enough to break the connection. Back to the drawing board, I guess."

"I was wondering..." Grace paused. Only one ghost in the room. Maybe this was the moment to ask Akira the questions she'd been thinking about.

"About?" Akira raised a brow.

"The whole unfinished business thing," Grace started.

"Doesn't work." Akira shook her head.

"But Rose's door — she only got it after Henry died, right?"

A hint of uncertainty creased Akira's forehead. "I think that's right. She and Sophia are watching movies at Nat's, so I can't ask her, but I'm pretty sure she said that."

"So maybe the door had something to do with Henry, then."

Akira rubbed her belly again, a rueful smile tugging at her lips. "It'll be a long time before we can ask him. Even if he remembers anything, and I bet he won't."

"I wasn't thinking about asking him," Grace said. "I was wondering..." Grace couldn't bring herself to say anything about Noah. What he'd told her, what she knew, it was private. It was up to him to decide what he wanted to share with other people.

But she had ghosts of her own.

"My dad suggested that maybe Dillon was a ghost because we couldn't let him go. Because we were holding him here." Her dad had specifically suggested that he was the one who'd trapped Dillon, but Grace wasn't sure he was right about that.

Akira looked taken aback. She frowned. And then she seemed to have much the same reaction as Grace herself had had, flickers of expression — doubt, thoughtfulness, more doubt, rejection, curiosity, more doubt — crossing her face at high speed. "I don't know. Wouldn't everyone become a ghost, then? It's not as if we ever want to let go of the people we love."

"I'm imagining knots in a tapestry," Grace said.

Akira shook her head as if to say she didn't understand.

"The fabric of life, the plan, it is what it is." Grace meshed her fingers together, like the warp and weft of threads on a loom. "Natalya can see the future because the future follows a pattern. Mostly. And then something happens." She twisted her hands together, then pulled them apart. "A new path. But some of us, we fight the new path. We hold on. We refuse to let go. The threads become a knotted mess, instead of a picture."

Akira wrinkled her nose. "You're suggesting I might need to have more conversations with relatives, you know."

Grace chuckled. "Sorry. Not what you want to hear. But I admit, I am wondering if there's something we could do to open Dillon's doorway. Not his unfinished business, but someone else's." She pressed her lips together, feeling a prickle at the back of her eyes.

"Not his dad," Akira said thoughtfully. "He's talked to Lucas. They're good. Not his mom, either, or he would have gotten it after he met her. She definitely thinks he should move on. Ghosts kind of freak her out."

"Really?" Grace blinked. She hadn't noticed that — and she couldn't imagine anything freaking Sylvie out — but she hadn't spent a lot of time with her brother's fiancée in the presence of ghosts other than Dillon. Not that she knew about, anyway.

"Little bit, yeah," Akira said absently, frowning. "Makes sense, I suppose. In her line of work—" She shrugged. "No one wants 'creating ghosts' to be part of their job description."

Her words trailed off and she frowned. "Nadira?" She pushed herself off the door she'd been leaning against since they entered the room.

"Stop that!" she said sharply. "Don't! Wait. No!" She was turning, watching something Grace couldn't see, her hands lifting, fingers spreading wide. "No, no, no, no!"

Lurching forward, she grabbed for the door handle. "This way. Go this way!" She yanked open the door.

"What's wrong? What is it?" Grace said.

Akira turned to her. Her eyes wide, she opened her mouth before gasping and clutching her stomach. Dropping her head to her chest, voice rasping in her throat, she choked out, "Get Noah. Run!"

Grace ran.

33

DILLON

"If I had a superpower, I would like to fly," Misam was saying.

"You're invisible and you can walk through walls, dude. Isn't that good enough?" Joe replied.

"No, it's boring. I can't do anything. If I was really invisible, maybe I'd rob a bank." Misam had his arms spread wide, Superman-style, leaning forward against the tug of his attraction to Noah, letting it pull him along. "Would you rob a bank if you could, Joe?"

"Nah, probably not. My mom wouldn't like it," Joe replied.

"Your mom wouldn't like it either," Dillon said, turning and walking backward so that he could see Misam while still following Noah.

"Maybe she would rob a bank with me." Misam abandoned his flying posture and skipped a few times to catch up with them. "If the bank belonged to bad people, she might."

"Pretty sure if you use your super power to rob banks, you're a super villain, not a super hero," Joe said, sounding amused. "No matter who the bank belongs to."

"All right, no banks." Misam sighed, before offering more hopefully, "But maybe Mama would like being a super villain."

"She'd have to wear a super villain costume," Joe said. "Spandex."

Dillon gave a snort of laughter, picturing Nadira's reaction to that idea. And then he froze.

Something had appeared in the hallway behind them.

"Uh, guys?" Dillon said, trying to make sense of what he was seeing. He stopped walking.

An amorphous cloud was drifting toward them, a mass of patches of light and dark, plumes of shadow trailing off behind it.

Joe turned his head to look at him, then followed his gaze. "Shit!" He grabbed for Noah's arm, his hand passing straight through and closing into a fist, then jumped in front of Misam, as if he could guard the little boy from the approaching darkness.

Misam looked, too. "What is that?" he started, before his mouth dropped open. "Mama?" he whispered the word, then shrieked it. "Mama!"

He hurled himself past Joe at the cloud. He passed right through it, his momentum toppling him over on the other side.

"Oh, no. Oh, no," Dillon murmured the words like a mantra, like a prayer. The Faraday cage hadn't worked, at least not the way they'd wanted it to. The bond between Nadira and Noah hadn't broken, but Nadira had been shredded. Her energy must have been drawn through tiny holes in the mesh that surrounded the room. She wasn't disintegrated, the way she might have been in the vortex, but fractured into hundreds, thousands, of particles of light and dark and color.

"Mama." Misam rolled over and gazed up at the cloud above him. She'd stopped moving.

The cloud hummed. Not words, not that Dillon could distinguish, but a blur of sound. Maybe it was Misam's name. Maybe it was just a hummed M.

"What is it? What's happening?" Noah was staring blindly down the hallway.

Grace appeared at the end of it. "Noah," she called. "Come back. Akira needs you!"

Noah didn't hesitate. He plunged straight through the Nadira-shaped cloud that he couldn't see and over Misam's prone body, racing down the hallway to Grace. The two of them disappeared around the corner.

The ghosts didn't move.

"Nadira?" Joe croaked. "Is that you?"

The hum got stronger.

"This is not good," Dillon said, his mouth dry.

"Way to understate," Joe muttered. He stepped past Dillon, approaching the vapors, then crouched on the ground. He held out his arms to Misam and the little boy crawled into them. Joe rose, taking a step back, holding Misam.

"Mama?" Misam looked toward the cloud, before giving a tiny whimper and burying his face in Joe's shoulder.

"Nadira?" Joe repeated.

The hum sounded impatient this time. And somehow distinctly like Nadira. There were no words, but the tone was right.

Dillon joined the others. He reached out, his fingers brushing against and then through the dark wisps that might have once been Nadira's shoulder.

"I'm gonna guess, you've never seen anything like this?" Joe said.

Dillon shook his head, feeling nauseous as he remembered the times that he'd let his car drive away without him. What if the airport walls had been shielded? What if he'd ever gotten far enough away from his car to visit his aunt in her lab? This could have been him.

"What do we do?" he said.

"We don't panic," Joe said firmly. He was patting Misam's back, with short quick strokes. "She's still here. We just need to... to put her back together. Somehow."

"Do you think it—" Dillon glanced at Misam and bit back the words. He remembered how much it hurt when Akira drove away from the airport. The pain had been like nothing he'd ever felt before.

And then there'd been the few brief moments when his grandmother's vortex had ripped him away from his car. That had been agonizing while it lasted.

Whatever had happened to Nadira, it had definitely hurt, but Misam didn't need to hear that.

"Do you think—" he started again, looking for an alternative ending to the words.

"Shit!" Joe exclaimed. Tendrils of Nadira were drifting away from them, back in the direction from which she'd come, like curls of smoke blowing in a breeze they couldn't feel. "Noah's gone too far away, he's pulling us. Dillon, run, tell him to get back here."

Dillon nodded and took off down the hallway, veering to the side to avoid crashing through the pieces of Nadira. He didn't think they would stick to him, not like Chesney had in the vortex dimension, but he really didn't want to find out that he was wrong. Not that Nadira would feel like Chesney — her essence would probably be spicy and warm and tart, maybe something like a lemon ginger cookie — but the thought was still horrifying. He didn't want to carry little droplets of Nadira away from the rest of her.

"Noah," he called as he ran. "Noah!"

He caught up to Grace and Noah at the doorway to Natalya's scanner room.

"A chair, let me get you a chair," Grace was saying to Akira. "You need to sit. Or lie down, maybe you need to lie down. The scanner table?"

Akira waved her away. She was folded over, gasping in sharp pants of breath, one after another, and then she exhaled in a long, slow sigh and straightened. "Okay, totally rethinking the natural childbirth thing."

"Are you okay?" Noah demanded. "Should we call someone? An ambulance?"

Akira snorted. "For Braxton-Hicks? No." But she rubbed the side of her mound of stomach, her expression worried. And then her eyes widened and she said, "But Nadira. Is she okay?"

"Not," Dillon interjected. "Big-time not."

Akira looked past Noah and saw him in the hallway. "What happened to her? I opened the door, but it was too late. She was being squished through the wall like it was a tube of toothpaste and she was the toothpaste."

Dillon shot a quick glance over his shoulder, making sure Misam wasn't in earshot. "She's vaporized."

"Vapor — what?" Noah spun to face Dillon. "What are you talking about?"

"You need to come back," Dillon told him. "And not move away from her. Pieces of her are drifting around like, like I don't know what. Like smoke. We need to put her back together somehow."

"How are we supposed to do that?" Noah said.

"What can we do?" Grace asked at the same time.

Akira shook her head, biting her lip. "I've got no experience with this. Vaporized implies particles, though. Particles should attract? Like diffusion versus condensation, maybe? Or maybe something to do with cohesive forces. Van der Waals? Zero-point energy? That could imply fields. Aether, maybe? Could ghosts be a form of aether? Maybe energy's always been nothing but a bad metaphor. But stronger bonds are better, of course. What could make an attractive force stronger?" She'd started off talking to the others, but by her last words she was muttering to herself more than to anyone else.

"What do we do?" Grace repeated.

Akira lifted her shoulders in a helpless shrug and stepped out into the hallway. She looked in the direction from which Dillon had come and grimaced. "Shit."

"Is it bad? Is she — what do you see?" Noah asked her.

Dillon looked, too, but the other ghosts weren't visible yet. At least not to him, but Akira had always been able to perceive their energy within her visible spectrum. He'd never even seen his grandma's energy, much less realized it was dangerous.

"A lot of very upset ghostly energy, heading this way," Akira replied. "And it's getting stronger by the second." She curved both arms protectively around her midsection.

Joe, still carrying Misam, rounded the corner of the hallway. There was no sign of the cloud of Nadira smoke.

Akira chewed on her lower lip and then her expression lightened. She took a hasty couple of steps backwards, back into the scanner room, and gave Grace a gentle shove toward the door. "Hey, I'm sorry about this, but I can't risk having a seizure, not with Henry. Lack of oxygen is not exactly best-practice prenatal care. And since I've recently discovered that EMF shielding works on spirit energy, I'm going to leave this one to you guys. Knock when it's safe for me to come out."

"Wait, what?" Grace started, but Akira was already pulling the door closed behind her.

Dillon breathed a sigh of relief. At least he didn't have to worry about Akira and Henry. They'd be safe in the scanner room.

"All right." Grace pressed her hands together, holding them before her mouth in a gesture almost like a prayer. "Disintegrated ghost. And we need to re-integrate her somehow." She looked at Noah. "Any ideas?"

Dillon had an idea. Not much of one, and he wasn't sure he liked it, but it was better than nothing.

"I could try doing what Rose did with the other ghosts," he said to Noah. "She gave them some of her energy. It made them solid."

It was the obvious solution. And how different from texting could it be?

"Didn't that make her start fading?" Noah responded.

"Yeah." Dillon swallowed. How faded could he get before he started losing himself? Before he became stuck on one sentence, one idea? And what would his fixation be? He hoped he wouldn't become some future ghost's angry man or singing lady, more annoying than human.

But Rose hadn't diminished, at least not yet. She was still as lively, with just as much personality, as if she were solid. He'd been watching her, hoping to see signs of deepening color, evidence that she was regenerating her own energy the way new ghosts could, but apart from the one day in the garden, he hadn't noticed any.

Still, he was a reasonably young ghost and he could get plenty upset. If he gave Nadira so much energy that it made him fade, it might freak him out enough to make him solid again. And it was worth a try.

"Who's fading?" Grace asked.

Joe and Misam were moving toward them, but slowly, walking backward. And now bits of Nadira were appearing, too, even more diffuse than when Dillon had first seen them.

"Dillon's suggesting he share his energy with Nadira. The way Rose did."

"But Rose isn't really a ghost. She's got that whole angel thing going on. Can't she do any sharing that needs to be done?" Grace was tapping her foot on the floor, a nervous, impatient jiggle of the leg that told Dillon she wanted to get moving, do something, anything.

"She's not here," Noah answered. "She and Sophia were watching movies at your sister's house."

"Besides, she's already too faded," Dillon added.

"Well, let's get her here," Grace said, not hearing Dillon, of course. She shot a glance at the closed door behind her and added, "Actually, that's an excellent idea. Let's get Nat here, too. I left my phone upstairs. Can I borrow yours?"

"Yeah, sure." Noah pulled out his own phone, unlocked it and handed it to her.

Grace stared at it. "Shit."

"What's wrong?" Noah asked.

She thrust the phone back in his direction. "I don't remember her number. I never dial direct. I need my phone."

"Right." Noah took his phone back. "Go. I'll—" He opened a hand to the hallway.

Grace raised her own hands and spread her fingers wide. She patted the air in a gesture that combined 'stop' with 'slow down' and maybe had some 'be careful' mixed into it, too. "I will be right back. Don't do anything drastic."

She paused, as if torn about leaving them, but Noah gave her a slight nod, and she shook her own head in response, then hurried away.

More of the Nadira cloud was drifting around the corner and Joe had stopped walking to wait for it. "Dillon?" he called. "Any ideas?"

"Akira says we need to make her stronger," Dillon replied, returning to Joe's side. "Stronger bonds attract better or something like that."

"Stronger? Like by getting her angry?" Joe reached out and poked at one of the wisps of fragmented Nadira. He pulled his hand back when it dissipated even more. "Okay, not that way."

"I know, I know." Misam wiggled in Joe's arms until Joe set him down on the floor. He stood in front of the gathering cloud and lifted his chin, eyes looking up toward where Nadira's face should have been.

"If you do not put yourself back together, Mama, I will ask Noah to take me to the place with the ladies in sparkly clothes." He waited, but the particles didn't start coalescing into his mother. "To lots of places with sparkly ladies, all the sparkly ladies!"

"Bound to be strip clubs in Florida, right?" Joe added with a jocularity that didn't match the grim look in his eyes. "Maybe Noah could take us to Miami. Lots of hot girls on the beach, right? And those thong bikinis, they're pretty close to naked."

Maybe the cloud solidified a little, but if so, it was so minor that it was barely noticeable.

"Mama, if you do not put yourself together, I will... I will..." Misam's lip wobbled. "I will be very angry with you. I will take Joe's side in all the arguments. I will say that *The Jungle Book* is the best movie, and that football should be called soccer, even though that is a stupid name, and that the Hulk is a better superhero than Iron Man."

The cloud hummed, but the pieces did not start reassembling themselves into Nadira.

"Than Iron Man, Mama," Misam said plaintively. "I am saying that strong is better than smart! Do you hear me?"

"Let me try to do the energy thing," Dillon said. He concentrated on Nadira, trying to focus the way he did when he sent a message to a phone. He tried not to remember all the electronic devices he'd killed while trying to learn how to send messages. Too much energy wouldn't hurt Nadira. It would probably help her. A good zap somewhere to the center of her might drag all those floating bits in like iron filings jumping to a magnet.

Except... it didn't. Dillon closed his eyes and tried harder, trying to push his energy into the amorphous cloud. But it wasn't like a phone. There was nothing to receive the energy, nothing to do with it. It felt like the energy just streamed straight through her and splashed against the wall on the other side of the mist.

He opened his eyes. More of the particles were gathering, but he didn't think it was because of anything he'd done. Noah was standing still next to them and the pieces of Nadira were collecting near him.

"Should we try, too?" Joe asked. "Like the TV remote, right?"

Joe had never managed to switch the channels on the television but Misam had. Dillon glanced toward the little boy. He wished he could see energy the way Akira could. Misam didn't look like he was about to open a vortex and their surroundings were unchanged, nothing getting fuzzy. How much energy did he have? Enough to safely give some to his mother without turning into a fader himself? Nadira would never want to be restored if it harmed Misam.

"What's happening?" Noah asked, voice tight, fists clenched.

"I don't know how to transfer energy to another ghost," Dillon said. "Rose does, but..." But Rose wasn't with them. And even if she had been...

"She's already faded," Joe said for him.

"Mama. Mama, please come back," Misam said in a tiny voice.

Joe grabbed his hand. "We can do this. You learned how to use the remote, we can figure this out, too. We will bring her back. You and me, buddy, we got this. Together, right?"

309

Misam lifted his chin and nodded, but Dillon could see how hard he was trying not to cry.

"Stronger," Noah barely breathed the word. "Stronger." He turned to the door next to them and rattled the handle. "This is medical supplies, right?"

Dillon tried to remember which room was which. He'd followed along on Noah's security rounds more than once, but he hadn't bothered to pay close attention. But it was the right location for it, near Nat's office and scanner. "Yeah, maybe. I think so."

"Medical supplies, gotta be a fail-safe lock," Noah muttered, before directing his words toward Dillon again. "Can you zap the passcode reader on this door? If the electricity goes out, it should unlock."

"Um, sure." What good were medical supplies going to do a ghost? But Dillon didn't ask questions. He just concentrated on the electronic lock until he heard a satisfying sizzle, followed by a thunk.

Noah shoved open the door and disappeared into the room. Dillon turned back to the others.

"We concentrate," Joe was saying to Misam, "and just, I don't know, think power. Power to your mom. Like all that power Sophia made before when she was really sad and mad."

Misam sniffled. "I said I would be angry, but I don't feel very angry."

"Forget angry," Joe said. "We don't want that vortex thing, anyway. We want... think love. Think lots and lots and lots of love, all your love, pulling your mom back together again like Super Glue."

Dillon had never tried loving a cell phone. That wasn't how he'd made his energy transfer happen. But he wasn't going to argue with Joe. It wasn't as if his approach was working.

He tried again to send energy in Nadira's direction. Akira had said maybe it wasn't energy after all. She'd mentioned aether, which as far as Dillon knew was some old drug that they used to knock people out in medieval times. Or maybe it was during the Civil War. Same difference, right?

But maybe she meant aether like essence, like the core substance a spirit was created from. Not molecules and cells, but memories and emotions, dreams and fears and hopes, personality and temperament — all of those intangible elements that added up to a human being.

No, not a human being — human beings were composed of matter and substance, too.

But a soul. An identity.

And Nadira's soul needed help. It was humming again, a sound more like a swarm of bees than words. Could she be trying to tell them something?

Before Dillon could decide what it could be, Noah was back, standing in the middle of the hallway.

"Where is she?" he demanded. "Is she here?" He must be hearing the hum, because he'd managed to find a spot almost directly in the middle of the cloud of particles.

"Yes," Dillon answered him with a frown. Noah looked disturbingly fey, eyes searching the hallway as if he could find them if he looked hard enough. But his mouth held a resolute line and he was rolling up his left shirt sleeve.

"What are you doing?" Joe let go of Misam's hand and took a step closer to Noah.

"Get back," Noah ordered, voice harsh. "This isn't for you."

"What isn't?" Joe didn't step away.

Noah opened his left fist. Dillon didn't recognize the sealed packet he held. But Noah turned it over and ripped it open, sliding the scalpel it held into his right hand.

"Blood makes ghosts stronger," he said simply. "Rose showed me. So I'm going to give Nadira some of mine."

"Whoa!" Joe protested. "Hold on."

Noah didn't pause. He took a deep breath as he poised the scalpel above his wrist, then with a quick, sharp strike, sliced his forearm from wrist to elbow.

34

NOAH

Blood spurted immediately.

And it hurt like hell, a deep pain that Noah hadn't expected. He grimaced, gritting his teeth. Dropping the scalpel to the floor, he pressed his hand against his inner elbow and turned his arm, letting the blood pool on the floor.

He'd done a good job. No hesitation, no half-hearted thin scratches, he'd managed to go deep into his arm, cutting straight through his own flesh without pause.

It probably helped that the blade was so sharp.

But he'd definitely hit the vein. The blood was gushing, not just oozing or trickling to the surface. The spray had hit his face, warm sticky drops on his cheek, and the puddle on the floor was growing wider quickly.

Maybe he'd done too good a job. If he'd wanted to die, he would have gone for his carotid, bending his neck and coming in from the side so that he didn't get stuck on his larynx. Or his leg, aiming for the big vein behind the knee. He'd seen a guy bleed out from a thigh wound once, and it had happened so quickly that there'd been no way to stop it.

"Is it working?" he asked over the ghosts' reactions. Joe was yelling at him, Dillon objecting less loudly, and Misam squeaking, alternating orders to his mother and to him. But he couldn't discern any words from Nadira.

He lifted his hand off his arm, releasing the pressure, letting the dripping blood flow freely.

More blood would help.

It had to.

It was running down his arm, trickling through his fingers. It was different when it was his. It looked redder somehow, deeper and brighter.

God, but there was a lot of it.

His stomach twisted.

The smell was different, too. Cleaner, he realized. Still that warm, sweet, metallic scent, but every time he'd smelled it before — really smelled it, the times when the odor was overwhelming, pervasive — it had been mixed with smoke and guns and sweat and fear.

This was just blood.

But his legs felt wobbly. He tried to concentrate on the real blood, his blood, but the memories were bubbling up. Joe's face, his eyes, the glazed look. The kid. Had he seen the kid? A glimpse of color — blue stripes — and then red.

So much red.

Noah dropped to his knees. The jolt of pain as they hit the hard tile floor was almost enough to distract from the pain in his arm and the worse pain of his memories.

Almost.

He hadn't tried to avoid the blood. It would seep into his jeans. The denim would absorb it, turning dark and stiff.

Brown, saturated, ruined, gone.

His hands felt cold. It was too soon for it to be blood loss. Just reaction, that was all.

"What the hell?" It was a female voice, but not Nadira's.

Noah glanced up, tearing his eyes away from the blood on the floor.

"Don't do anything drastic, I said!" Grace's cheeks were flushed, her green eyes snapping. "How is that not drastic?" She pointed at the blood.

It wasn't funny, but Noah wanted to smile anyway. She was so damn pretty, even prettier when she was mad. And she was definitely mad.

"*He's losing a lot of blood,*" Joe said, sounding worried.

"*It's working, though, isn't it?*" Dillon said.

"*Mama? Mama, can you hear me?*"

"*Is she getting stronger?*" Joe said. "*I think she's reforming. I can see her shape in the cloud.*"

"We need to stop that bleeding." Grace crouched next to him.

Noah shook his head. "Not yet. It's working."

"Working?" Grace's hands were poised in the air above his arm, as if she wanted to put pressure on the slice he'd made but wasn't quite sure how.

"Nadira, she's coming together." A cold sweat broke out on the back of Noah's neck. Was it the ghosts, creating a chill in the air? Maybe it was just him. His arm was throbbing in time with his pulse and nausea was settling in, his mouth both dry and gushing with saliva.

"Good for her," Grace said, a grim line to her mouth. "She's just going to have to do the rest on her own." Gingerly, she placed her hands on his arm.

Noah pulled it away from her, shaking his head. "I owe her. Owe them. It's fair." He swallowed, trying to hold the nausea back, along with the memories.

Joe had been dying, maybe dead already, and the emotions — the frustrated helplessness, the surge of red hot rage, the despair — were as real as they'd been then.

But he didn't want to see the rest, didn't want to remember. What had he done?

"You don't owe them your life." Grace grabbed for his arm. She didn't get a good grip on the cut, but her hands were already covered in blood. He was getting it on her skirt, too, smears of bright color against the blue. And on her shoes.

His lips curled into a smile. "Ruining another pair of heels. Sorry about that."

She made an exasperated noise. "They don't matter. You're already pale. You need to let me help you."

She pressed her hands on his arm. He tried to tug free, but she didn't let go.

"You don't understand. I've got to help her."

"Not by killing yourself. She's a ghost!"

"Yeah, because I made her one. Because I killed her."

She shook her head. "I don't know why you think that's true, but I'm pretty sure it's not."

Noah closed his eyes. He didn't want to share the details. He'd never told anyone about that day, never had to. By the time he'd woken up from his coma, the investigation was over.

And they'd given him a medal.

"Not to mention that I don't think that's how ghosts are made. Damn it." Her last words were muttered under her breath, her hands squeezing Noah's arm.

"We were out in the desert," Noah started. "We'd just passed through a village."

"You're still bleeding," Grace interrupted him. "The blood's not stopping." Blood was oozing up through her fingers, dripping down his arm.

"We came under fire," Noah tried to continue.

"No," she corrected him. "First there was an IED."

How did she know that? Noah stared at her. She was looking around the hallway, as if hoping a medic would miraculously appear.

"I know the whole story," she continued. "I've read all the files. The 15-6 report, the award recommendation forms, the commendations, all of it."

316

"What?" Noah blinked.

"I've got good sources. For a priority security clearance, I can get full access from the DOD." She grabbed his right hand and pressed it against his inner elbow. "Hold that," she ordered. "Hard."

She let go and began unbuttoning her shirt.

Noah blinked again, then shook his head. The hallway swam around him.

"Yeah, an IED." He licked his lips, his mouth dry. "I didn't spot it."

She frowned. "You and thousands of other people."

"Not thousands."

"Well, not then, not that day. But if IEDs were so easy to spot, Iraq would have been a much safer place, right?" She was folding her shirt, not neatly, but quickly, almost rolling it up and turning the fabric into a pad, letting the sleeves hang loose.

Noah might be bleeding out, but he wasn't so far gone that he didn't appreciate the sight before him. Her bra was midnight blue, trimmed with a delicate bow of cream-colored silken ribbon. It was probably ornamental. But it made his fingers itch to tug at the trailing ends, to see if untying its knot unwrapped her curves. Her really nice, soft, smooth, gorgeous curves.

He closed his eyes again.

"And you can't say you killed them because you missed spotting a bomb," Grace continued, as she placed the pad on his arm. "I mean you could, but that would be stupid. The person who made the bomb, the people who planted it, they're the ones responsible for its consequences."

Noah winced, part the pain as she tugged the sleeves of her shirt around his arm, part from the hard truth in her words. Maybe it was stupid to blame himself for Joe's death. But that had always been easier than acknowledging the others. As long as he was seeing Joe's eyes, he wasn't seeing what came later, what happened next.

"And unless a whole bunch of people told a whole lot of lies," Grace said, drawing the sleeves tighter, "you didn't shoot anyone."

"No," Noah agreed. Maybe he would have. It might have been instinct. If he'd had his weapon in his hands, would he have fired at anything that moved? But it hadn't happened that way.

Grace sat back on her heels. "So what did you do?"

"I grabbed the wheel of the truck. Joe had been driving. And I..." He stared down at her shirt on his arm, at the blood seeping up through the cloth. "I stuck my foot on the gas pedal and I steered it off the road."

He looked at Grace, meeting her eyes. "Into them," he told her. "I drove into them. Over them."

She took a breath. "The woman and the kid." She said it as a statement, not a question, but Noah nodded anyway.

"Ouch." Her expression didn't judge him. If anything, she looked sympathetic. "They gave you a medal for clearing the road. Valor under fire. Despite grave injuries, you made it possible for the rest of the convoy to get out of the ambush."

She sounded like she was quoting from some paper she'd read, but he nodded again.

"So you saved lives?"

He shrugged.

"And that doesn't make up for it?"

He shook his head. "I killed them. Nothing I do can ever change that. I'll blame myself forever."

"Aw, man, you shouldn't feel that way," Joe said, his voice low, worried.

But his words were almost drowned out by a sharp, *"Piffle!"* from directly above Noah.

"How ridiculous you are," Nadira continued. *"On what planet does a hijab protect one from an explosion that shatters vehicles? Do you really think Misam's t-shirt was more armor-plated than that stupid truck you were in? We were dead the moment that bomb went off. You could have driven over us with a dozen trucks and it wouldn't have made us any more dead than we already were."*

Noah froze.

318

"Mama, mama, you're back!"

"I was never gone," Nadira said, sounding irritated. *"Just not quite all here."* She sniffed. *"And really, the idea that blood would be good for me is revolting. I'm not a vampire."*

Noah wasn't sure whether he wanted to laugh or cry.

Grace tilted her head to the side. "Are you okay?"

"You blamed me, too." The words rasped out of Noah's throat. He knew Nadira did, had. She'd said so, often enough.

"Of course I did! I blame all of you American soldiers. What were you doing there, anyway? Some Saudi terrorists attack your country so you invade mine in response? Pure stupidity and greed."

But she heaved an impatient and frustrated sigh. *"And I much prefer to blame you than myself. I was told not to leave the house that day, but I was tired of being cooped up. I took Misam for a walk, knowing I would get into trouble for it. I simply thought the trouble would be a scolding from my mother-in-law about my impudent ways, not our deaths."*

"What's happening?" Grace asked.

Noah shook his head, dizzy with confusion. And maybe with blood loss, too. The floor seemed to be racing toward him, but he put his hand out and caught himself.

"I didn't kill them," he said. The kaleidoscope was spinning again, the world spinning with it.

Grace grabbed for his arm, squeezing the inner elbow as Noah grunted with the pain.

"Still bleeding," she said. "Maybe you didn't kill them, but I hope to hell you haven't killed yourself. Hold on, Noah. Nat's coming, I promise."

Down the hall, the doorway to Natalya's scanner room opened.

Noah lifted his head to look as Akira stepped out. She was cradling her belly and she looked pale, as pale as he felt.

"Um, Grace?" she started.

"What's she's doing out here?" Dillon said. *"We're too dangerous for her!"*

"Are you okay?" Grace said sharply, without letting go of Noah.

"I thought I wet my pants," Akira said, sounding tragic.

Noah wanted to reassure her. Accidents happened. He'd had a company commander explain it once, something to do with the limbic system and the fight-or-flight response, but he couldn't remember the details.

He couldn't find the words, either. His brain was too fuzzy, his vision a mix of light and dark spots. But he retained enough awareness to understand her next words.

"I don't think I did, though," she continued. "I think my water broke."

35

DILLON

THIS WAS A DISASTER. DILLON WANTED TO RUN AROUND IN
circles, screaming, and if it would have helped, he would definitely
have done so.

Instead he stood motionless in the hallway, halfway between
Akira and Noah. He and Joe and Misam had backed away from
Noah when Noah cut himself, not wanting to take energy from his
blood. When Nadira started reforming, Joe and Misam had ventured
closer, but Dillon had stayed where he was.

"It's too early," he told Akira.

"I know that," she responded, sounding grumpy.

"It's too early," Grace called from where she still crouched by
Noah. He'd fallen forward from his kneeling position, not unconscious, but definitely losing control. She was helping him to a sitting
position against the wall, while trying to keep pressure on his arm.

The amount of blood was horrifying. The red was so intense on
the white of the tile floor, under the bright hallway lights, that it
looked surreal.

"I know that," Akira repeated. "What the hell happened out
here?" But before either Grace or Dillon could answer, she grimaced

and folded over around her belly. She started panting, quick, sharp breaths.

"We need a doctor," Joe said. He was hovering over Noah and Grace, fists clenched.

Nadira had scooped up Misam and was holding him close, her eyes closed. She might have said she didn't need Noah's blood, but the expression of exhausted relief on her face told another story. Or at least revealed that it had been a close call.

"What did that feel like, Mama?" Misam was bubbling over with questions. "Did it hurt? Could you hear me? Were you talking to us?"

"The Hulk? Really, Misam?" Nadira answered him without opening her eyes, resting her lips on his hair.

He laughed, part relief, part glee. Leaning back, he put one hand on either side of her face, pushing them together until she pursed her lips. "Never do that again. Do you hear me?"

"Never," she agreed. "Shielded rooms, one more thing that we must stay far away from." She opened her eyes and looked down at Noah. He was slumped against the wall, eyes closed, face white, even his lips turning pale. His head was down, chin against his chest. "Is he going to be all right?"

"Not unless we get some help here," Joe replied.

Akira stopped panting and straightened. "I think you're supposed to elevate the injury."

"Elevate it?" Grace looked blank.

Akira lifted her arm above her head, as if she were a student answering a question.

Grace looked dubious, but she raised Noah's arm. She was using two hands, fingers clenched on the sopping shirt, but blood was still trickling through her fingers. "Hang on, Noah. Stay with me. Stay with me. Shit." She brushed her face against the top of her own arm as if she were trying to get her hair out of her eyes, but Dillon could see that she'd started to cry, tears spilling down her cheeks.

"Oh, hell," Akira said. She hurried toward Grace and the ghosts, skirting her way around Dillon. "None of you zap me, all right? Being premature is gonna be hard enough on Henry."

Dillon trailed along behind her, and the others backed away to give her room.

"This room's got medical supplies," Dillon told her, pointing out the room that he'd opened for Noah.

"Got it." She reached for the door handle.

"It's locked," Grace started as the door swung open. "Damn it," she breathed, then quickly added, "Look for a trauma kit. Nat's got them in there somewhere. Maybe one of the bottom drawers? Not like we have a lot of use for them, but…"

She let the words trail off because Akira was already inside the room, hunting through drawers. "Hang on, Noah," she said again, her voice soft.

Akira emerged, already ripping open the plastic bag surrounding the medical supplies, as the elevator door at the far end of the hallway slid open. Natalya stepped out, followed by Kenzi, Rose and Sophia.

Natalya immediately broke into a run, the others hurrying after her. She skidded to a halt next to them and shook her head. "Geez, Grace, really? In your underwear?"

Grace's smile was wan. She tried to wipe her face again, only succeeding in smearing it with blood. It mingled with the tears.

"Good lord, he did a really good job," Natalya said, eyes seeming to measure the quantity of blood surrounding them. "Was he trying to kill himself?" She didn't wait for an answer, glancing at Kenzi with a worried frown.

The little girl gave her a pleading look, her hands folded in front of her, but made no move toward Noah until Natalya nodded, adding a firm, "Gently."

Kenzi darted forward. With total disregard for the blood and gore, she placed her fingers on Noah's arm as Grace moved out of the way.

"Ooh, you killed him, after all," Sophia said as she arrived. "And I didn't have anything to do with it."

"He's not dead," Joe snapped. "He can't be. He won't be."

"He looks awfully dead to me," Sophia said. The words were callous, but her frown was uneasy.

"Kenzi will fix him," Rose said, but she looked uncertain, too. And then she wrinkled her nose, looking around at the others.

"If she has enough energy, that is," she added apologetically. "I'm not sure I can help her. I don't suppose I could borrow some of your energy?"

"Whatever you need." Joe held out his hand to her.

"Me, too," Dillon said.

"Me, me!" Misam waved. "I was very upset. I must have lots and lots of energy right now."

Nadira held him closer, but then said, only a little grudgingly, "I don't mind helping. This was stupid of him, but he did it for me. It was a generous thought, I suppose I can't just let him die."

Rose beamed at them all. "Lovely."

Akira bit her lip. "My water broke. Save Noah, but you might save some of that energy for Henry and me, too. He might need some help."

Rose clapped her hands together. "How exciting!"

Akira rested a hand on her stomach. "I'm not sure that's the word I'd choose."

Natalya pulled her watchful gaze away from Kenzi and reached a hand out to Akira. "You and the baby are both going to be fine. I promise."

Maybe she meant her gesture as reassurance but Akira passed her the pouch of medical supplies.

"Ah, thank you." Natalya's smile flashed. She squatted next to Noah and Kenzi as Noah stirred, his chin lifting. "Okay, that's enough, honey."

Natalya loosened the sleeves of Grace's makeshift bandage and let it drop to the ground as Kenzi lowered Noah's arm. The little girl stroked her fingers along the length of the incision. On his wrist, at the shallowest point of the cut, the skin closed, turning pink as a scab

324

began to form along his inner arm. At the deepest point, inside his elbow, the blood stopped seeping.

"Whoa. That's cool." Sophia peered over Kenzi's shoulder as the little girl swayed.

"Rose?" Natalya directed the word to empty air. She shot a glance at Akira and Akira nodded in reassurance of her own, so Natalya turned back to Noah.

"My pleasure," Rose said and put her hands on Kenzi's shoulders. The other ghosts clustered around her.

"What do we need to do?" Joe asked.

"Just relax," Rose answered. "You won't feel a thing."

Akira was watching, wide-eyed with wonder. Dillon couldn't see any energy flowing, but Rose's color deepened, the gold coming back to her hair, her skirt changing from its translucent pastel back to its original deep pink shade.

And he could easily see Kenzi bouncing back as if she'd never touched Noah at all. She shook herself like a puppy after a bath, and chirped, "Sizzles."

Noah's eyelashes fluttered. He lifted his head.

Grace sat down on the floor. She put her hands up to cover her face, maybe to hide her tears, or maybe to cry more freely, but stopped before she touched herself. She lowered her hands, fingers wide, as if she'd only just recognized that they were covered in blood.

Nadira was frowning at Joe, her expression puzzled.

"What is it?" Joe asked her.

"I was about to ask you the same thing." She tipped her head to the side, shifting Misam on her hip. "What is that behind you?"

Joe looked over his shoulder.

Dillon followed his gaze, then drew back, blinking in surprise.

It wasn't a door. It looked nothing like any door he'd ever seen. There was no doorknob, no hinges, no frame. And it wasn't a passageway, either. It didn't look like a hallway or an airlock or a cloud or any of the things that he'd ever imagined.

But the air shimmered with a vibration that practically begged for him to step into it. It wasn't exactly visible, but it was present in a way that made it seem as if it had always been there and always would be.

Joe poked at it. Gingerly.

It didn't move and his hand didn't disappear into it, but its essential door-ness didn't change. Dillon knew that if Joe turned around and took two steps forward through it, he would disappear into the shimmer as if he'd never been.

"It sparkles." Misam sounded awed.

Sparkles? Dillon frowned. He didn't see sparkles.

"Mama, mama, look!" Misam pointed over Nadira's shoulder.

Nadira turned her head and glanced behind her.

She had a shimmer, too.

Her mouth opened, then closed without comment. Carefully, she set Misam down on the ground and crouched to peer beyond him. Now that he was standing apart from his mother, Dillon could see that Misam had a shimmer of his own.

Dillon could barely breathe.

He wanted to look.

He was terrified to look.

But carefully, as if the shimmer might be a bird perched on his shoulder, he let his head drift sideways until he could see behind him.

It was almost like a soap bubble, a big one. Except it wasn't like a soap bubble at all. There was no roundness, no sense of a surface. And it wasn't a light. Dillon didn't know why Misam was saying sparkles, because there was nothing glittery about it. But at the same time, it felt like light, or maybe warmth, as if it was emanating energy just beyond his ability to perceive it.

"What is it?" Sophia asked. She was looking from one to another of them, her brow furrowed with puzzled concern.

"What are you looking at?" Akira asked.

"Doorways," Joe said, his voice hushed, reverent. "We have our doorways."

"But what happened?" Nadira said. "Where did they come from?"

"Maybe it was because Noah almost died again?" Joe replied.

"Or did die?" Nadira stood, but she put a hand on Misam's head. "For a moment or two, long enough to open a path that closed once before?"

Akira didn't look like she was paying attention anymore. She was panting again, entirely focused inward, one hand resting on the wall, the other curled into a tight fist.

Suddenly everyone was talking at once. Dillon let the words flow past him, too overwhelmed with his own emotions to listen to the others.

He had a door.

His own door, his own path. Whatever had been keeping him here, whatever had made him a ghost, his time in this dimension was coming to an end.

Akira stopped panting. "That doesn't make sense," she said, just as if she'd been part of the conversation all along. "Why would Dillon get a doorway just because Noah almost died? When I died before, no one got any doorways out of it."

"Maybe my grandma did?" Dillon offered.

"Maybe." She narrowed her eyes at him, sounding skeptical. "I suppose it's possible. When she was red, she didn't have a doorway or she would have used it. But I don't like it."

"Maybe it's because we all gave Noah energy." Misam leaned into Nadira. His eyes were wide with excitement, but he clutched her robe with a ferocious grip. "Maybe we needed to save his life, maybe that's why we were here."

"I would have given him energy, too," Sophia said, half sulky, half defiant. She couldn't see the doorways, Dillon realized. And she hadn't gotten one of her own.

"We didn't really save him, though." Joe nodded toward Kenzi. "She did it. We just helped her recover faster."

Natalya had been focused on Noah, but she looked up and frowned at Akira. "Dillon has a doorway?"

Akira nodded at her. "And the others, too." She gestured at Noah and the bloody floor. "I don't intend to ever emulate your method, but you did something right."

"I'm not sure it was this," Noah said slowly, staring at his arm. "I think maybe..." His gaze flickered to Grace and stayed. "Maybe I let go of something I'd been holding on to for a long time."

Grace met his gaze. She took a breath, then released it, and brushed away her tears, ignoring the blood on her hands. "Maybe. Maybe I did, too." She looked as if she wanted to say more, but then she shook her head and pushed herself to her feet. "I need to get cleaned up."

"Do you have a change of clothes here?" Natalya asked her.

As the living people began consulting on the practical details of their physical reality, Dillon turned his attention back to the other ghosts.

"Well. This is very exciting." Nadira didn't sound excited. She was looking at Joe. "I suppose we all go through our own doors now, to our own afterlives?"

"I suppose," Joe agreed. He didn't sound excited either.

"I didn't get a door," Sophia said. She wasn't crying, but she was staring at the floor. "I guess that means I stick around."

"You could come with one of us," Dillon offered but he already knew that Sophia wasn't going to agree. She wanted to see her parents. He glanced over his shoulder again, less tentatively. The shimmer was still there.

Sophia shook her head. Her nose looked like it was getting pink and her eyes were starting to glisten, but she lifted her chin and said, "I'll be okay."

Nadira and Joe weren't paying attention to her. They seemed to be engaged in some sort of wordless communication, but Misam let go of his mother's robe and took Sophia's hand. "Are you sure, Sophia? Won't you be lonely without us?"

As the two of them started talking, Dillon sighed.

For a fleeting moment, he was tempted to dive through his doorway like a character in an action movie escaping a hail of bullets.

He was ready to leave. He was tired of being a helpless observer to events in the material world. And more than that, he wanted to know what came next. He wanted to see his grandmother again. He wanted to find out what Rose's flying — metaphorical or not — would be like.

But maybe not quite yet.

Rose's doorway had lasted for all the years that Henry had lived with her, so a doorway, once it appeared, was probably pretty stable.

And how could he leave while Akira was in labor? So maybe he'd stick around to meet Henry again and make sure that the two of them were okay. And then there was his parents' wedding. And his aunt's wedding.

Plus, he wanted a chance to talk to Rose again, to try to persuade her to come with him. The universe was a dangerous place for spirits trapped on the material plane.

And if all that meant that he was around until Sophia had talked to her parents... well, there was nothing wrong with that.

He could wait until Sophia was ready.

3 6

NOAH

THE LAST WORDS NOAH REMEMBERED BEFORE GOING UNDER
were something to do with water. He remembered nothing from
being unconscious: no white light, no visitations from the welcoming
dead, not even a sense of mystical peace. He'd felt himself fading out
and then he was awake again, while his voices talked about doorways
and a little girl magically healed him.

Grace could say all she wanted about the science of werewolves
and cellular transformations, but Noah knew magic when he saw it.

Or delusion, he supposed. Maybe he really was dead and this was
the universe playing an elaborate practical joke. Or maybe he was
locked up in an institution somewhere, unconscious and dreaming.
Or maybe life really was one big virtual reality and they were avatars
believing they were alive while a computer controlled their environment.

It didn't matter.

He hadn't killed Nadira or Misam.

He hadn't killed Joe, either. But while he'd felt guilty about Joe —
hell, yeah, plenty of guilt — it had never been the kind that was

unbearable to look at, unbearable to even let his thoughts brush against. It was just normal old-fashioned survivor guilt.

The doctor was talking to him, Noah realized. He tried to pay attention, but the ghosts were all talking, too.

"*I suppose this is it, then,*" Nadira said.

"*I guess so, yeah.*" Joe sounded troubled. "*No reason to stick around. Although—*"

"Not so fast," Noah interrupted him. "I need to talk to you."

"You need liquids," Natalya corrected him. "And plenty of them. I can hook you up to an IV or you can start drinking, your choice, but decide now because it's time I started paying attention to the pregnant lady in the room. I don't like how fast her contractions are coming."

"Got it." Noah tried to push himself to his feet. The hallway spun around him and nausea surged.

"Careful." Grace grabbed his elbow.

"Got it," Noah repeated. His eyes met hers. She was a mess, but the green of her eyes was deeper than ever and held the same magnetic pull that they'd always had for him. He paused for a breath, wishing he knew how to share all the thoughts and emotions spinning around inside his head with her, but it was impossible. It felt like he'd dropped a boulder he'd been holding onto — and hiding behind — and everything left inside him was a jumbled, incoherent mess.

"You okay?" she asked him and he knew she wasn't only asking if he could stand on his own.

"Yeah." He let his gaze drop to her mouth. It would be totally weird if he kissed her now, but he wanted to with a bone-deep desire that was so much more than simple attraction. He wanted her the way his body wanted air to breathe, the way his soul craved joy. The way he wanted life itself.

"Liquids," Natalya ordered. "Lots of them. Grace, take care of it."

The moment broke.

Grace looked away from him and nodded at her sister, then took charge with her usual efficiency. Within minutes, Noah found himself alone in a restroom, holding a pile of neatly folded clothes that belonged to one of her brothers and a sports drink.

Or almost alone.

"Joe?" he said as he set everything down on the counter by the sink.

"*One and the same,*" Joe replied.

"Anyone else?" Noah asked, turning the water on. The blood drying on his skin itched, so he didn't wait for the water to warm up, just stuck his hands and arms under the cool stream.

"*Just me,*" Joe said. It sounded like he was standing at the sink next to Noah. If Noah closed his eyes, let the words be his only reality, he could imagine the two of them back in Basic, quietly rolling their eyes over the latest blasts from their drill sergeant.

But he didn't close his eyes. The water was running red, then pink down the drain. He watched it flow, then lifted his eyes and stared at his own reflection in the mirror. His scars didn't show, never had. But he'd always known that they were there.

Were they gone? He didn't think so. It wasn't that easy.

But he turned his arm up and eyed the half-healed cut that ran almost its length.

Maybe all his scars were now as faded as that one.

"*Pretty damn cool.*" Joe laughed. The sound held nothing but delight. But his voice sobered when he added, "*I'm glad. Really glad. It's not your time.*"

"It shouldn't have been your time either. I'm sorry." Noah took a deep breath. "I'm so sorry. I fucked up."

"*You didn't do anything.*"

"I let you get killed."

"*I was the driver. I should have seen that damn IED.*"

"Crew's supposed to be watching. Eyes open, remember? I was…" Noah scooped up some cold water and splashed it on his face, wanting the chill, the shock. He took another breath, and admitted the painful truth. "I was so fucking bored."

"*Dude. It was fucking boring out there.*"

Miles of sand. Miles and miles and miles of interminable dirt and desert and more dirt. It could be beautiful. The sunsets, in the wide expanse, with the haze of dust and shimmer of heat in the air, could steal your breath away. But the hours lasted like days, the days like weeks, except for the brief moments when time suddenly skewed, compressing and spiraling out of control. Joe's blood spurting through his hands had been the fastest forever imaginable. No time and an eternity.

He shook his head again, but this time not to shove the memories away. Instead, he let them come, let them wash over him. Joe's eyes, the emotion, grabbing for the steering wheel. He hadn't been thinking, only reacting.

"*You didn't do anything wrong,*" Joe said.

Noah wasn't sure that was true. But he wasn't sure it was false, either. Maybe it didn't matter. One way or another, it was over. It was time to let it go.

"*And what I did to you...*"

"What did you do to me?" Noah turned off the water.

"*I left you behind. Made you do it all alone.*"

Noah snorted, starting to strip off his bloody clothes. "You never left me at all."

"*Yeah. Sorry about that, too.*"

Noah pulled his t-shirt over his head and dropped it in the sink. "If you're gonna apologize, apologize for the right stuff. Remember that nurse in Germany?"

Joe laughed. "*She was hot.*"

Noah shook his head. It had been early days, soon after his injury. He hadn't gotten used to ignoring the chatter and a stream of irate Arabic had brought an abrupt end to an otherwise friendly second date. He turned the water back on and let it run over the clothes in the sink.

"*Grace is, too. You should go for it, man.*"

Noah didn't answer. He grabbed a handful of paper towels to clean up the rest of the blood.

"*I'm serious. The two of you look good together.*"

Looks weren't everything. But Noah didn't want to disagree with Joe. The kaleidoscope was still spinning and he didn't know what the world was going to look like when all the pieces finally fell into place. Grace — even covered in blood and tears — was still a millionaire CEO. And he... well, he didn't know who he was.

"*I guess I won't be here to see it, though,*" Joe said.

"You can stick around if you want." The words came unexpectedly easily.

"*Nah, it's time.*" Joe didn't sound happy about it.

"You sure?" Noah paused, half in, half out of the sweatpants Grace had found for him.

"*Yeah, I'm ready.*"

He still didn't sound sure, but Noah finished dressing before he asked, tentatively, "Anything you want me to do for you first?"

"*I know this might not be fun, but you could visit my mom, maybe. You don't have to tell her about the whole ghost thing, but maybe... I don't know. Bring her some ice cream. Butter pecan.*"

"I can do that."

"*And go see your mom, too.*"

Noah hesitated for a moment, but he turned his arm up and eyed the line along it again. It was still healing, much faster than it should, the scab now fully formed into his elbow.

Joe was right. Noah didn't know what he'd tell his family, if anything, but he was lucky to be alive.

He needed to do better at being alive.

"I will."

Someone knocked on the door.

"Noah?" Grace's voice. "You okay in there?"

"Almost done," Noah called back.

"*Good. Will you take me to see my parents?*" Sophia said at his elbow.

"*Sophia! You do not belong in there,*" Nadira hissed, but her voice also came from too close, as if she'd joined them inside the room instead of staying in the hallway.

"*Hey. Bathroom. Privacy, remember?*" Joe objected.

"*He's dressed.*"

"*I'm not looking.*"

Noah couldn't tell which scornful reply came from which female voice, but he bit back his smile and answered Sophia's question. "Not right this second. But yeah, I will."

He'd take a road trip. Joe's mom, Sophia's parents, his own family. Maybe by the time he got there, he'd know what to say to them. How to find his place there, the common ground that had escaped him for so long.

"*Thank you.*"

"*Good. Then...*" Nadira started before pausing.

"*Then it is time for us to go!*" The kid sounded jubilant. "*Are you ready, Joe? Are you ready?*"

"*I guess so.*" Joe didn't sound ready. He sounded grim.

Noah frowned. What was Joe thinking? Why was he worried?

"*We asked Rose whether different doorways might lead to different places,*" Nadira said briskly. "*She does not think so, but she can not say with confidence.*"

"*I was wondering that, too,*" Joe said. "*You hoping for Islamic paradise?*"

"*Well...*"

"*I hope it's a nice place,*" Joe said. "*I hope it's everything you deserve. You should go someplace great, you really should.*"

"*Pfft.*" Nadira's scornful noise was more of a gentle dismissal.

There was a momentary silence. Noah wished he could see the ghosts. What were they doing?

"*You deserve someplace nice, too,*" Nadira finally said. "*I'm sorry for all the unkind things I've said over the years. I know it was never your fault.*"

Joe's laugh sounded choked. "*No worries. It's been... well, yeah.*" He hesitated, before adding, "*I'll miss you.*"

"*If it happens that way,*" Nadira said. "*It might not. All our doors might lead to the same place.*"

"*Or they might not,*" Joe said.

Another pause. Noah turned the water off and started squeezing the excess out of his mostly-rinsed clothes.

"*Are you guys just going to keep staring at each other?*" Sophia finally spoke.

"*No, of course not.*" Nadira returned to her previous briskness. "*It is time to go. But—*"

"*Mama and me are both going through my door,*" Misam interrupted her. "*Do you want to come with us, Joe?*"

"*Through your door?*" Joe sounded surprised.

"*I will not risk losing Misam,*" Nadira replied as if that was obvious, before adding, "*If you wished to come with us...*"

"*Really?*" Joe asked.

"*You might not want to,*" she said quickly. "*I understand if you don't want to chance losing your, what is it, streets of gold? They sound very... pretty.*"

"*They sound cold,*" Joe said. Noah could hear the grin in his voice. "*And shiny.*"

"*Our paradise has much delicious food in it,*" Nadira said and Noah could hear that she was smiling, too.

"*Also, someday, probably, your, uh, husband,*" Joe said.

"*And his houris,*" Nadira's tone was acerbic. "*That shall not concern us. But if you do not wish to join us—*"

"*No, I do,*" Joe interrupted her. "*Very much. I... I would miss you.*"

"*And I, you,*" Nadira said.

Noah pressed his lips together to hide his smile.

"*Okay, you guys should stop staring at each other now,*" Sophia said.

"*Let's go, Mama, Joe. It is time! Goodbye, Sophia. Don't cry too much. Goodbye, Noah!*"

"*Allah bless you, Sophia. And you, too, Noah.*"

The words felt unexpectedly warm to Noah, as if Nadira truly meant the blessings she offered. He swallowed around a lump in his throat.

"*Goodbye, man. Take care,*" Joe said.

"Goodbye," Noah said, his voice husky. "And good luck. To all of you."

"*Goodbye,*" Sophia said. "*Don't take any wooden nickels.*"

"*Why would we do that?*" Misam asked. "*What's a wooden nickel?*"

"*I don't know, it's just something my grandpa used to say. If you see him...*"

"*We will tell him hello! We will tell him you are on your way and coming soon! You are coming soon, right?*" Misam's voice was moving as if he was bouncing around the room, from one person to another.

"*I hope so. If Noah will take me to my parents.*"

"I will," Noah promised again. "And I'll even talk to them for you."

"*Don't wait too long,*" Misam ordered.

"We won't," Noah replied. "We'll go right away."

"*Good, good,*" Misam said. "*Are we all set?*"

"*Everyone ready?*" Nadira asked.

"*Should we say goodbye to Dillon and Rose?*" Joe said.

"*They're with Akira in the prison room. I am not going back there.*" Nadira's voice was firm.

"*They know we are going,*" Misam said. "*Dillon said to say goodbye, Rose said something about time being a construct. I think it was a quote from a television show, but I don't know which one.*"

"*All right, then.*" Joe sounded resolute. "*Noah...*"

"Butter pecan," Noah replied. "I'll take care of it."

He wasn't going to cry. Not because of the humiliation factor — real men could cry, Noah knew, and technically he was alone in a bathroom, so what better time? But there was too much relief and honest joy in his emotions for the loss to hurt.

His voices, his ghosts, were going to be fine.

And so was he.

"*Mama, you hold my hand, and Joe, you can hold my other hand,*" Misam ordered. "*And I will lead the way into my doorway.*"

"*Do you think I'll get houris in this afterlife?*" Joe asked.

"*Ha.*" Nadira snorted. "*You will have to live without.*"

"*But Misam will get them, right? Maybe he'll share,*" Joe said, words teasing.

"*There will be no sharing of houris,*" Nadira said. "*Take Misam's hand before we leave you behind.*"

"*But—*" Joe started.

"*But nothing,*" Misam said. "*No arguing!*"

Noah smiled at the exasperation in his voice, and he was still smiling when the room fell silent.

37

GRACE

Henry was a girl.

She was also healthy, breathing well, and a good size for such a premature baby, but Zane was having trouble processing the surprise.

"But he's a girl," he said, for possibly the fifth or sixth time. He'd met them at the hospital, where Akira had delivered a first baby in record time. By early evening, the baby had been born, examined, measured, tested, pronounced beautiful, and half a dozen visitors had already come and gone.

"I know," Akira said, gazing in wonder at the bundle in the crook of her arm, just as Henry opened her mouth and yawned, tiny baby tongue lapping at her lips. "Oh, my gosh, she has the most perfect tongue. Look at how tiny it is."

"Are we gonna name her Henrietta?" Zane asked.

Akira made a face. "No, of course not. That's a terrible name."

"But..."

"We have time, we can think about it."

"How did we not know that she was a girl?" Zane asked. "You had an ultrasound. Two of them."

On the other side of the bed, Natalya smirked.

341

"You knew, didn't you?" Grace said to her sister.

Natalya widened her eyes but didn't respond.

Sometimes she could be so infuriating.

And other times... Grace couldn't help remembering the relief she'd felt at Natalya's arrival a few hours earlier. She'd been so sure Noah was dying, so sure that he wasn't going to make it. His survival was a miracle. Nat's miracle. Or maybe Kenzi's.

Or maybe the universe had listened to her own desperate litany. She hadn't been praying out loud, but she'd been making promises. And she'd felt something happen. Not something external, no warm light or beneficent glow, but a knot loosening inside her, a ball of anger and grief and agonizing pain releasing and floating away.

She didn't exactly forgive Dillon for dying. He'd been an idiot. But the thought didn't bring the usual pain. People made mistakes. Dillon's had been huge, but it wasn't like he could turn back time and reverse it.

And she'd made mistakes of her own. She'd just been luckier than him. Much luckier.

"Helen's a nice name," Akira said, giving a yawn of her own. "A little like Henry, a little like Eleanor. Sort of your mom's name, but not."

"Helen," Zane repeated after her, tracing a finger down the line of the baby's cheek. "I like it. Gentle, peaceful."

Natalya pressed her lips together, holding back her smile.

Grace narrowed her eyes at her, wondering about her sister's amusement.

Natalya patted Akira's arm and said, "We should let you guys get some rest. Congratulations again. And welcome to the world, baby Helen. You're going to like it here."

Akira and Zane tore their attention away from the baby long enough to make their good-byes, but they were already busy admiring her again as Natalya and Grace made their way to the door.

Noah was waiting for Grace at her car, leaning against the hood, his head bent over his phone. Grace's steps slowed when she saw him, then sped up again. She hadn't expected him, but she felt her heart lifting, a smile breaking out on her face as she came close.

"How long have you been waiting? You could have come inside." She didn't wait for him to answer, before adding, "The baby's fine, so is Akira. Four pounds six ounces so the littlest thing you've ever seen in your life, but healthy enough that she's staying with Akira in her room instead of the NICU. Probably for a few days, though, until she gets a little bigger."

"She?" Noah straightened, sliding his phone into his pocket.

Grace's smile widened. "A girl, yeah. That was a surprise. I think they're going to name her Helen."

"Nice name," Noah said.

Silence fell between them.

It wasn't awkward, but Noah's eyes were on her, steady, intent, dark with an expression she couldn't read.

Grace bit her inner lip. Her body felt like it was humming with the heat of her attraction, vibrating with the warmth of wanting him. What would happen if she stepped closer, pressed herself against him, lifted her mouth for his kiss?

But maybe she should tell him how she felt instead. What had Akira suggested? Say she was attracted, ask if he felt the same?

She didn't really need to ask, though. She could see the desire in his eyes. She took a step closer, opening her mouth, not sure what she was going to say, but he spoke first.

"I wanted to say good-bye," he said.

"What?" She fell back the step she'd just taken.

He thumbed toward his truck, parked a few spaces down from her car. "Heading out now."

"You're leaving?" Her voice sounded odd to her ears.

He nodded, his own smile fading. "Feels like the right time."

It was not the right time. It was totally the wrong time. Of course, anytime would be the wrong time, but still — they hadn't had a chance to talk. She hadn't told him anything: not what had happened, not what she thought, not how she felt, nothing.

"But are you well enough?" It wasn't what she wanted to say. "You nearly died."

"Yeah, I feel fine. Better than."

"That's good." Grace swallowed. She wanted to object. She wanted to tell him he couldn't leave. She knotted her hands together, fighting the urge to reach out and touch him. "Where are you going?"

"DC, to start. Taking Sophia back to her parents."

"Oh."

More silence. Grace's throat felt tight, choked. Not as if she was going to cry, but as if this moment — standing in the glow of an over-head light, surrounded by asphalt, the bright lights of the emergency room behind them — was a turning point in her life, a time when everything hung in a balance that she couldn't see.

"And then home, eventually. It's been a long time since I've been back. I need to see my family. Talk to them."

Grace couldn't argue with that. Family mattered.

Noah tipped his head, as if listening to a voice Grace couldn't hear, then nodded. "Go ahead. I won't go without you."

"Sophia?" Grace asked.

Noah nodded. "She's gonna visit the baby, and say good-bye to Dillon and Rose. They should still be there."

"Dillon? I thought he was—" She made a swooshing movement with her hand. "Out of here. Moving on."

"Not quite yet, I guess. The others have, though."

"That's good." Grace didn't know whether she was saying it was good that Dillon was still around or good that the others weren't — the words were automatic, just meaningless sounds as she gazed into Noah's eyes.

She didn't want him to leave.

Her father was right, Noah belonged in Tassamara.

He belonged with her.

344

"I wanted to thank you before I left," Noah continued.

'Thank you' was not a declaration of desire. Grace didn't want to be thanked.

"For what?"

His ridiculously beautiful mouth curved up in a smile. "Saving my life?"

"Oh. That." Grace's mouth twisted. She'd had plenty of time in the waiting room while Akira was in labor to consider every moment of the day's events. She shook her head. "No, I screwed up."

He raised an eyebrow.

"The scalpel you used was right there on the floor. If I'd thought for two seconds, I would have realized you must have opened the medical supply closet and remembered the trauma kits. I was using my shirt when there were fancy hemostatic coagulation bandages designed to stop bleeding two feet away from us." She sighed. "Well, maybe ten feet. Either way..." She shook her head again. "Don't thank me."

"I wouldn't have made it without you."

"I'm glad you did." More than glad, although she couldn't explain to him what his survival meant to her without getting into complicated stories about orange juice glasses and failing when she'd never had a chance. About guilt and forgiveness, holding on and letting go.

Plus, the world was better with him in it.

Not that he was going to be in her world for long, not if he was leaving.

"I wanted to apologize, too, for the short notice. Although it's not like you ever really needed another security guard." His wry smile invited her to share the irony, but she couldn't bring herself to smile back.

"It's not a problem." That sounded too abrupt and like she didn't care. She did care, way too much. She tried to smile. "Although the job will always be there for you, if you..." She let the words trail off.

If you want to come back, if you need a job.

If you miss me as much as I'm going to miss you.

Nope, she couldn't say that.

His eyes hadn't left hers. His gaze was searching. "So..." he started.

She tilted her head in question, not trusting her voice.

"We're alone," he said. "First time ever, really."

Her heart started to beat faster. She could hear it thudding in her ears. She stepped closer to him, stopping only when they were almost toe-to-toe.

"Are you shy?" she asked, lifting her face to his.

He ran his fingers up her arms, his touch light. "I admit, the crowd scene has been a little off-putting."

"Scared they might judge your technique?"

"Something like that." His hands reached her face. He cupped her cheeks, and for a moment just held her, looking into her eyes. Then he bent his head and took her lips.

She melted. For weeks, she'd been wondering about that kiss in the forest. Had it really been as good as she remembered or had her memory added flourishes?

It was as good as she remembered. Maybe even better. There was none of the awkwardness of a first kiss, the uncertainty of tasting a stranger. Instead, they fit together like they'd been designed for it.

His lips against hers were magic. Her brain turned off. All the worries, all the what-ifs, got lost in a flood of sensation. His hands against her skin, the rush of desire running through her veins, her body flushing with heat and lust.

Time stopped.

All there was, was the moment she was in, his scent, his flavor, his feel. She wanted him with a straightforward intensity that had nothing to do with tangled emotions.

And then he pulled away.

She him go reluctantly, but he leaned forward, resting his forehead against hers.

"Damn," he whispered.

She laughed, breathless, but a hint of tears stung the back of her eyes. He was going to walk away. She could feel it in his body, in the energy coursing through his shoulders and arms. She should let go of him, step back herself, but she couldn't bring herself to do it.

And then she did.

She let her hands drop to her sides. He was leaving and as much as she wanted him to stay, she could see that he needed to go.

"Sophia's back," he said. "She says the baby looks like an alien."

Grace's chuckle was genuine. "She's beautiful. For a newborn."

"I guess I'll have to take your word for it." He glanced at the hospital. "They're trying to sleep."

"Yeah."

He nodded. There was a pause, and then he indicated his truck with a tilt of his head. "I should get on the road. Long drive ahead of me."

She nodded.

They stared at one another for one more long silent moment.

And then he turned and walked away.

GRACE DIDN'T MOPE. OR AT LEAST SHE TOLD HERSELF SHE wasn't moping. There were two weddings to plan, adoptions to arrange, a newborn baby to hold, and a company to run. Who had time to mope?

But Maggie fed her comfort food every time she ate at the diner, Max asked her to come kayaking at least twice a week, and Zane moved the Ms. Pac-Man machine out of storage and back into his office. Mrs. Swanson tsk-ed, shook her head, and suggested lavender. Even Lucas was uncharacteristically gentle, although that might have been Sylvie's influence.

Only Natalya didn't seem to notice or care whether Grace was moping or not. But she had five children to take care of, and happy-ever-after with five children wasn't quite as simple as a few signatures on some dotted lines.

Still, the days passed and Grace did her best to keep a smile on her face. She was not unhappy, she told herself firmly. What had happened, after all? A cute guy came to town and then left. It's not like there was any more between them than a couple of kisses and a few intense moments.

And if she lay awake at night wishing for what might have been, the evidence was easy enough to cover up with some over-priced under-eye concealer.

Her smile finally wore off on the day of the weddings. Plural, because Natalya had easily welcomed the idea of a double wedding with Sylvie and Lucas. Grace served as maid-of-honor to both brides, juggling bouquets and bachelorette parties with her usual efficiency.

The early afternoon ceremonies were held outside, underneath a gazebo built for the occasion next to the lake by Natalya's new house. The guest list included Colin's enormous extended family, Sylvie's sizable extended family, every local employee of General Directions and more than a few who traveled to be there, plus most of the town.

The reception was picnic-style at the house, kids running everywhere, gigantic outdoor fans under tents trying to keep the crowd cool in the June heat, flowers and music and food and people... and after the ceremonies, the reception line, the posing for photographs, and the first toasts, Grace was just done with the whole thing.

She grabbed a glass of champagne from a passing tray and beat a retreat into the house. She wasn't alone inside — people were flowing through the house, with plenty of guests opting for the temporary comfort of air-conditioning, plus the catering crew working out of the downstairs kitchen — so she headed for the stairs. She'd find a quiet place to sit, maybe the third floor patio overlooking the lake. But on the second floor landing, midway up the split-back flight of front stairs, she could hear voices from the third floor. It sounded like a few of the older kids were waging some sort of video game war in the upstairs great room. Not exactly the peace she had in mind.

Wrinkling her nose, she paused on the second floor, debating. Unfurnished guest room, one of the kids' bedrooms... but no. Movie theater room, of course. There'd be a movie playing — Natalya had programmed a day's worth of kids' movies on the digital theater system and then locked it down to "entertain the smaller guests while avoiding arguments" — but at least no one would talk to her.

Grace slipped into the theater. It was empty. Perfect.

But a movie was just starting.

The Little Mermaid.

Damn it, Nat.

Grace sighed and took a seat in the middle row. She shouldn't blame her sister for playing one of her favorite animated movies. There was no way Natalya could know how personal it had become to her. It was just a movie.

But when Ariel sang about being the girl who had everything and still wanting more, Grace's mouth twisted. She had everything, too, but yeah, she wanted more.

She wanted Noah.

Ariel could sing all she liked about people and warm sand and answered questions, but she wanted her prince, too. And so did Grace.

So how was she going to get him? She'd let Noah go, feeling like it was the right thing to do, but if Ariel was willing to make a deal with the devil — sea witch, whatever — and give up her voice, surely Grace ought to be willing to get on a plane and at least tell Noah how she felt.

She was so lost in her head that she didn't even look when someone came into the room and sat down next to her.

At least not until he leaned over and whispered, "All right, point taken. She's not singing about wanting the guy, is she?"

Grace gaped.

Noah grinned at her.

He looked beautiful. Of course, he always looked beautiful, but he was dressed for a wedding — gray suit, a navy-striped tie, clean-shaven, his hair trimmed — and elegant was a good look on him.

But it wasn't just the clothes. His eyes had lost their shadows.

"You... you... what are you doing here?" Grace stammered.

"I was invited," he replied.

"Natalya called you?"

"No." His grin grew wider. "Not exactly."

"Not exactly?"

"She handed me an invitation the day we met. Told me I didn't need to RSVP. It's been sitting in my truck ever since."

"She—" Grace realized she was still gaping and closed her mouth.

"Everyone else called me, though. Everyone except you."

"Everyone? Who?" Grace demanded.

"Your dad. Your brothers. Sylvie. Even Akira, although I think that was just because Zane passed her the phone. She sounded pretty out of it."

"What did they say?" Grace wasn't sure whether to flush with embarrassment or go kill her brothers. It was one thing for her to decide to look for Noah; another entirely for her family to be talking to him.

"Mostly they offered me jobs. Your dad offered to spin off a subsidiary for me."

"What?" Grace's response was indignant. "He can't just do that." Did her father have any idea of the paperwork involved in separating corporate assets? They had enough problems with the SEC already.

"As long as I picked one that could be based in Tassamara," Noah continued. "Lucas and Sylvie offered me contract jobs. Zane suggested I work for Special Affairs, maybe part-time if I wanted to go to school. Akira..." He chuckled. "Akira asked if I wanted to be a nanny. I guess the baby doesn't sleep?"

"She's very lively," Grace confirmed. The theater room wasn't dark, but the lights were dim enough that she was searching his face, trying to catch every nuance of his expression. On the screen in front of them, Ariel was seeing Eric for the first time and falling in love.

What had Grace been saying? Oh, right, the baby. "Helen the Hellion, Zane's calling her."

"Yeah." Noah chuckled. "Like that encourages a prospective nanny."

"Are you going to be a nanny?"

"No." Noah picked up her hand and intertwined his fingers with hers.

"What are you going to do?" Grace felt breathless, like suddenly there wasn't enough oxygen in the room. Her heart was beating faster. All she could feel was the touch of Noah's skin on hers, electricity shooting along her body like the lightning on the movie screen.

"I have no idea," he said. "I took Sophia home to her parents. Those are some people who had life figured out until their kid broke their hearts. And then I went to visit Joe's mom, and then home to my own mom. All along the way, I was trying to decide what I wanted to do with the rest of my life, what kind of job I wanted, what my career should be."

"Those are some big questions," Grace said softly. He hadn't looked away from her. His eyes were on hers and he wasn't smiling anymore.

"Yeah." He nodded. "But they're not the important ones, not really." His fingers tightened around hers.

"No?" The warmth of his hand sent heat racing through her veins. His touch made it hard to concentrate on his words. But she knew what he was saying, she knew where he was going.

"No. What matters is where you are, and who you're with. I don't know what I'm going to do with my life, but I know I want it to be here. And I know I want you in it."

Grace couldn't speak — the happiness was too big, it felt like it was going to overflow and explode out of her in all directions.

"Although I'm not, you know, proposing marriage. Not before our first date, anyway," he added hastily, as if her silence was a sign of concern.

"No?" Her smile was impossible to contain. She beamed at him, wondering if her happiness was lighting up the room. But then she glanced at the screen. The storm was over, Ariel had saved Eric, and the movie was lighting up the room.

"That," she said, nodding toward the screen.

"That?" Noah looked confused. "You want to go to the beach?"

She laughed. It was joy, this feeling, Grace realized. Bubbles of happiness were popping and fizzing in her bloodstream. She drew their entwined hands toward her heart, leaning toward him as Ariel sang.

"Oh," he said, looking at the screen, putting the pieces together. "She saves him from drowning."

"And falls in love," she replied as he brought his face to hers.

"He does, too." He let go of her hand, but only so he could run his up along her cheek and into her hair. "But it's just their beginning."

"Yep," Grace murmured the words, her lips almost brushing his. "Be part of my world, Noah."

"Always," he replied and began to kiss her.

38

DILLON

The weddings were over.

The cake was cut and eaten.

The dancing was done.

And the Sheriff's department's scheduled hazardous waste disposal exercise — a full hour of confiscated illegal fireworks set off over the lake in a truly glorious display — was complete.

It was time.

"So you never committed any, like, major sins, right?" Sophia asked.

"For a person who thought death was the end of everything, you've gotten awfully worried about the rulebooks," Dillon said, following Akira up the path to her front door.

"Hey, if I'm going to join you in your afterlife, I'd like to make sure it's not gonna be any place too weird," Sophia said as they reached the porch.

"It won't be," Dillon assured her. He hoped it wouldn't be, anyway. He glanced over his shoulder at the reassuring soap-bubble shimmer of his doorway. It didn't look like it would lead somewhere horrible. And Rose had promised him it would be okay.

"So when are we going?" Sophia asked.

"As soon as I say good-bye to Rose," Dillon replied as Akira unlocked the door and they headed into the house.

He was surprised that Rose had left the reception early, but baby Helen had objected — strongly — to the fireworks and so Zane had taken her home. Rose had gone with them.

Akira had stayed to translate for Dillon which meant he had a chance to say a full good-bye to everyone — all of his family members and friends. It was one last opportunity to talk until they met again, someday down the road.

It had been an amazing day, The best part had been seeing his parents holding hands as they promised each other forever. Or maybe the best part had been watching Grace sparkling with happy energy as she danced with Noah. Or... well, it had all been good.

"This is it, then?" Akira said to Dillon, as she set her keys down on the table by the door.

He nodded, chest swelling with certainty.

This was it.

From upstairs, the impassioned cry of an angry baby carried through the house. Akira glanced at the stairs and sighed. "She wants me. I should go rescue Zane."

"Good luck with that," Sophia said. "That baby has good lungs."

Akira gave a wry smile. "Rose says Henry's just mad about being so helpless. Apparently she's starting to forget, though. She's beginning to sleep more."

"Will Rose be upstairs with her?" Dillon asked.

Akira shook her head and gestured toward the kitchen. "Not if the baby's still crying. She'll be out back. She doesn't like it that she can't comfort her." Akira yawned widely, then covered her mouth, blinking. "Sorry."

"You're tired. You should go to bed," Dillon said.

Akira nodded, but she didn't move. Her eyes were on Dillon. She bit her lip.

"Thanks for everything," he said. He opened his mouth, then

closed it again. It felt like there was so much more to say, but a universe of words wouldn't be enough to tell her how he felt, how grateful he was for everything she had done for him.

She ducked her head in an awkward nod. "You, too. I'm gonna miss you."

Dillon grinned at her. "Never know, I might be back." He tilted his chin up toward the sounds of the wailing baby. "I'll try not to be quite so noisy if I make it back that way."

She chuckled. For another long moment, they looked at one another, wordlessly saying all the things there were no words for, and then Akira exhaled, turned, and headed up the stairs.

Dillon headed toward the kitchen, Sophia trailing him, and through the back door. The yard was dark and shadowy, but the streetlights and moon provided enough light that the pool area was clearly visible.

Rose was sitting on the edge of the pool, feet dangling in the water, her back toward them.

The backyard boys were playing, the way they always did, running across the surface of the pool as if it weren't there. They were faders, all the color gone, but their bodies still distinct enough that Dillon could see their shorts and wide collars and the suspenders over the shirt on one of them

He sat down next to Rose.

"Oh, hello," she said, but she didn't look at him. Her head was tilted to the side, her eyes on the boys. "How were the fireworks?"

"Good," he replied.

"Really colorful," Sophia said, sitting down next to him. "And really loud."

"Mmm." Rose gave a murmur of acknowledgement.

"Who are they?" Sophia asked, nodding toward the boys. It was the first time she'd ever been in Akira's backyard. Noah had never had a reason to visit during the time he'd stayed in Tassamara, and Sophia had been traveling with him ever since he left.

"They've been here since before Rose," Dillon answered.

But Rose pointed, first to the one in suspenders, then the other. "That's Willie, that's Charlie."

"You know their names?" Dillon asked, surprised. The boys didn't talk. If you listened hard, you could hear them laughing sometimes, but mostly they just ran, spending their eternity in a perpetual game of tag.

"Oh, sure." Rose sighed, then turned to look at him. She smiled. "It's time?"

"Yeah." Dillon nodded.

He'd tried to think of ways to convince Rose to come with them, but none of the risks of being a spirit in the material world mattered to her. She wasn't in danger if a vortex opened up and she knew how to manage her energy. He'd been worried about her fading, but ever since they'd saved Noah, she just seemed to get brighter and brighter. These days she almost glowed.

And if she stayed, she could keep an eye on Henry, and maybe help Kenzi. He understood why she wouldn't come with them.

He still wished she would.

"All right, then." She scrambled to her feet.

"Are you sure you don't want to come?" Dillon said, following suit.

She wrinkled her nose. "Don't be silly. Of course I'm coming. But not alone."

Dillon blinked in surprise as Rose stepped out onto the water. Walking across the pool, she stopped in the middle of the boys' game of tag and spread her arms wide. The boys kept running. Past her and through her and then back again, and with every time through, they grew more solid, until she grabbed their arms.

"Is she coming with us after all?" Sophia asked as she stood up.

"I think she might be," Dillon said.

Colors flowed into the boys' forms, their hair growing dark, skin turning brown, shorts deepening to blue, shirts to white and beige.

With a laughing protest, one of them said, "No fair, Rose. You're not It!"

The other said, "Rose, Rose, are you going to play with us again?"

Smiling, Rose slid her hands down to hold hands with them and tugged them both toward the side of the pool where Dillon and Sophia stood waiting.

"Hello!" Willie, the younger of the boys, offered a gap-toothed smile to Dillon and Sophia. "Are you going to play, too?"

"Oh, jolly fun." Charlie swung on Rose's hand. "What are we playing?"

"Good question," Rose said. "I think it's time for a new game."

She smiled at Dillon and if her smile was a little wry, her eyes a little sad, he understood.

Leaving was hard.

But he grinned at her as he grabbed the closest boy's hand and said, "Let's go be butterflies."

It was time.

ACKNOWLEDGMENTS

A Gift of Grace took me forever to write. Okay, not forever. But close to four years, and it sure felt like forever. Along the way, it went through innumerable versions, multiple plots, and even some major character changes. I'm not sure how I persisted, but I'm pretty sure I couldn't have done so without the support of my writing buddies: Lynda Haviland, Angela Daniels, Joyce Bittle, and Tim Nutting. Thanks, guys!

I am also very grateful to my beta readers: Tim Nutting, Allison Hubble, Natalie Solomon, Barbara Gavin, Lynda Haviland and Carol Westover. Thank you for taking the time to point out errors, ask questions, and let me know what worked and didn't work for you. Letting go isn't easy, but your help made it possible. Thank you!

Thank you also to all the readers who've sent me nice emails over the years. When writing *Grace* became a marathon, your encouragement was the cool water and orange wedges that I desperately needed.

Finally, much thanks to my family. It's been a long road, with plenty of self-doubt along the way, but your faith in me never wavered. Love you!

AUTHOR'S NOTE

For a free short story about Maggie's arrival in town, plus news of new releases and giveaways, please sign up for my mailing list at www.sarahwynde.com.

And if your retailer allows e-book lending, please feel free to share this book with a friend.

Thanks for reading!

Find me online at:
www.sarahwynde.com
sarah@sarahwynde.com

THE TASSAMARA SERIES

A Gift of Ghosts

Akira has secrets. But so does the town of Tassamara.

Akira Malone believes in the scientific method, evolution, and Einstein's theory of relativity. And ghosts.

All the logic and reason in the world can't protect her from the truth—she can see and communicate with spirits. But Akira is sure that her ability is just a genetic quirk and the ghosts she encounters simply leftover electromagnetic energy. Dangerous electromagnetic energy.

Zane Latimer believes in telepathy, precognition, auras, and that playing Halo with your employees is an excellent management technique. He also thinks that maybe, just maybe, Akira can help his family get in touch with their lost loved ones.

But will Akira ever be able to face her fears and accept her gift? Or will Zane's relatives be trapped between life and death forever?

A Gift of Thought

Sylvie swore she'd never go back to Tassamara. She was wrong.

At seventeen, Sylvie Blair left her infant son with his grandparents while she went shopping. She never returned. Twenty years later, she's devastated to learn of his early, untimely death. But although Dillon's body is long since buried, his spirit lingers on.

And he's not real happy.

He doesn't like his mom's job—too dangerous. He doesn't like her apartment—too boring. And he definitely doesn't like her love life—non-existent.

But when Dillon decides that his parents should be living happily ever after, he sets them on a path that leads deeper and deeper into danger. Can Sylvie let go of the past and embrace the future? And can Dillon survive the deadly energy he unwittingly unleashes?

The Spirits of Christmas: A Tassamara Short Story

Akira's plans are simple: write wedding invitations, bake Christmas cookies, and eat red meat. (The last surprises her, too.) But when Rose, the ghost who haunts her house, asks for a favor, Akira can't say no. Although she's faced danger before, even death, a toddler who doesn't like peanut-butter-and-jelly might be her worst nightmare.

A Gift of Time

She thought she could see everything. Time is proving her wrong.

Ten years ago, Natalya's ability to remember the future cost her the life she wanted when her vision of her fiancé's death tore them apart. Ever since, she's considered her precognition more of a curse than a gift. How can she live in the present when the future looms so large?

But when the night she's long dreaded finally arrives, Natalya's vision and reality diverge. She and her ex, Colin, are drawn into a web of the unexplained, led by a mysterious little girl. Who is Kenzi? And where did she come from? The little girl might be the reason Fate has spared Colin's life, but could she also bring Natalya and Colin together again?

With Colin, Kenzi, her family, the townspeople of Tassamara, and a set of circumstances that nobody could foresee, Natalya must solve the puzzle of a lifetime. Her discovery that her gift is not the only one at work will change the lives of everyone around her, as time becomes precious in a most unexpected way.

The Wedding Guests: A Tassamara Short Story

Meredith Mulcahey doesn't have time for love but when unexpected guests attend Akira and Zane's wedding, her life will change forever. Will it be for better or for worse?

For fans of the Tassamara series, this short story (16,000 words) takes place at the wedding of the main characters from *A Gift of Ghosts*, after the events of *A Gift of Time*. One reviewer calls it, "a super fun, sassy, and supernatural story you don't want to miss!"

A Gift of Grace

The voices are driving him crazy. And he's driving them crazy, too.

For Noah Blake, pretending to be normal is getting harder by the day. A brush with death in Iraq has left him suffering from chronic auditory hallucinations. Ignoring the voices he hears isn't always easy, but Noah knows it's better than the alternatives.

Yet when a mysterious redhead hands him a seemingly innocuous business card, a new voice — that of a teenage boy — becomes too insistent to deny. It wants him to go to Tassamara. It swears he'll find help there.

It's bad enough to have hallucinations, but doing what they say is bound to lead to disaster.

Isn't it?

Also:

A Lonely Magic

Nothing is what it seems…

Fen, a street-smart, 21-year-old orphan with anxiety issues, thinks she has her life under control. Then a gorgeous stranger tries to kill her. WTF?

A mysterious boy, Luke, and his sexy older brother, Kaio, come to her rescue, whisking her off to a glamorous Caribbean island and supposed safety. But the island's atmosphere simmers with unnerving undercurrents. The brothers have secrets and Fen has questions. Who are they? How did they know she was in trouble? And what aren't they telling her?

When Luke takes her to a magical underwater city, she discovers answers more enchanting than she could have imagined. But the enchantment has dark edges. Fen finds herself caught in tides of romance, mystery, and political intrigue, with her life and the fate of all humanity on the line. If she hopes to stay afloat, she'll have to find courage she never knew she had.

A Lonely Magic contains no explicit sexual scenes or graphic violence, but Fen's not shy about swearing when she's under stress – and she's under plenty of stress.

---

36 Questions: A Very Short Story

Can answering thirty-six questions really make you fall in love?

Charlotte isn't convinced that speed-dating using the *New York Times'* "36 Questions for Intimacy" is going to be any better than any other form of modern dating. But she's willing to give it a try.

Discover the unexpected results in this short story (2400 words) that one reader described as "feel good" and another called "seriously fun."

87138983R00220

Made in the USA
Middletown, DE
02 September 2018